TRAITOR

TRAITOR

SANDRA GREY

Covenant Communications, Inc.

Cover photography by McKenzie Deakins
For photographer information please visit www.photographybymckenzie.com.

Cover design copyrighted 2008 by Covenant Communications, Inc.

Published by Covenant Communications, Inc.
American Fork, Utah

This is a work of historical fiction. Many of the characters, names, incidents, places, and conversations are products of the author's imagination.

Printed in Canada
First Printing: February 2008
13 12 11 10 09 08   10 9 8 7 6 5 4 3 2 1

ISBN 13: 978-1-59811-358-7
ISBN 10: 1-59811-358-5

This story is dedicated to all who stayed true to the faith throughout the horrific years of World War II, and continued to do what they knew was right in the face of unimaginable terror and persecution. We are grateful to them for their examples.

ACKNOWLEDGEMENTS

I am grateful to my husband, who has washed dishes, fixed dinners, negotiated peace settlements among six busy youngsters, suggested ideas, and encouraged and inspired me so that Rolf and Marie's story could be recorded. I could not have completed this book without him.

AUTHOR NOTE

Besides the fictional characters and situations portrayed in this book, *Traitor* depicts a multitude of historical people and situations. For those of my readers who are interested in distinguishing the facts from the fiction, I've included a section of historical notes at the end of the book to explain which aspects are facts and which are my own embellishments or deviations for the sake of the storyline. These notes are organized by chapter according to the first time the name, term, or event appears in the text. Enjoy!

ONE

Nothing could be more uncomfortable than the cargo bay of a Martin III Marauder, its insides and underbelly iced over in a windchill of twenty-below, dropping through the night sky from a cruising altitude of fifteen thousand feet to a mere six hundred feet. Nothing, that is, except falling out of said cargo bay into empty space with forty kilos of supplies and a parachute of dubious dependability strapped to your back. Not only is the roar of two eighteen-cylinder engines replaced with the scream of ice-cold air slashing at your ears and ripping at your throat, but you catch a terrifying glimpse of the darkened undercarriage of the American-made British bomber in the night sky before the sweat on the inside of your flight goggles freezes solid and you are free-falling into enemy territory without the benefit of sight, sound, or touch.

Marie Jacobson jumped, corkscrewing violently away from the underbelly of the bomber and tumbling toward earth, battered by a wall of wind that threatened to tear her limbs from their sockets. Her heart racing, she tried desperately to remember her brief training as she tumbled toward the clearing below. Her frozen senses became disoriented as she fell, and they failed to inform her of which direction the retreating plane flew and in which direction lay the approaching ground.

She felt a vicious tug at her backside and glanced up, squinting through the ice on her goggles in an attempt to see the white cloud jettison away from her body, disappearing for a fraction of a second in the darkness before opening to its full circumference with a sound that reminded her of enemy bombs exploding over the rooftops of London. The force jarred her slender frame and snapped her head back like that of a rag doll.

She had not been prepared for this. She'd had no time to think—about her reasons for coming to France, about the difficult path that had brought her to this point some six hundred feet above the frozen Rhône-Alpes, or about the fact that occupied France was one of the most dangerous places on earth for an American woman in 1943.

She clutched at her useless goggles and ripped them from her face, peering first upward in order to convince herself that the parachute really had opened, and then downward into the darkness below. Her eyes stung and watered, and she wiped impatiently at burning tears until finally she could make out the silhouettes of treetops against an ethereal gray background below her. A second later she located the flicker of four tiny lights shining upward from the small clearing. She prayed it was her welcoming committee that watched her descent—not a German patrol.

A gust of ice swept her parachute north of the clearing and she fought with the straps, hoping to correct the error. In the struggle her goggles slipped from her hands and disappeared from view, spiraling downward on their own trajectory toward some unknown destination. She didn't have time to think of the implications of a pair of British flight goggles discovered by the wrong person—the hazy gray-white of the clearing was rushing toward her at a rate that made her light-headed and pushed all else from her mind. She tried to relax, to ignore the panic tightening her chest muscles and making her want to reach for the earth instead of allowing it to come to her. *Stay flexible,* she cautioned herself through clenched teeth. *Don't tense up.*

She gripped the straps on either side of her body and took a deep breath as the clearing filled her vision and she found she could distinguish footprints in the snow. The impact, when she landed, knocked the breath from her body and sent shockwaves from her ankles to her skull. She crumpled into a ball and lay still as the immense expanse of fabric above her ballooned over her body and then sagged gently to earth.

For a moment there was complete silence. From somewhere in the clearing she could hear the hooting of an owl. The icy wind that had pummeled her body so mercilessly only a moment before now gently stirred the tops of the darkened trees. Ice particles moved about her in a gentle whirlwind, falling on the fabric of her parachute like the soft pitter-patter of a million marching insects. Finally her body accepted her attempts to breathe and she gasped in lungfuls of cold air. Her senses registered the damp snow against her back, and she could hear muffled footsteps running toward her.

She had made it. She realized she was trembling, not from panic like in those last moments before she jumped—but from relief. Soon Félix would find her, convince her she was still in one piece, and wrap her wondrously in his arms for the first time in two years. That was, of course, if the approaching footsteps were not attached to black boots, machine guns, and swastikas. She shivered involuntarily at the thought and forced herself to roll onto her knees, hanging her head momentarily while she focused on quieting her breathing. She knew she should be dislodging herself from the parachute harness, but the relief of her safe landing mixed with the fear of the unknown numbed her muscles and made them weak.

"Amélie?" Félix's whispered voice carried unmistakably, and Marie struggled to her feet, turning to distinguish the man she had missed so terribly from among the group of four Frenchmen approaching through the darkness.

Félix! Her joy at finally seeing her fiancé after two long years could not be disguised, and now he reached for her and pulled her close in one swift motion.

"*Sois la bienvenue, chérie!*"

Marie wrapped her arms around his neck and returned his embrace. "It's been so long! How I've missed—"

"We've got to hurry." Félix Larouche hugged her briefly before firmly dislodging her arms from his neck. He snapped the release on the parachute harness and helped her pull the straps from her shoulders. The parachute sagged to the ground one last time before he grasped the fabric with both hands and tugged it toward him, bunching it swiftly and efficiently against his chest. "We might've been followed."

Marie stepped back, nodding mutely. She was relieved to see him but at the same time felt a twinge of disappointment at his hurried greeting. *Such is war,* she thought, and she bent to retrieve the tiny spade strapped to her leg. One of Félix's comrades took it from her and bent to the task of digging a grave for her flight suit and parachute. Marie struggled out of the cumbersome suit and dropped it in the shallow hole. Another comrade reached for her pack, grunting softly as the weight momentarily unbalanced him, and then hefting it more securely onto his shoulders and turning away from her.

Félix swiftly wrapped the parachute tightly inside its straps and tossed it into the shallow depression, and another man covered it with soil and then snow, sweeping it with a branch to camouflage their efforts. Then Félix took Marie's arm and smiled briefly. "We really must get going, *chérie.* You all right?" His breath came in tiny clouds as he spoke.

Marie nodded silently and realized she was still shivering. "Nothing's broken."

"That's good. Follow me." Félix turned and led her away from the drop site. She slipped her gloved hand into his and felt his grip tighten comfortably around her palm. Her anxiety lessened with the familiar pressure and she moved with him toward the tree line.

* * *

"What's in the pack?" Félix gripped the steering wheel and bent his lean torso forward, his eyes riveted to the darkness ahead of the truck. Marie glanced at the Frenchman seated next to her. She could discern the shock of unruly hair beneath his cap and the determined set of his jaw as he negotiated the uneven trail. The truck passed between stately trees, which rose on both sides of the trail like sentinels standing regally, shoulder to shoulder, tapering forms pointing heavenward in a sky brilliant with stars. She watched as Félix swerved the truck deliberately, managing to miss the worst of a large depression in the road. The truck righted and continued downward, clinging tenaciously to the almost invisible road. Below them lay the darkened windows of a mountain village, heavily shaded and waiting for the end of curfew and the sun that would be rising in a few hours.

"Medical supplies," she answered. "Mostly morphine. Transistor radio tubes, money, food vouchers, several pistols, a few maps and documents . . ."

"Good girl."

"Are those your friends from Belley?" Marie nodded toward the canvas flap that separated them from the back of the truck.

Félix shook his head. "Local *Maquis*."

"Where's Jacques?"

"You'll meet him soon enough." He glanced over at her. "His code name is 'Bruno.' Make sure you call people by their code names—at least in public."

"I'll remember."

"You missed the drop zone. Troubles?"

"A strong breeze, that's all. I fought it but lost the battle. I lost my goggles, too."

Félix paused. "You lost what?"

Marie hesitated, sensing the worry in his voice. "My flight goggles."

"What do you mean, you lost your goggles?"

"When the wind swept me away from the drop zone. They slipped from my hands while I was trying to come back around . . ."

Marie recognized the tightness creeping into his voice. "What were they doing in your hands?"

"I was blind, honey. The ice . . ."

Félix shook his head. "You should've left them on. Do you realize what this means?"

Marie felt her defenses rising. "Yes, I think I do."

"If they search the area they'll find your goggles and the drop zone will be compromised." His glance held reproach. "People could die. Now we'll have to find a new site."

"Look, I'm sorry. I—"

Félix sighed. "Don't worry about it." He turned back to study the road. "It could've happened to anyone. Things like this have happened before. It's not your fault, *chérie.*"

Marie took a deep breath and forced herself not to say what she was thinking—that if it wasn't her fault, why had he tried to make her feel responsible? She studied him in the darkness, forcing herself to breathe normally around the tightness in her throat. She changed the subject. "You mentioned you thought you had been followed."

Félix squinted into the darkness. "One of my men thought he saw somebody before we gathered tonight, and we debated calling off the drop."

"If you'd been followed, wouldn't the Germans have arrested us by now?"

"Perhaps." Félix fell silent as he negotiated a difficult curve.

"Maybe they were tipped off but didn't know exactly where we'd be going."

"Their Alpine troops, their *Gebirgsjager,* will comb this mountain tomorrow, and they'll find your goggles . . ." Félix almost sounded bitter.

Marie's hands clenched in her lap. "You keep coming back to the goggles."

"Honey, I'm sorry." Félix sighed. "I don't mean to hurt you. But you'll find that here in occupied France little things can mean the difference between life and death." Félix relaxed his hold on the wheel and reached one hand to Marie's knee. "A cough, a look, a hesitation, a tiny piece of paper in the wrong hands—all these things could mean death to good men who are fighting this monster that is Germany."

Marie covered his hand with hers and watched him closely.

"These mountains are our lifeline, *chérie.* Most Frenchmen shrug their shoulders and submit to the occupation. Some even condone it. But a growing number of us refuse to surrender to Nazi tyranny. We disrupt the railways, steal supplies, impersonate German officers, and fight the enemy any way we can. We need the safety of these small mountain villages in order to survive." Félix glanced at Marie. "Did you know SS troops will crush whole villages suspected of harboring *Résistance?*"

Marie was shocked. "Seems like excessive retaliation for small acts of sabotage."

"Small?" Félix snorted. "Our efforts may seem insignificant to some, but these revolts strike at the Nazis where it hurts most—in their pride. The

British and Americans have finally recognized our usefulness and have begun to send us more agents, weapons, and supplies. Of course, Germany will strike back any way it can."

Marie watched her fiancé, awed by the intensity of his passion. "I remember when you told me the Germans had crossed the demarcation line, taking over the southern half of France," she said softly. "You were like a madman, pacing your office and flinging your students' papers across the floor. You told me then that the Nazi troops posed an even greater threat to the Résistance than the Vichy government."

"They're bent on our destruction. The Vichy are at least our countrymen, and at times they can be reasonable—or at least bribed."

"And the German garrison in Belley?"

Félix nodded. "They moved in not long ago, determined to flush out Bruno and his organization." He moved his hand back to the wheel. "Bruno says there is a new officer in charge there—one sent specifically to capture him."

"He's that much of a threat to them, then?"

"Bruno worked closely with Jean Moulin in Lyon. How the Gestapo would love to get Bruno into their torture chambers! His capture would practically cripple the Maquis movement in the Rhône-Alpes . . . perhaps in all of southern France . . ."

"Would he talk?"

Félix shook his head vehemently. "Never! Jean Moulin never talked—and he lost his life for it. Bruno would be as strong as Moulin."

The flap behind them lifted and one of Félix's comrades poked his head through. "We're finished back here. How do you want to work the distribution?"

"We'll talk about it later. First I want to get Amélie to the safe house."

Marie had thought she was prepared—had been told by her superior that she was prepared—but hearing Félix call her by her code name made her wonder. She realized she had entered a world only described in Félix's letters and British training pamphlets—a world filled with a fear she had not imagined. She wondered if her feelings were similar to those of young men going off to war for the first time—feelings of adventure and excited anticipation. She wondered how long it took those boys to be hit with the reality, the terror that burned your insides and clung viciously to the base of your throat. No heartburn pills could cure this burn, she thought, and she again clenched her hands together. It didn't help that Félix seemed so different, so cold. She knew he was feeling the burden of her safety and the safety of his men, but she realized he had changed. He was no longer the Félix she had known.

"Madame Guilbert's residence?" The man yawned and glanced at Marie.
"Until curfew is lifted."
"And the debriefing?"
"As soon as possible. There's much to do."

TWO

Madame Donatienne Guilbert's home lay comfortably situated between two larger homes on the non-assuming Rue de St. André near the outskirts of Belley. Félix introduced Marie to her hostess, and Marie instantly liked the woman, with her white hair, wizened face, and fearless gray eyes. Marie knew Madame Guilbert was taking an incredible risk in allowing her to stay, and she tried to express her gratitude but was cut off in mid-sentence.

"No no! It is *I* who must thank *you!*" the woman exclaimed. "You and your friends are welcome guests and will be safe here. They would never suspect me, for I am too old to cause trouble." Her smile was radiant in spite of several decaying and crooked teeth. She offered to fix a small meal for Marie, apologizing in advance for the quality of her coffee and the lack of meat, but Marie declined gently, explaining that she was tired and needed to sleep for a few hours before the other Résistance leaders arrived.

Félix grabbed her hand outside her bedroom door, warming it between his own and looking into her eyes. Marie saw in their depths a deep suffering and a fire of conviction that surprised her. He leaned close and kissed her briefly, and Marie closed her eyes, hoping to feel the surge of emotion that used to accompany his kisses. She was disappointed when it did not come. She wondered if disappointment would accompany every moment with her fiancé during this trip.

Félix felt her sadness and tried to reassure her. "I'm glad you're here. You're a breath of fresh air to me, *chérie,* and I want you to remember how much I love you, even when I seem distracted and harsh. The war—"

"Shh . . ." Marie touched his lips with her finger and then kissed him softly in return. "I understand a little of what you're up against, Félix. You don't need to worry. I'm here to help in any way I can."

Félix nodded, his eyes tired. "Sleep then, until I call for you. Do you think you can sleep?"

"I'm asleep on my feet already. I'll be fine."

"Good." Félix tried to smile, and he touched her cheek with a hint of the affection she remembered. "Don't worry about the meeting. It'll be short, and you will have important things to say that these men need to hear."

Marie nodded. "Thank you. I'll do my best."

He kissed her on the cheek and turned to go. Marie entered the bedroom and shut the door, locking it behind her. For a long moment she rested her head against the frame, closing her eyes and listening silently. She did not turn on the light, but relied on the moonlight filtering through the delicate lace curtains to provide the light she needed to move across the small room to the window, past the bed with its soft down comforter folded temptingly back. There she stood quietly, studying every shadow, every movement, for well over ten minutes. Then she turned the latch, grasped the edge of the window, and pulled it slowly upward. She slipped outside and landed on frozen ground, her boots silent as she pulled the window mostly closed behind her. Hugging her thin coat tightly around her shoulders, she circled the house until she reached the street, where she paused and looked carefully in both directions. Any German patrol would endanger her plans, she knew. Being caught outside after curfew was reason enough to be shot—just as much so as being captured doing what she was about to do.

Marie kept to the shadows as she had been taught and moved swiftly and silently toward her destination, keeping a lookout for danger. Her heart raced, more from fear and adrenaline than from the exertion. She realized that when she'd agreed to this task she'd had no idea of the peril involved. She'd only known that Director Marks had offered her a chance to join Félix if she would agree to complete one simple task.

Marie remembered the night the offer was extended. She had been walking home from Grendon when she was accosted by two men in business suits, ties, and bowler hats, who had greeted her in French when she tried to pass them on the sidewalk. They had called her by name and indicated that she was to come with them but had flatly refused to explain what was happening. Marie had spent the whole of her escorted walk to Baker Street mentally concocting terrifying reasons for her predicament.

Her solemn companions escorted her to the office of Mr. Leo Marks, head of SOE communications, whom she had met briefly upon her appointment to Grendon as a coder. He shook her hand warmly, dismissed her depressing escorts, and introduced her to another man in the room— dark-haired, middle-aged, and obviously French.

"Lieutenant Valois wishes to meet you, Marie. He is visiting from General de Gaulle's RF section and has heard about your successes as a coder at Grendon. He wishes to discuss with you a new coding system we are developing for the French agents. It seems he has need of your services." After that introduction had followed the most incredible, terrifying explanation of the reason for the secret meeting: Monsieur Valois wanted Marie to drop into France, test a new code system developed by Marks, and, if ordered by SOE, train the Résistance leaders and existing field WT operators in the use of the new system.

"You have wanted to join your fiancé, Miss Jacobson. Here is your chance."

It had taken several minutes and plenty of promises on the part of the Frenchman before she had accepted the assignment, and even after she'd agreed to it she felt trepidation. Her life was turning in a direction that she had not anticipated and that she was not necessarily enthusiastic about following. Sure, she would be allowed to see Félix again after an incredibly long time. But the atmosphere was not going to be ideal for rebuilding a romance, and she doubted whether he would be happy for her presence.

As her whirlwind training progressed, she often found herself giving in to the fears and worries that shadowed her adventure. She worried that her coding skills might not be up to the standards set by Director Marks. She worried that she would be arrested, interrogated, tortured, and perhaps killed by the Germans—and that Félix and his Résistance comrades would die because of her mistakes.

That fear was paramount in her mind at the moment as she made her way past an abandoned barn, through a moonlit church graveyard, and into a dilapidated, leaning cluster of homes that looked like they'd been empty since the first years of the war. She followed a narrow, weed-choked street, counting houses on her left until she reached the fifteenth structure. She hesitated then, swallowing forcefully against a fear that threatened to turn her limbs into stone. Her first assignment could be her last, she realized, if the Germans were listening.

She took a deep breath, glanced back down the street, and climbed the steps to the house. Inside, she continued down a hallway to a small room at the back, where a locked door confirmed that this was indeed the correct location of the wireless transmitter. *"A WT set will be waiting for you,"* Valois had said after giving her a list of instructions and directions to the location.

Marie slipped her tools from the pocket of her coat and easily manipulated the lock. She entered the small, darkened room and sat at the table, removing the old clothing and dusty bedding that had been thrown across the radio to act as camouflage. She then bent and unlaced her boot, reached inside, and from a slit in the lining worked free a small square of silk that might have been a lady's handkerchief if it weren't for the tiny letters printed on it. She smoothed the square in front of her and extracted a small pencil stub and scrap of paper from her pocket.

With a small torch held securely between her teeth, she bent over the paper and quickly drew lines at ninety-degree angles to each other, creating a crude graph that she then began to fill with letters, seemingly haphazard in their location and cluster, but nonetheless perfectly accurate in their effectiveness. She referenced the silk code key in front of her often, transferring the necessary information from the first line of the transposition keys printed there.

She took her time. The local *Funk-Horchdienst*, German message-interception units, would not begin looking for her until several minutes after she began to transmit—that is, if they were in the area at all. And then, with these new "worked-out keys"—often called WOKs—the fear all but disappeared that her message might be deciphered by the Germans even if it was intercepted.

She wanted the message to be perfect: no misspelled words, no misaligned columns, and definitely no mistakes in her security checks! Her message could be one hundred characters long instead of the poem code's required two hundred fifty, thus requiring less time on the air and less chance of detection. She believed in this new system and wanted her message to prove its effectiveness to SOE's signals directorate.

This was nothing more than a test transmission, according to Marks, but the information she was planning to send would be more than just a test. She wanted to alert Baker Street to the new developments in Belley: the new German officer in charge of the Belley garrison, the compromised landing site, the possibility that her drop had been observed . . .

Marie turned on the machine, raised the antenna, listened for a minute, adjusted dials, and began to transmit. Her finger touched the Morse pad gently, expertly, as if she'd been transmitting her whole life and not just for the past year. She felt the familiar cramping in her forearm and tried to relax, breathing deeply and evenly as she informed London of her arrival and added her warnings. Her message ended with her security code, which could easily be altered if she were captured, in order to alert London to her predicament.

Grendon's reply was almost immediate, surprising her with its speed. There was to be a supplies drop the following night, and because of the compromised site, news of the drop and new drop coordinates would be transmitted immediately through regular channels (meaning through Jacques's regular WT operator) in order to keep Marie's transmissions secret.

Marie was to schedule one more secret transmission for the following night at nine thirty—six hours before the drop. If the new code was deemed satisfactory, silks would be sent via the drop to be distributed to Félix and his comrades. Marie acknowledged London's reply and then signed off, stood, and moved to the front door to watch the street below.

All was silent. Apparently she had caught the Germans sleeping, and she prayed her next transmission would go as smoothly. She returned to the back room, pulled a small pair of scissors from her coat pocket, and cut along the top of the WOK, completely removing the strip of silk that had the key she'd just used printed on it. She hid the rest of the fabric in her boot and unraveled the thin silk strip between her fingers, shredding it until the symbols disintegrated along with the fabric. With her foot she swept the remaining residue into a trash-filled corner of the room. Then she lowered the radio's antenna and threw the old blankets and clothes back over the table. She quickly scanned the room, looking for signs that she had been there, and then she blew on the footprints and chair scuttle marks, displacing dust until it settled over her fresh marks, giving the appearance that several weeks had passed since someone had been there. She locked the door behind her, then moved through the house and back onto the darkened street.

THREE

How the tables have turned, Marie thought.

Félix should be the teacher, not her. But she had information to deliver that put her at the front of the room and Félix behind her. She swallowed, trying to eliminate the dryness in her throat as she gazed over the assemblage. In the sleepiness of early morning, the parlor seemed claustrophobic, crowded with eleven men and their hostess, Madame Guilbert, still wrapped tightly in her robe. Behind the blackout curtains Marie caught the first glimmers of morning, and she knew it would be light within the hour. She would have to hurry. Félix was anxious for the group to disperse without capturing the attention of too many people, and soon the street outside would be busy with its usual morning commute.

Marie was not used to addressing assemblies—especially with such information as this—and she would have much preferred Félix in the role of teacher, as he had been when they first met at Brigham Young University. She glanced sideways at her fiancé. His slender form relaxed in a chair to her left, and when he briefly met her gaze, she realized that even in such circumstances the memory still came unbidden. His classroom had been dominated by female students while most of their male counterparts fought the horrible war over in Europe. She had been young and impressionable, and he had seemed so sophisticated and charming. He had become increasingly impressed by her French, and she had been shocked and pleased when he'd offered her a job as his assistant.

"Mademoiselle?"

She cleared her throat. "In answer to your question, monsieur, it will be sometime next year. That's all I know."

"A little vague, don't you think?"

Marie looked at the speaker. He was a small man, bristling with a mustache and a beard, and the top of his head was thick with black hair. His dark eyes watched her and waited for her answer, as did those of every other leader in the room.

"It is enough to know that the Allies are coming," Félix defended her. "What would we do with more information? Leak it to our enemies? We are not all as strong as Moulin. If we knew the exact date and were caught—"

"Perhaps you doubt our allegiance, Dorian?" The little man seemed offended. "Perhaps you think we will sing the moment they begin to torture us."

Félix shook his head and rose to stand beside Marie. "I think nothing like that, Bernard. But you know as well as I that if we are captured and we resist, they have means at their disposal—"

"You talk of drugs? Scopolamine, perhaps?"

"Perhaps. It is likely they would use it."

"The Germans will see us suffer first. They love to see us suffer. Barbie made that all too clear with Moulin."

"Klaus Barbie is Gestapo," Félix corrected. "Members of the Gestapo love to see us suffer. But not all Germans are barbarians."

A murmur filtered through the group. Marie felt the tension in the room and turned to glance at Félix. It seemed an inflammatory comment to make in such an assemblage, and Marie wondered why he had risked it.

Félix recognized the question in her eyes and continued. "We've all had experiences with the Germans. But they aren't all in this war because they want to be. Remember, *our* service is voluntary—*theirs* is compulsory. I believe there are many good people among them." Félix felt the tension in the room and hurried to continue. "But the fact is they would destroy us if we were caught. And," he stared pointedly at Bernard, "if we were caught, we would be tortured and compelled to talk." Félix glanced again at Marie. "Let me just clarify, lest any of you think me a traitor, that I know *one* good German. I feel there are others, but that is not the issue here. War is not the time to talk of good people among the enemy. I should not have brought it up. Forgive me." He sat down.

Marie stared at her fiancé. His voice had caught when he'd mentioned "one good German." She realized this was a part of him she had never known—a part he had never shared with her. She wondered if he would ever tell her.

"Any more questions?" Marie glanced at the clock. They were running out of time. Soon the Germans would be patrolling Madame Guilbert's street and setting up random checkpoints throughout the city, and it would be difficult to disperse without attracting attention.

"How about the British?" A heavyset man in his forties raised his hand like a school boy. "You think they'll provide us with the supplies we'll need for these operations?"

Marie nodded. "The SOE and the American OSS are committed to this support. They're counting on your help in this invasion—they need your disruptions. The Germans need to be compelled to build up their defenses in places far removed from the actual landing sites."

Marie saw the question in their eyes. She clarified, "Which locations are not yet public knowledge, for reasons explained just now."

"How do things change, mademoiselle? We already stage disruptions— with or without the help of the Allies." The speaker was a lanky youth, stubble just beginning to roughen his features, who was leaning back in his chair with his legs stretched out, his hands shoved deep into the pockets of his wool pants. "How does your information—your presence here—change that?"

"Your efforts are appreciated by the Allies, monsieur. They want you to continue with your disruptions and be ready to intensify sabotage when the invasion draws near. They feel you are an integral part of next year's plans. They also want you to step up your efforts—Moulin's and General de Gaulle's efforts—to organize and cooperate with the several different Résistance organizations throughout France. You will be compensated with more supplies, agents, and fighters. I was sent simply to give you this message. Other than that, my presence here is of a personal nature."

"What do you mean, 'of a personal nature'?"

Félix rose to his feet and moved to Marie's side. Turning to face the assemblage, he slipped one arm around her waist. "After we win this war, Amélie and I are going to be married."

* * *

Marie felt as if a weight had been lifted from her chest and she could finally breathe. The message Félix expected her to give had been delivered, and now she felt a desire to curl up in a ball in front of a warm fireplace, pull a thick, soft comforter up to her chin, and sleep until the war was over. If not for her other mission, known only to herself and half a dozen people in London, that luxury might have been a possibility for her near future. But her stay might be of some duration if Marks received a go-ahead from de Gaulle. She yawned, hiding it discreetly behind her hand as she glanced around the room. Résistance leaders discussed the information she had brought with her into France, planning what would come next and discussing the possibilities. She watched her fiancé as he and Bernard studied a map of the Rhône River valley, discussing possible drop sites.

In a far corner she noticed a Frenchman standing alone, his back to the wall and a frown on his face. His dark skin stretched taut over prominent cheekbones, and his nose was crooked from some past injury. His stance suggested military, and a Basque beret hung low over dark eyes that remained active and aware of his surroundings. The set of his shoulders betrayed his watchfulness, as if he expected a disruption at any moment and was constantly prepared to respond. Like a cougar watching his prey he waited, one arm hovering near his sidearm, his eyes watching the assemblage with wary detachment.

Marie moved across the room to stand beside the man. "I've heard so much about you, Bruno."

Jacques's face remained impassive. "I'm sure none of what you've heard is true."

Marie smiled. "Dorian said you're his best friend." She used Félix's alias and was surprised when it slipped from her tongue as easily as Jacques's. "You've saved his life more than once, I hear."

"And he has saved mine."

"I'm glad to finally meet you."

Jacques studied her solemnly, his eyes hooded. "You understand, mademoiselle, that he won't allow his feelings for you to distract him."

"I understand. He is loyal to the cause, and I'm just glad to be here with him. I don't plan on distracting him."

"How long do you plan to stay?"

Marie hesitated. "I planned to stay a couple of weeks . . ." She glanced across the room to where Félix studied the map with Bernard. "It all depends on what he needs."

Jacques said nothing, so Marie continued. "I was naive, Bruno. I had no idea how busy he is, how all-consuming this battle is . . ."

"He loves you. Don't ever think otherwise. He talks about you all the time—about how after he returns to America he will marry you in his church."

Marie felt her eyes filling with tears and blinked them back fiercely. Jacques continued. "You are very important to him. Your church is very important to him. He is crazy about you, and about this Mormon religion he has joined. But he won't let anything get in the way of his work. Do you understand?"

"I understand."

* * *

"I have secured a position for you."

Marie looked up at her fiancé questioningly. "A position? What do you mean?"

"As a teacher at *La Maison d'Izieu,* the Izieu children's home." Félix sat on the sofa with his map. "It won't pay much—only room and board—but Madame Zlatin is a good woman who could use your help with the children in her charge."

Marie hesitated, and Félix misunderstood her hesitation. "Everybody works, *chérie.*" He smoothed the map next to him on the seat. "If you don't have regular employment it will look suspicious. Besides . . ." Félix gestured at the map. "The children's home is near our new drop site."

Marie glanced out the window. The last Résistance members had left Madame Guilbert's home, disappearing one at a time into the passing traffic with a proficiency borne of years of practice at fading into the woodwork. Marie stepped away from the window and moved toward Félix. She studied him for several seconds, smiling at his handsome brow wrinkled in concentration as he bent over the map. She felt a familiar tightness in the base of her throat, a sign she had come to associate with fear of the unknown—or looming panic. But she forced herself to move across the room and grasp her fiancé's hand. "All right."

"I'll make sure you get safely out of France after the invasion."

"I know you will." Marie smiled playfully. "Bruno said I would be a distraction and he's right. You don't need me around to distract you."

Félix laughed shortly. "Maybe you're just the distraction I need—to keep me from losing my mind."

Marie squeezed his hand. "At first I couldn't understand your passion."

"What do you mean?"

"Your passion for your countrymen's plight," she explained, sitting next to him on the sofa. "News of the Occupation angered you, I could tell. I knew you loved me, but your loyalty to your countrymen runs deep, and I knew I had to let you go." She took a deep breath. "It was the most difficult thing I've ever done."

"Why was it so difficult?"

Marie laughed lightly. "I was determined to become your wife, graduate from Brigham Young University, and settle down in some southern Utah town to raise a family."

Félix grunted, smiling impishly. "You didn't expect much, did you?"

Marie hesitated. She knew he was joking, but there was an undertone to his comment that suggested irritation at her words. She felt a twinge of hurt and lowered her voice. "There was a time when you had the same feelings . . ."

Félix sighed, then turned and put his hands on her shoulders. "And I still feel that way, *ma chérie.* But right now I'm busy with other things, important things! My countrymen are fighting a formidable enemy—one that would stop at nothing to exterminate us." He shook his head, and Marie noticed the deep furrows that had etched themselves in his brow since she had last seen him in America. "And now Bruno says this new Nazi officer is infamous for his ability to unravel the secrets of the Résistance."

"Do you know him?"

Félix shook his head. "I doubt it. He's a major from Hamburg. Supposed to be fluent in French and English. He's an intelligence officer working under Major Schellenberg." Félix leaned his elbows into the map on his knees and rubbed his fingers tiredly into his temples. "*Ai,* what I would give for this war to be over . . ."

"Can't you rest? It's been a long night." Marie touched his arm, fearful at the change in him. Where was the energetic, charismatic man she had fallen in love with? What had happened to the sparkle in his eyes and the smile she was used to? Not once since she arrived had he smiled at her in that special way she treasured. Again, she felt the twinge of fear that had bothered her all morning. She felt urgency now—an urgency to leave France and return to the safety of her father's home in southern Utah. She had been so excited to return to France, to be here with him and help him with his work. But now that she was here she felt more alienated from him than before she'd come.

"Sweetheart . . ." Félix moved his arm around Marie's waist, his tired eyes searching hers. "I told you I'm glad you're here, and I mean it. Don't ever think I'm not. I'm looking forward to the day this horrible conflict is over so that we can be married. But now I must concentrate on our battle. Many lives are at stake, and Bruno and I are responsible for them. You do understand?"

Marie steadily returned his gaze. "I understand."

"That's my girl." Félix turned back to the map. "Now I have to study this new drop site—we must get the new coordinates to the Allies. My source tells me there will be another drop tonight, and we've got to prepare."

"How can I help?"

Félix gathered two corners of the wrinkled map and began to fold it inward. "You can inform our contact while I coordinate the new location with Bruno."

"Who is your contact?"

"He owns a café not far from here. He'll get the word to our men." Félix set the folded map aside and turned his full attention to Marie. "You will go to the café at the corner of Place des Terreaux and Chapelle. You will sit at the counter and order a cup of coffee and a croissant—with marmalade. The barman will tell you he's out of marmalade and ask if you'd like a substitute. You will decline, saying that you will take your croissant plain."

Marie listened carefully. Félix took her hand and folded several coins into her palm while he continued. "Your little exchange will tell our contact all he needs to know. Don't rush. Read the paper. Talk to people sparingly. If you're pulled into conversation, stick to your cover story. Pay the barman and leave when you see me cross the street."

"Why coffee?"

Félix hesitated, as if unsure what she meant. Then he shook his head. "Marie, if you're concerned about the Word of Wisdom, you needn't be. France doesn't even have access to coffee made with real coffee beans. The coffee they serve nowadays is brewed with grains—another effect of this war. And besides . . ." His brow furrowed slightly. "You don't want to draw unnecessary attention to yourself. Everyone orders coffee. Any more questions?"

Marie shook her head.

"Your exchange with the barman is a coded request that our comrades meet at a certain location after curfew, where they will help us distribute the supplies we receive. I'll pass by the café five minutes after you enter. Observe which way I go and walk the same direction a few minutes later. Someone will be watching you to make sure you aren't followed."

"Where will you go?"

"After I talk to Bruno about the new drop site, we'll get our radio operator to transmit the new coordinates to London. And then we'll go find Hervé."

"Hervé?"

"Seventeen years old. Barely knows what a gun looks like, let alone how to use one. He's young and inexperienced, but his enthusiasm for our fight matches that of men twice his age. He'll never forgive the Germans for what they did to his parents."

"What happened?"

"His parents were arrested and murdered for harboring *maquisards* after an attack on a German convoy."

"How awful!"

"For the last six months Hervé and his brother have been living under assumed names here in Belley, carrying forged papers provided by the British." Félix stood, gathering up the map as he rose. "You'll find that everyone has a story—most of them inspired by German oppression."

"You mentioned someone will be there to watch me outside the café. Will I see him?"

Félix shook his head. "No. But he'll be there."

"Will he follow me into the café?"

"No." Félix looked apologetic. "When you're delivering your message you'll be on your own. It's better that only one person—" Félix stopped abruptly, looking uncomfortable.

Marie watched him steadily. "It's better that only one person be arrested instead of two—is that what you were about to say?"

Félix closed his eyes. *"Chérie . . ."*

"Don't worry." Marie squeezed his hand. "I want to help. You don't need to worry about me." She stood, then bent and kissed him on the forehead. "I'll see you at *La Maison d'Izieu*. I'm to wait there until you come for me tonight, right?"

"I'll come for you."

"I love you, Félix." She whispered his given name and touched his unruly hair. "And I'm proud of what you're doing."

FOUR

Marie paused at the curb across the street from the café and took a deep breath. A chill breeze whispered across the wet stone and combined with the odors of foul *ersatz* coffee, baking bread, and cheap cologne. The aroma invaded her nostrils, heady in its intensity. Across the street and three doors down a bakery opened its doors, admitting the first few women at the front of a bread line that blocked the sidewalk and disappeared around a corner. A passerby made a derogatory comment about the Germans and was immediately shushed by his wife as two of the offending party strolled down the street. One of the soldiers glanced through Marie and then away, as if her presence was not worthy of his attention, and Marie was grateful for the tattered coat and sensible shoes that made her blend into the crowd. She'd been through an intense orientation before she came, but there was only so much one could learn in a British classroom. *Each situation is different,* she thought, *each assignment totally original in its experience and implications.* She licked her dry lips and glanced casually at the retreating backs of the Germans. She realized that if she paused any longer she would surely be discovered, so she stepped purposefully from the curb.

The café was pleasantly busy, not in a crowded, stifling sort of way, but full enough that she felt confident she would not be singled out. The room drifted with a thin film of cigarette smoke, illuminated by a cheerful bank of large windows at the front of the store that let in the morning light. Lacy curtains that looked like they could use a good washing spanned the windows at chest height, giving the patrons privacy as they ate but allowing them the view of passersby on the street. The only shadow in the room originated from the mandatory Nazi flag hanging prominently from the top of the window, its swastika waving lazily in a cool morning breeze and its shadow crawling across the floor like a dark hand reaching for its victim.

Marie walked up to the bar, purposefully ignoring the other café patrons. She slid onto a stool and reached for a newspaper, casually scanning the headlines until the barman moved in her direction. She noticed his irregular gait and realized with pity that one of his legs was shorter than the other. "Coffee please," she said, "and a croissant. Any chance of marmalade?"

The man shook his head. "No, mademoiselle, I'm completely out. I'm sorry." He hesitated and then asked, "Perhaps you would like a substitute?"

Marie shook her head. She realized her hands had begun to tremble and she gripped the newspaper tightly. "No, thank you. I'll take it plain."

"Very well." The barman turned away, his expression betraying nothing. He filled her cup and placed it in front of her with a croissant on a chipped plate. Marie tossed the coins Félix had given her onto the counter and pretended to read the paper, her right hand picking absently at the roll. At first her apprehension kept her from noticing anything more than headlines, all of which seemed to condone the war and the situation in France. *Relax!* She berated herself silently and forced herself to read an article. In spite of the tightness in her chest she realized the newspaper's contents angered her. She wondered what turncoat would write that the occupation was boosting France's economy. What idiot would claim that a work program that took young men from France to compulsory labor in Germany would be a great benefit to not only the young men but to the families they left behind? Representatives of the Vichy government admonished their fellow Frenchmen to do their duty and register their lineage, reminding Jewish citizens to display their stars at all times and carry their properly stamped documents.

"Pretty awful stuff, isn't it?"

Marie looked up from the paper, startled. "Excuse me?"

The man sat three seats down. Marie studied him surreptitiously, remembering what one of her instructors had taught—that she should always pay attention to people without displaying too much interest. He sat casually, seemingly at ease, his left elbow resting on the countertop and his body turned in Marie's direction. His light brown hair was cut short, and the faintest shadow of a beard deepened the curve of his jaw. He smiled at her. His smile—pleasant and non-assuming—touched his dark blue eyes, wrinkling the skin at their corners. Broad shoulders hinted at his height and strong hands played with his hat on the countertop as he spoke.

"Your coffee. Don't you like it? They say it's the best France has to offer." The last was said with a sardonic twist of his lips, and Marie stared at the man in confusion. "I'm not sure what you mean."

The man gestured. "You pushed your cup away without even tasting it, as if you didn't want it."

Marie looked down at the counter and felt a shiver run up her spine. Her cup sat on the counter *behind* her newspaper, where she wouldn't have been able to reach it without setting the paper down and using her left hand. When had she pushed it away? While she was reading the Vichy article that so annoyed her? It had been unintentional, she knew—habit borne of a lifetime of abstinence. But what terrified her was that she had let her guard down for just a moment, and her little gesture of dismissal had caught the interest of one of the locals and endangered her errand—and possibly her life.

She made a face. "It's disgusting. Can't get used to *ersatz* coffee."

"Then why did you order it?"

She feigned irritation at the man's intrusion and angrily met his gaze, her hands clammy on the newspaper. "Look, monsieur, it's really none of your—" Her breath suddenly caught in her throat as she realized it was not just her own folly that unnerved her—it was the man himself. His appearance was just a little too meticulous—his wool coat a little too expensive, his dark shirt a little too tailored. His hair lay a little too neatly and his hands were a little too clean. When he stood and moved to the empty seat next to her his step was a little too casual for the military background suggested by the set of his shoulders. Marie felt her muscles tense as if they would bolt for the door of their own accord, leaving her skin sitting casually at the counter.

"You're new here." It was a statement, not a question. "Where are you from, mademoiselle?"

Marie sat frozen to her seat, glaring at his handsome, terrifying face. *Where is Félix?* She realized not enough time had passed, and she felt her throat go dry. Wetting the inside of her mouth, she forced herself to speak casually. "Paris."

"Every newcomer says they're from Paris these days." His deep voice was pleasant, but she sensed an accusation in his words. "So what is a young woman from Paris doing in the middle of the Rhône-Alpes? Especially at a time like this?"

"You mean, because of the war?"

"Not the most beautiful time of our lives, is it?"

She shook her head in agreement and found herself drawn to his eyes and trapped there. She wondered if he could see what she was thinking and sense her fear, and she forced her gaze away from his. At that moment she saw Félix pass the café window. Without looking inside he turned and crossed the street, striding purposefully past the bread line and around a corner. Suddenly Marie felt completely alone in hostile territory, and she quickly averted her eyes from the retreating figure.

The man next to her glanced at the window and then back at her. "Waiting for someone, mademoiselle?"

Marie had a sinking feeling in the pit of her stomach, realizing that her casual glance in Félix's direction might have placed them all in danger. She had no idea who this man next to her was, but her instincts told her he was not there to discuss her choice of beverage. Félix had warned her there were *collabos*—Frenchmen who spied for the Germans—everywhere, and on her first day it seemed she might have been cornered by one. She set her paper deliberately on the edge of the counter and rose from her seat. "Monsieur, I am sorry." She tried to smile cordially but couldn't manage more than a grimace. "I cannot stay."

She was turning to go when his large hand closed lightly around her elbow. Startled, she turned and found him gazing at her. His eyes held in their blue depths an interest—an *empathy*—that she realized he was trying to hide from her, and she felt her terror deepen.

"Mademoiselle, don't worry." He sighed, and Marie imagined she heard genuine sorrow in the sound. "Not everyone in France is your enemy."

His words shocked her and washed over her like cold water. Her head felt light and she felt her heartbeat accelerating. Terrified, she pulled her arm from his grasp and walked with as much dignity as she could muster from the café. Crossing the street she began to turn in the direction Félix had gone. Then, hazarding a quick glance over her shoulder, she saw that the man from the café stood in the doorway, his hands in his pockets, watching her. Worried for Félix's safety, she turned in the opposite direction, counting on her invisible bodyguard to eventually intercede and get her to where Félix wanted her to go.

* * *

When Marie began encoding her message that evening, her experience in the café still upset her, and she realized her hands shook slightly as she drew her graph. *I'm not cut out for this,* she thought, and she imagined for a moment the warmth of her father's home in St. George, Utah. She remembered bringing Félix home to meet her dad at her mother's funeral, their quick hike in the red rocks and the heat of the sun soaking into both the rough sandstone and their backs. Then the lead of her pencil snapped, bringing her sharply back to the present, where the crisp cold moonlight outside shone faintly through a broken, dirty window in war-torn France. She used her fingernails to cut through the wood of her pencil and managed to produce a tiny amount of lead.

She thought about the man in the café, and a shudder ran up her spine. His deep, mesmerizing eyes and incredible voice could not mask the danger that lurked behind his every word. His smile had been charming—disarming, even—the kind of smile that caused women to swoon; possibly even more so because the owner of the smile seemed unaware of its effect. But Marie's senses warned her that this man was either a German or in league with the Germans, and that his interest in her presence in the café had not been just happenstance. Marie had told Félix what had happened and had described the man, but besides a slight concern for her safety and a reminder to be careful what she said to strangers, he had been too preoccupied with preparations for the evening's drop to give heed to her worries.

As the day wore on, her unease grew until it was a living presence inside of her that tightened her chest muscles and sapped her strength, screaming constantly that something was wrong.

She had come close to betraying her evening sked to her fiancé, ready to tell him all about the new silk codes and her orders to send test messages to London. She wanted to tell him that she had been ordered to contact Grendon that evening, and that she planned to tell SOE that the drop had been compromised and should be postponed until the next full moon. Instead, she had whispered, "Honey, if there were something wrong, would you be able to sense it? Would you be prompted?"

Félix had thought about her question, the look in his eyes telling her he was disturbed by it, and then he'd answered her frankly. "Marie, I've forgotten what it feels like to receive a prompting from the Holy Ghost. Everything is dark, terrifying, and dangerous right now. War does that, and it completely debilitates our ability to receive promptings." He put his arm around her shoulder and continued. "Your fear is normal—you're new. Soon you'll learn to live with it—on a daily basis, I'm afraid."

It was nine thirty, and in front of the WT unit she bent again to her task, alternating between silk and graph as she produced the sequence she would transmit. She didn't agree with Félix, she realized. Certainly an evil environment could not keep a good person from receiving a prompting! Evil would never be more powerful than good, her father had once said—unless we allowed it to be.

Her fingers again produced their Morse magic, warning London that the Germans might know of the drop and recommending that it be postponed. She'd made it halfway through her security code when the front door exploded inward and heavy footsteps approached the room at a run. Without thinking, she grabbed the silk key and launched herself through the glass window, shielding her face from glass shards with her arm. She landed on her back and shoulder in the snow, crunching her bones excruciatingly and sending a howl of pain from her lips. She scrambled to her feet and fled into the shadows, feeling rather than hearing the shouts of *"Halt!"* and the bullets raining down on her from the shattered window. She saw a van and a troop transport parked outside the house where she had been transmitting and wondered how long it had taken them to pinpoint her location. *I couldn't have been on the air for more than five minutes!* she realized with a start.

Her heart pounded in her chest, and her pulse screamed in her ears and throbbed through her neck and bruised body like a speeding freight train. Her feet flew over the snow and onto the back porch of another abandoned house, but her boots slipped on the icy planks, threatening to surrender her to the Germans approaching from behind. With every ounce of strength she had left, she launched herself into the closed door, turning the handle in case it was unlocked, but forcing the door with all the energy her slender frame could muster until it fell inward on rusted hinges. She ran down a hallway, dodging broken furniture and bashing her shins against an over-turned table in the darkness before finding a door on the opposite side of the house and exiting onto a weed-choked driveway. Without hesitating to see if her pursuers might have approached around the sides of the building, she ran as fast as her legs would take her across the driveway, over a waist-high stone wall covered with winter-dead grapevines, and into a neglected, decades-old apple orchard thick with underbrush.

There Marie rested, hiding in the bottom of a weed-choked ditch until her breathing slowed and she could decide what to do. She watched the darkened shapes of her pursuers and knew that she had momentarily eluded them. But she suspected that within moments torches would be lit and search dogs released, and no escape would be possible. Staying as close to the ground as she could, she followed the ditch, stepping in snow and standing water and ice up to her ankles until she could no longer feel her toes inside her useless boots. Her path led her through the orchard and through a field still thick with last year's cornstalks. The drooping leaves were blessedly soggy and silent as she moved through their shadows.

Her pursuers must have been counting on apprehending her at the table, she realized, for they seemed disorganized in their pursuit and not sufficient in numbers to search the whole countryside. *Lucky for me,* Marie thought, and she hurried away from the scene of the crime.

FIVE

In different circumstances Marie Jacobson could have climbed the mountain behind her to its summit and seen the panorama of the Rhône as it snaked around the village of Izieu and headed back to the northeast. In the morning darkness the reflection of the full moon on the river would be visible for miles in both directions, and she would see the tiny community below her gradually awaken. Blackout shades would be lifted. Businessmen would migrate in the direction of their respective offices in the surrounding communities, and factory workers on bicycles would sound bells as they navigated uneven streets. Children dressed in multiple layers would clutch the hands of over-worked housewives on their way to the market. To the villagers of Izieu, the war might have seemed insignificant: no German troops patrolled the village streets, and, tucked as Izieu was high in the mountains east of Lyon, not much happened to remind the villagers of the war.

In the darkness Marie heard the wind moving the treetops at the edge of the clearing. An icy breeze carried the noise past her on its way down the mountainside toward the village. Her hands felt numb and she raised them to her mouth, blowing on them in a futile attempt to keep them warm. Her shoulder-length hair refused to stay tucked beneath her wool beret, and her brown locks escaped and fell into her eyes on a regular basis. She huddled behind a tangle of bushes at the edge of the clearing and wrapped her coat tightly around her slender frame, trying not to shiver too violently in the bitter darkness. Her shoulder hurt from her catapult through the window six hours before, and she knew the arm of her coat where she had shielded her face from the glass would be in shreds. Other than that, she had been fortunate in her escape from the German detection unit.

It still bothered her that she hadn't been able to receive confirmation from the coders at Grendon that her message had been understood. She was positive she'd been cautious—she could not imagine she had made mistakes in her coding. But as there was no way to confirm that her message had been deciphered in time to inform the RAF, there was still a strong possibility that the drop would take place tonight.

Félix's arm brushed her shoulder as he shifted position next to her. She turned and looked at him affectionately. His dark hair looked characteristically unruly and his cap sat at a rakish angle. She watched the rise and fall of his chest as he used his binoculars to search the clear night sky. After a few minutes he laid down the binoculars, pulled off his gloves, and blew on his hands, rubbing them together vigorously in an attempt to regain feeling. He glanced in her direction and smiled, his dark eyes crinkling in the way meant especially for her. He leaned his face close to hers and whispered, "Glad you're here, *chérie.*"

She smiled back at him. Perhaps she'd been mistaken. Everything was fine. It had just been her overactive imagination that had caused her such trepidation, and it was as he said: while she was in France she would just have to learn to live with the anxiety she had felt today—perhaps even on a daily basis.

On the opposite side of Félix, Jacques Bellamont checked his ammunition and adjusted the Stenmark slung across his shoulders. His movements were silent and efficient, his military training evident in the way he handled his weapon.

On the other side of Marie, a fourth member of their group fumbled nervously with his rifle. Seventeen-year-old Hervé's breath escaped in short bursts as he shifted position in the snow. He had every reason to join the Résistance, Marie thought, remembering Félix's account of the boy's misfortunes.

The wind moaned through the trees, howling like a wounded soldier. It penetrated Marie's useless coat, heavy woolen trousers, and thin leather boots. She wrapped her arms around herself and shivered. Above the moaning of the trees she thought she heard another sound. She looked at her fiancé, her eyes questioning.

Félix nodded encouragingly. "It won't be long now, Amélie. Are you all right?" She nodded and returned his smile, and they both listened to the low rumble of an approaching aircraft.

Jacques whispered, "Hudson light bomber. She'll be here in a moment." Félix, Jacques, Hervé, and Marie removed flashlights from underneath their coats. At Félix's nod they left their hiding place and entered the clearing. Their task was to take formation and indicate the drop zone to the approaching plane. Marie moved into position near the middle of the formation, her flashlight still unlit as she waited for the signal.

The snow-packed clearing gleamed white in the moonlight. A full moon was imperative for a drop: the pilot had to be able to locate the site, and, at an altitude of three hundred feet, moonlight would make the contrast between trees and meadow snow visible to the plane's navigator. Once the crew located the pinpoints of light from the formation on the ground, the plane would increase altitude and circle for another pass, then drop its cargo as it flew a second time across the clearing.

Several moments passed and the low rumble intensified above the trees. A dark shadow passed above the far edge of the clearing, and Félix turned on his flashlight and shined the beam directly upward into the night sky. Marie, Jacques, and Hervé followed suit, holding their lights steady while Félix signaled the plane with short flashes of pre-arranged code.

The twin-engine bomber crossed the clearing and disappeared above the opposite tree line. Marie heard its engines fading for a few moments before it circled to again pass overhead, this time at an altitude of six hundred feet. As it appeared the second time, its shadow spilled a line of shapes that blossomed in the darkness—seven mushrooms floating downward in the empty night sky. Its task complete, the bomber continued west toward Lyon.

Marie and her three companions watched as the gray shapes floated silently toward their position. Jacques spoke then, and his quiet voice carried across the clearing. "Gather them quickly. Someone will report to the Germans." Many villagers, though amicable during the day, would not hesitate to inform the occupiers of a plane circling the high meadow after midnight.

Félix ran for the first parachute. Once the attached canister had settled in the snow, he grabbed the billowing material and rolled it into a tight bundle against his chest. With a small knife he dislodged the parachute straps from the metal canister and threw the fabric aside. He grasped the metal tube and pulled it rapidly toward the edge of the clearing.

Another parachute deflated in the snow near Marie. She approached, capturing the heavy fabric and tugging it away from the cylinder. Following her fiancé's example, she rolled it into a tight bundle against her chest and threw it to the side. She then unsheathed a small knife and sawed at the harness. The straps took several precious moments to separate from the canister and Marie glanced anxiously across the clearing at her friends. Except for the cylinder she still struggled to dislodge, they had pulled the last of the canisters into a pile. Félix moved in her direction and Hervé disappeared into the trees, heading for the road to bring the truck.

Marie wrestled with the container. Taller than herself and at least three times her weight, the canister refused to budge. She pushed her unruly brown hair out of her face and bent again to her task. She gave the object a tremendous heave and her feet slipped in the snowy grass. She was struggling to rise when her peripheral vision registered a small, almost imperceptible flash of light at the edge of the clearing. She froze, halfway to her feet, but when she turned in the direction of the light it had disappeared.

Marie's heart missed a beat as she saw Félix drop to the snow and motion for Jacques to do the same. Panic rose in her throat as she realized someone was watching the clearing. Marie watched Félix release the safety on his Colt automatic and Jacques slip the Stenmark carefully from his shoulder. Now that the plane had come and gone, they found themselves in a precarious situation. Whoever waited for them would act soon, moving in to capture them and confiscate the supply canisters. Marie realized the moon's illumination of the clearing not only benefited the passing aircraft but also anyone interested in their activities.

Crouched in the clearing, Jacques and Félix held their weapons ready. From the road below the clearing Marie heard gunfire. She felt sick. *Hervé! They found Hervé!* She clutched the handle of her knife tightly, as if the small blade could offer protection against a barrage of machine-gun fire.

She jerked back defensively when a spotlight flooded the clearing, its strong light exploding inside her head and forcing her to raise a hand to protect her eyes. For one agonizing second she tried to convince herself that she was dreaming, that in a moment Félix would awaken her from this nightmare and take her home. Twenty feet from Marie, Félix raised his weapon and fired at the floodlight, shattering the glass and throwing the clearing back into darkness. In the ensuing confusion Félix shouted her name as he bolted for the cover of the trees. Marie stumbled after the sound of his voice, struggling to keep her footing in the snow while her eyes fought temporary blindness. She heard shouts behind her and the whistle of bullets moments before her hands brushed the foliage at the tree line. Blinking rapidly, she forced herself to push onward, and her eyesight returned just as her fiancé's hand grasped her arm.

She struggled to keep up with Félix's headlong flight. Up ahead Jacques passed beneath the trees and Marie felt the sting of snow on her cheeks as powder dislodged from branches and filled the air. She heard shouts behind them and she tugged Félix's hand.

"What about Hervé?"

"There's nothing we can do for him." Félix glanced in her direction, his eyes worried. "Somebody's betrayed us to the *boches*."

The terrain changed, sloping upward. Branches laden with snow tore at Marie's arms and clouded her vision. She clutched Félix's hand and glanced over her shoulder. Their movements left a path in the snow, and the moonlight would make it easy to follow. "Who would have known about the drop?"

His grip on her hand steadied her as they negotiated the slippery face of a boulder.

Jacques whispered from above them, "They're right behind us."

Félix reached his friend and pulled Marie up beside him. "We have darkness on our side—at least for the moment." He glanced up the slope. "We need to find a place to hide."

"Hide?" Jacques snorted. "The new German major is a bloodhound. I'm sure he's down the hill, hot on our trail."

"We might get lucky."

"Let's keep moving," Marie said. She touched Félix's sleeve. "You're right. We've got to find a place to hide."

Félix pulled Marie forward, following Jacques deeper into the forest. Behind them Marie could hear the sounds of pursuit, and panic gave her the strength to keep up with her companions' rapid pace. She tried to ignore the sounds behind them, but she couldn't help imagining that any moment would bring the echo of a rifle and the burning pain of a bullet tearing through her flesh. She wondered what it would be like to die.

"Up ahead." Félix pointed, indicating a small stream cutting across their path. He wasted no breath explaining but simply ran in the direction of his discovery. On the opposite bank the ground sloped gently downward for several hundred yards before rising again toward the summit. The depression acted as a natural wind tunnel, channeling cold morning air across the slope with a force that had cleared the entire area of its covering of snow. "If we cross the stream we'll have that slope to hide our tracks," Félix explained as he turned to follow the streambed, searching for a way to cross the icy flow. "We haven't much time."

Jacques shook his head. "The major is no fool, my friend. He'll never even miss the snow."

"We'll take whatever time it buys us—even if it's only a few minutes." Félix's eyes searched for a crossing.

Marie glanced down the stream. "Over there—a tree across the stream."

"It looks sturdy." Félix moved passed her. "Let me go first; a tumble in this cold water would kill you." He tested the log with his foot, then carefully stepped onto the center and leaned forward. It settled under his weight but held steady. Félix then placed one foot in front of the other and advanced across the stream until the tapering trunk bowed under his weight and disappeared into the swirling blackness. He hesitated momentarily and then jumped and landed in the snow on the opposite bank.

Félix turned and gestured urgently for Marie, and she stepped out onto the log, forcing herself not to look at the swirling darkness below her. The water moved swiftly underneath the makeshift bridge, and she grasped a branch for support. Balancing herself, she maneuvered across the tree trunk like a tightrope walker. At the point where the trunk's narrow tip submerged in the current, she lunged toward the opposite bank and landed securely next to Félix. Jacques quickly followed her across, then turned to grasp the end of the makeshift bridge and work it back and forth until the trunk splintered from its base and slid into the swirling stream, spinning lazily in the current as it continued down the mountain and out of sight. "Anything for a few extra minutes, right?" With that, Jacques shifted the strap of his weapon and disappeared into the trees.

They continued downstream for several hundred yards before turning across the valley, staying under cover of the trees wherever possible. For several minutes Marie heard nothing but the movement of the creek behind them and wondered if perhaps they had outmaneuvered their followers.

But the thought ended abruptly. Behind them, gunfire erupted and a branch near her head exploded into kindling. Startled, she jumped sideways. Another shot followed immediately, brushing her cheek as lightly as a feather before burying itself with a dull thud into a tree trunk in front of her.

Félix glanced at her as they ran. "Are you all right?"

Marie nodded, but her eyes were wide with dread. No training could have prepared her for the stark terror of being tracked by a gunman. Somewhere behind them a German sniper had them in and out of his sights, and he was taking advantage of every opportunity to fire in their direction. Marie forced herself to swallow her fear and move forward.

They reached the other side of the small valley and began to climb the slope. For several minutes the ground rose gently and the tree cover thickened, the tangled branches pulling at their legs as they ran. Félix spoke, his breath coming hard and fast. "They're not alpine troops—maybe we can still outrun them."

Jacques disagreed. "Not if that new major is with them. Whoever's back there has managed to track us without a moment's difficulty."

"What do we do now?" Marie felt the strain of their rapid ascent in every muscle. Up ahead the mountain steepened considerably, and the jagged rocks pushed skyward as if holding back the stars. Between boulders the silent shadows of trees rose toward the summit.

Her fiancé studied the terrain. "All right, Bruno. Any ideas?"

Jacques wiped the sweat from his forehead. "If we try going around, they will easily close the distance. As it is, we have them at a slight disadvantage—higher ground, you know."

Félix glanced at his friend and a look of understanding passed between them. "Remember the summer before we went to Paris?"

Jacques chuckled grimly. "How could I forget? Best hunting trip we ever had."

Félix turned to Marie and explained, "His brother convinced us we'd be safe from predators if we had the higher ground." He pointed through the trees toward an outcropping halfway up the slope in front of them.

Marie looked where her fiancé pointed and saw moonlight reflecting off the smooth surface of the rocks. Her jaw dropped. "And how do you propose we get there?"

He shrugged.

"It's too steep . . ." Marie looked in disbelief from one man to the other. "What, exactly, are you two planning?"

Again Jacques and Félix glanced at each other. Félix spoke. "*Chérie,* we're about out of options. The Germans have us at a disadvantage."

"So you're turning to fight." Marie felt her throat tighten. "You're going to see how many Germans you can ambush before they get us."

Félix spoke. "I know this is hard to understand, but we've got no choice."

"There's got to be another way. I can't accept this as the only option!"

"There's no way around, honey. No way but up. Unless you want to surrender to the Germans . . ."

"Perhaps we should."

"Honey, you know what will happen if we do. I know they briefed you on what would happen . . ."

Marie's gaze faltered. They would torture her. They would try to squeeze information from her about the Résistance and the Allies' plans. She would hold her tongue, and the Germans would consider her stubborn and torture her more. She would be beaten senseless and wrapped in bandages and thrown on a couch for other prisoners to see, just as Jean Moulin had been in Lyon. The thought made her legs go weak. She took a deep breath. "They'll kill us if we try to hide up there."

"They'll try." Jacques sounded impatient. "But we'll pick them off one by one as they climb the slope."

"Yes," Marie shot back, "until your ammunition gives out. Do you think they'll leave you alone then? They've probably already sent for reinforcements."

Félix interrupted. "*Chérie,* we have to try."

Jacques nodded toward the valley behind them. "The sun will be rising soon, my friends. We need to get this thing done." He turned and headed resolutely for the slope.

Félix spoke softly. "There may be a way to escape on the other side of the outcropping leading to the summit. I want you to find one and see how far you can get. Perhaps you'll be lucky . . ."

"I won't leave you—I can fight . . ."

Félix kissed her on the forehead. "I believe it, *chérie.* You've been a fighter ever since I first met you."

Marie ran toward the outcropping with Félix close behind. With every ounce of energy she had she attacked the slope, clutching at the terrain with her hands and elbows, her knees and boots. She hurried between clusters of trees, pausing to rest briefly, wrapping her arms defensively around a trunk and trying not to look at the drop-off falling away into blackness only inches from their path. She heard Félix behind her and quickened her pace. Above her, Jacques had reached the last stretch of trail before the outcropping. The moon illuminated the rock formation above her, and sporadic gunfire accompanied her efforts as sharpshooters below tried to pluck them from the face of the cliff. Jacques disappeared over the edge of the nearest boulder. He kept his head below the level of the rocks as he motioned for them to hurry.

Marie fought a morbid desire to turn to see their pursuers, who were hidden somewhere in the darkness behind them. She clawed her way toward Jacques while Félix whispered encouragement from behind. He grasped her waist and lifted her the few remaining feet upward until she was able to grasp Jacques's outstretched hand.

As Jacques took hold of her hand, Marie's world exploded into a nightmare. Félix's strong hands on her waist shuddered violently and loosened. At the same instant she heard the sharp burst of machine-gun fire below them and multiple bullets striking their target. With a moan, Félix leaned agonizingly against Marie's legs and then rolled away, pulled by gravity toward the valley below. He twisted like a rag doll and crashed through the underbrush, bouncing as he fell. Marie screamed and struggled to free herself from Jacques's grip.

"He's dead, Amélie. We've got to let him go."

"I can't leave him! *I can't leave him!*" Using her free hand she peeled at Jacques's fingers, clawing violently until he swore and released her hand. She slid several feet down the slope before finding her footing.

"Amélie," Jacques whispered from above her, "I can't be caught. You understand, don't you?"

She nodded, and after one last haunted look in her direction, Jacques disappeared.

Marie turned and sprinted down the slope, willing her legs to stay under her as she careened downward. Shock and disbelief kept her eyes dry and her body numb. Félix would be all right. He had to be all right. She reached the valley floor and ran toward Félix's twisted body. She ignored several dark shapes following her and flung herself to her knees next to the still form in the snow. Reality struck as her hands lifted his head into her lap, and she tried not to glance down at his mutilated torso. Something wet and sticky ran across her wrist and pooled at her side. His breath, shallow and weak, escaped his crushed chest with effort. Marie stroked his hair and repeated his name over and over as if she could think of nothing else to say.

"You need to . . . return to America." Félix struggled to form the words.

Marie fought her tears. "You'll make it—I know you will." She forced a smile. "Remember, Jacques says you're too stubborn to die."

Félix's lungs fought for air. He tried to lift his hand to touch Marie, but it dropped uselessly back into the snow. "You'll be all right, *chérie*. I know how strong you are . . ."

Her voice shook. "I'll be all right."

"You'll go back to your family . . . in Utah . . ."

She smoothed back his damp hair and kissed his forehead, which was sticky with sweat. "I love you, Félix," she whispered.

"Marie . . . I love you too . . ." All code names disappeared along with pretense, and Marie stroked his forehead gently.

A sound to their left startled Marie and she jerked her head up sharply. Ten yards away a tall German officer appeared in the shadows of the trees. He moved deliberately toward her, followed by several soldiers brandishing rifles. She watched him approach, her apprehension growing with his every step. His shiny black boots sank into the snow and his dark overcoat trailed down past the tops of his boots to brush across the frozen grass. Darkness masked his face, but as he drew close, Marie sensed a familiarity in his stride. She watched, horrified, as he paused next to her and bent to one knee in the snow. From under the brim of his visor cap the German officer studied her unruly hair and defiant eyes, and she recognized the man from the café.

Marie felt defeated. She cradled Félix's head in her arms and tried not to shudder. The officer's eyes searched hers, reading her fear and pain. "How is he?"

"He—he's dying." Her voice trembled with accusation as well as fear.

The officer leaned closer to study the man in her arms, and then for a split second he froze, letting out a strangled gasp. Whirling, he shouted in German at his men, and two soldiers turned immediately and raced down the slope. He removed his overcoat and laid it over Félix, tucking it around the tortured body with a gentleness that surprised Marie. "I will get a doctor for him, mademoiselle . . ." The man's voice sounded strangely tight, and Marie stared at him, surprised.

Suddenly she felt her fiancé's body convulse in her arms. She looked down at him and was startled to see him staring at the German officer, his eyes wide and unnaturally bright. Félix seemed to recognize the man, and he whispered incoherently, urgently. He again struggled to raise his hand off the grass and this time succeeded in clutching weakly at the edge of the German officer's tunic. Marie glanced from her fiancé to the officer and was shocked to see similar feelings mirrored in both men's eyes. Félix struggled again to speak, but the effort was too much and with one last agonized gasp he let go of the German officer's uniform. Then his hand fell back into the snow and he went still against Marie's chest.

"*Félix!*" The scream wrenched from her lips, and at the outer perimeters of her grief her mind registered the German officer crouched next to her with a stunned expression on his face.

Finally the man turned to her and placed a gentle hand on her shoulder. He sounded sorrowful as he said, "Please stand up, mademoiselle."

She recoiled from his touch, and when he rose to his feet and offered her his gloved hand, she refused his assistance and clung to Félix's body. Another soldier reached down and grabbed her by the arm, hauling her firmly to her feet and escorting her away from Félix. She turned to look one last time at her fiancé and saw the German officer dropping again to one knee next to Félix Larouche's lifeless form.

SIX

When the Italian Zone turned management of their affairs over to the Germans, they left southern France in a state of unrest. With the Italians, at least, citizens felt as if they had an iota of control over their own futures. The Italian armies, with their friendly ways and casual supervision, did not spark such hatred in the Résistance and *maquisards* as did the German garrisons that quickly intimidated their way into the formerly Vichy communities.

"Intimidation" might not be the best description of the Germans' tactics in Belley in November of 1943. Just the simple fact that they were enemy forces determined to crush the opposition sent French citizens into a quandary. How could they continue their way of life with the regulations imposed by the hated German *boches?*

When they first arrived the previous year, the Germans tried to be cordial with their reluctant neighbors, and officers were under orders to treat the local populace with respect and to try to limit confrontations whenever possible. But under the circumstances it was understandable when greetings were ignored or mothers bodily pulled their children away from approaching troops in order to avoid contact. As time passed, however, a percentage of the good citizens of Belley and surrounding communities softened toward the Occupation. A pleasantry here, a conversation there—and since the "non-fraternization policy" imposed on the troops by the new Nazi major extended only to the exclusion of trysts with members of the opposite sex, as time went by and many citizens relaxed their distrust of the Germans, on a weekend it was not uncommon to see Germans and Frenchmen drinking together in the cafés along the Place des Terreaux or in many other establishments throughout the city.

The major himself never made an appearance in these drinking circles, and so his reputation developed principally by what information passed between drunken soldiers and their local drinking buddies. Members of the Résistance gained a reluctant respect for the new German officer while they friendshipped his young troops and enticed them with any available alcohol. They plied the inexperienced *boches* for information on the major's plans and the major's movements, and when their unwitting German subjects became too drunk to do more than babble, the Frenchmen carried the information to their superiors.

The Nazi major had his own spies and gained a good amount of information in return. It seemed the Allies had plans for the coming year—plans that included the cooperation of Résistance cells in France and Belgium—and might be trying to implement those plans now. There had been reports from *départements* throughout France of an influx of Allied agents over the past weeks, as if Charles de Gaulle was organizing some sort of enormous Résistance activity—possibly to distract the Germans and keep them looking in the opposite direction. Rumor in Lyon held that the Allies were planning a massive invasion for the first part of next year—and the major's orders from his superiors gave high priority to the apprehension and interrogation of all Allied agents and Résistance fighters. Therefore, a good bit of German espionage also took place among the drinking circles of Belley. The major's spies had discovered the pending arrival of the American woman and had tracked her and her French connections to his *département*. He had taken it upon himself to find out as much as he could about her, and when his source had pointed her out in the café yesterday morning, he had been ready to arrest her. But he had cautioned himself to be patient, realizing she might be more helpful to him on the street than in an interrogation room—at least for the time being. Especially if she could lead him to the Résistance leader his sources referred to as "Bruno."

Major Rolf Schulmann had been tracking Bruno for weeks—ever since being assigned to Belley and hearing of the elusive escape artist who terrorized German garrisons from Lyon to Marseilles. Several times the major had come close to apprehending Bruno, but each time Bruno had managed to slip away undetected. Evasive as a ghost, Bruno always seemed one sabotage ahead of him and one contact richer—until today.

Until today, Bruno could have brushed by Schulmann on the street and the major would never have known. But this morning when the fourth member of the Résistance group managed to escape, even when cornered, the major wondered if the man might be the elusive Bruno. When the floodlight in the clearing had showed him the man's face, he had realized he'd seen the man around Belley, laughing and drinking with off-duty soldiers in the cafés and teaching in the *école primaire* during the week. In fact, Major Schulmann remembered the man had once spoken with him—a brief and innocent request for the time initiated by the man himself in front of a café on the Place des Terreaux. If this man were actually Bruno, then Schulmann finally knew his real name, and the American woman he had captured could help track him down.

As his driver turned the black Citroën into the Place des Terreaux, Rolf Schulmann could see the two sixteenth-century towers of the Château de Lafont in the distance. Soon the entire structure would be visible, with its classical European architecture and Roman-inspired stone arches. The château belonged to a Monsieur Jean-Motier Boisseau, but the major had requisitioned it for the Germans' use after his arrival this year. His troops had applauded the change—from a low stone barracks on the outskirts of civilization where dinner was served chuckwagon style in the courtyard, to the luxurious mansion in the center of town. Monsieur Boisseau had not been enthusiastic about the situation, but what could he do? These were the Germans, not the Italians. So he had shrugged his shoulders and moved in with his eighty-year-old mother in Lyon.

The major's driver turned into the stone courtyard of the Château de Lafont. Several trucks and a lorry were parked in front of the wide stairway, and as his vehicle circled the courtyard he saw metal cylinders stacked amid bundles of parachutes in the open back of one of the trucks. The confiscated Allied supplies represented a dismal failure for Bruno and a severe blow to the *maquisards,* who would be expecting the armaments and provisions donated by the Allies. His troops would have returned several hours ago with their prisoner, since the major had opted to complete a bit of unfinished business at the location of the Frenchman's death before returning to Belley. He waited for his driver to open the door, then he stepped onto the cobblestones and stretched, his strong body upright and his back slightly arched as his long arms reached skyward. He stifled a yawn and moved toward the stairs.

Major Schulmann's entire body ached from the morning's exercise. He had severely underestimated Bruno's tenacity, and he and his troops had paid for it physically. At least none of his troops had been shot. He wouldn't have to write condolences to some widowed mother in Germany saying that her only son had been shot in the line of duty and had died a hero of the Third Reich.

Entering the main reception area, the major removed his overcoat and handed it to his aide. He walked across the marble tiles and climbed the grand staircase toward the second floor and his office. Partway up, he stole a glance downward to where the staircase spiraled into the darkness of the cellar—used as a dungeon in the sixteenth century and a prison for POWs during the Great War. He found it ironic that just twenty-five years later, dungeons used for German prisoners in 1918 should now house Germany's enemies. The woman he had arrested early that morning now waited in a cell below him. The major paused, thinking. Even though she would help tremendously in Bruno's capture, something about her troubled him. He continued on and, reaching the second floor, followed the hallway to his office. Closing the door behind him, he adjusted his sidearm, absently snapping the leather cover over the Luger's grip. He tossed his hat onto the desk next to a book and a photograph of his wife.

Major Schulmann sat behind his desk and leaned his head into his hands. He'd had a headache ever since the capture, and now he tried to lessen the pain by massaging his temples. He couldn't get the American woman out of his mind. He remembered her headlong flight to the dying man's side though she could easily have been mowed down by the major's men. Perhaps her haste had been what saved her life. His soldiers had been startled by her actions—no one in their right mind would rush *into* the enemy, especially without a weapon—and the slight figure hurtling down the mountainside had clearly been unarmed.

What bothered the major was the woman's obvious attachment to the man killed in the raid. He thought about the dead Frenchman. He had been shocked and dismayed to see the man lying there in the snow—his soldiers had only been obeying the major's orders when they'd shot the fugitive down from the mountainside. How could his soldiers have known . . . ?

If the major had known Félix Larouche was among those he was pursuing up the mountainside, he would have moved heaven and earth to bring him in alive.

* * *

Blindness causes one's other senses to sharpen dramatically, Marie thought as she squinted into the darkness of her confinement. And that blindness, coupled with barely concealed panic, fear of the unknown, and morbid anticipation of the future, could change a person—*like a wild animal cornered.* She leaned her head sideways until she felt the cold moisture of the stone wall pressed against her cheek. Her knuckles gripped the edge of the rough-hewn bench and she breathed in the smell of centuries-old decay. Her heart beat so loudly she was sure her two guards, laughing and conversing at the foot of the darkened stairway, would be able to hear it if they paused for breath. She swallowed, wishing for a glass of water to reduce the acrid dryness that coated her tongue and the roof of her mouth.

She thought about Félix, his body twisted grotesquely in the snow at the base of the precipice, his pain-filled eyes staring into hers and his grip weakening on her hand. *Why won't the tears come?* She remembered how he used to hold her face in his hands and smile into her eyes, laughing with her and telling her how much he loved her. He used to unexpectedly swing her up into his arms and carry her, protesting wildly, through the doorway into her classroom or across a busy intersection. She remembered once when she had complained about having too much to carry and he had offered to carry her textbooks. Before she could protest, he had swept her into his arms, books and all, and carried her, shrieking and laughing, the remaining three blocks to her apartment.

Marie reached to touch the cold stone pressed against her face. Condensation made the wall slippery, and she scratched absently at the surface with her fingernails. She was dry-eyed, numb. She realized it would be impossible to cry; she felt like she had died with Félix, and dead people did not cry.

The loud jangle of a telephone startled her back to the present. One of the guards answered it, still laughing at whatever he and his comrade had been discussing. Marie heard the mirth in his voice quickly change to respect as he listened and responded to the speaker at the other end. He replaced the receiver and said something to the other guard. Then lights came on in the corridor outside her cell, and Marie heard footsteps approaching. She straightened, staring at the small square of light at the top of the door while she tried to breathe normally. She realized she was not ready to face an interrogation—could a person ever be ready to face torture? Her knees trembled and she doubted she had the strength to stand. She swallowed, and the bitter taste of her own saliva caused her empty stomach to rebel, forcing stinging acid up her throat and into her mouth as the terror of her predicament overwhelmed her.

The door opened, flooding her cell with light from the corridor. "On your feet. *Schnell!*" One of the guards reached to lift her from the bench, and his fingers dug into her upper arm. She rose on shaky legs and moved toward the door, trying to breathe against the nausea and fear that tightened her chest and made her light-headed. She then walked between her escorts down the corridor and up the curving staircase, leaving the dampness of the basement for the grandeur of the château's marbled entry before continuing to the second floor.

At the top of the stairs the guards escorted her down a hallway to a large office near the far end. As Marie entered, her eyes swept the room, taking in a framed photograph of Adolph Hitler among a group of loyal supporters on the wall behind the major's desk. A coat stand in the corner held an assortment of objects—several hats, a common gray wool scarf, and a bulky woolen coat that reached almost to the floor. She looked at the desk and noticed her French identification papers spread haphazardly across its surface along with the morning's newspaper, a small package tied with twine, an address book, and several other documents written in German. A small pencil holder fashioned in the frivolous shape of a fish held several pencils and pens protruding at uneven angles from its backside, and a mug of what looked like clear, cold water reminded her of her thirst and forced her to swallow uncomfortably.

Light from a narrow window fell on a small, framed portrait of a young woman, which was propped against a telephone on the desk. The photograph captured Marie's attention, and she studied it closely. The woman stood centered in the shot, her light hair tied back in a youthful ponytail that made her look sixteen. She wore a white dress that fit snugly around her pregnant middle, and she stood on the banks of a river with several other people. She looked happy, and her smile made her eyes sparkle. Wind whipped at her hair, capturing wisps that had escaped the ribbon and flinging them in haphazard abandon around her delicate cheeks and smiling lips. She had one hand raised as if to block the sun, and her clear eyes focused on a position to the left of the photographer, as if the object of her affection stood nearby. It seemed a beautiful morning in a serene setting, and the people in the photograph were obviously in high spirits.

Marie was startled from her thoughts by the sound of a door opening at the opposite end of the room, and she looked up to see the German officer from the mountainside approaching the desk. She straightened to face him, trying to mask the fear that involuntarily enveloped her. Her hands clenched as she tried to remember her training—*"A Nazi officer's presence is intended to have a powerful effect on a prisoner. The cut, color, and insignia of the uniform have been meticulously designed to project superiority, power, and authority."* Standing here in the commanding presence of this officer, she could now understand the reasoning behind those statements, so mocked by the young cadets behind the backs of their instructors. In the light hanging from the ceiling she now saw details she had missed in the morning darkness. The officer was a *Sturmbannführer*—the German equivalent of a major, she noted, recognizing the insignia she had studied in her crash course with SOE. His gray visor cap displayed the SS eagle and *Totenkopf* embroidered in silver bullion over a dark gray background. His dark gabardine wool tunic was buttoned to his throat and had silver and white piped collar tabs with the SS insignia on the left collar and the four pips of a Nazi major on the right. His broad shoulders displayed the braided silver epaulets of a high-ranking officer, and his double-breasted tunic was belted at the waist with a wide black leather belt, aluminum buckle, and cross-strap. His trousers were of the same material as his jacket, and they tapered to his knees and then disappeared inside black leather boots with knee-high uppers. On his belt he carried a leather gun holster and small straight dagger in a silver-inlaid scabbard. Black gloves completed the ensemble, and Marie felt the whisper of panic that had probably been intended by the sight.

The major removed his cap and hung it on the stand before turning to look at Marie, and she forced herself to meet his gaze. Again she was struck by the intensity of his dark blue eyes, and when she realized he could read her emotions she fought the urge to look away.

He was a walking contradiction, she thought. His tall, muscular frame suggested power, but his large hands reminded her of those of a carpenter rather than an interrogator. She wondered if he might just prefer a quiet fishing excursion to an afternoon spent in the Führer's illustrious service. He obviously exemplified the Aryan purity so preferred by the Nazi Party, yet his eyes held nothing of the cold cruelty Marie had expected to find in an SS officer. Instead, she remembered her first impression of him from the café—that this was a man who tried to hide his emotions behind a facade of duty. The picture on his desk suggested he was capable of feeling. Could it be a picture of his wife? *What must it be like to be married to a Nazi officer?* Marie shuddered at the thought and felt a twinge of compassion for the woman in the photograph.

The major did not take his seat but instead remained standing. Perplexed, Marie wondered what he would do. It all seemed so wrong—this was not what she was expecting. Except for the uneasiness created by his authority and rank, she might have been entering a businessman's office for a job interview. She stood stiffly in front of him, determined not to allow his civility to throw her off balance.

The major issued a short command, and without a word the guards saluted, turned, and left the room. Marie sensed that the officer was accustomed to having his commands obeyed without question. He studied her carefully, and she felt uncomfortable under the intense scrutiny of his gaze. When he spoke, his French was perfect and his voice companionable, almost gentle. "My name is Major Rolf Schulmann of the Allgemeine SS. I am here in Belley under direct orders from Major Walter Schellenberg. My assignment in Belley is to gather intelligence on the members of the French Résistance in this district." Major Schulmann picked up the photograph from his desk. "As I entered I noticed your interest in this photograph." He held it out to her. "Please, feel free to take a closer look. This is my wife, shortly before the birth of our child."

Marie awkwardly accepted the picture with shaking hands. It unnerved her that a Nazi interrogator would talk to her as if she were his equal. *Trying to show he is human,* she thought. The absurdity was that if she allowed herself to look into his eyes, he actually seemed it. She lowered her head and studied the photograph so she wouldn't have to look into his eyes.

"She is beautiful," she said.

"Yes, she is."

"Is she here with you—in Belley?"

"No."

"When will you get to see her again?"

Major Schulmann frowned. "Not for a very long time."

"It must be difficult to be away from your family." She handed him the photograph, and he set it carefully on the desk.

"It is, mademoiselle."

The conversation made her uncomfortable. Marie shifted uneasily and could think of nothing else to say.

She felt his scrutiny. "You are young, mademoiselle. How old are you?"

"Twenty-four."

Without warning he casually switched to English. "And what prompted you to come to France?"

Marie's heart skipped a beat and she forced herself to breathe calmly. The major knew more about her than she had expected, and it unnerved her. She forced her brows to pucker slightly as if she did not understand.

He smiled at her attempt to look bewildered and continued in English, "Why did you come to Belley?"

"Je ne comprends pas."

"Si, vous comprenez. Yes, you *do* understand, mademoiselle, and if you cooperate it will be easier for both of us."

Her heart pounding, Marie shook her head and frowned, feigning confusion.

Major Schulmann sighed. "Your name is not Amélie Leduc. Your real name is Marie Jacobson and you are an American citizen. I knew before you were captured that an Allied agent had arrived in my district. I knew you were coming to France even before you lost your goggles over the Rhône-Alpes. Now tell me, please, why you are here."

Marie shivered at the mention of her infamous goggles and felt defeated. Surrendering, she switched to her native tongue. "To visit a friend."

"The British went to a lot of trouble to finance an excursion to visit a friend." Schulmann smiled. "Please tell me the real reason you are here, Marie Jacobson."

Marie met Schulmann's gaze and said nothing.

"I have asked you politely to cooperate. Answer my question, please."

Marie could feel her heart beating faster. She forced herself to keep silent.

"You were arrested under suspicion of collaboration with members of the Résistance. You were in the hills above Izieu with members of the Résistance. You were assisting the Résistance in accepting supplies from the British. Again, I will ask you, why are you here?"

Marie said nothing.

"The SOE trained you extensively, didn't they? You were taught never to give away information under interrogation." Schulmann sat behind his desk, his eyes on hers. "You are afraid of me, Miss Jacobson?"

Marie lifted her chin defiantly.

"They are meticulous in their training, are they not?" His eyes darkened slightly. "But I am also meticulous in my interrogations, mademoiselle. I will take as much time as I need to in order to discover the truth. So . . ." He leaned back in his chair, his eyes never leaving her face. "Either you will cooperate, or we will be together for a very, very long time."

* * *

Marie felt the headache begin as a suggestion at the back of her neck and radiate downward between her shoulder blades, where the tension tightened her muscles and stiffened her back. By the time Major Schulmann offered her lunch, her entire skull throbbed as if pounded by a sledgehammer. Every question he asked skillfully probed at her ability to maintain the tattered remnants of a cover. He knew she was an American. He stubbornly stuck to English, and Marie had to admit he had an excellent command of the language. She wondered where he had learned it—his perfect pronunciation could have placed him in the center of Times Square and no native speaker would have been the wiser. He knew when she had parachuted into France—and where she had done so, thanks to her own error. He knew she'd been trained by the SOE. He knew she'd been working with members of the Résistance, and he'd alluded to knowing that the men on the mountainside with her had been Résistance leaders. She waited, cautiously wondering what else he knew.

Schulmann picked up her French identification papers from the desk. "These documents are forged, mademoiselle. Where did you get these papers?"

"From a contact. I don't know his name."

Schulmann changed the subject. "Did Félix Larouche secure a position for you as a teacher at *La Maison d'Izieu?*"

She started at his mention of her fiancé, then swallowed uncomfortably. "They needed another teacher. The director was kind enough to . . ."

"Who at *La Maison* is involved with the Résistance?"

Marie's eyes grew wide. "How should I know that, sir? I've been there only once, for a brief few hours. I was told they needed another teacher, and they were kind enough to give me a job—that's all."

Schulmann's lips twisted slightly. He leaned forward, lacing his fingers together in front of him. His voice softened and he watched her closely. "Tell me about Félix Larouche."

His words brought back her grief at losing the man she loved, and she stubbornly shook her head, refusing to answer his question.

"Was he this 'friend' you mentioned?"

Marie recalled the major's perplexity as he stood over Félix's body. She said, "You recognized him from somewhere, didn't you?"

Schulmann frowned. "No, mademoiselle, it is *my* turn to ask the questions. You will answer, please. What is your relationship to Félix Larouche?"

Marie dropped her eyes. "He was my fiancé. We were to be married after the war."

"Ahh . . ." Major Schulmann leaned back in his chair and studied her. "I am sorry for your loss."

His words twisted like a dagger in her heart. She raised her head, her dark eyes flashing. "How can you possibly say such a thing?" She pointed at the portrait of the woman on his desk. "If your wife was murdered and the murderer said, 'I am sorry for your loss,' how would it make you feel?" Suddenly she stopped, terrified at her own impertinence and wishing she could take back her words.

Major Rolf Schulmann's face remained impassive. He studied her thoughtfully and then shifted his eyes to look at the portrait. For a moment he was silent. His voice when he spoke was controlled, soft. "You are right, Marie Jacobson." He hesitated. "However, even though it is hard for you to believe, I *am* sorry for your loss. It is never easy to lose someone you love."

Marie stared at him, fighting back tears. She hated that his words disarmed her and left her feeling vulnerable. She met his gaze and saw in their blue depths a flicker of compassion. For some reason it angered and confused her, and she had to look away.

He spoke gently. "That will be all for this morning." Without another word he stood and left the room, and Marie covered her face with her hands and wept bitterly.

* * *

In the late afternoon the guards again escorted Marie from her cell. This time they mounted only one flight of steps and she was deposited in a large, empty room that might once have been the château's main parlor. Now it was devoid of furnishings, and the curtains hanging at the large windows seemed dingy and cheerless. The light filtering through the trappings carried a slight orange tinge, and the setting sun cast long shadows across the marble floor. A small table and two wooden chairs were all that graced the empty expanse, and Marie wondered what the room must have looked like furnished in all its finery of years past.

Major Rolf Schulmann waited for her. He moved from the window where he had been standing and approached the table. "Miss Jacobson." Schulmann spoke in English and gestured to a chair. "Please. Sit down. We will begin." Obediently, Marie sat, and the major took the chair opposite her at the table. He waved the guards away and smiled at her. "I hope you don't mind, mademoiselle—I must ask you more questions about your fiancé."

"I would prefer you didn't, sir."

"I understand it is a difficult subject . . ." He seemed about to show sympathy, but then he decided against it. "This morning you told me Monsieur Larouche was your fiancé. How did you meet?"

"At the university."

"In Paris?"

Marie hesitated.

"I know you spent your first several years there with your parents, Marie—your father, Monsieur William Jacobson, and your mother, Irma."

She relented, shocked at his knowledge of her background. "It was a university in America."

Schulmann shifted position and looked at her in surprise. "Félix Larouche was with you in America?"

"He was student teaching at the university, and I was in his class."

"When was that?"

"Almost three years ago."

"What did Monsieur Larouche teach?"

"French."

"But you learned French in Paris, did you not? Why did you take a French class at the university? I should think you spoke it as well as your teacher."

"Félix taught everything French—French language, French literature, French history. I met him in his French literature class."

"And you and he were together at the university before he returned to France to join the Résistance. What university did you attend?"

"A private university in the West."

"What university?"

Marie hesitated, annoyed. What did it matter what university she'd attended? Major Schulmann again asked the question.

"What university, Marie?"

"Brigham Young University—in Utah."

Major Rolf Schulmann leaned back in his chair. Folding his arms, he studied her silently for a moment, and to Marie it seemed her answer had given him more information than she had intended. Marie tried to hold his gaze, uncomfortable under his intense scrutiny but determined not to look away. She clasped her hands tightly in her lap and wondered when the torture would begin.

"Why did your family move to the United States?"

Marie shrugged. "My mother wanted to live in Utah."

Major Schulmann frowned. "And how did you feel, abandoning your country?"

"I love France, sir. I have many happy memories of Paris as my home. But I was a child when we moved to the United States. It was my parents' idea."

"Where are your parents now?"

Marie hesitated. "My father is in the United States—at our home in southern Utah. My mother died almost three years ago."

His gaze was penetrating. "These questions make you uncomfortable."

"No, sir." Marie paused. "*You* make me uncomfortable."

Schulmann shrugged, his expression sympathetic. "And I can do nothing about that. I would only suggest you cooperate fully and you will not have to be uncomfortable much longer." He tapped the table with one hand. "Tell me about Jacques Bellamont."

Marie's heart skipped a beat. "Who?"

Major Schulmann smiled tightly. "You are persistent, Miss Jacobson. You pretend not to recognize the name, even though he was a member of your group in this morning's expedition." He sighed. "His code name is Bruno. Does that help you remember?"

"We're told little about each other. Why would I be told Bruno's real name?"

The major studied her carefully. Then he glanced up at the ceiling and said, "He made a valiant effort to escape this morning. But my men are well-trained . . ." He trailed off and returned his gaze to Marie's face, his expression unreadable.

Marie felt sick. *"I can't be caught. You understand, don't you?"* She remembered Jacques's parting words and realized Félix's friend would have fought to the death rather than allow himself to be taken. And she remembered the silence of the château basement and knew she was the only prisoner. They had not brought Jacques back from the mountains. She felt an unreasonable surge of anger at the German sitting across from her, and at the same time she realized that the last fragment of her cover story had disintegrated. She relented.

"What is there to tell? He was Félix's best friend."

"Tell me about Jacques's Résistance work."

Marie shook her head. "Why would he confide in me?"

"You are an agent for the Allied forces. The Allies sent you to help him with something—something important enough to train you and drop you here in my district. What are you supposed to do here?"

Marie held his gaze, unblinking. "It seems we are back to the same question, Major Schulmann. You are mistaken—"

Schulmann waved her objections aside. "I know, I know. You planned to marry Monsieur Larouche. But you have another reason. You traveled to Great Britain with the Women's Army Corps and spent several months training with SOE before parachuting into France. You carry forged identification papers. You are hesitant to tell me the real reason for your return to France . . ."

Marie was silent.

He folded his arms and frowned at her. "I have my sources, Marie. I have been a police interrogator for the German government since I was twenty-six, and for the past five years I have been perfecting my interrogation techniques. If I want to get something from a prisoner, I can get it."

Marie felt a chill run up her spine, but she lifted her chin and said nothing.

Major Schulmann sighed. "Tomorrow things will be different, mademoiselle. Unfortunately, your stubbornness makes it difficult for me to keep you safe. I was contacted today by my superiors in Lyon. They plan to send a Gestapo officer to observe your interrogation. I am concerned that if you do not cooperate he will take you back with him to Section Four headquarters." Schulmann stood and walked to the door. "You refuse to cooperate, and I am concerned for your safety." He opened the door and gestured to the guards standing in the hall. "I will see you tomorrow, mademoiselle. It is late. Try to get some sleep. And . . ." He sighed. "Try to be a little more cooperative tomorrow."

* * *

Marie was still asleep when they came for her. It was impossible to keep track of time in the darkness of her confinement, and when they pulled her from her cot and half dragged her into the corridor her feet became tangled and she fell. Her heart pounded with the suddenness of her awakening, and it took a few moments before she remembered where she was. The guards unceremoniously hauled her to a standing position and carried her up the stairs.

Morning light streamed though the windows as they entered the first floor of the château. This time her guards escorted her past the second floor to the attic, and the last flight of stairs was so narrow they had to ascend single file with Marie in the center. At the landing she waited while her guards opened a heavy wooden door. They ushered her inside and closed the door behind her.

It took a moment for her eyes to adjust to the gloom. The air floated with dust particles that tickled her nose and throat and made her eyes water. She stood with her back against the door and saw light filtering into the room through a dirty window at the far end of the long, narrow expanse. Her bare feet stood on floorboards worn smooth and uneven, and she felt a nail under her heel that was beginning to work its way up from the plank. The attic ceiling vaulted at a precipitous angle into shadows, disappearing where the dim morning light from the small window could not reach the peak. Cobwebs thick with dust and dead flies hung in long strands from the ceiling, waving gently in a breeze she could not feel.

Two men stood in the center of the room. Marie immediately recognized Major Schulmann, who stood with his hands clasped behind his back and his boots spaced evenly beneath his strong shoulders. The smaller man beside him stood still as a statue, his face inscrutable in the backlighting from the window.

A wooden table and a single straight-backed chair were the only pieces of furniture in the room, and Major Schulmann placed one hand on the back of the chair. "Mademoiselle," he began in French, "have a seat, please." The major's voice hinted at the seriousness of the occasion.

"I prefer to stand."

The shorter man had neither moved nor spoken. Major Schulmann came forward and took her firmly by the elbow. "I insist, Marie. Come and sit down." Something in his grip on her arm terrified her, and she allowed herself to be led to the chair. She could see the smaller man more clearly now, and what she saw in the dim light made her blood run cold.

He wore the dark uniform of the Gestapo, immaculately tailored, with every button buttoned and every crease perfect. His cap rested under one sinewy arm, and his whole wiry frame must have been no taller than Marie herself. He defended his smallness with an arrogant lift of his sharp chin and nose, and his thin lips were pressed naturally into a severe, uncompromising line. His cheekbones jutted prominently, defending deep-set eyes that held a terror all their own: one clear-blue eye stared from the right side of his face with an icy disdain so evil that it caused Marie to shiver, and the other, set even deeper within the recesses of his skull than the first, was nothing more than a purplish-gray mass encased in a wrinkled eye socket. His defect held her mesmerized as might a cobra ready to strike, and from the malicious smile playing at the corners of his mouth as he watched her, she realized that he knew of the snake-like fascination his deformity held for his prisoners and that he relished capitalizing on the repulsive sight.

The major had told her the Gestapo would eventually become involved. She began to tremble. Her hands would not stop shaking and she was silently grateful for the chair. *Dear Heavenly Father,* she prayed silently. *Please help me. I don't think I can do this alone.*

Schulmann spoke from beside her chair. "Mademoiselle, this is Captain Bernard Dresdner from Gestapo headquarters in Lyon. He is here to observe our session. For his benefit we will speak only in French. Please answer our questions carefully. Please be as accurate as you can." He retrieved a stack of photographs from the table. "We will speak about Jacques Bellamont." He shuffled the pictures in his hand, selected three, and placed them face up on the table in front of Marie. "You have met with Résistance leaders, I am sure, to update them on SOE's activities. We need your assistance to identify the men in these photographs."

Marie stared dispassionately at the photograph of Jacques Bellamont walking from a café, a young woman draped prettily on his arm. His face was turned in his companion's direction, Marie saw, but she realized his eyes were scanning his surroundings instead of paying attention to her apparent chatter. *Always alert,* she thought, and she smiled inwardly, relieved. The major was trying to get her to identify Jacques, which meant he was still alive. They had not been able to catch him.

"Who are the men in these photographs, Marie?"

Marie realized she was in a dangerous situation. If Jacques truly had escaped in the mountains, then possibly the major had not gotten a good look at him. She didn't know if the major already knew one of these photographs was of Jacques and he was just testing her willingness to cooperate, or if his knowledge of Jacques was through reputation only and he needed her help to identify him from the photographs. If Jacques's identity still remained a secret, she did not want to be the one to reveal it. She looked up at her interrogator, hoping to discern what he already knew. Major Schulmann returned her gaze steadily, but his eyes were hooded so that it was impossible for her to read his expression. She took a deep breath. "I told you yesterday I was not introduced to anyone, sir."

"I find that hard to believe, mademoiselle, considering Jacques was your fiancé's close friend."

Marie said nothing.

"Which one of these photographs is of Jacques Bellamont?"

"Félix does not tell me everything, or introduce me to everyone . . ."

"You deliberately avoided my question, Marie."

Marie hesitated. She glanced up at the major, then at the Gestapo captain behind him. Captain Dresdner had begun to pace, his one good eye watching her intently—*like a cat ready to spring,* she thought with a shudder.

"I'm sorry, Major Schulmann . . ." She felt her heart beating loudly, traitorously, and she looked back at the major. She swallowed her fear and spoke, her voice barely over a whisper. "I cannot answer your question."

A sharp staccato of German exploded from Captain Dresdner. He strode to Marie's chair and with one fist dealt a stunning blow to the side of her head. Marie felt the world turn upside down as explosions of light filled her vision. She flew sideways off her chair, viciously cracking her skull against the sharp edge of the table before the floor lurched toward her and her already bruised shoulder struck it with crushing, bone-jarring force. Before she lost consciousness, she heard a sharp, angry German exclamation from Schulmann, followed by a defiant retort from the Gestapo captain.

* * *

Someone knocked incessantly at the door, and Marie rushed to open it for Félix. But when she opened the door the knocking continued. Félix was not at the door. The Gestapo captain with the dead gray eye stared at her. He said in accented French, "Identify the men in these photographs."

Marie opened her eyes. Someone had returned her to her seat. In the haze of the attic Major Schulmann was standing close at her side with his arms folded across his chest. His eyes watched her closely. In front of her, Captain Dresdner stood waiting for her answer, his hands hanging loosely at his sides. The knocking continued relentlessly, and Marie realized it was actually a tremendous pounding in the side of her head. She reached up and felt something sticky and wet above her left ear. She looked at her hand and was shocked to see blood on her fingers.

Dresdner leaned close, his face devoid of emotion except for the dead iciness of his glare. "Identify these men, mademoiselle."

Marie trembled. "I do not recognize them, sir."

With one hand Dresdner grabbed her jaw in a cruel grip. His fingers ground painfully into the sides of her throat, making her light-headed. "You are so beautiful, even for an American woman. But I can easily change that." His hand wrenched at her jaw, forcing her head back until she was required to meet his gaze. His voice was smooth and evil. "You are naive, Miss Jacobson, if you think I will not strike you again. This time you may not recover." He released her abruptly and Marie's hands went protectively to her throat.

Major Schulmann spoke. "Answer him, Marie."

Marie felt a trickle of blood across her ear. Her head pounded and she felt nauseated. She tried to swallow past the pain in her throat, and her voice came out as little more than a whisper. "My answer could cost Jacques his life—and possibly the lives of others as well."

Captain Dresdner stepped back and looked at the major. "Obviously, gentle persuasion will get us nowhere."

Major Schulmann moved away from Marie. "Your definition of 'gentle' amuses me."

"Are you questioning my methods, Major? You know you are in no position to question what I do."

Major Schulmann answered sharply in German before moving to the attic door. His firm knock produced Marie's guards, and they moved obediently to her chair. Dresdner was talking rapidly in German to the major when the guards removed her from the room and half carried her back to her cell.

SEVEN

Marie slept fitfully. Her sleep crawled with horrific nightmares that constantly woke her. Once, when she turned over, she felt blood on the mattress from her wound, and pain clawed at her head as she slipped back into restless slumber.

The nature of her dreams changed. She was crouching with Félix in a frozen meadow. His head rested in her lap and she felt sticky blood in his unruly dark hair. His eyes were open and he tried to tell her something. Marie leaned closer in order to hear his words. *"I know him."*

She awoke. Her cell was dark and cold. No windows shed moonlight on their prisoners here in the dungeons of the château's cellar. She heard a rat whispering across the floor before she again drifted into unconsciousness.

This time her mother called to her. Irma Jacobson stood on the step of their tiny villa in Paris, and Marie ran toward her through the front gate. The flower garden Marie and her mother had so painstakingly planted bloomed with every color of the rainbow, and birds sang from the old apple tree. Her mother smiled at Marie and held out her arms. Marie ran into her mother's embrace and felt warm and at peace. Her mother held her gently and sang a song from Marie's childhood.

Then her mother said softly, *"Trust him."*

In the next instant her mother, their Paris home, and the feeling of peace disappeared and were replaced by a black whirlwind of unintelligible whispered threats and the clatter of a train coming toward her through the darkness. She couldn't see the train itself—only its headlight moving rapidly in her direction. In a panic she tried to move aside but could not make her legs respond. She reached down and felt the cold steel track. The sound of the train faded, but the headlight continued toward her at an alarming speed. Terrified, she cried out.

She opened her eyes to see a powerful light shining in her face and two figures moving behind the source. In the darkness beyond the shapes she could see that her cell door stood open.

Fingers touched the wound above her ear and she flinched. "Careful—hold still, please." The words were in badly spoken French. "You will want to hold still, even if this hurts." The fingers left her skull and returned a moment later with a rough cloth bathed in the heady smell of alcohol. When it touched her wound Marie gritted her teeth, forcing herself not to scream when the pain seared her skull like a firebrand.

A voice spoke from behind the flashlight. "Make sure she is stabilized for the trip. She will need to be healthy enough to be interrogated." Marie recognized the voice of Major Rolf Schulmann.

Fingers continued to busy themselves about her head. "I've seen worse. I'll do my best."

Marie closed her eyes and tried not to flinch. The pain lessened somewhat but continued throbbing mercilessly through her skull and down her neck.

"I need to administer morphine, mademoiselle. Please lie still." Marie felt the pinch in her arm and pressure as the doctor injected the painkiller into her vein. The doctor removed the needle and tossed it into his bag.

"Major . . ." Marie's words were no more than a whisper.

"Yes, mademoiselle." Schulmann moved closer.

Her lips felt dry. "You never struck me."

"Excuse me?"

"You interrogated me for two days and never struck me."

Major Schulmann was matter-of-fact. "There are more effective methods of interrogation than torture. How much did you tell Captain Dresdner while you lay unconscious on the floor?"

Marie whispered, "Thank you, Major Schulmann."

Schulmann did not respond.

"Do you mind . . . if I ask . . . what will happen to me?"

"Captain Dresdner has received orders from his superiors. He will be taking you to Gestapo headquarters tomorrow afternoon. He plans to continue your interrogation in Lyon."

Her throat constricted and she found it difficult to breathe. A cold chill swept through her body. Gestapo headquarters! She thought about the Résistance leader Jean Moulin. In Lyon they interrogated him and tortured him, beating him until he died. They would kill her there. "Please, Major . . ." Her voice trembled. "I've told you everything! Félix never told me the names of anyone important—"

"Miss Jacobson." Schulmann cut her off firmly. "I am not here to interrogate you. That is out of my hands. You are no longer under my jurisdiction."

"Don't you believe anything I've told you?"

"It doesn't matter what I believe. You're no longer my concern."

She felt the primal terror of a cornered animal and struggled to rise. Behind the two men her door stood open. In her panic Marie imagined herself lunging past the two men and through the door of her cell. But the drug coursing through her bloodstream sapped her body of the ability to carry out her wishes, and Schulmann caught her before she reached a sitting position. She fought weakly to escape, and he held her firmly against the mattress as he addressed the doctor. "Restraints, please." Marie felt straps tighten around her upper arms and gradually she forced her body to relax. The major released her and stepped back.

"Proceed with your examination, Doctor."

The doctor turned Marie's face to the wall and probed at the wound. "Significant bruising along the skull and jawbone. Bruises to her neck. A small break in the skin approximately one centimeter in length. She should have stitches if she is to heal properly."

"Stitches, then."

"Considering what will happen at headquarters, she could get by without them. Infection will set in, but . . . ah . . . it might not matter."

"Give her stitches."

"As you wish. Shall we take her upstairs?"

"No. Here in this room."

"It will be difficult, Major. I have supplies with me but the lighting is inadequate. We would need to turn on the—"

"This will have to do."

"All right. Hold the light steady, please."

Marie waited, staring at the mildewed wall near her face. She listened to the labored breathing of the doctor as he bent past the bulk of an overly satisfied paunch to rummage through his supplies. He straightened and sat heavily on the edge of the mattress next to Marie's restrained arms. In the flashlight's glow she watched shadows of his hands moving next to her head. His pudgy fingers worked to thread thick gut onto a curved hook. Marie could see the shadow of the needle, and its size frightened her. She closed her eyes so she wouldn't have to watch.

For several minutes she gritted her teeth each time she felt the sting of the needle and the indescribable sensation of razor wire passing through her flesh. The doctor tied off the last stitch and snipped the gut close to her scalp. "Keep it clean, mademoiselle. Try not to get it wet." He covered the stitches with fresh gauze and taped the bandage securely. Then he turned away from her and returned his tools to the bag.

The major spoke, his words low and firm. "Please listen, mademoiselle. This is important." He turned and gestured for the doctor to leave. While the doctor lumbered obediently from the room, Schulmann turned back to Marie. "I know you are afraid of what lies ahead of you. I can only suggest you cooperate fully with Captain Dresdner and the Gestapo. You might have more control of your future than you think."

Major Schulmann paused to let his words sink in. Then he continued deliberately. "If you talk, they will listen. If you do not talk, they will hurt you."

Marie lay silently on the mattress, her face to the wall.

"Are you listening, Marie?"

"Why are you telling me this?" Marie turned her head, wincing as the movement tugged at the new stitches.

"Because someday you might be able to return to America if you are intelligent enough to do as I say. Your father would want that, wouldn't he?"

"You told me I was no longer your concern."

"That's right. You are not my concern." The major turned to go. "Can I get you anything? Coffee? It's real coffee, not that horrible substitute they serve in the cafés."

"I don't want it. Thank you."

"This might be your last chance for a long time."

"I don't drink coffee, Major Schulmann, but thank you anyway."

"You are unique, Marie Jacobson."

"Major . . ."

Schulmann stopped. He did not turn around.

"You have kindness in you, Major Schulmann."

For a moment the major hesitated, turning halfway toward Marie. He opened his mouth as if to speak. But instead he shook his head and left the room.

* * *

Snow fell heavily as Marie exited the château and walked with her guards down the stone steps to the courtyard and a waiting Renault. She wore the same clothes she had worn the morning Félix died—her wool trousers still carried bloodstains, reminders of the early-morning tragedy in the mountains above Izieu. Her thin coat did nothing to stop the cold, and her feet already felt numb in their leather boots. A clean bandage covered the wound above her ear, and aside from tenderness at the location, her headache was gone. From the back seat of Captain Dresdner's car she glanced up at the windows of the old mansion, feeling an idiotic desire to see the major one last time. She saw no one.

Captain Bernard Dresdner sat to her left. He pulled out the key to her handcuffs. "Shall I unlock you?" His face remained expressionless, his one blue eye characteristically cold.

"Yes, please."

The Renault pulled away from the door of the château. The tires crunched on snow as the driver maneuvered the vehicle into the street and drove north out of Belley. They would pass the first checkpoint and turn west toward Lyon. Marie shuddered, only partially from the cold.

Dresdner dangled the key ring tauntingly in front of her face. "On second thought, I'd better not. You might try to open the door and throw yourself into the snow."

Marie was silent. The thought had actually occurred to her. But with her hands manacled she had little hope of escape.

Dresdner grabbed her wrists and jerked her around to face him. "How about a compromise, mademoiselle? I will unlock *one* of your wrists. Will that be agreeable? I want this to be an agreeable trip—don't you?"

Marie nodded silently.

Dresdner inserted the key and freed her right hand. He then reached her left hand above her head and, hauling her several inches off the seat, locked the free end of the handcuffs to a steel bar bolted to the roof. Marie found herself caught halfway to her feet: she couldn't straighten her legs, and even with her arm outstretched she couldn't sit comfortably.

"There, now, Miss Jacobson, isn't that more agreeable?" Captain Dresdner relaxed in his seat and smiled mirthlessly. "Our trip usually takes two hours, but with this snow we might be lucky to make it there by night-fall. Please make yourself comfortable and enjoy the ride." In the front seat, the two German guards looked back and smirked at Marie's discomfort.

"I see the good major patched you up." Without warning Dresdner took hold of her bandage and ripped it from the side of her head. Marie winced as hair came off with the bandage. "Stitches! Wait till they see this at headquarters!" Dresdner's hand came up and touched the swollen wound gently, almost caressingly. When he spoke, his words made her throat constrict. "I wonder how many times I can strike this spot with a wooden club before the stitches break."

Marie pulled her head away from his fingers. She tried not to show the leering captain that she was afraid. Her legs were beginning to shake in their unnatural position. She remembered times as a youth when she would sit against the wall with her friends, their knees bent and their backs flat against the wall. It had taken stamina and physical strength to hold the position, and they would stay pressed against the wall until their legs shook. When they could no longer bear the agony, usually after less than five minutes, they would drop laughing to the ground. But this was no game. The thought of spending three hours hanging from her wrist was more than she could take. *"Heavenly Father . . ."* Her lips trembled. *"I need Thy help. I can't go through with this! I can't do this! Please intervene! Please help me!"*

Dresdner seemed mesmerized by the slight movement of her lips. "Praying, Marie?" He laughed mirthlessly. "Good idea. You'll be doing a lot of that."

* * *

Major Rolf Schulmann did not watch the car pull away from the château courtyard. Instead he sat at his desk and ran his finger thoughtfully over the framed image of his wife. The woman's smile seemed incongruous in such a place, he thought, yet her face cheered him—and helped him keep his course.

Schulmann replaced the photograph on his desk. The Renault with its prisoner and idiotic Gestapo captain had gone, and he imagined that Captain Dresdner would lose no time in grinding his prisoner's spirit into submission. Schulmann knew Dresdner well enough to assume Marie Jacobson's life was already becoming a living hell.

In the interrogation yesterday Captain Dresdner had done what Schulmann expected: He used his position as a Gestapo officer and the safety of Schulmann's family as leverage. The major would turn the prisoner over peacefully to the Gestapo, or his loved ones would disappear deep into the concentration camps of Nazi Germany.

Of course Schulmann would comply. Captain Dresdner would be allowed to remove the American prisoner to Lyon on one condition: the interrogation techniques for which Dresdner was infamous not be utilized until Marie Jacobson was out of Schulmann's jurisdiction.

Rolf Schulmann allowed himself a momentary thought of the American girl he had arrested on the mountainside that fateful morning. He had a fleeting image of her slender frame bent agonizingly over Félix Larouche in the snow. He couldn't condemn Derek for shooting Félix; Derek saw the fugitive and responded precisely as he'd been trained to respond. How was Derek to know of the scribbled message in a book, the life-altering rendezvous on the banks of a river, and the deep friendship that had developed between Félix and Rolf four years before?

Something about Marie Jacobson concerned him. He could understand Félix's unfortunate dedication to a misguided group of Résistance fighters. After all, Schulmann's government had disrupted their lives in ways some found difficult to accept. But Marie—he had to assume the worst. He hated interrogating women. The thought sickened him. He hated the ease at which they melted into tears and spilled their guts. His superiors were pleased with the results, but he was not. Marie had surprised him. She hadn't begged or cajoled—at least not until he'd told her she would definitely be transferred to Lyon. Then the look of fright in her wide brown eyes had unnerved him. He hated that.

There was a knock at Schulmann's office door. He rose to his feet and straightened his uniform. "Enter."

The man who entered the room was close to Schulmann's height, but all similarities ended there. Where Schulmann was clean-shaven and serious, the newcomer was unshaven and had a glint of mischief in his brown eyes. His black hair reached almost to his shoulders, and he had it swept back under one of the many caps he used when he disguised himself as a Frenchman. A gray scarf was wound once around his throat and hung loosely over the shoulders of his dark wool coat. Schulmann could see the grip of a Stenmark submachine gun protruding from beneath his coat. Stenmarks were preferred by *maquisards,* he knew, because of the ease with which they could be disassembled and hidden under one's clothes. Beneath the man's coat, his shirt, belt, and pants were French-made. He wore thin, fur-lined snow boots with wool pants tucked into their tops. Except for the weapon hidden under his coat, SS Lieutenant Hans Brenner looked like a French citizen ready to leave for work at the factory.

"You look like you've just been ordered to the Russian front, my friend," Brenner commented with a sardonic smile.

Rolf smiled faintly.

"Something's bothering you. I know you, and I can tell you're struggling with something."

Schulmann nodded. "You remember that year we ran away and spent the summer with friends in Berlin?"

Brenner smiled. "You and I had the adventure of a lifetime. Wished we'd never have to go home. That was when we joined the Party . . ."

"Exactly," Rolf agreed. "But something else happened that summer as well. Do you remember the two twins, Dustin and Ellery?"

Brenner nodded. "We met them at the university and spent the evening drinking . . . I remember we invited them to join us and our friends on a hunting trip, and then you started having second thoughts."

"That's right."

"I remember arguing with you—we needed the break, and the twins were as excited as we were. It turned out your feelings were right."

Rolf smiled grimly. "I couldn't explain the apprehension I felt. I would never have imagined the twins would rob Conrad, Gil, and Emil at gunpoint, much less shoot them and leave their bodies in a ravine. I felt ill when the snow finally melted in the spring and we found their bodies."

"So you're having second thoughts about today's expedition?"

Rolf shook his head. "What I felt about the twins was hard to describe. It was a feeling of anxiety, even a little fear—as if someone or something were trying to warn me of danger. No, I'm not having second thoughts about today." Schulmann looked at the lieutenant. "Just wondering what we'll find out about the American girl. Wondering if she'll be worth it."

"You're worried about your family."

"I'm always worried about my family."

"And you always will be." Brenner sat on the edge of the major's desk. "You've got the Führer's eyes on you, and he's not going to allow you to make mistakes. It's your own fault, you know."

"I know. But I had to do what I did . . ."

"Your convictions will be the death of you, just you wait and see." The lieutenant folded his arms. "Not that I'm complaining—but don't ever say I didn't warn you."

"You warn me every time we see each other, Hans. I appreciate your concern, but I have to do what I think is right."

Lieutenant Brenner grinned at the major. "Won't you come with us? It'll be just like old times."

"Wish I could." Schulmann retrieved his hat from the desk and moved toward the door. "But I've got a small errand that will take me a couple of days to complete. Besides, Dresdner would recognize me and that would ruin the whole thing. That's why you're perfect for the job, Hans—he's never had the opportunity to meet you."

"Not yet, at least." Hans grimaced. "A problem I will try my hardest to correct."

The major smiled. "I'm sure you will. And I'm grateful." He clapped Hans on the shoulder. "I'll join you when you reach St. Étienne. Is your team assembled?"

Lieutenant Brenner gave a mock salute. "Ready to move, sir."

"What will you tell your boys?"

"I'll tell them Captain Dresdner cannot be trusted. He plans to kill the prisoner. The American will not tell him anything and information vital to the Third Reich will die with her. For the good of the Fatherland she must not be taken to Gestapo headquarters. I'll tell them that." Brenner moved toward the door. "And what do I do with the good captain?"

Schulmann hesitated. It would be easier to eliminate the vile man now while they had the chance. But Dresdner's testimony that *maquisards* had kidnapped Marie Jacobson would be necessary at Section Four. "He needs to live so he can testify in Lyon."

"Understood. Anything else?"

"Yes. At first Marie Jacobson will think you are members of the French Résistance, so don't give her any false hopes of freedom. Watch her closely until you get to your destination. I should be able to join you by the end of the week."

"I understand."

"And Lieutenant . . . Hans . . ."

"Yes?"

"Thank you."

Lieutenant Hans Brenner grinned and strode purposefully from the room.

* * *

Snow fell heavily as the black Renault slowed at a checkpoint northwest of Belley. On either side of the road the landscape lay frozen and dormant, covered with thick misshapen blankets of snow. Just outside the guard shack two German soldiers huddled over a fire they had built inside half a metal drum. Reluctantly they left its warmth to approach the Renault.

"Papers, please." The man at the driver's window stared at Marie from beneath his fur cap. For a second she recognized pity in his gaze. He shifted uncomfortably in his boots and turned his eyes self-consciously away from her to watch the driver. The other guard drifted to the opposite side of the car and stamped his feet, hugging his hands into his armpits. He did not seem interested in the passengers in the car but instead watched his comrade as if anxious to bolt for the guard shack as soon as the papers were returned to the driver.

Another vehicle, a dark blue Citroën, pulled in behind them and waited patiently, its powerful engine idling and sending steady clouds of steam from the car's exhaust into the cold afternoon air. Finally the guard handed the papers back to the driver and, with another sympathetic look in Marie's direction, waved them on. The car behind pulled forward and Marie saw the guard bending toward the driver's window before snow and distance erased the scene from her sight.

As the miles crawled by, Marie discovered a way to relieve the excruciating pain in her leg muscles: she shifted back and forth from one leg to another, keeping her movements as hidden as possible. She worked with the movement of the car, trying to make it look as if she was being moved back and forth by the car's movement. But she rested first her left, then her right foot while they drove toward Lyon, and Dresdner seemed reluctantly impressed by her stamina.

The Citroën again pulled in behind them, and this time it honked its horn rather violently at the black Renault. The Citroën swerved back and forth on the icy road, trying without luck to pass the Gestapo car. Dresdner looked through the rear window and swore. "What do they think they're doing?"

"Seems they want to pass, sir." The driver looked through the mirror at his boss, waiting questioningly for orders.

"Keep driving. They can wait their turn." Dresdner turned his back disdainfully to the swerving car behind them and settled comfortably into his seat. He glanced at Marie and then dismissed the sight of her.

He's bored. I'm not swooning fast enough for him, she thought, and she clenched her teeth against the pain, determined to hold on as long as necessary.

Behind them the owner of the Citroën rolled down his window and leaned out, shaking his fist and yelling. Dresdner's driver watched the spectacle anxiously in the rearview mirror.

"Captain—"

"He's drunk. Carry on."

At that moment the Citroën accelerated and drove in a very fast, very sober straight line, directly into the rear fender of Captain Dresdner's black Renault. The impact threw Marie toward the rear window but the handcuffs stopped her short, cutting viciously into her fettered wrist. The heads and necks of both guards and the driver snapped back sharply. Dresdner had his head near the back of the seat and suffered only minimally. With the driver stunned from the blow, the Renault swerved wildly to the right and plowed headfirst into a snowbank. This time Dresdner's head and upper body snapped violently forward and contacted the back of the driver's seat with a hollow thud. He crumpled unconscious to the floor. The driver cracked his chin and neck on the steering wheel and sat stunned, holding his jaw and moaning. Both guards struck the windshield and shattered the glass. They lay bloodied and unconscious, and Marie's wrist burned from the pressure of her body. Her legs shook as she struggled for a footing, and she crumpled again to the length of her arm. Ignoring the excruciating pain in her wrist, she twisted around and fumbled with her right hand through the Gestapo officer's clothes for the key to the handcuffs.

Dresdner groaned and flinched. Marie swallowed her panic and continued to search for the key. If he regained conciousness and realized what she was doing, he would punish her mercilessly. She forced herself to keep searching.

The blue Citroën responsible for the accident pulled to a skidding stop beside the disabled Gestapo car. Three men in civilian clothing jumped out and approached at a run. They carried weapons and wore caps pulled low over their eyes.

Maquisards! Marie's hand closed around the small key in the inside breast pocket of Dresdner's uniform. She pulled it quickly from the awakening captain's body and reached to unlock her wrist. She willed the hand holding the key to stop shaking and was finally able to insert the key in the cuff. A moment later her left hand was free and she lunged for the door.

One of the attackers opened Captain Dresdner's door and hauled him unceremoniously out into the snow. The small man lay there in a pitiful heap, moaning and clutching his head with both hands. Others pulled the driver and guards out and threw them on the ground next to Dresdner. Two of the armed civilians covered the heap of wounded flesh with their guns while another moved around to Marie's door.

"Mademoiselle?" He held out his hand to Marie, and with his help she exited the black Renault on shaky legs.

"You are lucky, *chérie.*" The long-haired man nodded in the direction of the Gestapo officer. "He is a murderer. You would not have survived the interrogation."

Marie stared at the man and he flashed a brilliant smile. His French was choppy and incorrect, his accent unmistakably . . . German.

EIGHT

Marie gratefully accepted the coat draped around her shoulders. Her left wrist hurt where the handcuffs had bruised her skin, and her whirlwind rescue left her head spinning. She stared numbly at the man who had spoken. He took her arm and led her quickly toward the Citroën. "Stay here, mademoiselle." He spoke politely, but his hands on her shoulders pressed her firmly onto the back seat. "We will be leaving soon." He closed the door and returned to the prisoners.

Marie rubbed her left wrist and watched as the three men ordered the Gestapo captain to his feet. Dresdner struggled to rise, holding his head and moaning loudly.

One of his captors nudged him with his automatic. "Give me your coat."

Dresdner glared at the man and made no move to obey.

The man reversed his weapon and smashed it into the stomach of the Gestapo officer, who doubled over, crumpling like an aluminum can. "Give me your coat, monsieur—are you so dim-witted you would lose your life over a coat?" He hauled Dresdner to his feet. "Your coat *and* your boots, if you please—German pig!"

Captain Bernard Dresdner slowly removed his coat and then, at his captors' insistence, his tunic, breeches, and long shiny boots. He stood forlornly in the snow in socks and long winter underwear, his body pitifully small and thin now that all the trappings of power had been removed. Watching from the back seat of the car, Marie almost felt sympathy for the slight man standing shivering in his underwear. Almost. She watched as her rescuers bound Dresdner securely, dragged him away from the Renault, and threw him to the snow next to his comrades. Then the long-haired vigilante with the German accent turned and shot a bullet into the Renault's gas tank, and the stranded vehicle exploded, sending a ball of flame heavenward and shrapnel in all directions. The Citroën rocked violently and Marie instinctively ducked, shielding her face with her arm.

"We must hurry, mademoiselle." The man with the long dark hair and dark eyes slid in next to her and tossed Captain Dresdner's clothing at her feet. His two companions took the front seat and the Citroën pulled forward. Soon the Gestapo car, now a burning wreck, was far behind.

Marie studied the man next to her. "You're not Résistance. You're German."

The man nodded, unconcerned by her insight. His hand ready on his weapon, he watched the road behind for any sign of pursuit. The driver accelerated as fast as possible on the icy road and within seconds they had rounded a bend and lost sight of the Gestapo car. Thick black smoke billowed upward, and Marie knew the burning vehicle would soon capture the attention of the Germans. Her rescuer watched for several moments longer and then his grip relaxed on the stock of his rifle. He turned and settled comfortably in his seat, smiling at Marie. "Lieutenant Hans Brenner." He gestured toward the driver. "Our chauffeur is Derek." The Citroën continued to follow the winding mountain road. At times, falling snow completely obliterated the outside world, but Derek seemed unconcerned. He drove the large car down the mountain pass with a confidence that unnerved Marie. "And this . . ." Brenner indicated the last member of their group, ". . . is Lancelot."

Lancelot looked back at her and grinned. His face swam with freckles and his hair was strawberry blond. He looked like he was not yet twenty.

"Lancelot looks young and naive, but don't let his looks fool you." Hans Brenner grinned and reached across Marie to slug the redhead. "Lance here has a wife and three *kinder* at home. Also, he's killed more men then there are days in a month. He's ruthless."

"Yeah," Lancelot agreed. "Don't mess with me."

Hans continued. "Are you all right?"

Marie nodded.

"Dresdner really had it out for you, didn't he?"

Marie said nothing but watched the lieutenant warily. She winced when Hans grasped her wrist and studied it. He shook his head and smiled at her. "Good thing we got here when we did."

"But why—why rescue me from your own Gestapo?"

Hans removed his cap and smoothed his long hair with his free hand. "Our job is to make you disappear."

"You mean you went to all that trouble just to shoot me?"

"Not as easy as that, mademoiselle." Brenner replaced his cap. "Captain Dresdner lives by the common Gestapo philosophy that the end justifies the means. His methods do more harm than good. So we're hiding you from the Gestapo. The Führer has some use for you. He does not want you damaged."

Marie shuddered at Brenner's choice of words. "So where are you taking me?"

"You'll know soon."

Marie rubbed her wrist. "More interrogation?"

"Probably."

NINE

"Keep your head down, mademoiselle." Hans kept his attention on the road outside. In the distance Marie could make out angular shapes in the shadows—buildings completely enshrouded in a blackness imposed by the mandatory curfew. Toward the center of the town rose an ancient cathedral, the silhouettes of its stone towers reaching heavenward as if in prayer. As they approached the darkened city, Marie caught a glimpse of thatched rooftops before Hans's strong grip on her shoulder forced her to the floor. "Do not move, mademoiselle—we are passing the *manufacture d'armes*—the arms factory." He covered her with a blanket and rested his rifle haphazardly across her back. "There is a guard station. They will look inside the vehicle."

Derek slowed the Citroën and approached the checkpoint at a cautious pace, and Lancelot cocked his pistol and hid it under the coat on his lap, angling it toward the driver's side window. He mumbled, "Sure would hate to have to kill a countryman . . ."

"No need. We've changed back into our uniforms, so they'll never suspect us." Hans lifted his legs and crossed his boots on Marie's back. "Besides, they're only gendarmes—local Vichy police. At night the citizens of St. Étienne— the *stéphanois*—always pull the worst watch. And not only am I their superior, but I'm also going to be drunk and completely unreasonable." Marie heard the pop of a cork and Hans gulped a goodly portion of a bottle's contents.

"Careful, Lieutenant—you *will* be drunk if you continue." Lancelot glanced back at Hans.

"I hold my liquor well. You know that."

Derek looked back doubtfully through the mirror at Hans. "What do you want me to say to them?"

Hans took another long drink. "Nothing. I'll do all the talking."

Derek glanced nervously at Lancelot as they approached the mobile guardrail spanning the road at chest height. Two Frenchmen in the uniforms of the Vichy *gendarmes* approached the Citroën, their weapons held casually in the crooks of their arms and their flashlights ready. The taller of the two approached Derek's window and bent to peer into the car, training the beam of his torch around the inside until it landed on Hans's face.

Hans let out an expletive, his voice loud and slurred. "What's the meaning of this? Watch where you point that light, you idiot!" He struggled convincingly to right himself on the back seat, failed, and settled back into his slump. Beneath the blanket Marie bit her lip to avoid yelping—Hans's black boots were heavy, and the sharp edges of his heels had dug viciously into her back when the lieutenant tried to right himself.

"Pardon me . . ." The gendarme lowered his flashlight and strained to see Hans in the back seat. He started noticeably when he recognized the insignia of an officer. "Lieutenant!" He saluted from his crouched position, managing to bang the knuckles of his hand against the window frame in the process. "Good evening, Lieutenant. Let me see your papers, please."

Hans swore again, and his words ran into each other as he shouted, "What do you think we are? *Maquisards?*"

The man smiled uneasily. "Forgive me—there have been reports of French outlaws impersonating German officers."

Hans surged upright, his face mottled with rage. Marie groaned inwardly and knew her back would be severely bruised. "Forgive you? *Forgive you?!*" Hans gestured with the half-empty bottle. "You're a complete *imbecile!* Don't you know who I am?"

"No, sir, I'm sorry, I don't."

Hans gestured violently with his bottle. "I am Lieutenant Arnold Schaeffer—second in command to the Section Four *Obersturmführer* Klaus Barbie!" Hans's voice grew progressively louder. "You could be shot for suggesting I am an imposter!"

The man was shaken. "I—I never meant to accuse you of—"

"Yes you did!" Hans pounded the seat and glared at the young *gendarme.* "I order you to tell me your name, monsieur. I am going to report you to the *Kommissariat* myself!"

The man retreated from the window, his face as pale as the snow surrounding the guard shack. He turned and shouted to his comrade, who hustled to raise the guardrail. The first gendarme then hastily waved the vehicle forward, and Derek gunned the engine and pulled away from the checkpoint. For good measure, Hans launched the half-empty bottle through the open window at the man. "Waste of a good bottle," he mumbled as he pulled the blanket off Marie.

"Are you all right, mademoiselle?" The slur was gone and Hans seemed his old jovial self. "My eternal apologies for your suffering."

Marie rubbed her mutilated spine. "Don't mention it," she mumbled, and she slid back onto the seat.

They drove through the streets of St. Étienne, a community shrouded in darkness and silence. Except for an occasional stray dog or cat, Marie saw nothing moving on the city streets. She wondered if Résistance cells hid here, blending into the general populace and trying not to catch the attention of the Gestapo at Section Four in Lyon. She realized she would have to find a way to contact the Résistance if she were going to make it out of France alive.

They crossed a series of railroad tracks and continued west out of St. Étienne. Buildings gave way to clusters of trees and farms as the Loire River valley approached, and to the left, a smooth black expanse of water shimmered in the moonlight.

"River Loire." Hans gestured. "There's a large castle somewhere around here—nice place for an outing."

"Not exactly on our agenda, is it?" Marie commented.

"Not tonight."

"Now will you tell me where we're going?"

Hans shrugged. "A village of no consequence—St. Victor-sur-Loire, fifteen kilometers from here. We will wait at a small villa for further instructions. Sorry . . ." He smiled apologetically. "I'm not allowed to tell you more right now."

"Fair enough." Marie turned her attention to the darkness outside.

* * *

Marie must have slept, because the sound of her door opening startled her. She lifted her head from the seat and stared, disoriented, at Lieutenant Hans Brenner. Behind him she could make out the dark shadow of a stone wall rising two stories until it met the overhang of a wood-shake roof. Shutters framed windows set deeply into the stone structure, and a heavy wood door with a brass knocker stood slightly ajar. Hans helped her from the car and gestured toward the house. "Lancelot will point you in the right direction, mademoiselle. The washroom is near your quarters, at the rear of the house."

Marie climbed three steps and entered the villa, the strangeness of her surroundings heightened by sleep-induced confusion. She entered the foyer and passed the grand front parlor furnished richly in antiques and brocades, then followed the redheaded German soldier up the stone steps and down a long hallway where musty air suggested that the residence had been vacant for some time.

"In here, mademoiselle." Lancelot indicated a door on her left and Marie walked past him into her room. Lancelot turned on a light. "Stay here until somebody calls for you. Lieutenant Brenner said there's no need to lock your door unless you try to escape."

Marie studied her new prison, dropping her coat on a small wicker chair and moving around the perimeter of the room. On the wall opposite the bedroom door a window interrupted the textured stone, draped with velvet tapestries that ran luxuriously through her fingers but smelled of mold. Next to the window stood an ancient armoire, carved out of black walnut and cherry wood. It stood taller than her and reeked of mothballs. She opened the doors and ran her hands through dresses, coats, skirts, and blouses, all relatively new. She closed the armoire and turned to see Lancelot yawning in the doorway. He indicated the armoire with his chin. "The lieutenant said to use what you need."

Marie nodded, grateful to finally have a chance to change out of her bloodstained clothes. Lancelot closed the door and Marie sat on the edge of her bed. She looked at her hands and realized they were shaking. Clenching them tightly, she concentrated on breathing evenly, steadily. She felt overwhelmed by the events of the day and wished a good night's sleep could eradicate the memory of Dresdner's evil face so close to her own. She bent and tugged at her boots, loosened the laces, and pulled them from her feet. She slipped out of her trousers and studied the crusted, black blood that was the only physical reminder of her fiancé's death. She found a soft nightgown in a drawer next to the bed and pulled it over her shoulders. Padding on bare feet across the floorboards, she turned off the light and moved to the window. She lifted the blackout curtain and peered into the night. Below her, a cigarette glowed yellow against the blackness, and she knew one of her German companions guarded her window. Dropping the curtain, she threw herself across the comforter, ignoring the dust that rose in a tiny cloud from the pillow. The last thing she remembered before she drifted into unconsciousness was the sound of a telephone ringing somewhere in the villa.

* * *

She slept, a dreamless, uninterrupted sleep, until the next day's late-afternoon shadows stretched across the corridor and stairs outside her room. When she finally awoke, disorientation lasted for a moment before she stood and stretched. She felt monstrously hungry, but she craved a long warm bath more than food. She padded barefoot across the hallway to the bathroom, grateful there was no one currently occupying the tiny room. In fact, the villa was as silent as death, as if her German guards had abandoned her here in this strange, empty residence in the middle of France.

At the door of the small washroom she paused with her hand on the knob. She squinted at the stairway through dust particles suspended in translucent rays of light, her senses heightened as she listened for any signs of life below. Not a sound. She looked to her left past her bedroom door and noticed two more doorways and a window facing north. Her hand slipped from the knob as she moved in that direction. Passing the first doorway, she paused at the second and touched the knob lightly, then turned it slowly and silently until the latch gave and the door hung free in her hand. With the same gentle caution, she moved it inward until she could see the edge of a desk and the cord of a telephone. She hesitated, studying the small office through the tiny crack and listening for signs of movement until she was satisfied it was empty. Closing the door, she moved to the next and found it locked.

Her hands trembled, and she hugged them close against her nightgown. She contemplated returning to the safety of her room and preparing for a warm bath, but she postponed the idea. Her luck would hold, she argued with herself, and if her captors were occupied elsewhere, she had to make use of this time. She moved silently and swiftly across the corridor and down the stairs. At the bottom, she hesitated, listening to muffled voices carrying from the basement. Two voices. She glanced through the parlor window across the corridor and saw the empty driveway and the shadows of trees stretching across the gray snow and a stone wall. One of the men had apparently left with the car, and two others chatted in the basement. She left the relative safety of the stairwell and tiptoed across the foyer, silent as a mouse, and risked a quick glance in the direction of the stairs leading downward to the kitchen. Her feet whispered across cold marble tile as she crossed the parlor and entered a corridor on the other side.

More doorways. She passed several bedrooms with doors ajar, their disarray typical of male inhabitants, before ascending another stone stairway, this one narrow and dark, as if unused. It carried her to a small sitting area and another stairway to the attic, and she paused on the landing and studied the solid oak door in front of her while her ears registered the distant rumble of an approaching automobile. She moved forward and tested the handle and found it locked. She turned and escaped the way she had come, running silently down two sets of stairs and through the corridor, hesitating for a split second when she saw Captain Brenner's large Citroën parked outside the parlor window. He slammed the door and moved toward the villa, and Marie ducked below the level of the windowsill and ran. She sprinted across the parlor and halfway up the stairs before she heard the solid door opening heavily on its iron hinges. She took the last steps as if the entire German army was on her heels and managed to flatten herself against the wall of the corridor before Hans's figure passed through the doorway. He glanced casually up the stairs before proceeding through the foyer and down toward the basement kitchen, and Marie exhaled slowly, her body relaxing against the cold stone wall.

* * *

Marie stretched out as far as she could in the warm water. Her toes appeared at the opposite end of the tub, and when she pulled them down, her knees broke the water's surface. She slid down to her chin and closed her eyes. The world faded, and for a few moments she drifted luxuriously between consciousness and sleep. Reluctantly she pushed her shoulders up out of the warmth and reached for the large bar of soap. It looked like the kind her mother had used to scrub off her adventures when Marie was ten years old and little more than a street urchin loose on the streets of Paris. She ran the bar over her shoulder and down her arm. The soap smelled better than she remembered, and she began to feel clean for the first time in at least a week. She thought about her mother and about her dream. *"Trust him."*

Trust him? Trust who? Major Rolf Schulmann? She imagined she wouldn't see him again. The thoughts of him and her incarceration in that moldy cellar sent shudders of cold down her warm spine. She would probably never have to be in the same room with him again—hadn't he said she was no longer his concern?

But who had orchestrated her escape from Captain Dresdner? Marie frowned uncomfortably at the thought. She was still a prisoner. Nothing had changed in that regard. But her present situation was infinitely more pleasant than the alternative. Marie touched the bruises on her left wrist and reached up to feel the tenderness of the stitches above her ear. She would most likely be dead by now if it had not been for Hans's assistance. Lieutenant Hans Brenner and his men had saved her life—or at least postponed the end thereof. Marie shifted uncomfortably. Hans had made it clear he was acting under orders from higher up. Who had ordered him to kidnap her?

Major Schulmann. It had to be Rolf Schulmann. She had sensed a kindness in him, totally incongruous to his uniform and the horrific regime it represented. But why would he order her to be kidnapped from someone representing the Third Reich? Deep in thought, Marie shampooed her hair, lathering her long dark curls completely before taking a deep breath and sliding her head under the water, ignoring the doctor's orders to keep her wound dry. Her fingers massaged her scalp, carefully transversing the stitches above her left ear. She stayed under water as long as she could hold her breath, and she watched through the waves of her hair as sunlight from the bathroom window danced on the water. Tiny whirlpools shimmered and waved above her head, stirring her dark hair in a gentle, undulating rhythm.

Her knees were getting cold. Marie straightened them slowly under the water and her head broke the surface. Reaching for a towel, she stood and vigorously rubbed herself dry. She wrapped her hair tightly in the towel and twisted it above her scalp. Stepping out of the tub, she reached for a dress and undergarments she had found in the armoire. Marie fingered the dress for a moment and wondered who had been its original owner. It looked worn but still serviceable. Removing the towel from her hair, Marie pulled the dress over her head and smoothed the skirt, which flared below her knees. The fine cotton of the bodice was light blue, and buttons marched up the front to meet the V of a modest neckline. Buttoning the bodice, she looked at her appearance in the mirror and then moved closer and reached again to touch the wound at the side of her head. Captain Dresdner's energetic removal of her bandage had not done as much damage as she had thought—the waves of her hair almost covered the location. Marie reached for a comb next to the sink and ran it gingerly through her hair, and as she combed she realized it would take some time for her life to regain semblance of normalcy.

* * *

Major Rolf Schulmann hesitated at the gate, his eyes studying the small cottage in front of him. It was just as he had remembered it, with its leafless rosebushes, whitewashed stone, and the small concrete fountain resting in a frozen garden. The shed to the left of the house still leaned noticeably on its foundation, and the wooden planks of the shed door still hung precariously on rusted hinges. Layers of naked vines with a thin film of frost covered the shed's walls and a good portion of the stone structure of the house. If it were not for the sound of an army truck passing in the street behind him, he would have thought not a day had passed since he last stood on these steps.

His neck muscles constricted painfully at the thought of what lay before him. He dreaded this meeting as much as he had dreaded anything in his life. He remembered returning to the market as a child, his earlobe painfully twisted between his mother's thumb and index finger, to tell the owner he had stolen a small toy. Not only had he been mortified by the experience, but he had also embarrassed his mother, whose sense of right and wrong was interspersed with the realization that her son's theft had tarnished the family's image. If for no other reason than that it was embarrassing for a well-to-do family to have a thief for a boy, she made sure he did the right thing.

Rolf's gloved hand rested on the latch of the gate. Even though this present reparation could also be considered compulsory, no one would fault him if he chose to say and do nothing. Even though his mistake could also be considered a theft, it had been in the line of duty and therefore did not necessarily need his remorse or his repentance. Rules in wartime tended to bend into strange shapes, full of justifications and necessities that oftentimes overruled one's conscience. But he couldn't live with the feelings that churned inside his chest and urged him to do this thing—not only for the sake of the feelings of an individual he barely knew, but also for his own peace of mind and a sense of right and wrong that could not be silenced. Taking a deep breath, he lifted the latch and opened the gate.

He hesitated as he reached the first step, studying the house in front of him. Even though the steps were swept and the walk had been cleared of snow, his senses registered the subtle clues of vacancy. He had been so determined to complete this task that he failed to notice the silence surrounding the structure. Little things, like the removal of snow, were indications that someone lived there, but to Rolf everything was too still, and there was a feeling of vacancy—as if someone only cared for the home in order to make it look inhabited. Just in case his feelings missed the mark, Rolf approached the front door, removed a glove, and knocked. His knuckles made a hollow sound in the stillness, and as he had expected, there was no subsequent response from inside. His ears had been trained to detect even the smallest of movements, and so he remained still to listen.

He heard nothing. Concerned, Rolf stepped back and returned his cold hand to the comfort of its glove. He forced himself to breathe calmly and evenly, his expelled breath hovering in the cold air as he contemplated what to do next. He should feel elated. The house was empty—did that not clear him of his obligation? He turned and descended the steps, walking thoughtfully toward the gate. As he approached his car, his brow furrowed and he glanced back at the house. Perhaps the woman had been gone for some time. Considering the circumstances, she could possibly be in hiding. If that were so, then the task of finding one old Frenchwoman in occupied France would be like finding a needle in the proverbial haystack. But as hard as he tried, he couldn't shake the feeling that he should not give up. Somehow he had to finish this. He knew he wouldn't be able to live with himself otherwise.

* * *

Marie turned off the light and raised the blackout curtain to watch the ground below. Forty-eight hours ago they had arrived at the ancient villa that stood overlooking a bend in the precocious Loire. According to Hans, several times a year the river changed directions in some spots, and flooded in others. Mist from the river blurred her vision and she squinted, watching carefully for any signs of movement through the darkness. After a few minutes she recognized familiar shapes in the mist: stone walls ran the length of the drive and encircled a small abandoned garden. They rose out of the haze like shadowed mounds of sticky buns sprinkled with powdered sugar. In the afternoon she had followed those walls into the vast fields and riverbanks, conscious all the time of Derek trailing behind. Her captors seemed willing to allow her freedom—to an extent. When they had reached the main road, Derek had called her back and insisted she return to the villa.

Marie continued to study the darkness below her window. The shadow of an old peach tree grew from the slope to her left, and beyond that lay a crumbling stone shed. To her right Marie could see nothing but blackness, indicating that the river lay less than a stone's throw from the walls of the villa. She stood unmoving at the edge of her window, not wanting to attract attention to herself. She wanted to be satisfied that there was no guard. Last night it had been Lancelot. The night before, Hans said it had been him. By default tonight should be Derek's turn to stand beneath her window, but he was nowhere to be seen. She continued to watch.

After fifteen minutes she was convinced Derek was not hiding behind a stone wall or peeking up at her window from around a corner of the villa. She padded softly to her bed and slipped into trousers and her boots, then moved to the door. She tried the knob and found it locked from the outside, and she hesitated, her ear pressed to the rough surface, listening for any sign of life. Satisfied the corridor was empty, she left the door and again crossed her bedroom. She pulled the sheet from her bed and ripped the material into long, thick strips, then tied them together and secured the makeshift rope to her bedpost. To her chagrin the thick rope barely reached the windowsill. Marie then combed the room in search of a pair of scissors or any object with a sharp edge. She pulled open every drawer and sifted through all the clothes in the armoire. Finally she discovered a small hand mirror, which she placed on the floor and carefully crushed under her shoe.

Selecting a shard of glass, Marie attacked the comforter, slicing through its cushiony insides and separating strips of cotton and batting. Carrying the strips to the window, she added them to the sheet-rope until she was positive her feet would reach at least within safe dropping distance from the ground. Gathering the soft coil of makeshift rope in her arms, she studied the ground below her until she was positive Derek was indeed shirking his duty. Satisfied, she tossed the fabric out into the night.

It looked easier than it actually was. Grabbing hold of the rope and allowing herself to drop from the solid safety of the windowsill took all the courage she could muster, and when she had fallen to the length of her arms she hung there, terrified, willing herself not to look at the ground two stories below. She searched with her feet for a knot between strips and stood on it, forcing her boots not to slip and praying the tie would hold. She allowed her arms to loosen slowly until her weight lay completely on the knot between her boots. Then she slipped her hands downward and again grasped the rope, allowing her weight to shift between her hands and her knees and feet until her head finally came level with the top of the first-story parlor window. Relieved, she let go and landed in the snow at the base of the wall, crumpling as she landed in order to absorb the shock. Standing on unsteady legs, Marie brushed the snow off her hands and knees and glanced up at her windowsill, grateful to be down.

"Not too original, mademoiselle—I think I've seen that technique in some American movie."

Marie whirled toward the sound of the voice, almost losing her balance on the uneven terrain. Squinting through the mist, she saw an all-too-familiar figure relaxed against a stone wall. His arms were folded, and his dark overcoat was draped casually across his wide shoulders which were hunched ever so slightly forward as he watched her intently. After a moment, Major Rolf Schulmann pushed himself upright and moved toward her, his gait as natural and relaxed as a stroll on the beach.

"Where did you think you were going, Marie?"

"Fishing."

"Mind if I come along?"

"You'll scare the fish."

Rolf laughed, and then his eyes darkened. "A little cold for an escape attempt, don't you think?"

"I wasn't planning to wait for summer, Major Schulmann."

"I understand." Rolf nodded. "And I apologize that I must curtail your enthusiasm. But there are several highly sensible reasons why you should not continue with your plans. First . . ." Rolf pointed down the gravel drive.

"That road is the only way out, and there are soldiers stationed in a guard shack not far from here. Second . . ." He indicated the direction of St. Étienne. "That city is crawling with Germans and Vichy—and you cannot be planning to swim across the river in this weather. Third . . ." He folded his arms and studied her in the darkness. "You have no papers and it's after curfew, which means we would shoot you first and ask questions later. And finally, most important, mademoiselle . . ." He shook his head sadly. "I have traveled all the way from Belley to spend more time with you, and I can't imagine losing my chance to get to know you better."

"I thought I was no longer your problem."

"I've decided to make you my problem."

Marie watched him soberly. "I guess under the circumstances I could postpone my outing." She shrugged away from his proffered hand and walked toward the front of the villa, her back ramrod straight and her head held high. When they reached the door, Rolf produced a key, inserted it in the lock, and turned it twice before pushing the heavy door inward. He then stepped back and bowed slightly, indicating that Marie was to precede him through the entry. She allowed him to lead her through the grand front parlour and down the stairs to the kitchen. Derek and Hans sat at the table eating bratwurst and drinking coffee.

"Look what I found near the river, Derek." Rolf shed his overcoat and pulled a chair away from the table for Marie.

Hans laughed, exuberantly tipping his chair back against the wall. "I knew she'd do it!"

Derek blanched, choking on a mouthful of bratwurst as he scrambled to his feet. "When—when did you arrive, sir?"

"Over an hour ago." Rolf combed the kitchen for edibles. "I've been watching the entertainment outside."

Marie glowered at the major and folded her arms defiantly.

"You missed a good show, Derek." Rolf shook his head sadly. "If you had been where you were supposed to be . . ."

Derek mumbled an apology, still shaken from the major's unexpected entrance. Glancing forlornly at his unfinished dinner, he scrambled over Hans's legs and hurried from the room.

Marie watched Rolf warily. "Why are you here?"

Rolf poured hot water into a cup and added a spoonful of honey. He placed it on the table along with a loaf of bread. "Captain Dresdner returned to Belley rather shaken, Marie. It seems *maquisards* assaulted him, torched his transportation, and left him to die in a snowbank. It happened in my area and it would seem suspicious for me *not* to search for you—under the circumstances." He searched for a bread knife. "You were a valued prisoner and will be sorely missed by the Gestapo. They will waste no time searching for you."

"Wish I could have seen it." Hans speared his sausage and took a big bite, grinning around a large mouthful. "The old rope trick, eh, Rolf?"

Marie ignored Hans. "You speak in the past tense, Major. You forget I'm still a prisoner."

"Of course you are. But at least you are not in the Gestapo's loving care."

"Will they look here?"

"Highly unlikely." Rolf indicated the food in front of him. "Won't you join me? The bread is excellent—no sawdust."

Marie shook her head.

Rolf continued. "Why would Maquis kidnappers bring you here? No, the *Gebirgsjager* will be focusing their search in the Rhône region where guerillas are known to operate."

"*Gebirgsjager?*"

"German alpine troops." Hans interceded cheerfully. "Mountain combat forces considered some of the best fighters in the Führer's army."

Unable to locate a knife, Rolf picked up the loaf and broke it. "Hans is one of them—one of the *best* of them—which is another reason why you would not have succeeded tonight."

Hans let his chair slam to the floor. "Now, I really should be modest . . . but how can I argue with the truth? He's right. I *am* the best."

Rolf smiled. "You'll notice Hans is about as humble a guy as you'll ever meet."

"Influenced by your noble example, Major." Hans downed the last of his bratwurst and emptied his mug, then stood and moved toward the door. "Speaking of 'humble,' Rolf forgot to mention this villa belongs to his family."

Marie stared at the major.

Rolf bowed. "My contribution to the war effort, mademoiselle. Or, I should say, my *deceased grandparents'* humble contribution."

Hans yawned. "I'm off to bed—that is, after I confiscate one long, hazardous rope." He winked at Marie, laughed, and closed the door behind him.

Marie studied the major. "Why did you order Hans to kidnap me?"

Rolf returned the bread to the table. "Because I have more questions for you."

"All your questions would have been answered by the Gestapo."

"Yes, I'm sure they would have told me everything they discovered—after they buried you."

"What do you care?" Marie's voice rose. "You've captured me, killed my fiancé . . ." Her voice caught. ". . . Imprisoned me and interrogated me for two days, and now you care if the Gestapo kills me?"

Rolf watched her carefully. "Marie, there's something I need to find out about you—something important." He hesitated. "I might be able to help you—I might have a need for your services."

Marie's jaw dropped, and she rose to her feet. "How *dare* you even *think* . . . !"

For a split second Rolf's face reddened, then he scowled darkly. "That's not what I meant, Marie. There's no need to be afraid of me."

Marie stood resolutely, her hands clenched into fists. "What exactly *did* you mean, Major?"

"I can't explain right now." Schulmann pushed his chair from the table, glancing at his meal as if he had suddenly lost his appetite. "But I can tell you your future depends upon what I decide over the next few days."

"Really? So if I answer your questions to your satisfaction than I walk free?"

"No. But you'll be better off than if you refuse to cooperate."

"And what if I fail your little test?"

"I haven't decided. I might send you the remainder of the way to Lyon."

Marie felt the unreasonable panic at the base of her throat at his words. "You mean my life is in your hands."

"You could put it that way, yes."

"You Nazis love to play God, don't you?" Marie shook her head, amazed. "You think you have the authority to decide whether a person will live or die—based on your own twisted definition of right and wrong."

"Look at it however you wish, mademoiselle. I'm not going to argue with you tonight."

"O mighty one." Marie bowed mockingly. "I would *beg* permission to retire to my room."

Rolf sighed. "Pleasant dreams, Marie Jacobson."

TEN

If only her mother could see her now.

Marie smiled at the horror her diminutive French mother would have shown to see her down on her knees picking a lock. Her training had prepared her for more than a parachute drop and poem codes, and her newfound skills would help her to alert Baker Street to her predicament. She listened for the telltale surrender of the locking mechanism under her hands, her hairpin only slightly more awkward than the tools she had relinquished in Belley. She suspected this attic door hid a wireless set—she'd seen the aerial when she'd glanced up at the roof during a walk on the riverbank with Derek.

With an almost imperceptible click, the lock yielded. Marie straightened, listening for signs that the Germans in the bedrooms below had discovered her activities. Lancelot's foul snoring continued rhythmically, and Marie exhaled slowly, returning her attention to the task at hand.

Wooden floorboards. A small, dirty window. Cobwebs hanging from the rafters. Dusty, stale air. The attic brought back memories of Captain Dresdner, and her fingers moved unbidden to the stitches at the side of her head as she remembered his fist connecting with her skull with a force she would have thought impossible from such a small man. She shook off the memory and forced herself to focus on the table in front of her, feeling a swift wave of euphoria at the sight of the large radio set displayed temptingly on its surface. Walking toward the heaven-sent object, she reached inside the sleeve of her nightgown and extracted the silk WOK. *Thank goodness for the tailors at The Thatched Barn,* she thought. At Director Marks's request they had worked their camouflage magic on her boots, producing a small sleeve inside the lining for hiding her silk code key. She had managed to keep her WOK hidden away from the detail-oriented eyes of the female guard who searched her after her capture. Marie had been required to remove all her clothes, which were then examined closely for any hidden weapons, documents, and suicide pills. Somehow her WOK, in its hiding place, had evaded their inspection.

Her euphoria gave way to panic as she realized she had no means of cutting and destroying the key sequence she was about to use, but she forced herself to proceed, convincing herself she would find a way to destroy the line of text as soon as she returned to her room. She slid onto the chair and faced the set, her eyes flitting expertly over the controls. The model in front of her was similar to the one she had learned to use in cryptography school in Bedford.

She took a deep breath. This might be the WOK's first real test, she realized, to discover whether an agent transmitting in a dangerous environment, with no way to encrypt her message on paper and with nothing but her WOK and a memorized poem to assist her, could still manage to transmit a message without deadly errors or double transposition. Hesitating for just a second, Marie turned on the power and reached for the headset.

Her hands darted between the silk, with its lines of codes, and the machine, her Morse pattern cramping her forearm as she tapped. She felt a drop of perspiration slide across her ear and she brushed at it impatiently. Her unexpected traffic might not be heard by the coders of Grendon, or in her haste the columns might be misaligned or her words misspelled. Then it would take Director Marks himself to decipher her indecipherable. That is, if the Germans didn't hear her first.

She added her security check at the end of her message and sat back to wait. There was no response, and she realized she probably had not been heard. Field operators were supposed to transmit at pre-arranged times, but no one would be expecting her call. She would just have to pray some insomniac with nothing better to do would be listening. Glancing at the closed door behind her, she again attacked the machine, re-transmitting the encryptions as quickly and as accurately as she could. She knew her life expectancy diminished with every second on the air, and she tapped out her indicator key phrase and flew immediately into her message, a growing worry that it was useless tugging at her consciousness. Grendon wasn't listening—at least not on her frequency. Her fingers slowed, and when large hands lifted her from her chair and threw her bodily to the floor, she had the fleeting thought that it really didn't matter.

"What do you think you're doing?" The uncharacteristic fury in Major Rolf Schulmann's voice cut her deeply, and the dark anger in his eyes and the steady gun in the hand of Lieutenant Hans Brenner at the major's side convinced Marie that her life was finally over. She recoiled, raising her arm in an instinctive attempt to protect herself from a bullet.

"Stand up." Rolf's voice held a mixture of disbelief and anger.

"Want me to shoot her?" The absence of Hans's usual cheerfulness convinced Marie he considered this infraction more than just a second-story rope trick. She felt cold as she stared at his gun. Shock robbed her body of function, and she lay where she had fallen.

"Does he *need* to shoot you, Marie?" Rolf towered over her, his hair sleep-ruffled but his eyes penetrating. She met his gaze and realized the anger in his eyes could not camouflage another emotion—one that eluded her but, she realized, one that troubled her even more than his anger.

Shaken, she whispered, "No."

"On your feet."

She struggled to rise, and the major grasped her upper arm and pulled her to a standing position. "Do you realize what you've done?"

She didn't answer.

"When the *Funk-Horchdienst* comes searching, it's *you* they'll find. Did you honestly think you could get away with it?"

Marie glanced at Hans, who held his gun steady, then back at Rolf. "I knew the risks."

Rolf turned to Hans. "Get me a paper and pencil, Lieutenant."

"Any chance they got her bearings?"

"We have to assume. They know this is a military facility, but they might stop by all the same."

Hans glowered at Marie as he lowered his weapon. "I'll be back."

Rolf turned his attention back to Marie, and their eyes locked. "Are you trying to make this difficult for me?"

"Let go of my arm."

For a moment Rolf didn't move, as if reminding her she was in no position to tell him what to do. Then he released her and stepped back, his eyes never leaving hers. "Explain yourself, mademoiselle. What message were you trying to send?"

Marie shrugged. "My location. I wanted to let them know where I am."

The major studied her carefully, and Marie recognized the elusive emotion in his eyes: Major Rolf Schulmann was disappointed. Surprised, she shifted uneasily, realizing she could handle his fury—she could even demonstrate a little of her own before her demise—but the incongruous thought that he might be disappointed in her shook her resolve. She felt her gaze wavering, and then she finally dropped her eyes, hugging her arms against her nightgown and waiting for his response. His disappointment no longer confined itself to his eyes but filled the room and wrapped itself uncomfortably around her, shaking her determination in a way that stunned her. He turned, straightened her overturned chair, and gestured toward it. "Sit, Marie. We have work to do."

Marie complied, her back stiff and her eyes averted, and Hans returned bearing a piece of graph paper and a small pencil. He placed them on the table in front of Marie and then turned and left the room.

Rolf tapped the paper in front of her. "Write the message you transmitted, encoded exactly as you sent it." He picked up her silk WOK and studied it solemnly. "Use this key. I assume this is yours?" He handed it to her.

She knew he would hear the bitterness in her voice. "Why encode it? Why not just tell you what I meant to say?"

"I have my reasons. Begin, please." Rolf turned away and stood silently at the attic window, his back to her. Marie remembered her teachers' admonitions to refuse—to deny, resist, and be prepared to take her secret to her grave. Then she remembered a darkened basement cell, stitches, and a man who showed her kindness completely foreign to his position. *Trust him.*

She looked at the paper. "How will you know I'm writing the same message?"

He sighed. "It doesn't matter."

Marie was confused. "Why?"

Rolf folded his arms and didn't turn to look at her. "Just start writing, Marie."

Ten minutes later her pencil stilled. Rolf turned away from the window, walked to the table, and picked up her paper and the silk WOK. He studied her writing silently, then folded the paper and slipped it into his pocket along with the code key. He produced a pair of handcuffs, then grasped her wrists in one hand and locked them together. "You've raised a new set of questions, mademoiselle—questions I must have answered before I can help you." He walked to the door and opened it, then turned briefly to study her before closing it firmly behind him.

Marie stared after him, confused by his actions and terrified of the unknown. She had a thousand unanswered questions of her own, and she wondered if she would ever understand what the major was doing. Why had he brought her here? What did he mean to find out? Marie glanced down at her wrists and felt the cold steel against her skin. She put her imprisoned hands on the table in front of her and dropped her head onto her arms.

* * *

Three hours later Rolf Schulmann returned with Hans Brenner. Without preamble the major laid her coded message in front of her, followed by two others written in his own handwriting. There was something vaguely familiar about them, and Marie stared in disbelief before turning questioning eyes to Rolf.

"Your messages from Belley." His voice had an edge to it, as if he were holding his anger in check. "Decode them."

"What makes you think these are mine?"

"I *know* they're yours, Marie. I don't just 'think.'"

"How do you know?"

"They have the same transmission signature—your personal touch." He shook his head. "You of all people should know it takes as little as two intercepted transmissions for an operator's signature to be recognized. Once we've intercepted one of your skeds we can recognize your traffic whether it originates from Paris or my neighbor's basement." He tapped the back of her chair. "Besides, your security checks are similar. Even if we had missed both your Belley messages—we did miss half of the first—we would have known just from your security check that it was the same person. You might as well run an announcement in the daily paper."

Marie stared at him in shock, and Rolf reached for her handcuffs, inserted a key, and freed her hands. He continued. "You were lucky to escape my direction-finding officers in Belley; they would have shot you first and asked questions later." His hand rested on her shoulder, and he repeated his order. "Tell me what they say, Marie."

She took a deep breath. "How will you know . . . ?"

". . . if you're telling the truth?" Rolf indicated the most recent message. "I've already deciphered today's message—you used selections from a poem familiar to me, Marie: *The Road Not Taken,* by Robert Frost. One of my favorites, I might add." His brow knit. "Only it was not decipherable in the usual way, and it was not until I utilized this ingenious little handkerchief you supplied for me that I was finally able to break your code." He held up her silk WOK and dangled it in front of her face. Marie ignored the silk and kept her eyes on the three papers in front of her. Behind Rolf, Hans Brenner stood with his arms folded, silently watching both Marie and the major. Rolf continued. "I assume you meant to remove and destroy the indicator keys you had just used—before we interrupted. Am I right?"

"Each indicator is random, Major Schulmann. You won't be able to use that silk—"

"I know that already." Rolf paused, straightening the silk on the table next to the three square papers. "But you underestimate our *Funk-Horchdienst.* They have been working steadily to decipher your transmissions ever since your traffic was intercepted near Belley."

"Perhaps, as you say, your coders are incredibly talented." Marie took a deep breath and forced herself to speak calmly. "But *I* cannot decode these two transmissions without the key, and the key has been destroyed."

"Yes, but you know what messages you encoded, mademoiselle." His hand tightened perceptibly on her shoulder. "Write them down."

Marie picked up the pencil and began writing, hesitating at intervals as she recalled those two nights in Belley. She finished writing the first—her "test message"—and turned to the second. This one posed a problem: not only had her message been freelance, but it had had emotions attached to it that distracted her and hindered her concentration. She struggled with her memories—her distress that had built ever since that morning in the café, her worry that the drop would be compromised, the subsequent arrival of German soldiers and the chase, and the death of her fiancé and her own capture. Major Schulmann stood at her side, monitoring her progress, and she tried to ignore him as she concentrated on her task. A headache had been building for some time, and now she rubbed at her temple with her left hand, trying to alleviate the pain as she wrote.

Finally, she finished and laid the pencil on the table. Major Schulmann locked her wrists together, then bent past her to retrieve all three papers and the silk. "You will wait here, mademoiselle, while I check what you have written against what my coders in Belley are preparing for me." She finally turned to look at him, and he continued. "If you lied and your messages differ from what my coders deciphered in Belley, or if your transmissions to London in any way endanger the lives of my men, I will escort you immediately to Gestapo headquarters in Lyon."

* * *

Marie stood near the window and watched the sunrise. She felt exhausted, numb, and she had tried without success to forget the disappointment in Rolf Schulmann's eyes when he had pulled her away from the WT set. Why had it affected her so? Why would she care if she had let him down? What had he expected of her, and why had he been so disappointed in her actions? She turned when she heard the door open. Major Schulmann entered alone, and at his request she returned to her chair at the table.

"Ingenious, these silks, mademoiselle." Rolf smoothed the cloth again on the table in front of Marie. "My men are excellent decoders, but your messages might have caused them more than their usual amount of grief without this device." He unlocked her wrists and arranged six sheets of paper in front of her. "They succeeded, though—as I knew they would."

Marie studied the messages. Aside from a few spelling errors in the decoded messages, Rolf's coders had done a perfect job—as if someone had handed them the destroyed code keys on a silver platter. Director Marks would be devastated when he learned that his silk codes could be so easily compromised. Her eyes scanned both her writings and the original messages intercepted and decoded by the *Funk-Horchdienst*. Rolf read them aloud. "Arrived safely, debrief in four hours. New German officer at garrison Belley, drop site compromised, new coordinates required before next drop . . ." Rolf glanced at Marie. "I admit you're a talented coder." He moved his index finger to the second, leaning over Marie's shoulder as he read. "Germans aware of drop. Abort and reschedule . . ." The major shook his head. "If you had mentioned this message to your Résistance fiancé and any of my men had been shot on the mountainside, I would have considered this message your ticket to Lyon." He straightened, and she could feel his eyes contemplating her from above. "You are lucky, mademoiselle."

"You Germans keep telling me that, Major, but to be honest, I don't feel lucky right now."

"Nevertheless, you are fortunate, Marie. I chose not to arrest you in the café, you escaped my direction-finding units, my men didn't shoot you when you came flying down that mountainside, and you're not in Captain Dresdner's clutches—at the moment. Yes, I consider you *very* lucky."

"You forgot to mention how lucky I am to be here in France."

"That's one thing I've been curious about, mademoiselle. In fact, I've been so curious that I decided to do a little research after you left with Dresdner. I had questions about you—questions that did not seem to be resolved by your answers. So tell me, why send a young woman with no military training and half a college degree into France?"

Marie pressed her lips firmly together.

"Would I be far off to suggest that you were sent here to test this new coding system? I take it SOE is finally aware of how my teams love your agents' poem codes?"

"They're aware."

He reached for a chair and sat down facing her. "A hypothetical benefit of the new system would be faster transmissions, therefore less airtime and less chance an agent would be discovered. Rolf nodded toward the messages on the table. "None of these messages come close to the old poem codes' two-fifty rule, and none of your traffic even reached the fifteen-minute average of codes past. Can you explain it to me?"

Marie sighed. "It's a long story—and I won't explain it to you."

"I'm good at stories, especially long ones. So let me guess." Rolf settled back comfortably in his chair and stretched his legs out in front of him. "SOE knows we devour your agents' poetry for breakfast, and in order to save more lives somebody dreams up a new system that doesn't require memorization and therefore can't be tortured out of a captured agent." He folded his arms and watched Marie closely, a hint of a smile playing at the corners of his mouth. "You travel to Britain with the WAC, attend cryptography school, and, because of your dual nationality, flawless French, mathematical skills, and pretty smile, are approached by SOE to join their pool of ladies breaking codes at Grendon. You're eager to do anything in your power to beat *'Les Boches,'* and perhaps prolong the life of your Résistance fiancé, Félix Larouche, who is fighting the enemy in France. Am I right so far?"

Marie felt her pulse pounding at the base of her throat, but she said nothing. The major leaned forward, watching her intently. "Perhaps the daughter of renowned structural engineer and Parisian professor William Jacobson was then recruited by some representative of the Free French leader in exile, General Charles de Gaulle, who resides at the moment, I believe, in Algiers?" When Marie did not comment, Rolf continued. "After the last war your distinguished father was consulted several times on matters of state by General Philippe Pétain, head of France's Vichy government. At the time Pétain was acquainted with your father, Charles de Gaulle was a staff member of General Pétain in Paris—I believe he was responsible for recruiting your father to assist in rebuilding much of what the Allies destroyed during the conflict with Germany.

"A friendship developed between your father and de Gaulle, and when a new war threatened France, General de Gaulle contacted your father and invited him to join him in London to assist in coordinating the Free French movement. Am I right?"

Marie shook her head. "My father lives in the United States—he did not move to England."

"I understand. But you knew of the connection between de Gaulle and your father." It was a statement rather than a question.

"That has nothing to do with my decision to come to France, Major. I came to be with . . ." Marie felt her emotions rising to the surface and she swallowed hard, forcing herself to maintain control. She pushed the image of Félix's lifeless body to the back of her mind and glowered at the culprit in front of her.

Rolf ignored the daggers she was mentally throwing at him and continued as if she had not spoken. "Your father took several trips to England with your mother while you attended the university in Utah. You knew of those trips and were understandably curious. One day you confronted your father and he told you about de Gaulle and about the general's efforts to organize rabble guerilla cells in France into one cohesive unit—the Free French."

Marie couldn't help herself. "Where do you come up with such nonsense?" She felt her face redden at the thought that this German could know so much about her personal life. "You're a talented storyteller, sir, but not much of a historian."

Major Schulmann's lips twisted. "Perhaps not a historian, mademoiselle, but I *am* an intelligence officer—this is what I *do*."

"There's no way you could find out these things about me without an outside source—" Marie stopped, realizing her thoughtless words had all but confirmed his story. She sat back, mortified, mentally kicking herself for her stupidity. Terrified, she glanced furtively in the direction of the window, as if either her body or her useless cover story were just about to take a plunge into the river below.

Rolf leaned back again, the look on his face telling her that he was amused at her mistake but that he had already known his information was valid. "There is a twist to this story that I don't understand," he said. "And if you do not volunteer a solution I'll have to invent my own. How does Commander Henri Giraud, co-president with de Gaulle of the *Comité Français de la Libération Nationale,* fit into the picture?" Marie had never heard of the name, and she knew her confusion was evident to the German officer. Schulmann continued. "Both Giraud and de Gaulle met in Morocco at the beginning of this year—for a reason I don't have the talent to discover." He smiled at Marie, as if conceding the possibility that he was not as knowledgeable as she might think him. "I assume that since Giraud also liaisons with the puppet Vichy government, and General de Gaulle is not on speaking terms with Pétain, there must be some sort of understanding between the Vichy and de Gaulle organizations."

"But I thought the Vichy government was collaborating fully with you Germans—they have bowed to your every wish and agreed to all your Führer's oppressive rules."

"Not *all,* Marie. Why do you think we came south?"

Marie was silent.

"The Vichy collaborates with my government, yes. But at times it seems a token allegiance, that's all. Philippe Pétain, I believe, is not wholly convinced of the Führer's goodwill. Because he is not completely compliant, under the rules of the 1940 armistice that makes his authority forfeit." Rolf fingered the silk WOK lying on the table in front of Marie. "So perhaps Pétain secretly authorizes President Giraud to research the possibilities to find a way to cooperate with General de Gaulle and the Free French behind our back. We have no proof of this betrayal, of course, but it makes sense that after we break our end of the bargain and cross the demarcation line they might find a way to express their disappointment.

"Perhaps Giraud decides the best way to help the two rival French governments secretly cooperate is to help de Gaulle's agents and freedom fighters coordinate more effectively with both the SOE in Britain and the OSS in America. Both organizations, working together to help the Free French, could theoretically put a stranglehold on German forces in France when the Allies invade."

"What does all this have to do with me?" Marie broke in. "Or SOE's decision to change the coding system, for that matter?"

"Patience, mademoiselle. I will arrive there shortly." Rolf continued. "You understand that the United States recognizes the Vichy government and England recognizes de Gaulle's Free French. A disagreement like this might seem minor in the grand scheme of things, except for the fact that the Allies are planning to invade sometime next year—a point we Germans accept as fact, by the way, and are preparing for accordingly—and any frivolous squabbles between the two French authorities can undermine the Résistance in France and the rest of the countries the Allies plan to invade. So at de Gaulle's suggestion, Giraud meets in London with your father, bringing with him de Gaulle's request that Monsieur Jacobson lend his considerable intelligence to the effort of finding a way to assist the guerilla organizations in France.

"Your father, kind and religious man that he is, sees this as a way he can save lives and perhaps assist his important friend in unifying the Free French forces. On a personal note, he has a future son-in-law in France whose life is at the mercy of SOE's procedures, and an intelligent, motivated daughter who has also joined that organization. He visits both de Gaulle's and SOE's headquarters in London. He understands from SOE's director of communications that we Germans are having a field day with the agents' existing system of poem codes, which are easily detected and deciphered, keep the agents on the air for longer than is safe, and can be tortured out of an agent if he is captured. After several weeks of research, he suggests to President Giraud that lives could be saved if the existing secret French code used by de Gaulle could be reworked.

"Your father suggests to Giraud that there might be a way to implement a new system that has been created by SOE and is beginning to be implemented by other agents in the field—but the system has not yet been tested using the secret code de Gaulle's agents are using. Professor Jacobson recommends strongly that the code be tested and implemented as soon as possible, and de Gaulle sends a representative to SOE to negotiate implementation of the code."

Marie's head was beginning to spin. "You thought this up all by your-self?" was all she could think of to say.

Rolf laughed. "With the help of sources within SOE and de Gaulle's organization."

His words sent shockwaves up Marie's spine, and she knew the expression on her face would be impossible to hide.

Rolf watched her carefully. "How did you expect we would know where to be in order to intercept your transmissions? How do you think we have the capability to decode your Belley traffic without the code keys you destroyed?" He indicated the silk in his hand, and Marie felt the warmth in her cheeks rise at the thought that her whole mission had been doomed to failure from the beginning. She felt an unreasonable anger forming inside her chest at the thought that she had been a pawn in the hands of Pétain's Vichy government.

Rolf ran his finger across an unused code key imprinted on the silk. "Pétain has his agents among Grendon's coders, it seems. We were given the new key you would use within hours of your arrival in France, along with your name, specific background information, such as your father's connection with de Gaulle, and the exact times of your transmissions. All we had to do was locate your WT site and bring you in."

Marie felt nauseated, and she clenched her hands together in a death grip. "Does General de Gaulle know the Vichy government is double dealing with the Résistance?"

"Probably not—unless he suspects, now that you have disappeared."

"Why me?"

Rolf shrugged, and Marie thought for an instant that she saw pity in his eyes for her predicament. "All I can figure is that your father made an enemy of General Philippe Pétain when he chose to follow de Gaulle instead of returning France and assisting the new Vichy government. Perhaps Pétain's British agents informed the Vichy leader that you were recruited by SOE, and then Pétain ordered his agents to convince de Gaulle to recommend you to SOE's director of communications for this particular job."

"Making it possible to kill two birds with one stone." Marie's voice had a bitter edge.

Rolf nodded, and now the sympathy in his eyes was unmistakable. "First, undermine the Free French by compromising their new coding system, alerting us to its existence and training us in its use. And second, send the daughter of traitor Jacobson into a situation where she is sure to be captured, tortured, and most likely executed for spying."

"I'm not a spy."

"The Gestapo sees you as one, Marie." Rolf shook his head. "How unfortunate your second message was received at the Grendon coding center by Pétain's agent, who probably had been told to volunteer for that shift, and who recognized the message's significance and deliberately misspelled three of your five indicator words so that it could not possibly be deciphered in time for London to abort the drop. How different things might have been . . ." His voice softened slightly. "It's too bad they sent you into France at this time, mademoiselle; you could have been safely at home, your Félix might still be alive, and you wouldn't have had to be here with me."

Marie pictured a young French woman, loyal to the German occupiers, sitting at her station and calmly transposing letters and hatting columns, making it look as if the field agent transmitted the message that way, and then turning and handing the tortured message to her supervisor, explaining apologetically that the transmitting agent must be under great duress because she had just sent an indecipherable. Could the supervisor get Director Marks on the line and ask him to assist? Oh, and by the way, there was no way to ask the agent to retransmit, as she had broken off unexpectedly and might have been captured . . . Deflated, Marie stared dazedly at Major Schulmann. He leaned forward and took her hands in his, and Marie was too numb to pull away.

"Yes, I believe you *are* lucky, Marie Jacobson: You are lucky to be alive. But I'm concerned for your well-being."

"I'm glad to know of your concern." She meant for her words to be sarcastic but realized she was too tired to try that hard.

Rolf studied her solemnly. "The part you play in the war is only a fraction of my concern, Marie. There is something infinitely more important that will influence your future."

She looked up at him then, her eyes questioning. "Major, I—"

"Not now, mademoiselle—I'm tired, and so are you, I imagine." He stood, straightening his back in a long stretch. "It's been a long and eventful night, and we both could use a rest." He smiled tightly. "An informative, productive session—don't you agree?"

Marie said nothing.

Rolf turned to go, and Marie watched his back as he moved to the door. "I recommend you rest for a few hours, Marie. I will expect you in my office at ten o'clock, ready to continue our conversation."

ELEVEN

Under her hands Marie felt the hard surface of a wall, and she allowed her fingers to follow its shape as it rose and fell with each unique stone. She watched as the woman exited the villa and held out her arms, and Marie walked obediently through the gate and up the path. Through flowers lovingly planted and painstakingly cultivated she walked, her eyes watching the woman standing near the villa. The apple tree was still loaded with ripe fruit, and the air exploded with the fragrance of a summer garden. She knew what her mother would say before the sweet woman opened her mouth. *"Trust him, Marie."*

She opened her eyes and stared at the ceiling of her room. Never before had she experienced a recurring dream, and this one in particular troubled her every time she had it. She threw back her blanket and sat up, turning so her feet could slide to the floor. The cold floorboards sent shivers up her body, clearing sleep from her head and reminding her of her predicament. On bare feet, she padded over to the window and pulled up the blackout shade to let the morning light flood into the room. Below her, Lancelot sat with his back against the stone wall and his arms wrapped around his rifle, hugging it to his chest as if it would afford him insulation against the cold morning air. He looked up at her, and she waved cheerfully down at him.

Returning to her bed, Marie pulled off her nightgown and slipped her head through the neckline of a dress from the armoire. She glanced at her reflection in the small mirror above the washbasin and was dismayed to see how gaunt her face seemed. Her cheekbones were beginning to protrude, and her eyes were shadowed from days of anxiety. She ran a comb through her hair and realized it did little to repair the damage, so she hastily pulled the curls away from her face and tied them back with a string. Her dark brown eyes looked unnaturally bright, as if she were always on the verge of tears. Every emotion seemed to stand out in bold relief in their depths, and she worried that the major would be able to read her every thought. Disheartened, she turned and left the room.

Major Schulmann looked up from the telephone when she entered his office. He was dressed as he had been when she'd first met him: wool coat, dark shirt and trousers, and thick boots. This was the first time Marie had seen him out of his uniform since the café in Belley, and she was curious. She hovered by his desk and waited for him to hang up the phone. He nodded at her solemnly and spoke into the receiver. "Of course not. I've already been away too long. I can only spare a few more days." He listened for several moments and then spoke again, his voice rising slightly. "I'm sure you would, Major. But the truth is, it's not my fault. Dresdner insisted upon transporting the prisoner without an escort, even though I offered . . ." He paused to listen. "No. He flatly refused. Said he couldn't wait—" Rolf stopped, as if someone had interrupted on the other end. "My advice would be to have your agents scour the mountain villages between Belley and Aix-les-Bains. She would be dependent on the *maquisards* for cover, but she's going to have to make a move sometime—she'll want to get back to Allied territory." Again he listened. "No. I cannot. And that's final. Tell Dresdner to clean up his own mess." Rolf slammed the receiver and gave Marie a wry smile. "Seems no one can find the American girl."

"I came to ask what you need me to do today."

"Go with me on an outing to the river."

"An outing?" Marie blinked. "It's freezing outside. Do I have a choice?"

"Certainly." Schulmann reached for his hat and covered his neatly-combed hair. "You can come with me or you can sit locked in your room all day with Derek staring up at you from below. Of course you have a choice. We'll be leaving in fifteen minutes."

"If I'm going to get dirty, perhaps I'd better find something a little more suitable to wear."

* * *

Mist rose eerily from the river's surface as the Citroën pulled to a stop on a bluff overlooking the water. Hillsides rose steeply from the water on every side, and a carpet of trees forested the precipitous slopes, their dull winter gray blending with the blue-gray of the water below. A particularly long hill rose in front of them and stretched warily across the near end of the river like a large, lazy crocodile. On the lower end crouched the ruins of a castle. Its walls seemed hunched and its tower tall and alert, as if the presence of the man and woman on the bank gave it cause for alarm.

"Grangent Castle," Rolf said, nodding in the direction of the ruins. "I used to spend summers here with my parents and best friend."

"Hans?"

Rolf nodded. "Growing up we were inseparable."

"Seems you still are." Marie smiled faintly.

Rolf returned her smile, and for just a second Marie caught a glimmer in his eyes that might have been akin to companionship.

"You ever rowed a boat?" Rolf pointed in the direction of the shore, where a tiny wooden skiff lay halfway on the sand, its back end bobbing on the river's cold surface.

"Never. Is this your latest plan to get rid of me?"

Rolf laughed, and the sound softened the edges of Marie's dislike for him. "On a day like today it would be criminal not to enjoy the river. Don't worry, I'll take the controls." He descended the slope toward the waiting skiff.

A few minutes later they were gliding past the castle on the hill, and Marie watched the tower slipping away as they followed the current of the river. She gripped both sides of the flimsy craft and glanced at the major. He sat facing her, his shoulders and arms hunching as he dug with the paddles and then rippling forward and then backward with each powerful stroke. He confused her—his methods of "interrogation" so far had not followed the pattern presented to her by the British as being the norm. Where were the straps, the rubber clubs, and the metal bars? Where were the excruciatingly long sessions and the bright lights? Where were the chains and the mind-softening drugs? Marie clung to the sides of the skiff as a larger wave shook her seat. It didn't make any sense. Nothing made sense; treating her wound, kidnapping her from the Gestapo, being here with her on this river . . . Why would he risk his life and reputation to remove her from the Gestapo captain's clutches?

She watched his shoulders rolling with each stroke. He rowed rhythmically, each stroke as strong as the last, as if the exertion could not tire him. Certainly he must worry that somebody would find out, that he would be punished. They crossed a slight eddy, and the boat momentarily twisted sideways until his powerful strokes again pointed them into the current.

"Caught many salmon in these waters as a child." Rolf didn't even sound winded. He steadied the boat against the current and stopped their gentle movement away from the castle. "Shot my first rabbit in those hills," he said, pointing across the river at a wooded slope barely visible in the mist.

Marie giggled, then quickly smothered the sound behind her hand. She couldn't help it—his conversation seemed so out of character for a German officer. She remembered having similar thoughts when he'd entered his office the first day he interrogated her.

"Hans fell out of the boat once and nearly drowned in the current," Rolf said. He turned and saw the expression on Marie's face. "Not what you were expecting, is it?"

She shook her head. "Not at all."

He watched her closely, his blue eyes serious. "Tell me more about your family."

"I thought your sources already did that."

Rolf shook his head, ignoring the edge to her voice. "Not everything."

"Why should I?"

"Because I asked you to. Don't question me."

He suddenly seemed preoccupied, impatient. Marie took a deep breath. She reminded herself to tread carefully with him—hadn't he suggested her life depended on her cooperation? She forced herself to begin. "During the Great War my father was an engineer with the American Expeditiary Forces. But then, you probably already knew that."

Rolf's lips twisted. "Some of it. Go on."

"He was assigned to the Corps of Engineers to help demolish bridges to keep the Germans out of Paris." Marie hesitated and glanced sideways at the major before continuing. "Whenever Dad and his friends passed through the streets, people would cry, blow kisses, and sometimes give them bouquets of flowers. He said he felt like a hero even though he hadn't seen combat. He and several of his buddies billeted with a well-to-do family in a little village south of Paris. He used to tell me of the manure piles—the *fumier*—by the front door." Marie smiled, warming to her story. "Seemed the French considered this a sign of wealth and thrift, but Dad couldn't get used to the notion—not to mention the stench—and used to complain mightily to his hosts.

"One night the boys returned from the village, all of them drunk except for my dad. He was supporting one of his more inebriated friends and wasn't paying attention to where he stepped. In the darkness he and the friend he was supporting tumbled headlong into that pile of fresh fertilizer, and the daughter of their host—my mother—witnessed the accident. She couldn't stop laughing, and she called him 'Monsieur Fumier' for days. When my father was transferred, he and Mom agreed to write, and when the war ended they were married."

"Your mother had never left France, then?"

Marie shook her head. "Not until years later, when Dad convinced her to go with him to visit his relatives in the United States. She agreed, mainly because she wanted to go with Dad to the temple . . ." Marie trailed off awkwardly and fell silent. Major Schulmann looked at her intently, and she could see a curious stirring of emotion in the depths of his blue eyes. He said nothing for some time, and Marie wondered if her mention of a "temple" had alienated him. She could not imagine that a Nazi officer would understand about eternal marriage, let alone want to hear about it. She felt again the oppressive truth of her captivity and remembered that the man sitting in front of her was her enemy. "I'm sorry, Major Schulmann." She turned away from him and stared out across the river. "I don't wish to bore you with my stories—or my beliefs."

"Tell me about the temple in America."

Surprised, she turned to look at him. He smiled faintly. "It seems to be important—at least to your mother . . ."

"It was." She studied him hesitantly before continuing. "The temple is located in Utah—in the western United States." She took a deep breath and continued. "Dad was a Mormon—a member of The Church of Jesus Christ of Latter-day Saints. He taught Mom about his beliefs, and after several years she too joined the Church." Marie glanced at the major. He had not batted an eye.

"The missionaries told Mom about eternal marriage . . ."

"Eternal marriage?" He had a strange light in his eyes.

"Marriage that does not end with death. We call it being sealed. Mom wanted us to be sealed to Dad for eternity, so they started saving money to travel to America."

"The closest temple is in Utah."

"That's right."

"So, was your family sealed in the temple?"

Marie nodded and watched a heron fly low over the surface of the river until its graceful wings disappeared into the haze. "I remember how happy my parents were, and how beautiful they looked together all dressed in white . . ." Marie stopped. Something as sacred as that memory should not be shared with a Nazi—not even to prolong her life.

"And what about you and Félix?" Schulmann prompted. "Were you planning to be married in the temple?"

"Of course. Nothing less would do for Félix. For both of us. I can't imagine loving anybody and then promising to love them only for this life." Marie felt her emotions rising dangerously toward the surface, and she lashed out irritably. "Don't you have anything better to do than torture me with memories?" She felt tears forming at the corners of her eyes. "Don't you realize what you've stolen from me? Félix and I were to be married for *eternity!*" She paused. "That's something a man like you will never understand."

"Maybe not." He seemed unruffled by her remarks. "But I want to hear about it anyway, Marie."

"Why?"

"It intrigues me. You intrigue me—you and your beliefs. Sometimes I wonder . . ." He hesitated.

"About what, Major?"

"If there hadn't been a war . . . maybe you and I could have been friends."

Marie sat silently, shocked at his words.

"Maybe you would have married Félix and you and he would have moved to Paris . . ." Rolf looked out over the river. "And maybe I would have visited you two there, and we would have formed a lifelong friendship."

"Instead, you killed him." Marie's voice was bitter.

Rolf turned and studied her, his face impassive. "Such is war."

Marie frowned. "And how did you know Félix Larouche? Perhaps you had spent time with him in the cafés? Perhaps you deceived him, like you did me? Made him think you were a Frenchman loyal to the Résistance so you could infiltrate his organization?"

Rolf shook his head. "Nothing like that."

"How did you know him, then?"

Major Schulmann dug in with the paddles, turning the boat against the current to head back in the direction they had come. "This isn't the right time to tell you, Marie."

"Why not? I've been straightforward with you. I've answered your questions, haven't I?"

"Yes . . . because I required it." Rolf smiled sadly. "When you tell me what is in your heart because you *want* to—*then* I will confide in you."

* * *

Rolf tapped his desk impatiently. "I understand it is out of my jurisdiction. But it affects my district, my security, and the security of my men. This is the *Résistance* we are talking about—not some *Luftwaffe* deserter." He listened to the irritated voice on the other end of the line and reminded himself to keep his own impatience under control. "That's right. The woman is connected to the Résistance. And yes, I do think an old Frenchwoman's whereabouts is important enough to tie up three men each day for as long as it takes." He grimaced at the receiver, holding it away from his ear as the voice on the other end rose in volume. "You should calm down, sir—remember what the doctor said about your blood pressure." He hesitated. "Yes, I will assume complete responsibility for the surveillance. I only ask that you lend me the manpower until we can detain the caretaker. Someone is caring for the cottage, and he will help us track down the owner."

Rolf hung up the phone and paused with his hand resting heavily on the receiver while he sorted through the conversation. He shook his head to clear it and glanced out the window. *Hans is on guard duty,* he thought, and he straightened. He decided to go outside and join him.

Major Rolf Schulmann approached his friend, who was standing with his back pressed against the frozen garden wall. "Any problems?"

Lieutenant Brenner glanced at his comrade and shook his head. "None. Tonight Rapunzel seems content to wait it out in her tower, although from the tension I felt between you two when you returned this afternoon, she might just try to strangle you in your sleep."

Rolf laughed. "I'll be vigilant."

Hans turned to face Rolf. "Seriously, Rolf—you're taking a great risk. Have you thought what might happen if the Gestapo decides to check up on your activities? What if they managed to intercept the message that little vixen sent last night?"

"I've thought about it." Rolf leaned against the stone wall next to his friend. "And it's a risk I have to take—for the moment."

"So you haven't decided yet?"

Rolf shook his head. "She's afraid of me. She's determined to keep me at a distance. She shares her memories grudgingly and refuses to trust me."

"Is she worth the risk? I mean, as a woman she *is* incredible—but is she worth the danger to your family?"

"She might be."

"Is she who you thought she would be?"

"Yes."

TWELVE

In the kitchen Marie settled into a chair next to Hans. Derek and Lancelot sat at the other end of the table, arguing heatedly in German, their decibel level rising and their fists punching the air for emphasis. Hans sat munching a slice of bread and gulping coffee, seemingly unconcerned with the fight. His gun lay in its holster next to his plate on the table along with his dark leather gloves. Marie eyed the gun silently. If she stood she could easily sweep it from the table, tear it from its holster, and turn it on the men in the room. She chewed on her lip and contemplated the possibility.

She glanced up at Hans's face and realized he was watching her interest in the gun. "Got something on your mind, princess?"

She felt her cheeks redden. "Where is Major Schulmann?"

"Gone to Lyon." Hans downed the last of his coffee and pushed back his chair. "Business. Should be back this afternoon."

"Mind if I take a walk by the river?"

"Mind if I go with you?"

"Since when have you started asking my permission, Hans?"

Hans smiled. "I'd sure hate to have you fall in. The major would skin me alive."

"On one condition."

"What's that?"

"Don't trail after me like a rabid dog. Derek does that and I hate it!"

Hans turned out to be an interesting companion, once Marie could see past the unpleasant fact that he was there to keep her from running away. He showered her with stories from his childhood, touching briefly on the death of his parents and his years living with the pastor of the village parish and his wife. He told her of his introduction to Rolf's family and their decision to allow him to come and live with them. "When we were growing up, Rolf and I never went anywhere without each other," he said. "When one of us skipped school, the other tagged along. We cheated off each other's papers and terrorized his parents. We fished, hunted, and skied together, and we watched each others' backs. If one of us got sick, the other did also. We drank together, laughed together, and usually fell in love with the same *Fräulein*." Hans grinned, and his smile stretched from ear to ear. "There is no one to compare with my friend Rolf. I would do anything to help him, mademoiselle—*anything*."

"You make him sound like a good person."

"The best." Hans studied Marie. "You see him as an enemy—a monster, perhaps. He keeps you a prisoner. You see the side of him that you want to see."

Marie frowned. "What other side is there? He killed someone I care for, Hans. He killed a good man who was fighting to rid France of a plague greater than any the world has ever faced. He holds me hostage and stubbornly refuses to tell me what he plans to do with me."

"Yes, and you came to France to help your friends kill *us*. What's the difference? Do you think he loves killing? Do you honestly think he enjoys chasing *maquisards* and slippery Allies?" Hans scowled. "He doesn't hate you, Marie. He doesn't hate Félix or the Résistance fighters or the Americans or British. I doubt 'hate' is even in his vocabulary!" Hans paused. "Do you know where he learned English?"

Marie shook her head.

"Chicago. When he was a teenager he spent three years in America. Then, after a year with me at the *Universität zu Berlin,* he returned to America to attend the University of Chicago, and I decided not to follow him, although his parents would have supported me. Worst decision I ever made. We drifted into different paths. He studied law and graduated cum laude, while I studied what the Nazis wanted me to study and graduated with a military career and a handshake from Hitler."

Marie said nothing. Hans continued. "He's not in this war because he chooses to be. Don't forget that you're as much a threat to him as he is to you." He turned Marie to face him. "If you could ever get past your own self pity you would realize he saved your life. While you sit in your tower and plot your escape, he is planning how to hide you from the Gestapo until the war is over. Do you realize what a dangerous, impossible task that is? And don't even begin to think he'll let you go, Marie; a wolf allowed to run free always returns to the chicken coop." He paused. "Do you realize how much he's risked for you? Traitors are executed, Marie. And so are their families. You'll probably survive the war—but he might not. And all because he helped you."

* * *

While Marie and Hans walked by the riverbank, Major Rolf Schulmann returned to the villa and went straight to his office to call Belley. Lieutenant Meer relayed the message that Rolf's agents had managed to detain the caretaker of the abandoned cottage outside Paris. Rolf asked, "Did the caretaker explain what happened to the residents?"

"The prisoner refuses to talk, except to say he only tends the grounds and has no knowledge of who lived there or their whereabouts. Paris wants to know what you want done with the man—says they have no reason to hold him."

Rolf lowered his head and rubbed his temples wearily. "Tell them to bring him here to the villa. Tomorrow, if possible. I'll take care of him."

"Very well." Meer hesitated. "And when will you be returning, sir?"

"Soon. Is everything all right?"

"Fine, sir. It's just that . . ." Again the young lieutenant hesitated.

"What?"

"Bruno's been stirring things up a bit." Lieutenant Meer sounded exasperated. "Came after our shipment of munitions. He and his men managed to disable three panzers—and they killed two poor souls sent to guard the supplies."

"Any of my men?"

"Neumann was wounded, that's all. Doctor says he'll recover quickly."

Major Rolf Schulmann hung up the phone and climbed the main staircase with purposeful strides. He crossed the hallway and entered his bedroom. At the side of his bed he paused and stared out the window. Snow was beginning to fall, and he watched the tiny flakes pass between his window and the river below. Then he noticed two figures moving up the hill toward the villa: Hans Brenner and Marie Jacobson. He watched them thoughtfully for several seconds before turning away from the window.

After a pause, he removed his hat and sidearm and laid them on the bed in front of him. Then he knelt at the foot of his bed. "Dear Father in Heaven . . ." His words were whispered. "I have been worried about what to do with the American woman. I have tried for several days to discover what Thou wouldst have me do. She was important to Félix, and because of Félix I have tried to get to know her better. There is much about her that is good, Father." Rolf hesitated. "I have decided on a plan and I need to know if it's in accordance with Thy will . . ."

Rolf continued, his visor cap beside him on the bed and his Luger pointed haphazardly in the direction of the window. His brown hair bowed over his large hands and his knees pressed against cold floorboards. In Hamburg the American missionaries had taught him how to pray, but for most of the war he had been on his own—the idea of searching out members of the Church in Vichy France was unthinkable for a man in his position—so his prayers were as he chose. "It's risky, and there are a thousand ways it could go wrong. But for the sake of Hélène's and my family—and the life of the American girl—I need this idea to work." Rolf's hands clenched slightly and his head dropped lower. "Please help me . . ."

He never felt completely alone. The missionaries had told him about the Holy Ghost—how it would comfort him and help him if he kept the commandments. For the last four years he had tried to cultivate closeness to the Spirit, and had felt reassured many times when otherwise he would have felt completely overwhelmed.

". . . and please tell Hélène I love her." He could almost imagine that his beautiful young wife attended his interrogations, and the thought that she might be present helped keep him on track. He had imagined her presence during every session with Marie Jacobson. It was comforting; besides not wanting to disappoint his Father in Heaven, he would never want to harm someone with Hélène looking on. He wouldn't want to disappoint her.

Rolf heard footsteps and hurried to end his prayer before jumping to his feet and turning to see who approached his room.

"Praying? *Again?*" Hans's grinning face peeked in at the doorway.

"You should try it sometime, Hans." Rolf couldn't help smiling. Hans always lifted his spirits—even when he was teasing him mercilessly about his beliefs.

"The day I pray is the day I die," Hans said. "I don't need any god dictating *my* life. Besides, prayers are for the weak. You should know that, Rolf."

The major shook his head, smiling. "Call me weak, then, because I couldn't get by without prayer." Rolf then looked at his friend and his expression sobered. "I've made up my mind, Hans."

The lieutenant slipped into the room and closed the door behind him. "What's it going to be?"

Rolf opened a drawer and removed an envelope, which had been sealed and addressed. Inside was a single sheet of folded paper with a letter written on Major Rolf Schulmann's letterhead. "Keep this on your person at all times. It explains your orders in case you are questioned. Most likely you won't need it until you reach your destination, but keep it with you anyway."

Lieutenant Brenner accepted the envelope and hid it under his coat. "When?"

"Tomorrow morning."

"That soon? Are you going to tell her?"

The major shook his head. "Better she find out later. I'll be heading back to Belley tomorrow evening. It seems Jacques Bellamont has been harassing the garrison mercilessly, and Lieutenant Meer is ready to panic. He's young and inexperienced and I'd hate to see him fail."

Hans folded his arms and studied his friend carefully. "Are you sure? Is she worth the risk, Rolf?"

Schulmann returned his friend's gaze. "I believe she is."

* * *

From the deepest recesses of her dream, Marie's mind registered a tremendous pounding on her door. Rolf entered the room, dressed in full uniform and carrying Marie's coat. "Get up. You'll have to leave immediately."

Marie sat up and stared at the major, disoriented. "Captain Dresdner?"

"Maybe. I only know we'll have company soon. Grab your things quickly."

Marie gathered her meager belongings and pulled on her boots, then followed the major rapidly down the hallway toward the back stairs. Rolf grabbed her hand and held it firmly in his while they negotiated the uneven stone steps. Marie resisted the impulse to wrench it free—under the circumstances, she was grateful for his guidance. With her other hand she clutched her belongings close while the major led her through the empty kitchen, past a hallway leading to the servants' quarters, and through the rear door. Outside they hastened through the snow toward the waiting Citroën. Derek already sat behind the wheel and had the engine idling steadily. Lancelot and Hans arrived close behind Rolf and Marie, their weapons slung loosely over their shoulders and their fingers hastily buttoning their uniform tunics.

Rolf helped Marie into the back seat and closed the door. He then turned to Hans and they talked in low voices. Marie strained unsuccessfully to hear the conversation through the glass and, suddenly fearful of her future, hugged her coat and few articles of clothing tightly against her chest. Rolf clasped Hans's shoulders and Hans said something that made Rolf laugh. Then, with a brief wave, Hans jogged around the rear of the vehicle and slipped into the back seat next to Marie.

Rolf turned to watch Marie, his face impassive in the darkness. She returned his gaze and felt a momentary twinge of regret that her stubbornness had kept her from getting to know him better. *He has good in him,* she realized again, and she watched him as the Citroën pulled swiftly forward. Derek immediately turned a corner and the rough stone of the villa's walls hid the major from view.

* * *

When Captain Bernard Dresdner and two of his aides pulled up to the front door of Rolf's villa, the major was not surprised. He had felt a strong warning earlier in the night, and that feeling had pestered him until Marie was finally on her way under the excellent care of his best friend. So when the diminutive Gestapo captain entered the villa, Rolf was at peace.

Dresdner walked into the foyer, removed his gloves, and glanced casually up the stairs. "I decided to stop by and see how the search is proceeding."

"Curious, considering you're outside your district."

Dresdner smiled tightly. "You need to tend to your own business, friend."

"In that case . . ." Rolf stretched lazily. "Daylight is over an hour away, I'm rather tired, and I have a full day ahead of me and need to get some rest." He smiled. "You're right. I do need to stay out of your affairs. You have a search to conduct, Captain. You may show yourself out."

"I'm interested in seeing your villa."

"You mean you want to search the place."

"No, I've not yet had the opportunity to see the home you have so graciously donated to the Third Reich." Dresdner smiled. "I've never had the privilege of joining the officers here for a weekend of relaxation—"

"That's because you've never been invited."

Dresdner scowled. "You're out of sorts this morning, Major. I am here out of courtesy, and I expect to be treated with respect."

"By all means, Captain." Rolf bowed stiffly at the waist. "I will contact Major Nieman and inform him that one of his officers is making a social call to my villa, and that he is to contact you here if he needs you."

Dresdner's face darkened. "Major Nieman knows I am searching for the American girl."

"And how does that search bring you here?"

"I have reason to believe you knew of her disappearance."

"Of course I knew of her disappearance," Rolf snapped. "I am trying to recover her." He smirked. "Did you actually imagine I somehow helped her escape and then hid her here?"

Dresdner grimaced and said nothing.

"You're wasting your time, Captain Dresdner." Rolf frowned. "You are meddling in my affairs and insinuating traitorous activity, and I resent both the interference and the accusations." He glared at Dresdner. "If you must search the villa to see if I have the spy hidden in some musty closet, then I suggest you get started." He indicated the staircase with a grand sweep of his arm. "Because after you finish, I am going to report you to your superiors, and I want to accumulate as much evidence of your insubordination as I can." Rolf paused. "I can't imagine Major Nieman knows either your plans or your whereabouts this beautiful morning."

Dresdner's complexion darkened to an unattractive shade of purple, making his mutilated eye socket appear even more pale and sickly so that it stood out in grotesque relief to the rest of his face. "You stand on dangerous ground, Major Schulmann. I resent your words and your attitude. You are obstructing an investigation and accusing me unjustly, and I will not let it pass." He turned toward the door. "I cannot prove you helped her escape, Schulmann—not yet. But I plan to do an extensive investigation of my own . . ."

"You might want to find the girl first, and then perhaps she can fill in the details." Rolf turned his back on the captain, dismissing him. "I wish you luck." He climbed the stairs.

Dresdner reached for the doorknob and then turned. "This is not the end of it, Major Schulmann. Be advised, I will find out the truth."

Schulmann ignored him and walked down the hall.

THIRTEEN

In the twelfth century, Roman conquerors were amazed at the impassable thickness of the forests they encountered east of the Rhine River. They referred to the area as the impenetrable Black Forest and, after a halfhearted attempt to clear the dense, tangled mass, decided the area was not worth their time. It was not until the sixteenth century that Christian monks took an interest in the forest and began to sequester themselves in hermitages tucked deep inside its twisted growth. Little by little these religious hermits cleared and pushed back the trees, attracting more men of God, who built monasteries and pushed the trees back even more. Villages sprouted from the clearings, and farmers succeeded in subduing the forest—at least in the river valleys.

In the center of the southern Black Forest region Marie and her escorts followed a road winding north along the banks of the Weise. The river was inconsequential compared to the Rhine that formed much of the border between France and Germany. But to the inhabitants of this region it meant the difference between prosperity and hunger. Hans tapped Marie's arm and pointed. "Belchen. The highest peak in the Black Forest region. Can't compare with the Alps, but we're proud of it just the same."

Marie looked where he was pointing. "We?"

"Used to climb to the top of that thing with Rolf and hide out for days." Hans grinned like a kid at Christmas. "In the winter we'd ski till after dark. Knew this place like the back of my hand."

Marie looked up the snowy slope of the mountain. Past the checker-board of snow-blanketed trees, the upper slope was smooth and white. The morning sun reflected off the rounded east face of Belchenmont and momentarily blinded her.

"You ever been skiing, mademoiselle?"

"Only once. My parents took me east of Paris for a winter outing." Marie's eye caught a small movement near the top of the mountain. She pointed. "Vacationers?"

"I doubt it, although this whole region is a popular vacation spot for the SS. Most likely Alpine troops training for winter combat."

"Alpine troops train here?"

Hans nodded. "I've just been transferred here to work with the new recruits." Hans pointed in the direction of the slopes. "That'll be me up there tomorrow."

They passed through a small village. Nestled in the whiteness of the clearing, with the thick snowdrifts spilling over into the small river, the community looked deserted.

"Frohnd," Hans explained. "Still too early to see the local wildlife."

Marie smiled at his words and pulled her coat snugly around her shoulders. The cold from outside penetrated through to the car's interior, and she dreamed of a warm fireplace—or at least a warm bed. She wondered if being warm was in her future.

"Up ahead is Wembach. A ways farther and we're in my hometown, Schönenberg."

"You were born there?"

"And lived there with the pastor's family after my parents died." Hans leaned forward and tapped Derek on the shoulder. "After Wembach, take the road east of town to Schönau. I've got to report in. You keep the prisoner with you in the car."

Derek nodded.

Hans settled back in his seat and pointed at a passing farm. "Most houses here are built almost exclusively of Black Forest wood. Very little is used from outside the area. The villagers and farmers are almost completely self-sufficient—at least they used to be, before the war. Now their food is rationed and they have to send a large percentage of their crops to the troops. The German army needs its wine, you know." Hans grinned.

As they drove into Schönau, Marie realized the staff car they drove was one of the few vehicles visible on the streets of the tiny community, and it captured more than a few curious glances. But two German soldiers and a woman were not overly impressive in a village frequented by SS officers on furlough, so the villagers' interest was short-lived. After a few minutes Hans tapped Derek on the shoulder. "Stop right here."

Derek pulled the Citroën to a stop next to a small wooden building with a thatched roof and green shutters. Hans exited the car and disappeared inside. Three minutes later he returned, and Derek turned the Citroën north out of town.

"Put on your wig, mademoiselle." Hans had bought a blonde wig for Marie in Belfort, and now she obediently donned it over her dark curls and secured it with a few pins. She replaced her hat and studied her surroundings, and as they passed through the village center the first thing Marie noticed was that there were almost no young men. Women with baskets or small children hurried about their morning business with an air of gloom. They were composed enough on the surface, but the feeling here was one of loss. Marie imagined there were few of these women who had not lost a husband, son, brother, or sweetheart to the war. She realized her pity for their sacrifices transcended any cultural and moral boundaries; the loss of a loved one hurt, no matter what side the loved one had fought on.

"Turn here and follow the river."

They were driving through an open valley. To the right the river occasionally wound parallel to the road, and at times they drove close enough for Marie to see the heavy snowdrifts along its bank, which were jagged where large chunks of snow had lost hold and fallen into the water. On both sides of the river the mountains eventually took over from the meadow, rising in wide dramatic sweeps from the valley to the tree-lined summits. The road in front of them didn't show more than a depression in the snow's surface. Vehicles didn't come this way often.

They eventually abandoned the river and wound through the white meadow toward the tree line. Once, Marie found herself grasping the edge of her seat as the Citroën slid toward the side of the road, but Derek compensated with the wheel and the tires dug in, grabbing the road's surface until the car was again moving toward the trees.

The vehicle moved at a snail's pace through the cover of trees until they had completely circled to the back side of a small hill. Derek continued to wrestle with the steering wheel, trying to keep them on the road—or at least what was visible of the road. Belchen was prominent in the view offered through the car's windows, and Marie watched the tiny dots of skiers at the top. They looked like ants atop a giant mound of sugar. They scattered down the slope, following each other in confused zigzags. Tiny puffs of powder escaped from behind their skis and drifted up into the cold air.

The scenery changed as they left the tree line and entered a vast meadow. Here the snow deepened and the road entirely disappeared. Derek continued to fight the wheel as they rounded a bend, and ahead of them Marie saw a large farm sprawling the length and breadth of the clearing.

Tucked behind the hill, the farm was completely invisible from the river road.

Derek maneuvered the Citroën through an open gate and followed a stone wall toward a small cluster of buildings. Toward the center of the clearing stood the main house, a gigantic two-story wood structure situated among smaller outbuildings like a mother hen guarding her offspring. A wood-shake roof angled steeply to a peak, its shingles shiny with moisture and completely free of snow. The snow that had abandoned the steep roof now lay in enormous piles around the perimeter. An immense flue constructed directly in the center of the top ridge spouted dark smoke and hinted at welcoming warmth inside. Adjacent to the stone wall sat a small cottage wrapped in a white blanket, and icicles hung from the roof almost to the ground. They passed a barn and a large workshop huddled close together as if desperate to keep each other warm. Several tool sheds had been transformed into nothing more than steep mounds of snow with depressions to show the location of doors.

The Citroën pulled past the cottage, workshop, and barn, and as they approached the main house, a large sheepdog appeared from around the corner and enthusiastically announced their arrival. A woman appeared on the doorstep, and a bundled figure with a shovel looked up from his labor, leaned the shovel carefully against the house, and moved to stand beside the woman. Marie noticed a pronounced limp as the man negotiated the front steps.

Pulling to a stop near the front porch, Derek killed the motor, exited the vehicle, and opened the door for Hans. Lieutenant Brenner approached the house and greeted the man and woman. He pulled a letter from the inside pocket of his uniform jacket and handed it to the man, said a few words to the woman that Marie could not hear, and stepped back to wait while they read the letter. The woman looked up from the document to study Marie, who was still sitting in the back seat of the car. Handing the letter back to the lieutenant, the man nodded as if the contents of the letter met with his approval. The woman moved toward the Citroën with the sheepdog following eagerly at her heels.

Lancelot opened the door for Marie, and she stood to face the woman. Marie was surprised at the kindness she saw in the woman's blue-gray eyes. Wrinkles at their corners aged her, betraying the heavy psychological effects of the war, although Marie was sure the woman was not much older than herself. A wisp of blonde hair escaped her head scarf to brush lightly against her high cheekbones. Her face was thin and pinched, but the loveliness of her eyes hinted at the beauty she once had been.

Her careworn face softened as she smiled at Marie, and she spoke French with a thick, comfortable accent. "The lieutenant says you now will be 'Giselle Frank,'" she said. "You are welcome in our home, Giselle."

Marie was momentarily taken aback. She felt like she was meeting the gracious hostess at a dinner party, and she wasn't sure how to respond. She looked questioningly at Hans. Lieutenant Brenner joined them by the side of the car to explain. "Giselle, meet Frau Sandler. You will stay here with her family until you are summoned." Hans must have noticed the flicker in her eyes, because he added as an afterthought, "Derek and Lancelot will be rooming in that cottage." He gestured in the direction of the small cottage near the drive. "I will get a room in the village. So you will not think of taking any journeys on your own, understood?" He smiled.

Marie nodded. She understood.

Herr Sandler approached the Citroën and studied Marie from beneath the brim of his hat. He considered her guardedly, and she in turn studied him. His weather-beaten face suggested a lifetime in the outdoors, and his hands, twisted and discolored, looked as if they had been broken and never correctly set. His face betrayed concern, and he spoke to Hans in German.

Hans answered him at length and then turned to Marie. "Just so you understand completely, mademoiselle, you are under house arrest. You are in the custody of Walter Sandler and his wife."

Frau Sandler spoke in her heavily accented French. "The letter said she will tutor the boy. Is there not danger in this? What if she teaches him to hate his countrymen?"

"She will only teach what you want her to teach. Besides, it is a cover only. She does not even need to speak to the boy, let alone teach him." Hans turned to Marie, gave her an exaggerated salute, and moved to the other side of the car. "I'll be back in a few days to see how you are doing."

Derek and Lancelot unloaded their gear and headed toward the cottage, lifting their boots high as they negotiated the deep snow. Lieutenant Brenner slid behind the wheel, waved once, and then turned the Citroën back in the direction it had come. The sheepdog followed the retreating vehicle to the gate, barking and snapping enthusiastically at the tires.

Frau Sandler called after the dog. "Bandit, *Halt!*" She turned to Marie. "The lieutenant said you might try to escape."

Marie flinched but said nothing.

"Our nights are cold, Fräulein. Extremely cold. You would be in grave danger . . ."

"I understand."

"And besides, my husband and the two guards in the guest cottage—"

"Frau Sandler, I understand. Thank you for your worry."

Frau Sandler nodded, satisfied. She watched Marie silently for a moment, and her eyes held an expression of guarded pity. "I am sorry we have to meet like this. I am sure you are a nice person, Giselle. I am sure most Americans are nice. It is too bad, this war, yes?"

"Yes. It is too bad, this war."

Frau Sandler's voice softened. "You must be hungry. You look like you could use a good meal and a long bath."

For the first time Marie relaxed. Her relief seemed to satisfy the woman, who gestured for Marie to follow her inside.

When Marie stepped through the doorway she was surprised at the enormity of the room she had entered. Low ceilings suggested cozy family gatherings in a room that otherwise might have seemed overly immense. An enormous stone fireplace wide enough for a grown person to lie down inside dominated the far wall. Flames flickered welcomingly in the hearth, and above the fireplace a rough-hewn wooden mantle protruded from the stone. Several picture frames and porcelain figurines gave the mantle surface a pleasingly cluttered appearance. Marie noted with interest a large, ornately carved wooden clock hanging on the wall above the fireplace, and instinctively she moved toward it. She stood beside the hearth and studied the elaborate explosion of vines, leaves, grapes, and delicate blossoms—all carved of wood. The clock stood approximately two feet tall, and every inch of its surface showed intricate detail. It was the most beautiful timepiece Marie had ever seen. Like a child who equates the sense of touch with sight, Marie reached out and caressed its ornate surface. Her fingertips brushed against leaves and followed the curvature of vines and grapes. Suddenly, two leaves that arched together above the carved numbers of the clock swung open, and a tiny wooden bird shot toward Marie's face. Startled, she stepped backward and watched as the little bird rocked on its perch and whistled nine times.

From the other side of the room Frau Sandler laughed good-naturedly at her surprise. *"Kuckucksuhr."* She pointed at the clock.

Marie was confused. "What?"

"Kuckucksuhr." Frau Sandler repeated the word slowly, and then she imitated the high-pitched whistle of the bird. "Kuckuck! Kuckuck!"

"Ah . . ." Marie smiled. "Cuckoo clock."

"That is right." Satisfied, Frau Sandler turned toward the kitchen. With one last look at the clock, Marie followed her.

As she stepped through the door of the kitchen, Marie surveyed the room. She wondered whether it were possible for a kitchen to be large and cozy at the same time, because that was how she would describe this room.

In the far corner another fireplace was glowing. This one had a long iron hook hanging from the stone above the fire, and an iron kettle hung from the hook. Steam rose from the kettle, and the smell of food that permeated the room wrapped itself around Marie. She inhaled deeply.

Frau Sandler stood at a heavy wood table and cut half a loaf of round black bread. She gestured toward a seat at the table across from her. "Come. *Setzen Sie, bitte.* You will eat." Marie gratefully sank into the chair, and Frau Sandler placed bread on a plate in front of her. She ladled a thick porridge from the kettle and set it next to the bread, then filled a mug with coffee and set it beside the food.

"No. *Danke.*" Marie used the one German word she knew to indicate that she did not want the coffee.

"But Giselle, you are tired and cold. You need to drink."

"No, thank you, Frau Sandler. I do not drink coffee."

Frau Sandler stood there, staring at Marie with a puzzled expression. Then a light flashed across her face and she smiled. "Ah! I see. Just like him." Shaking her head, she swept the cup to the other side of the table and returned to the stove. She extracted another mug from a small cabinet and filled it with hot water from a metal pitcher near the fire. She placed it on the table in front of Marie.

"Thank you, Frau Sandler." Gratefully, Marie wrapped her hands around the warmth of the mug and sipped the steaming liquid. Frau Sandler's words confused her. What did she mean when she said that Marie disliked coffee "just like him"? It hadn't sounded like she was referring to her husband.

"Berta. My name is Berta." Frau Sandler sat opposite Marie and sipped from the rejected coffee cup.

Marie smiled. "All right, then. I am sorry about all of this, Berta."

"Do not worry, Fräulein—you are welcome for as long as you want"— Berta corrected herself—"have to stay."

* * *

Rolf studied the older man carefully. The caretaker of the small abandoned cottage outside Paris sat hunched at the kitchen table in the basement of the villa. His eyes remained lowered as Rolf scrutinized him from his standing position on the opposite side of the table. The man must have been at least fifty, perhaps older. It was hard to tell people's age when war burdened them to the point that their bodies began to record the stress. The ravages and sorrows of war didn't express themselves only in a person's mind—but also in the external display of wrinkles, gaunt expressions, sagging skin, and thinning hair. The caretaker's lean body displayed a goodly percentage of these effects, and his bony hands trembled as they held the steaming mug. Rolf assumed the trembling indicated both fear and infirmity. The man seemed pleasant enough, the deep creases around his mouth suggesting easy laughter and a pleasant demeanor. At the moment the man displayed neither, but seemed bewildered and fearful. He licked his lips. "I never lie, Major, I promise! I do not know who owns the house—or where they have gone."

"I have no reason to doubt you, monsieur. You are probably telling the truth." Rolf moved closer to the man. "But who pays your salary? You say you were hired to care for the cottage—to make it appear occupied." Rolf smiled. "You do your job admirably, I must admit—you almost had me fooled." He picked up the coffeepot and refilled the man's mug. "So who pays you to care for the property?"

"It is a different person each week, monsieur. Sometimes a boy on a bicycle will stop me on the street, or a girl will leave a loaf of bread with the money hidden inside on my doorstep." The man took a careful sip of the hot liquid. He repeated, "It is different each week."

"Very well." Rolf set the pitcher back on the table. He glanced silently at the only other person in the room, the man who stood leaning against the closed door of the kitchen stairs, his face devoid of all emotion as he watched the proceedings. He met Rolf's glance and dipped his chin slightly, in an almost imperceptible nod that would have escaped the scrutiny of all but the most astute observer. The old caretaker was not an astute observer and therefore completely missed the exchange between Rolf and the man. Rolf turned back to the caretaker and continued. "I see no need to detain you. You have been treated fairly, I hope. And I wish you a pleasant journey back to your home."

The caretaker stared at Rolf, bewilderment evident in his hesitation.

"Go on," Rolf said. "You are free to go."

The man stared at the major for another long moment before standing, and then he swayed slightly before regaining his balance and walking to the door. He opened it, hesitated, and glanced back at Rolf. For just a moment, Rolf imagined he saw a flicker of hatred in the man's eyes before he slipped through the heavy wooden door and disappeared into the night.

Rolf's plainclothes officer waited for a full minute before moving away from the kitchen door and following the caretaker silently into the darkness.

FOURTEEN

The hallway was not empty when Marie exited the washroom; a small boy stood near the top of the stairs and watched as she closed the door behind her. His hair was a sleep-ruffled brown and his eyes were large blue pools in a four-year-old face. He studied her soberly, clutching a carved wooden soldier in one pudgy fist and a small chunk of black bread in the other. Crumbs fell intermittently to the floor as he stared at Marie. Then his cheeks dimpled.

"Mami." He said just one word. Then he turned and ran on pudgy legs down the hallway to the stairs.

Marie watched him go, puzzled. He had seemed startled. His one word might have been referring to Berta down in the kitchen. Frau Sandler was obviously his mommy. But he had spoken it softly, reverently, to Marie. Marie moved slowly after him down the stairs and saw him standing near the foot of the couch, watching her descent with wide eyes. When she smiled at him he brought his fist to his mouth, bit into his bread, and chewed thoughtfully. His eyes never left her face.

Marie sank to her knees in front of him. "Hello."

The boy chewed his bread and stared at her.

"My name is Mar—Giselle," Marie quickly corrected herself. "What is your name?"

The boy was silent, but he reached up and reverently touched Marie's cheek with his wooden toy.

"Giselle." Marie repeated her alias and pointed at herself. Then she lightly touched the boy's chest with two fingers. "What is your name?"

The boy responded. "Alma."

Marie was surprised. It was an uncommon name for a tiny German boy. It was an uncommon name for any boy.

Suddenly Alma spoke excitedly at the top of his voice and gestured with his little toy soldier, all the time staring at Marie. Marie listened to the barrage and wished she understood German. Frau Sandler entered from the kitchen to watch. "The boy is telling you about the toy. His father made it for him before the war. He thinks you are his mother."

Marie sat on the couch and looked at Berta. "Then, you're not . . ."

Berta shook her head. "I am his *tante*—his aunt." The woman indicated the large room. "This is his father's home. We are here only to care for the boy and manage the farm while the father is away."

Marie looked back at Alma. "And what happened to his mother?"

"His mother? She died last year."

"That is so sad. She was your sister?"

"Yes."

Alma moved closer to Marie, his eyes searching her face. He touched her knee tentatively. Marie wrapped her arms around him and pulled him onto her lap. He smiled happily and stuffed more bread into his mouth.

"What should I do, Berta? I don't want him to think I'm his mother. That would be cruel."

"How would it be cruel, Giselle? He was too young to remember his real mother, and every day he asks me, 'Will Mami come and play with me today?'"

Marie hugged the little boy close. "Hasn't anyone explained to him that his mother is dead?"

"*Nein.* His father I do not understand. He tells the boy his mother had to go away for a while but they will see her again someday." Berta raised both hands in a sign of exasperation. "So the child keeps asking."

Marie looked at Alma, her face thoughtful. "Berta?"

"Yes?"

"He has an unusual name. Where did he get his name?"

Frau Sandler moved to the couch and sat next to Marie and Alma. "That I also do not understand. What kind of name is Alma? The father should have given him a German name he would be proud to carry. Why not name him after his grandfather, or his great-grandfather? Why take a name out of a ragged little book to give to a young boy? How can he grow to be a great man with a name like Alma?"

Marie was silent, her thoughts in turmoil. Berta's husband drank coffee, so her comment about Marie not drinking coffee "just like him" had likely referred to Alma's father. The man had given his son the name of a prophet from the Book of Mormon, and he was telling Alma they would be reunited with his mother someday. Marie felt a familiar warmth spreading through her body at the discovery. This little boy's father was a Latter-day Saint. He'd had to leave his son to fight on the wrong side of an evil war, and he had faith that in spite of it all his family could be eternal. It seemed incongruous that a German soldier could be a faithful member of the Church, but at the same time the incongruity seemed hopeful and true. Marie remembered how the people of Alma in the Book of Mormon had been in bondage to the wicked priests of King Noah and had been threatened with death if they prayed to their God. So they prayed silently as they shouldered their mandatory burdens. They stayed faithful in the worst of circumstances.

Frau Sandler's voice interrupted her thoughts. "Be his *Mami* for a few days—or weeks. He will face cruel reality soon enough." Berta touched the little boy's cheek fondly. "He could use the happiness."

Alma watched Marie, his chubby cheeks and mouth covered with crumbs. Smiling, Marie bent and kissed him tenderly.

"I'm sure you'll see your Mami again someday. But for now I'll play the part." The boy watched Marie's face eagerly, not understanding her words but responding to the gentleness in her voice. "At least until I have to leave or your daddy gets home and sets things straight. All right?"

Alma nodded. "Mami."

* * *

When Major Rolf Schulmann arrived at the stone courtyard of the Château de Lafont, Lieutenant Meer hurried down the wide stone steps to meet him before Rolf had even exited his vehicle. The man looked anxious.

"What is it, Lieutenant?" Rolf left his suitcase for the driver and hurried to meet his young officer. "What happened?"

"Your plainclothes officer—the one you sent to follow the old man . . ."

"Yes?" Rolf felt a sense of foreboding as he waited for Meer to catch his breath.

"The Maquis followed him, sir." Meer hesitated. "Shot him execution style and left him floating face down in the Rhône."

FIFTEEN

December 23, 1943

The Third Reich gave every German citizen the illustrious duty of contributing to the war effort. Even the local Hitler Youth groups became involved; the Führer sent his *Hitlerjugend* often to the doors of every resident to collect scrap metal, clothing, and food supplies. Even when they had nothing left to surrender, the German people were required to give. A few potatoes discovered in a pantry would be immediately confiscated for the German army. The military always came first. Starvation did not constitute a valid reason for resistance, and hiding supplies from the military usually meant severe punishment.

Citizens of the many war-torn communities turned to farmers for assistance. Often young children were sent secretly into the country to secure a few potatoes or an occasional sausage. If Providence provided anything edible, the children were instructed to hide it carefully for the trip back to the cities. Anything discovered by the military would be confiscated.

Living in the country gave the Sandlers a few more options than other folks, but Frau Sandler grumbled constantly about the scarcity of vegetables and the quality of the sausage they procured from the neighboring farm. Since many Germans had not seen a sausage since the first year of the war, she usually kept her grumbling to herself. Walter often consoled his wife with the reminder that they lived on a farm and probably would never go hungry.

Frau Sandler made their bread with whatever ingredients most closely resembled those used before the war, and sometimes, if they were lucky, their goat gave a few ounces of milk. Berta had been illegally hoarding supplies for Christmas, but after four years of war there were little, if any, of the necessities that had come to be seen as luxuries.

At breakfast the day before Christmas Eve, Marie had her usual cup of hot water, and Berta, feeling it was her duty to protect her incarcerated guest from the throes of starvation, kindly added a little milk and honey— another luxury the bees at the opposite end of the vineyards had consented to provide the previous year. Berta wrapped the honeycomb carefully in wax and burlap and hid her tiny store in a milk pail deep in the cellar. She gambled no Hitler Youth troops would discover it there, and so far they had not. The honey came out for special occasions or when her sweet tooth dictated. Alma had a little on his bread, as did Berta. Walter refused any, insisting on leaving it for the others.

Snow began falling for the second time that day. It let up around noon, and Marie took advantage of the break to take Alma outside for a bout of exercise. They released the goat and let her run, and she tore about the yard with Bandit, stopping intermittently to chew on anything that looked like it might have nutritional value. Marie and Alma wandered past Walter's workshop and through the orchard to the edge of the forest. The boy pointed excitedly up the hill and spoke rapidly in German. Marie had been working on her German and understood the words for "father" and "tree," and she squeezed his hand affectionately. He obviously missed his father and was describing his memories of outings in the woods. What a wonderful dad he must have! Marie wondered if she would ever meet him, but then she immediately dismissed the thought. She had no desire to meet any more German soldiers—Latter-day-Saint or not—than she already had. At least until the war was over.

Marie and Alma waved at the two guards at the guesthouse, and they waved back. Berta kept them supplied with food and warm bedding, and for the most part, they left the family alone. Weekends they took turns escaping to the town with Hans, and they usually didn't return until early in the morning.

It started to snow again before Marie and Alma made it back to the house, and Berta met Alma in the kitchen with a warm slice of bread and honey. Alma ate ravenously while Marie took the bucket and went to milk the goat. Perhaps there would be enough for cream over their bread this evening. She wondered, but did not hope.

The goat was ready and willing to return to her warm stall. Marie gave her a handful of corn and laid her cheek against the goat's back as she extracted the warm liquid. Her thoughts drifted as they often did while helping in the stable, and she thought about Félix. Whenever she thought about her fiancé her throat seemed to constrict and she had to blink back the tears. She thought this time about his death. Major Schulmann had said he regretted her loss. She wondered if a man like the major could even begin to imagine her suffering.

Marie thought back to that first semester with Félix at the university. It had been an afternoon similar to this. It had been snowing, and he'd held her hand as they climbed the steep path behind the Maeser Building. She remembered how they hadn't been able to stop laughing as the path got progressively steeper, its surface slick with new snow. They'd met another giddy couple navigating the path down and ended up in a monster snowball fight.

Marie looked in the bottom of the bucket and sighed. The goat had rewarded Marie with her usual half pint of milk. She returned the animal to the stall and carried the bucket toward the house. The farm's location in this hidden valley cost them an extra half hour of daylight on winter days, and Marie shivered against the cold.

She thought about her father. What would he be doing right now? Surely by now he would suspect her capture. There had not been word from her in over a month, and her silence would worry him. She wondered what designation the War Department would give her: Missing in Action? Prisoner of War? Killed in Action?

A large Citroën blocked the driveway near the guesthouse. In the fading light and falling snow Marie could barely see Derek and Lancelot talking with a tall uniformed officer. Lieutenant Hans Brenner, she thought, here to take them to town to get drunk and celebrate Christmas. She thought for the thousandth time about escape. Not that she felt in any danger from Berta and Walter, but she needed to get back to Allied territory. This would be her first Christmas away from her father, and somehow she needed to contact him and tell him she was all right.

She glanced again at the Citroën. The three men were watching her, and in the fading light she could not make out Hans's features. She had forgotten how tall he was.

She entered the kitchen door and closed it quickly against the cold. Berta stood by the fireplace, stirring a kettle hanging near the coals. She indicated the door to the living room with her chin. "Alma is in there. He is waiting for his father's return."

Marie set the bucket next to the stove and wiped her hands on her apron. "His father is coming home tonight?"

"If he can get away. They might let him have a few days' leave over Christmas." Berta tasted the contents of her kettle with a long-handled spoon. "Last Christmas he missed his wife terribly. This year might be too difficult for him. The boy will be so disappointed."

"He sounds like a loving father. I'm sure he will come home."

"In a snowstorm like this he might not."

Marie reached for a towel hanging near the stove and turned it over. "Where is Alma's father stationed?"

"Southern France. He is an officer in a small district near Lyon."

Marie started when she heard the name of the city where the Gestapo had tried to take her. She forced herself to respond lightly. "That is close to where I was visiting my fiancé."

"I see. And you were captured."

"Yes."

"What were you doing in France, Giselle? Do you not have family in America? Were they not worried for you?" Berta moved away from the fireplace and began shaping round loaves of bread dough that would soon be rising on the table near the oven.

Marie dipped her hands into the sink and grasped a dishcloth and a small bowl. She scrubbed the bowl until all traces of food particles disintegrated and disappeared into the soapy water. "I had a small mission to perform, in exchange for being reunited with my fiancé for a few days."

"And your fiancé, he was also an Allied agent?"

"No, a Résistance fighter."

"Ah . . ." Berta nodded as if all were now clear in her mind.

Marie selected a coffee mug and scrubbed vigorously. Behind her she heard the front door close, and Alma's voice rose excitedly. Most likely Walter returning from the workshop. Marie turned to greet the man.

Her smile froze, and her mind barely registered the sound as the mug she had been washing slipped from her hand and shattered on the stone floor. Major Rolf Schulmann stood in the entrance to the kitchen, holding an excited Alma in his arms. His tall frame completely blocked the doorway, and the little boy had his arms tightly around his father's neck and his face happily buried in the stiff collar of his uniform. Rolf's eyes locked with Marie's, piercing through her as if he could read her emotions. In unguarded moments she had wondered if this were his home, but she had refused to accept the idea. Now it seemed her nagging suspicions had been correct, but they had done nothing to lessen the shock of being once again in close proximity to the man. Now here she was standing in his kitchen, her heart already lost to his sweet little son.

"Rolf!" Berta, startled by the sound of the breaking mug, now moved toward the major. He extended his free arm, pulled his sister-in-law to his chest, and smothered her in a warm embrace.

"Berta, you look as beautiful as ever." He kissed her cheek.

"We weren't expecting you until tonight."

"I couldn't wait to see you—and my son." He turned to smile at Alma, who busily hugged his father's neck with both hands. "Alma is happy with you—I can tell."

"Alma is a joy to have around, Rolf. We love him as if he were our own son." Berta kissed her brother-in-law on the cheek, careful to keep her floured hands away from his uniform jacket.

"My eternal gratitude, sister." Rolf's eyes again sought out Marie. She had not moved from the sink, nor had she retrieved the broken pieces of the mug. Frozen in place, her eyes remained riveted to the man in front of her.

Berta saw her expression and spoke. "I did not tell Giselle who you were—as you requested."

"You have done well, Berta. *Danke.*" Rolf spoke to his sister-in-law but kept his eyes on Marie.

She felt vulnerable, betrayed, and . . . frightened. That he would be the father of such a wonderful boy . . . That he, of all people, should be the LDS father who named his son after a Book of Mormon prophet and according to Berta was such a devout Mormon . . . It did not make sense. It felt all wrong. No, not wrong, just strange. Impossible. Almost as if he could profess to believe one thing and act the complete opposite of his beliefs. Sensing Marie's resentment, the major released Berta and moved toward her across the kitchen. "Mademoiselle." Holding his son in one arm, he inclined his head politely. She recoiled at his greeting and said nothing. She couldn't imagine how to respond to him—how to treat him politely. She wished to run from the room, to do anything besides stay in the same room with this man.

"Mami!" Alma chortled from his father's arms and followed his outburst with an enthusiastic monologue in his father's ear. Major Schulmann's eyes widened as he listened and focused with increasing interest on Marie. She realized the small boy was explaining to his father that his mother had finally returned, and she felt her face flushing scarlet.

"I'm sorry, Major Schulmann. I—I should have found a way to tell him . . ."

Berta came to her rescue. "I advised her not to, Rolf. The boy is lonely enough without his father around."

Major Schulmann nodded. But he did not contradict his son's enthusiasm. Instead, he ruffled the boy's hair with his free hand and asked him a question in German. Alma nodded energetically and looked at Marie.

"I asked him if he likes having you here." Rolf's words to Marie were gentle. "He seems to love you very much." He did not seem angry with her for the deception. In fact, he seemed determined not to correct it—at least not yet. The kindness in his voice unnerved her and deepened her inner turmoil. She was not prepared to forgive this man, and his kindness only made things worse. Reading the look in her eyes, Rolf acknowledged her once more with a nod and returned to his family. Marie sensed she had upset him and tried not to care. Turning deliberately away from the touching home-coming scene, she bent to clean up the pieces of the broken mug and wipe the dishwater from Berta's clean floor. She felt a slight tremor in her hands and wondered if it was because of her fear of this man's power, his unnerving kind-ness, or because his presence reminded her of the brutal death of her Félix.

Félix. Fighting back her tears, she dug into her task with increased determination. What good would tears do her now?

* * *

At dinner Alma insisted on sitting between Marie and his father, and so Marie was not required to look often in the major's direction. But she found herself eating silently, uncomfortably. Rolf was courteous and polite to her, but he didn't try to include her in the conversation. In fact, after a few minutes he turned to her and explained that because Walter struggled with French, they would speak in German. Would she feel offended? Marie assured him she would be fine, and so her silence became complete.

She could tell Berta was delighted to have her brother-in-law home. The woman chatted incessantly to him, her face animated and enthusiastic. Major Schulmann seemed to have a multitude of questions for her, and Marie supposed they were talking about her a good portion of the time. Berta would be reporting to Rolf how things were going, and how Marie had been getting along. In a way, it disturbed her to know she was being discussed—it reaffirmed her knowledge that she truly was a prisoner.

Marie removed her dishes from the table and rinsed them in the sink. Setting them upside down to dry, she excused herself, took her coat off the hook by the door, and let herself out into the night.

The snow had stopped falling and now lay under her feet, deep and new. Bandit greeted her at the porch step, leaping and barking with the joy reserved for members of his family. He lobbied anxiously to be let inside out of the cold, but Marie knew Berta was adamant about him staying out of the family's living quarters. Marie stooped and gave him a sympathetic pat on the head before walking toward the workshop. Bandit followed, knowing she would not complain if he followed her into the warmth of Walter's domain.

Marie loved the workshop. In a way, it reminded her of her father's workshop back home. Sawdust shavings filled the room with a sweet smell, and she inhaled deeply of their fragrance. Walter's workbench held an assortment of clock pieces in various stages of completion. Moonlight filtered through a ragged curtain, reflecting off the polished surfaces of several *Kuckucksuhr* hanging on the wall. Herr Sandler had completed four in the past week and they hung graciously, awaiting Walter's trip to the market. Because of the war they would not bring much—most likely a trade of some kind: coal for the fire, flour, a few potatoes, perhaps a bit of sugar. Berta would be happy for whatever he could buy.

Marie ran her hand along the carved surface of a clock in progress before turning away from the workbench to look out the window. Suddenly, it seemed as if the dam she had carefully built around her emotions burst, and her tears flowed freely. Marie didn't try to brush them away. Instead, for the first time since that morning above Izieu, she allowed herself to cry uncontrollably. Bandit pressed against her leg and whined, sensing her distress. It seemed as if every pent-up emotion, every desperation, every fear, sorrow, and disappointment spilled out with her tears, and Marie lowered her head into her hands and sobbed quietly near the window. She didn't notice when Bandit left her side and joined his master in the doorway. Major Schulmann stood there, one hand on the dog's large head, watching Marie silently until she sensed his presence and turned. With a cry, Marie rushed at him, raising her fists to pummel his chest mercilessly. They never reached him. Rolf's strong hands closed around her wrists and held them locked in an iron grip, inches from his chest.

"Marie . . ." His voice was soft.

"You . . . you killed him. *You killed him!* Let me go!"

"I can't."

"Please, please let me go!" Marie's fierce anger at this man erupted in fresh sobs. "Please let me go home to my father."

"Marie . . ." Rolf spoke gently. "I can't let you go back. At least not yet. I thought Hans explained it to you."

"Sometimes I think it would've been better if you'd left me with Dresdner." Marie looked up at him, her words bitter. "At least then I would have been free of you and all you represent."

"You have no idea what he would have done to you." She felt his thumbs rub against her wrists as he paused, seeming to formulate his thoughts. "Félix loved you very much, and he would have wanted to marry a Mormon girl. He was that kind of man. Nothing less would do for him."

His mention of her fiancé shook her. "He hoped the war would be over soon."

"He would have been disappointed." Rolf's words were gentle, as if he didn't want Marie to think he meant to be argumentative. "You would have been, also."

Marie shook her head. "I'm not naive, Major Schulmann. I know Germany is strong. I know you are aggressive and self-confident. You think you'll be able to resist any threat of invasion and still keep your footing in France and other countries."

"That's not what I meant."

"Why did you bring me here, Major Schulmann?" Marie lifted her chin. "What would make you do such a thing?"

Rolf shifted his feet, but he did not release Marie's hands. "I cannot let you continue to operate as an agent in France, Marie Jacobson, nor can I release you to the Allies to share with them everything you know about us. And . . ." Rolf hesitated, as if he wasn't sure he should say what he was about to say. Finally he continued. ". . . I could not let my sister in the gospel be tortured, raped, and murdered by the Gestapo. Even if you are an enemy spy."

Marie shivered, her hands shaking in the major's. For a moment she could not think of what to say. It seemed incredible that he should be a member of the Church also, and want to protect her because of that connection. "Because I am LDS, you wanted to keep me safe?"

"And because you were special to Félix. He would have expected that."

"Why didn't you tell me you were a Mormon?" She shook her head. "You let me go on and on about eternal life and families and . . ."

"I had to find out if those things were important to you, too."

"You were testing my conviction?"

"I warned you I needed to decide . . ."

"That was not fair, Major, and you know it."

"I never imagined it was. But it was necessary."

She tried to remove her hands from his grasp, but he held her firmly. "And what about your wife?" she asked, "Alma's mother? You never told me she was dead."

"It was none of your business, Marie." Rolf explained. "What good would it have done me to tell you?"

She stood silently for several moments, considering his words. When she spoke, her voice shook slightly. "It bothers me that you talk about the man you murdered as if you knew him. If you did, that makes what you did to Félix even more despicable." Marie twisted her hands from his grasp and stepped out of his reach.

"Félix Larouche was important to me, too, Marie." Rolf shrugged his shoulders helplessly. "Someday I'll be able to explain it to you. But he was in the wrong place at the wrong time and my men responded exactly as they were trained. It was unfortunate."

"Unfortunate?" Marie stared at him in horror. "You justify his murder and then you eulogize him as if he were a saint?"

"This is war, Marie. Félix knew the dangers when he involved himself with the Résistance."

Marie moved past him, and he didn't try to stop her as she wrenched open the door of the workshop and plunged into the moonlit snow outside. After a few yards she heard Major Schulmann pulling the door closed and the sound of his footsteps following her to the house. In a way, she felt sorry for treating him as she had. But her memories of Félix were too raw, too close to the surface. She couldn't talk about him yet—especially not to the man responsible for his death.

Entering the warm kitchen, she passed Frau Sandler at the table. Berta saw the tears on her face and looked concerned, and her concern only deepened when her brother-in-law entered the kitchen close behind Marie. Marie hurried through the family room and up the stairs without another look in Rolf's direction. Behind her, she heard Berta's question in German, and the Major's short reply. He seemed unwilling to explain the whole situation to her, and Marie realized she was relieved. Much as she respected the woman, she didn't think her conversation with Rolf was any of Berta's concern.

She was grateful Rolf felt the same.

SIXTEEN

December 24, 1943

In the middle of the night Marie heard the sound of footsteps leading down the hallway. Curious, she slipped from beneath the warmth of her blankets and tiptoed to the door of her room. The hallway was empty, but she could hear the footsteps continuing down the stairway toward the main living area. Sometimes Alma wandered through the house listlessly before he found his way to the bathroom, so Marie left her room and went below to assist the sleepy boy.

The living room was silent except for the ticking of the *Kuckucksuhr*. From the stairs she could see him huddled in a pitiful heap on the couch. She reached the bottom of the staircase and walked toward him across the darkened room. As she approached the figure on the couch she realized it was too large for a small boy. She hesitated, her heart pounding as she looked at the form huddled in the shadows.

The form shifted, and she took a horrified step backward as it uncurled from the couch and rose silently to its feet. It moved toward her and she continued to retreat from the shape until her heel caught on the edge of the staircase and she lost her balance. Terrified, she crouched where she had fallen and watched the figure of a man approach, walking noiselessly across the floor until he was less than three feet away. Then she saw his eyes and she screamed. Captain Bernard Dresdner reached toward her, his dead, gray eye glowing in the darkness of the room. She tried to escape, but the stairs behind her were impossible to climb. She felt Dresdner's hands close around her throat and frantically she struggled against his grip. He squeezed harder, pressing her down into the staircase and closing off her windpipe.

Suddenly his hands were no longer at her throat and his face changed into that of Major Schulmann. Rolf spoke softly, soothingly. "It's all right, Marie."

"Captain Dresdner . . ." Marie began, and Rolf lifted her to a sitting position and wrapped an arm around her shoulders to support her. She felt disoriented, and when her hand brushed against the staircase she struggled to remember her reason for being there. "He—he was sitting on the couch, and then he . . ."

Rolf listened silently, and when she finished he shook his head. "Dresdner has made quite an impression on you, hasn't he?"

She felt sheepish. "I realize now it was just a dream. I'm sorry to wake you . . ."

"No need to apologize." The major lifted her and carried her to the couch, then he sat beside her in the darkness. "Captain Dresdner is an evil man, and what he did to you would haunt anyone's dreams."

Marie looked at him silently. His hair was ruffled, and he had his tunic hastily buttoned across his chest. She wondered if he had heard her leave her room and had followed her down the stairs.

"You thought I was trying to escape." Her voice was accusing.

He almost smiled, his mouth twisting in a way that intrigued her. "At first I had my suspicions. But when you began weaving as you descended the stairs I realized you were asleep."

"Sometimes Alma needs help going to the bathroom . . ." she defended herself, feeling foolish.

"I understand."

His eyes locked with hers and she felt the intensity of his gaze. Deep inside she realized she did not hate him as she had thought. But the fear of his position and his role in her life overwhelmed her and she looked away. "If I tried to escape, what would you do?"

"I would advise against it—not in this weather. You'd freeze to death before you reached the next town."

"That's not what I meant. What would you *do?*"

"I would bring you back." His words were matter-of-fact.

"But what if I asked you to let me go—as a favor to a sister in the gospel? What if I promised not to harm you—or Hans—in any way?"

Major Schulmann's face was sober. "Marie . . ." He paused as if trying to formulate exactly what he wished to say. "You need to understand something. In times of war, sometimes personal feelings have to be set aside."

"But what if your war is wrong?"

"Right or wrong, it wouldn't matter. What does matter is that your work for the Allies causes the deaths of German troops—men who have wives and sons and daughters who would never again feel their husband's and father's arms around them because of you. It's not just me who would be harmed."

Marie looked at him silently. Rolf continued. "Your country's soldiers would kill me on sight. They'd stop at nothing to see me destroyed. Don't you agree? What about Alma? Don't you think I want this war over so I can be with my son again?"

"Of course."

"I would do anything to protect my son. You have to understand that."

"Alma is a wonderful boy. But would you really do *anything* to protect him?" Marie shifted position on the couch and turned to face him. "Think of Dresdner. You told me he would be willing to do unspeakable things to me in order to uncover the truth. Basically you're saying the end justifies the means."

"Not necessarily."

"According to you, that seems to be the Gestapo's rationale."

"But 'doing anything to protect my son' could have a spiritual application." Rolf watched her intently. "Remember Captain Moroni? He was willing to do anything to protect his family, his people, his religion, and his land."

"Yes, but he was also a good man."

Rolf flinched. "I try to be a good man."

"I know you do." Marie felt rotten. "I've seen kindness in you where there logically should have been nothing but cruelty. I know you are LDS and supposedly have the same code of conduct as other God-fearing members of the Church. But I have a hard time understanding why you would give blind obedience to a corrupt government run by evil people." Marie realized she was treading on dangerous ground, but she couldn't stop. "How can you see Hitler as anything but evil?"

"It is *not* blind obedience." Rolf's voice was tight. "I am *required* to serve my country. Germany is not the free country America claims to be. I cannot always do exactly as I wish."

"But can you understand my confusion, Major Schulmann?" Marie wet her lips nervously. "You mentioned Captain Moroni, and I agree that he was willing to do anything to protect his freedom. But his cause was just. He never used the same reasoning to claim an allegiance to the Lamanites. He always had a desire to do what was right. The Book of Mormon calls it the 'Spirit of Christ.'"

Rolf quoted in English, "For behold, the Spirit of Christ is given to every man, that he may know good from evil; wherefore, I show unto you the way to judge; for every thing which inviteth to do good, and to persuade to believe in Christ, is sent forth by the power and gift of Christ; wherefore ye may know with a perfect knowledge it is of God. Moroni seven, verse sixteen."

Marie hesitated, and she realized her face betrayed her surprise when the major's lips twisted wryly. "Did you think only Allies had copies of the Book of Mormon?"

"I—I had actually never given it much thought."

"Just like you never thought I could be a Nazi and a Mormon at the same time."

"Rolf, I . . ." She stopped, flustered. This was the first time she had used his first name, and she was mortified. Quickly she corrected herself. "Major, I only meant that I had not realized you knew the scriptures so well."

Major Schulmann sat silently watching her. Over the fireplace, the *Kuckucksuhr* bird left its hiding place and whistled three times in the stillness. Rolf spoke. "I used to be more like Dresdner. I had career plans that didn't include anything that invited anyone to do good works or believe in Christ. But then I learned about the gospel and my whole outlook on life changed. I do what I do now because I must—not because I enjoy it or believe it is right." He rose to his feet and towered over her. "And, yes, I agree that my government is corrupt. But you have no right to judge me." He grasped her arm and pulled her up to join him.

"I'm sorry."

"I know you're confused. I'm not your typical Mormon, perhaps. But you have to remember that wartime is never normal." He leaned close. "You need to trust me."

Marie said nothing. Inside, her confusion was nowhere near resolved, but his words made sense and he seemed willing to forgive her callousness. She allowed him to lead her back up the stairs to her room.

Alone in her bedroom, everything was silent. She had once been at a crossroads in her life—sometime in her early teenage years—and the scripture Rolf quoted had awakened in her a sense of her own worth as a daughter of God. She remembered what a religion professor at BYU had taught—that the Spirit of Christ is a light that helps someone recognize the truth when it is presented. Also, the light of Christ can act as a conscience—regulating and modifying behavior that might otherwise be completely devilish.

With one hand she rubbed her throat and thought about the Gestapo captain who had invaded her dreams. She had no doubt he would be capable of doing what Rolf had said. He was pure evil, of that she was certain. What about Hitler? Did he have the light of Christ? Marie thought about the war raging about her and shivered. She climbed into her bed and wrapped the blanket around her shoulders and tucked it under her chin. How could a man like Hitler—or Dresdner—have the light of Christ? It was impossible.

But the scriptures said that every man had been given the Spirit of Christ.

Perhaps people like Hitler had lost the Spirit of Christ. They made terrible decisions that caused them to lose it. Hitler was not born with a swastika in his fist. Dresdner did not torture all his classmates in school. Both of them made decisions along the way that changed their hearts. Marie remembered what the Book of Mormon said about hard hearts. She remembered how Mormon described the Nephites as being "past feeling."

Past feeling the light of Christ!

Hadn't she been taught that refusing to listen to the Spirit made the Holy Ghost withdraw? And when it had completely withdrawn, wouldn't the dark, downward spiral of that individual be swift and sure? Marie lay down with her head on her pillow, watching the darkness outside. Dresdner was in that dark, downward spiral that culminated in blackness and despair. He had fully blocked out the light of Christ.

What about Rolf? Marie turned on her side to completely face the window. Rolf Schulmann was a product of the same Hitleristic society. He was an officer for the Third Reich just like Dresdner. But the feeling that surrounded him was not darkness. He had faced some of the same choices as Dresdner. But somehow he had made the right decisions. Marie closed her eyes and thought about the major, and an unbidden feeling of warmth enveloped her. The feeling surprised her, but she did not push it away. Instead, she thought about the kindness in his eyes when he looked at her and the soft deep timbre of his voice when he said her name.

* * *

She opened her eyes with a start. Daylight flooded her room and warmed the iciness of the morning. Slowly, Marie lifted her feet to the cold floor and stood, wrapping her blanket securely around her against the morning chill. Walking to the window, she looked out into the meadow. A tall, misshapen figure composed of multiple appendages was moving through the snow toward the house. It was Major Rolf Schulmann, carrying an exuberant Alma on his shoulders and pulling a Christmas tree behind him. The tree left a path of brushed snow behind them as they approached the house, and Marie felt a twinge of homesickness as she watched the scene. It looked like a painting on a Christmas card.

Rolf saw her standing at the window. He said something to Alma, and the tiny boy looked up and gave an enthusiastic wave. Marie could hear him yelling and pointing excitedly at the tree. His exuberance upset his balance and he almost tumbled backward. His father's hold on his legs was all that saved him from tumbling headlong into the bushiness of the Christmas tree.

Marie laughed at the spectacle and returned his wave. Turning away from the window, she pulled on a blue dress she had brought from the villa and smoothed her hair. A trip to the washroom mirror confirmed she was presentable, and she hurried down the stairs, admitting to herself that it was not just Alma she was eager to see when he passed through the door.

"*Tannenbaum,* Mami! *Tannenbaum!*" The five-year-old could not contain his excitement and burst through the front door, boots, snow, and all, to run into Marie's outstretched arms.

"He's telling you it is a Christmas tree." Rolf came through the door behind his son, smiling at Alma's enthusiasm. "He wants you to put the angel on top this year." He stopped and studied Marie in the blue dress.

"That must be a great honor," she said with a smile.

"It is to him. He remembers when I held him up high to slip it onto the top branch last year."

"You won't try that with me, will you?"

He smiled. "Not if you don't want me to." Hesitating, he asked, "Where did you get that dress?"

Berta came in from the kitchen. She glanced at the snowy footprints on her wood floor but said nothing. Instead, she admired the tree Rolf was leaning in the corner of the room. "My, but it will do nicely! Will you need to trim the height a bit, do you think?"

Rolf pulled the tree to a standing position and studied it critically. "Well, it does brush a bit. Maybe a few inches . . ." He reached for a pair of shears.

"*Nein!*" Alma grabbed his father's sleeve and tugged incessantly. Schulmann looked down at his son and smiled. "All right, if you want it to stay like this, I won't shorten it." His son did not understand his father's French but seemed satisfied with the soothing tone of his voice. He skipped around the sofa to retrieve a wooden soldier from the windowsill.

Marie waited for Rolf to ask her again about the dress, but he didn't.

She was grateful for the Major's continued use of French in her presence. He was courteous in that way, and if Walter was in the room he always begged her forgiveness before switching to German. He didn't need to include her in conversation, she knew. In fact, he seemed to want her to understand as much as possible, as if he sensed she would feel less a prisoner if she were treated with respect.

His behavior seemed incongruous. She always expected him to act the proud German officer, but here, in his own home, he seemed the exact opposite. He treated his son and his household—even Marie—with respect and deference. He was courteous to the Sandlers and loving to his son. He had not raised his voice or been sharp or impatient with anyone—even with her. In fact, the only time she could recall hearing him raise his voice was in Belley when the Gestapo captain struck her.

Rolf spoke to Berta. "I'll have the tree stand ready before breakfast."

"That will be good. This tree smells wonderful."

Marie asked, "When will we decorate it?"

Rolf leaned the tree back against the corner of the room. "Tonight. You can help Berta with the majority of the work, but Walter and I will light the candles."

"Candles? You use *real* candles?"

Rolf nodded. "If you've never seen candles on a Christmas tree, you're in for a treat."

"I'm sure it must be beautiful."

Major Schulmann studied Marie closely. He seemed for a moment to want to say something to her but changed his mind. Instead, he reached for Alma's hand. "We'd better get you out of here before you melt all over Berta's floor. Let's go make that Christmas tree stand."

With a bounce of delight that sent a shower of snow cascading in every direction, Alma grabbed his father's hand and followed him toward the door. Rolf nodded at Marie as he passed.

* * *

Major Schulmann fashioned a wooden base and secured it to the trunk of the tree. When he stood it up in the corner of the living room, it filled the room with its scent. Marie crushed one needle between her thumb and forefinger to drink in the lovely fragrance. For as long as she could remember, she had enjoyed the smell of pine trees. And this tree seemed extra fragrant.

The morning had passed in a whirlwind of preparation. Berta had showed Marie how to make a traditional German stollen—or at least a wartime version of the delicious treat—using dried fruit brought by the major. Rolf had also brought apple cider wassail—to the delight of Berta and Walter. To Marie the preparations for Christmas in the Schulmann household were new and different, but not at all unpleasant. She helped wherever possible and, still somewhat uncomfortable, tried to avoid the major as much as she could. The majority of the morning passed with Marie and Berta in the kitchen and Rolf, Alma, and Walter in the workshop.

Berta wiped her hands on a towel. "Lunch is ready. Would you bring the men from the workshop?"

Marie retrieved her coat from its hook and pulled her arms through. She reached for her gloves, but then she hesitated. "Berta? What does Major Schulmann think of me?"

"What do you mean?"

Marie pulled one hand into a glove. "I mean, why would he risk his life for me?"

Berta shrugged. "I thought it was obvious. At least it is to me, since I've seen you two together."

Marie's eyes opened wide. "What is obvious, Berta?"

Berta moved away from the stove. "Well, you both try your hardest to avoid each other, and when you meet accidentally you're polite and nothing more."

"That could mean we can't stand each other."

Berta smiled. "But it could also mean you are trying hard not to fall in love."

"What?" Marie felt her cheeks grow warm.

"At least I think *you* are trying. Rolf has fallen already."

Marie stared silently at the German woman.

Berta continued. "I think you're ignoring your feelings and trying to keep your fiancé alive in your mind. But you will never find a man as kind-hearted and loving as Rolf."

"He's a Nazi officer!"

"And perhaps you should know the reason why."

Berta gestured to Marie, and Marie moved to the table and sat next to the woman, clutching her empty glove in both hands.

"When Rolf joined the Mormon church, he became the most loving, attentive husband imaginable. At least *I* thought so. Even my Walter could not compare." Berta smiled. "Walter would get impatient every time I asked him why he couldn't be more like Rolf.

"Then Hélène died." Berta tapped her fingers thoughtfully. "Their second baby was breech and Hélène died before the doctors could operate. They tried to save the baby, but he suffocated. Hélène's death prompted Rolf to do what they had been discussing for several months—leave the Nazi party and move away from Germany.

"He went to his commanding officer and told him he wanted to resign. The man told him he could not leave; his services were required by the Führer. Rolf told him he could not bring himself to do some of what was required of him. He explained that he had joined the Mormon church and did not want to offend his God.

"His commanding officer became angry. He told Rolf if he ever asked to be released from duty again his son would disappear. Also, he threatened to reassign Rolf immediately to the eastern front."

Marie was shocked. "I didn't realize it was like that."

"It happens to a lot of soldiers."

"I can't believe a government would do that to its citizens!"

Berta's brows knit. "Doesn't your government have some sort of mandatory service?"

"Well, yes. I guess it does. At least during wartime."

"And what happens if the young man refuses to serve?"

Marie shrugged. "He could go to prison."

"Well, I guess there's not much difference."

"But the government would never harm the man's children!"

"Compared to America, Germany is a small country. What if every man refused to fight?"

Marie was silent.

"Rolf's life is complicated, Giselle. He is trying to balance his beliefs with his obligations to the Fatherland. He knows if his balancing act fails, he will lose his family. Many in his position would be cruel, as I am sure you know. But Rolf Schulmann is not one of them. Don't ever think he is."

Marie felt tears forming, and she tried to blink them back. She recalled how Rolf had ordered her wound stitched and dressed, even though the German doctor alluded to the idea that she would not survive long enough to heal completely. She thought about her escape from Captain Dresdner's cruelty. The major had trusted her enough to hide her from the Gestapo here with his family—and had put them all in grave danger if she were discovered. He was much loved by Berta and Walter, and adored by his young son. She thought about the way Rolf looked at her. She could imagine his eyes on her, and his deep, gentle voice in her head. "Oh dear!" Marie felt distressed. "I've misunderstood him so completely—about him being a Nazi . . ."

"He understands how you feel."

Marie spoke, her voice subdued. "I'd better go get the others." Quickly she exited the kitchen and plunged through the snow toward the workshop. Her thoughts were in turmoil. Her face felt hot and flushed. Rolf—in love with her? What a strange and terrifying idea! In a way it made her even more anxious to escape, to get back to England and safe territory. She didn't doubt Rolf had been caught in a terrible situation. But how could she ever fall in love with a Nazi?

She remembered her dream—her mother telling her to trust him. Félix telling her he knew him. Her throat constricted at the memory of her fiancé. How could she love anyone as much as she loved Félix? She reached the door of the workshop and scraped the snow off her boots. Inside she heard sounds of childish laughter, and she opened the door to see Rolf swinging Alma in a huge arch over his head. Walter sat at the workbench, carving something small and delicate in his hands.

Rolf looked up as Marie entered. Alma called out "Mami!" and scrambled from his father's embrace. His little feet carried him quickly across the wood shavings and into Marie's arms.

"There, little one." She patted his back affectionately. "It's time for your dinner. Tante Berta calls."

Walter stood, placing the delicate carving on the bench in front of him. *"Mittagessen?"*

"That's right—lunch." Rolf nodded, and Walter headed for the door with Alma.

Marie hesitated. One part of her felt a desire to talk with the major about the things Berta had told her. The other part of her wanted to run from him, to stay as far away from him as she could. She looked at him and willed herself to stay.

Rolf walked toward her. She felt his approach as a physical thing. His hand lifted and brushed her cheek lightly. His eyes looked deeply into hers. "What's wrong?" His voice was soft, and she shivered at his touch and at the sound of his voice. But she didn't know what to say. She looked back at him and willed him to see the confusion in her eyes.

He did. He dropped his hand and shook his head. "You still don't know what to think of me."

Marie said nothing, but she knew her eyes betrayed he was right.

SEVENTEEN

December 24, 1943

When they arrived at the lake, Marie worried they would stand out like a sore thumb—showing up in a military vehicle. She shouldn't have worried. They parked in a line of several SS staff cars and joined a throng of holiday revelers that swarmed with uniforms. Several military fathers skated with their children on the frozen surface of the lake, and a multitude of women circled, laughing and chatting with the soldiers. On this Christmas Eve, at least, it seemed war was the last thing on anybody's mind.

Rolf opened Marie's door and offered his gloved hand. With a hesitant smile she accepted, allowing herself to be assisted from the vehicle.

"Are you sure this is all right?" Marie indicated the soldiers intermingling with the locals. "Won't somebody recognize me?"

Rolf shook his head. "Not likely. Only Captain Dresdner has seen you before, and he's not going to be given holiday leave—not after losing a prisoner." Rolf and Marie smiled at each other, and she realized he was still holding her hand.

Alma clambered out of the car behind Marie, and she slipped her hand out of Rolf's to crouch in front of the small boy. "You'll catch your death of cold without your mittens." She pulled them from his pockets and slipped his tiny fingers inside.

Alma chattered a question. Rolf translated. "Will you skate with us?"

Marie smiled at the small boy's eager face. "Of course, munchkin. I wouldn't miss it." She stood and pulled on her own gloves, which Berta had kindly donated. She held out her hand. Alma happily seized her gloved fingers and moved toward the ice.

Marie could feel the eyes of the major on her as they moved away from his car. "Munchkin?" he asked.

She returned his smile. "Oh, just a name for very little people—from a recent movie. Stars Judy Garland."

"Judy Garland. I've seen her movie *Listen, Darling*—my wife adored Judy!"

She still wasn't used to the intensity of his gaze, and she found herself drawn more than once into the depths of his eyes. She felt he could read her every secret and understand her every emotion when he looked at her. A few times since he had surprised them for Christmas she had been betrayed by her feelings, and she didn't want him to see the conflict inside of her. So now as they laced up their skates together, their shoulders almost brushing as they both bent to help Alma, she felt the same familiar confusion inside of her. She was drawn to this man, she knew, but she tried desperately to fight her feelings. She thought instead of how much she hated what he stood for, and how she feared his power and position. The truth of the matter was that he was a Nazi officer, and she was his prisoner of war.

Or was that the truth? Never had she felt less imprisoned! She glanced around her at the festive sight. *Not a gloomy face in this crowd,* Marie thought as she struggled to pull herself to her feet.

"Let me help you." Major Schulmann reached one gloved hand to pull her up. Marie hesitated momentarily, but then accepted his proffered glove. Both skates sped out from under her in opposite directions, and she captured his arm in a desperate bear hug. Holding on for dear life, she mumbled against his sleeve, "I regret to inform you that ice skating is not one of my talents."

Rolf chuckled and pulled her unceremoniously to a standing position. "Do you think you'll stay up if I let go?"

His arm around her, however necessary, was unnerving. "Yes! Please let go."

He released her and she promptly fell down. Not gracefully, either, like in the movies. She hit her backside and lay in a heap at the major's feet. Rolf laughed uproariously and reached to help her again. Marie marveled at the rich timbre of his mirth. He seemed at ease with her, and that, coupled with his incredible laugh, made this whole embarrassing spectacle worthwhile. She found herself laughing with him as they struggled together to get her back on top of her skates.

Again his arms were around her and he held her steady. "You haven't skated before, I see."

"Not since I was Alma's age." Marie grinned down at the little boy, his eyes wide and curious as he observed his father's attention to his surrogate mother. "There was a little place in Paris where my mother took me once. I remember I fell a lot then, too."

Marie glanced back at Rolf. He was watching her intently, and she caught a flicker of something in his eyes that took her breath away. This was so different from what she had expected . . .

Without warning he bent and kissed her and she felt his arms tighten even more around her waist. For one glorious moment Marie allowed him to hold her, the shock of his kiss spreading rapidly and numbing every inch of her body. Then, as quickly as he had kissed her, the mood changed, and she felt him stiffen against her and whisper in her ear. "Marie. I need you to hold still."

"What?"

His voice fell to an urgent whisper. "Please, just do as I say."

Something in his voice frightened her. "What do you mean?" She found herself whispering also, her face close to his. He kissed her again, briefly this time, and loosened his hold slightly. "Don't say a word." She saw him glance quickly over her shoulder, and she felt a sudden knot of fear at the base of her throat. Unable to turn around, she wondered who was approaching from behind.

"Major Schulmann! What a wonderful surprise!" The voice spoke French, but the accent was German.

Rolf shifted Marie firmly against his left side so he could reach with his right arm to shake the hand of the speaker. "Major Klein. A pleasure."

"What a long time it has been!" The new officer gripped Rolf's hand briefly between both of his own. "I haven't seen you since before your transfer—it's been at least a year!"

"At least." There was a warning in Rolf's embrace that kept Marie still. His voice was unnaturally tight as he asked, "What brings you this direction?"

From her position against him she could now see the officer Schulmann addressed. She would have needed several minutes to correctly pick him from a lineup of bulldogs: he was short, stocky, and bowlegged, with arms like those of an Olympic heavyweight. His cheeks hung loose and moved as he spoke, and the flesh of his face carried a distinct grayish hue. She could see no hair beneath his uniform cap, and his small beady eyes almost disappeared in folds of flesh. The meticulously clipped mustache protruding from his upper lip and nose would have been the only thing to give him away, she mused. That, and the fact that the petite woman on his arm looked like a Cheshire cat. Despite the aura of languorous glamour surrounding the woman, her body was frail, her nose sharp, and her blonde hair had seen healthier days. She studied Marie with her nose slightly wrinkled, as if Marie were a piece of bad meat in the butcher shop—or competition for her husband.

"I'm here for the holidays."

"So are you still stationed in Hamburg?" Marie could feel Rolf's heart beating rapidly against her shoulder.

The officer shook his head, causing his jowls to jiggle. "As a matter of fact I've just been transferred to southern France—Section Four."

"Lyon!" To Marie, Rolf sounded both surprised and dismayed.

"Near you, if I remember correctly. Belley, am I right?"

"You have a good memory."

"I'm headed to Lyon now, but I decided to take a bit of a detour first—nothing like a Schwarzwald Christmas. Don't you agree, Major Schulmann?"

"Best place on earth."

Major Klein's beady eyes shifted to Marie, and he winked at her. Marie stared back steadily and felt sorry for the man's wife.

"I'm intrigued with your date, Major. Introduce me to her."

Marie felt Rolf's arm tighten around her as if he were protecting her from the man. "This is Giselle Frank. She has been tutoring my son since I was transferred to France. She has been a gift from God—in more ways than one." Rolf lowered his head and kissed her again, the meaning to his words evident to his fleshy counterpart. She saw the gleam in Major Klein's eyes as he watched the kiss, and she felt a profound dislike for the man.

"She's a rare find, that's for certain." Major Klein's eyes raked her appreciatively, and Marie forced herself not to recoil but rather to smile back at him as if she were pleased with his attention. Rolf continued to visit with the officer, and she was grateful Major Klein didn't try to include her in the conversation. She remembered Rolf's terse warning to keep quiet, and she kept obediently still against his side.

Klein didn't bother to introduce his wife or acknowledge her existence. In fact, Marie wondered if Klein were intentionally excluding the woman from their conversation.

Rolf asked, "What is your assignment in Lyon?"

Klein turned his attention from Marie back to her companion. "I've been sent to help Barbie implement the *rafle* system in the Vichy zone." He smiled enthusiastically. "Great things are happening at Section Four. You probably feel left out in your remote assignment."

"I manage to survive the solitude."

"Perhaps you hadn't heard, but Klaus Barbie has approval from Berlin for several more trains this coming year." Klein looked positively radiant at the news.

Marie looked up at Rolf and caught the flicker of anger in his eyes.

"Is that so?"

Major Klein warmed enthusiastically to his subject. "Marvelous news, isn't it? The Führer at first wanted to send the trains to Paris and northern France, but Barbie managed to convince him that production in those areas has been significantly reduced. There are so many smaller regions with untapped potential—like yours in Belley, Major—that could fill quotas without all the headaches a sweep causes a larger community. Barbie convinced the Führer that if we work *with* the locals to clean out their communities of undesirables, the results will be impressive."

Undesirables? Marie looked up at Rolf in alarm. What was Major Klein talking about? For a few moments his conversation had seemed to be about the transportation of war goods. A distribution of supplies—perhaps French supplies appropriated and sent to German troops across Europe. But *undesirables?* That sounded more like war criminals or prisoners. She watched Rolf's face for his reaction, but his eyes were unreadable, even cold, as he riveted his complete attention on the Section Four officer.

"And how do you propose we work with the locals?" There was a strange edge to Rolf's voice that chilled Marie. Worried, she watched him closely.

"The *milice!* Darnand has promised full cooperation in the effort. And the local *gendarmes.* They will do whatever you require."

"The *milice* are nothing more than local thugs."

"Then we make it worth their while." Major Klein's brows knit, as if he had just realized Rolf was not sharing his enthusiasm for the subject.

"There's not much to choose from in my district." Rolf's voice was clipped.

"Ah, but Klaus Barbie feels differently," Major Klein answered with a hint of irritation in his voice. "He has ordered a train for your region this spring. You will receive your official orders and notice of required quotas soon after you return."

"I'm busy with other affairs. Résistance groups are escaping into the mountains, setting up elaborate operations with the help of the Allies . . ."

"My friend, we all share your problems. But the Führer has given highest priority to implementation of the Final Solution, as you are well aware."

"I am."

"Then you will find a way to comply." Major Klein smiled pleasantly. "Of course, I will help you as much as I can. With the problems your region has with the Résistance, I can probably influence Barbie to be lenient with you—at first. For the spring shipment I will recommend a quota of forty *kopf* from your area. Then, when the next train is ordered, you will have your local rebels under control and will be ready to produce even more. The Führer will be pleased to know of your support."

Rolf said nothing, but his eyes smoldered. Major Klein seemed not to notice. He again turned appreciative eyes on Marie, and she cringed, unconsciously moving closer against Rolf's side. Klein's eyes glittered as he smiled at her. "So how do you like your new home, Fräulein? Where did you say you were from?"

Rolf's arm tightened a fraction of an inch in warning, and Marie said nothing. Rolf spoke for her. "Major Klein, it has been a pleasure. Much as we would like to stay and visit with you and your lovely wife, I must insist that I be allowed to skate now with my son and his beautiful tutor. The sun will be setting soon and I have yet to fulfill my promise to my boy."

"Of course!" Major Klein had not taken his eyes off Marie, and now he straightened and turned to Schulmann. "You must come and visit us in Lyon one of these days, Major."

"I will have to do that. And, as always, your presence is welcome in Belley."

"I'm glad to hear that." With a formal bow and click of his heels, Major Klein ushered his wife away.

Rolf watched them go and then turned to Marie. His eyes, she noticed, were still smoldering.

"What is it?"

Rolf's arm around her loosened, but he did not release her. He shook his head. "Marie, I've just placed you in grave danger. I would never have brought you today if I'd thought there was a chance you wouldn't be safe. I thought there was no one who could possibly recognize you here . . ."

"But why is Major Klein a threat to me?"

"He'll be working near Dresdner on a daily basis."

Marie immediately felt chilled. She took a deep breath and spoke, her words sounding unconvincing even to herself. "Perhaps they won't have much opportunity to talk to each other. Or, if they do, maybe it won't come up . . ."

"Perhaps." Rolf's voice was heavy. For a long moment he seemed lost in thought, his hand absently rubbing her back as he studied the retreating figure of Major Klein. Then he straightened and took a deep breath, looking down at Alma and smiling brightly at the small boy's upturned face. Affectionately, he touched the knitted cap on his son's head. "Anyway, Alma desperately needs our full attention now, don't you agree?"

Marie nodded.

"Can you stand on your own?"

"Of course," she joked. "You're being overprotective." They smiled at each other, remembering her unceremonious crash just minutes before.

So much had happened in fifteen minutes, Marie thought, as she watched Rolf's tall frame stoop to adjust his son's ice skates. The lightheartedness they felt as they first stepped to the edge of the lake had all but disappeared upon the arrival of the new Lyon major with his news that had so distressed Rolf. *Trains. Undesirables. Quotas.* The conversation didn't make sense to Marie. For all she knew the two officers could have been discussing some business venture or acquisition of supplies. But there was a sinister undertone to their conversation that made Marie shudder.

Rolf looked up and watched her soberly. "Are you all right?"

"Just a little cold, I guess. I'm fine."

Rolf bent and took Alma's small gloved hand in his. "I have a tradition to keep and then we can go. Will you skate with us?"

Marie looked at father and son and smiled. "You've got to be one of the most beloved fathers of all time, Rolf Schulmann. Look how he adores you."

Rolf glanced affectionately at his son and then back at Marie. "You deserve an explanation for my behavior. I will give you one, I promise."

Marie said nothing.

"Will you come?"

Marie shook her head. "Next time around. Let me try to get my feet to stay under me for a moment. You go on ahead."

With a smile, Rolf skated past her with his son in tow. Marie watched them go, Alma's tiny arm stretched upward and clasped in the large hand of his father. His tiny legs moved at double the major's pace as he enthusiastically skated across the ice. Several times the boy slipped and hung suspended from his father's grasp as his feet searched for the ice below. He giggled uncontrollably, and Marie heard again the pleasant rumble of Rolf's laughter at his son's enjoyment. Marie stayed exactly where she was, her feet carefully positioned so as to cause the least amount of movement. She concentrated on keeping her ankles straight and her knees exactly under her. She watched the major and his son. And she felt Rolf's kisses on her lips.

After one time around the lake, Rolf returned to her side, his son in tow. Alma's face was red and shining with delight.

Rolf extended his free arm in her direction. "Ready? I have an extra hand."

Marie smiled. "And I will need it!" The three of them headed onto the ice again, Rolf acting as anchor for Alma on one arm and Marie on the other. Laughing uncontrollably, they made their way around the lake. As they skated Marie felt the fear and trepidation of moments before lift—at least temporarily. Strangely enough, at least for the moment, she felt completely at ease with this man and his son, on this very extraordinary Christmas afternoon in the middle of war-torn Germany. Rolf squeezed her hand, and she saw that he was watching her, a smile on his lips. "Still cold?"

Marie nodded. "But it's worth it—to be here with you and Alma."

"I'm glad."

Her concentration on her skating was so complete that she didn't notice the approach of a Nazi officer behind her. But his sharp words in her ear frightened her so badly her legs shot out from under her and she again found herself sprawled on the ice. Shiny black boots stood inches from her face, and the owner of the boots guffawed loudly. She felt a large hand close around her elbow and a voice giddy with mirth above her head. "Why, princess! I had no idea you'd be so overjoyed to see me!" It was Lieutenant Hans Brenner.

Marie allowed him to haul her to a standing position. "Hans! What a pleasant surprise!"

Hans laughed again. "You're quite nimble on your feet, aren't you?"

"Major Schulmann has been giving me skating lessons."

"I can tell." Hans grinned at Rolf. "And how are things in Belley, Major? Quiet?"

"So far. The dog is off licking his wounds. He'll be back, though."

"Think he suspects you?"

"Possibly."

"And who was that officer just now?"

"A possible disaster."

Marie watched the two friends talk and realized she owed a great debt to these two men. She thought about what Hans had said to her as they'd walked along the riverbank near Rolf's grandparents' villa. Hans was still worried about Rolf, she could see. He had told her Rolf might not survive the war because he was protecting her. She thought about her rescue from the Gestapo that afternoon on the road from Belley, and silently she slipped her hand into Rolf's. It was unplanned, but when she realized she had done it she didn't try to pull away. Rolf said nothing, but his hand closed over hers and brought it close against his chest. She felt the beating of his heart through his coat, against the back of her hand.

Hans noticed the exchange, his sharp brown eyes glancing from Marie to Rolf and then back to Marie, but he did not comment. Instead, he stretched and patted his stomach. "Sure want to thank you, Major, for this transfer. Haven't had such a fine time since the start of the war. The food's great and the company's incredible." He grinned sideways at Marie.

"Giselle's off limits, Hans."

"I see that. How unfortunate. But luckily, there's a whole Schwarzwald teeming with women who would kill to spend time with an officer as handsome as me."

"Humble as always." Rolf smiled affectionately at his friend.

Hans bowed deeply toward Marie. "I am your humble servant, Mademoiselle Giselle. Call me whenever you need me. For anything. Anything at all."

Rolf slugged his friend on the arm. "I said, 'Hands off,' Hans, and I mean it. But I expect you to look after her."

"Oh, I'll look after her all right." Hans touched his cap at Marie. "You won't have to worry a minute, Major Rolf. Your American spy is secure."

* * *

The ride to Rolf's estate was quiet. Alma, exhausted, had fallen asleep in the front seat between Rolf and Marie. Rolf drove silently in the darkness, one arm on the wheel and the other around his son. Marie turned her head to study the major's profile. He seemed lost in thought as he watched snow falling in the path of the headlights.

"Rolf?"

He glanced at her briefly in the darkness.

"I've never thanked you properly for your kindness—in Belley and . . . after." Marie shifted her body so she could face him and continued. "I've repaid your kindness with thoughtless words and an unwillingness to see you for who you really are. I'm so sorry."

Rolf watched the road and said nothing.

"You're a wonderful father—and a good man. I—I'm grateful to you for everything you've done for me." She took a deep breath. "I believe I owe you my life."

"You're still afraid of me." His voice was quiet.

"Of what you represent, yes."

"If only—" Rolf stopped suddenly, as if he had decided not to say what was on his mind. Instead, he asked a question.

"Did the SOE teach you what to do if you encountered an enemy?"

Marie hesitated. "I'm not—"

"That's right, I forgot," Rolf interrupted her. "You're not supposed to admit to being an agent. All right—let's suppose an agent for the Allies encounters the enemy and has a chance to kill him. Do you think she would do it?"

Marie smiled. "She?"

"Just for the sake of argument, let's suppose the agent's a 'she.' And while we're at it, let's say she's a Mormon."

Marie hesitated. "Kill him?"

"That's right. Would she do it? She's obviously been trained to do it—so would she?"

"Perhaps she's not trained to kill. Not all agents are—I mean, I've heard not all agents are . . ."

"Would she kill him—if she could?"

Marie frowned. "Why are you asking me this?"

Rolf glanced at her solemnly. "Just wondering if a Mormon girl could justify killing an enemy soldier—if she were an agent for the Allies. Would she do what she was trained to do if the situation warranted it?"

Alma shifted on the seat between them, settling his head comfortably onto his father's lap.

"What about 'Thou shalt not kill'?"

Rolf gently stroked his son's hair. "The Book of Mormon is full of examples of when killing is justified, Marie: Nephi, Ammon, Moroni . . ."

"I don't know what to say, Major Schulmann."

"Maybe that's a good answer." Rolf looked at her gravely. "I would hate to think this Mormon girl might be a danger to the enemy soldier's family."

Marie's eyes grew wide. "You really think I would—"

"No, I don't. In fact I know you wouldn't. If I had felt even the slightest danger I would never have brought you to Germany."

Marie bit her lip and said nothing.

"So because you've been so loving and kind to my son, and because he calls you 'Mami,' and because you're so . . ." Rolf paused, and his voice broke. ". . . so important to me . . ." He reached toward her and gently touched her cheek, his fingers lingering. ". . . I will trust you with my family's life." His voice was a whisper. "Will I ever have reason to think you aren't trustworthy, Marie?"

Marie captured his hand in hers and leaned her face into its warmth. She blinked back tears. "No, Rolf. I promise. You won't."

EIGHTEEN

December 24, 1943

Rolf lit the candles on the Christmas tree, and to Alma's delight, his father allowed him to light the last candle, raising him high onto his shoulder so Alma could reach with the long, tapered candle to the wick and touch the tips together until the final candle sputtered into flame. Rolf lowered his son to the floor and accepted the candle Alma offered him, then bent to hold it in front of the boy's happy face. Taking a deep breath, Alma blew out the flame, leaving a wavering wisp of smoke rising toward the ceiling. Marie stared in awe at the multitude of tiny flickering stars beginning near the top of the tree and cascading downward until the tree seemed blanketed in undulating light.

With great pomp and circumstance, Rolf presented Marie with a delicate silk angel, and she climbed onto a kitchen chair to reach the top of the tree.

"Bravo." Rolf mimicked Alma's enthusiastic applause, grinning at Marie as she perched atop the chair. Then he swung her into his arms and deposited her on the rug.

Berta took her brother-in-law's arm. "You must sing for us, Rolf. You know that's as much a tradition as lighting the Christmas tree."

Rolf smiled down at her. "If you wish."

Alma clambered onto Marie's lap and snuggled down with his home-made pint-sized panzer tank. His father had presented it to him when they'd returned from skating, and the boy and tank had been inseparable ever since. Marie felt the softness of Alma's hair under her chin as she watched Berta sit at the piano and adjust her position on the bench. Walter handed his wife a stack of music, and she busied herself arranging it in front of her.

Rolf joined Berta at the piano and she looked up at him expectantly, fingers poised to play. Rolf was not in his uniform, opting instead for a soft sweater and dark slacks, and Marie was grateful for the change, especially on this night. His strong frame looked more at ease, his bearing was less stiff and military and more like a father—and a friend. He looked across at her and smiled. She found herself returning his smile.

Berta played the first few notes, and Marie instantly recognized the opening strains of "Silent Night." Then Rolf began to sing, and his rich baritone filled the room and wrapped itself around Marie and Alma on the couch.

> *Stille Nacht! Heilige Nacht!*
> *Alles schläft; einsam wacht*
> *Nur das traute hochheilige Paar.*
> *Holder Knabe im lockigen Haar,*
> *Schlaf in himmlischer Ruh!*
> *Schlaf in himmlischer Ruh!*

The candles on the Christmas tree flickered as a slight draft entered from the kitchen. Marie felt Alma press against her, and she wrapped her arms around him. The music was hauntingly beautiful, and she felt tears well up in her eyes.

> *Stille Nacht! Heilige Nacht!*
> *Hirten erst kundgemacht*
> *Durch der Engel Halleluja.*
> *Tönt es laut von Fern und Nah:*
> *Christ, der Retter ist da!*
> *Christ, der Retter ist da!*

Rolf watched her as he sang, and even though she could not understand the literal translation of his words, the feeling behind them was obvious. Marie found herself unable to pull her eyes from his, and his voice provided the feeling of peace that surrounded her.

> *Stille Nacht! Heilige Nacht!*
> *Gottes Sohn! O wie lacht*
> *Lieb aus deinem göttlichen Mund,*
> *Da uns schlägt die rettende Stund.*
> *Christ in deiner Geburt!*
> *Christ in deiner Geburt!*

The last strains of the song faded into the silence of the room. Nobody spoke. Marie felt frozen in place, and she could not pull her gaze from Rolf's as he stood silently beside the piano. Berta turned and noticed her brother-in-law's gaze and, curious, followed the gaze to Marie.

Rolf moved toward the couch. "Giselle, do you sing?"

Marie nodded.

"Do you know Adolphe Adam's adaptation of the French poem 'Minuit, Chrétiens'? It is called 'Cantique de Noël.'"

"Yes!" Marie smiled. "That is, I know it in English."

"Then will you sing it with me—in English?"

Marie moved Alma from her lap onto the couch and joined Rolf at the piano. Berta found the music and spread it in front of her, and Rolf wrapped an arm around Marie's waist as Berta began to play the introduction. Marie reveled in the warmth of the major's arm around her, holding her firmly to his side. She began to sing, and she felt a shiver of delight when their voices blended in perfect harmony:

> *O holy night! The stars are brightly shining,*
> *It is the night of the dear Savior's birth.*
> *Long lay the world in sin and error pining,*
> *Till He appear'd and the soul felt its worth.*
> *A thrill of hope the weary world rejoices,*
> *For yonder breaks a new and glorious morn.*
> *Fall on your knees! Oh, hear the angel voices!*
> *O night divine, O night when Christ was born;*
> *O night divine, O night divine.*
>
> *Led by the light of Faith serenely beaming,*
> *With glowing hearts by His cradle we stand.*
> *So led by light of a star sweetly gleaming,*
> *Here come the wise men from Orient land.*
> *The King of Kings lay thus in lowly manger;*
> *In all our trials born to be our friend.*
> *He knows our need; to our weakness is no stranger,*
> *Behold your King! Before Him lowly bend!*
> *Behold your King, before Him lowly bend!*

As the final verse began, Marie heard the waver in Rolf's voice and looked up in surprise. His eyes were wet. He noticed her gaze and pulled her closer.

Truly He taught us to love one another;
His law is love and His gospel is peace.
Chains shall He break for the slave is our brother;
And in His name all oppression shall cease.
Sweet hymns of joy in grateful chorus raise we,
Let all within us praise His holy name.
Christ is the Lord! O praise His Name forever,
His power and glory evermore proclaim.
His power and glory evermore proclaim.

Berta played the last notes and then the room went still. Alma had fallen asleep on the couch, and Walter was their only audience. Rolf did not let Marie go for a long moment. And for that moment, Marie felt completely at peace. For that moment the war was not raging around them and Rolf was not a Nazi officer and the enemy. For that moment the spirit of Christmas was as strong as she ever remembered, and she could not imagine a place where she would rather be. Her hand instinctively came up and touched the arm around her waist.

Berta spoke. "It is late. Walter and I will be attending the midnight Mass. Will you come, Rolf? Giselle?"

Marie felt the major shake his head above her. "I promised Lieutenant Brenner that tomorrow I would assist him with his troops. I need to make an early start."

With his words the serenity of the moment dissolved and the war again swirled about them like an evil, raging flood. Silently Marie removed Rolf's arm and moved away. He did not resist.

Berta looked at Marie. "And you, Giselle?"

Marie shook her head, a feeling of gloom descending over the warmth of the evening. "Thank you, no."

Berta nodded as if she had expected Marie's response. She left the piano and moved toward the coatrack. "We'll be gone until quite late—there's always a large supper after the Mass, although with this war I don't know what they will find to serve." She smiled at Rolf. "We don't want to miss your departure in the morning. Please don't forget to say good-bye."

"I wouldn't dream of it. But I will be back for a few hours on Sunday before I leave for Belley."

Walter held Berta's coat for her as she struggled into the sleeves, and then they disappeared into the night, releasing a cold wave of air into the warmth of the room. The fire wavered, dimmed, and then regained its steady intensity. Other than the ticking of the clock above the fireplace, the room was silent. Marie busied herself gathering the cups from their wassail. She could feel the major's eyes on her and turned to him.

He smiled softly. "For a moment the war did not stand between us."

Marie looked away. "For a moment."

Rolf moved toward the sleeping boy on the couch. "I wanted to thank you for your kindness to my son."

"He's a treasure. I've grown fond of him."

Rolf turned at her words to look at her. "You are like the mother he does not remember."

Marie shook her head. "I would never dream of replacing her."

"I know you wouldn't. But your presence here has given him someone to love."

"He has Berta."

"I've been clear with him on that point. Berta is his aunt—not his mother." Rolf's voice was soft. "He needs a mother."

Marie stared at the major and could think of nothing to say. He moved closer to her. "Marie, you have no idea what your presence in my home means to me."

"Rolf . . ."

"When I saw you for the first time I wasn't prepared for you. And when I saw you with your fiancé in the clearing and realized who he was . . . Marie, you are so beautiful . . ." He touched the side of her face and she could not pull away. "Ever since I first saw you I've been haunted by your face."

She felt an intense longing for everything to be all right between them, for the war to be just a bad dream. For him not to be a Nazi officer. For Félix's death not to trouble her. Closing her eyes, she concentrated on the gentle touch of his fingers against her face and neck. Then, as he had earlier that day, he bent and kissed her. For a long moment she allowed him to embrace her and she tried to forget the reality of their situation. But it was no use. She could not justify the war—or his part in it. "Please," she whispered, "let me go home."

His voice was sad. "I cannot."

Marie felt desperation rise in her throat. "Rolf . . . I beg you . . ."

"Shh . . ." His fingers touched her lips and silenced her. "Don't say another word about it. Until the war is over, I cannot let you go."

"I was starting to believe there was a side of you I could trust . . . that I could allow myself to feel—"

"Marie, I love you. I love you so much it hurts. I wish you would try to trust me."

"How can I trust you?" Tears welled in her eyes. "Rolf, I'm your prisoner. I'm an American and you're a Nazi. We're about as far apart as two people can be and still inhabit the same planet."

"We have more in common than you give us credit for."

"If you're talking about the gospel, yes, I admit you're right."

"That's not a minor thing, Marie."

"But the war still gets in the way."

"Maybe because of the war we need each other even more."

Marie looked into his eyes. "Rolf, you're a wonderful father and obviously a faithful member of the Church. You treated me with respect in Belley and saved me from a man who would have murdered me. I felt the incongruity of your position the first time you interrogated me in your office. And I felt the goodness in you even when I was locked in a cold cell in that basement." Marie found herself unable to stop the tears. "And I love the way I feel when I'm in your arms . . ." Marie began to sob, and Rolf pulled her to him.

Rolf's breath moved her hair. "Marie. Tell me what I can do to help you feel better."

"I don't know." She shook her head. "I don't know what to think of you—of us." She turned and buried her face in his shoulder. When she continued, her voice trembled. "And you knew my fiancé—my Félix . . ." Marie choked on his name and stopped talking.

"I've never told you how I knew Félix, have I?"

Marie stiffened and pulled away from him, moving across the room to stand by the window. Cold seeped through the glass and she had to rub her arms to stay warm.

She whispered, "In the mountains you recognized each other." For a moment Alma's regular breathing was the only sound in the room. Then she said, "Tell me how you knew Félix Larouche."

Rolf moved to stand beside her at the window. "Félix Larouche was a student at the University of Paris. There, he met two young American men on their way to Germany. They claimed to be missionaries."

"Yes, I know. He told me this."

"Well, then you know he bombarded them with questions—like any good student would—and ended up joining the church they represented.

"In 1939 I was working for the government as an intelligence officer specializing in interrogation. I had a young wife and a child on the way. I was stationed near Hamburg at a time when the Führer was extremely interested in the activities of foreigners in the area, and we detained and questioned many. Because I spoke both English and French, I found myself interrogating most of the foreign prisoners in the area.

"In August of that year I was given two prisoners to interrogate. Two young American men had been detained at the train station by our police as they passed through my district. They carried with them names of contacts in Holland, Denmark, and France and had several religious books written in both English and German in their possession. The two young men claimed to be Mormons—missionaries for the Church of Jesus Christ of Latter-day Saints." Rolf gave a short laugh. "That name was so outrageous I knew they must be spies. I decided to give them a thorough interrogation. I think at the time I was more worried about what my superiors would think than if the Americans would survive the ordeal.

"I had them taken to an interrogation room, and I began to question the younger of the two—a scared little boy from Idaho. He stood up well to my questions and refused to admit to any intelligence activities. He told me repeatedly that he and his friend were leaving Germany under orders from their president. That bothered me, and I told him he was admitting to working for the president of the United States. He still denied he was an agent.

"I decided questions were getting us nowhere. I ordered both boys strapped to chairs in the basement. After searching their mouths thoroughly for cyanide capsules—I didn't want them committing suicide before I could find out what I needed to know—I picked up an iron bar and prepared to break a few bones. Perhaps pain would loosen their tongues."

Marie felt suddenly ill. That this man would have been capable of such atrocities terrified her. Rolf continued. "The younger boy did not cry, but he closed his eyes and began to mumble something I could not hear. This was my first opportunity to use torture and I was admittedly a little nervous. But I had learned in training that my feelings were to be swallowed in the will of the Führer—extreme methods were justified if the outcome was in the best interest of the Reich. I raised the heavy iron bar and swung with all my strength at the boy's kneecap."

For a moment Rolf paused. Marie could feel her heart accelerating. Sickened, she closed her eyes and waited for him to continue.

"What happened next is still difficult to describe. I managed to swing halfway, and suddenly I felt the hand holding the iron bar imprisoned in the strongest grip I have ever felt. At the same moment I lost all feeling in my legs and dropped like a puppet with its strings cut. I could not move. Both boys were staring at me as if they'd seen a ghost. The guards attending me panicked and fled the room, one of them tripping over my useless legs as he ran for the door. Outside, I could hear them shouting for help.

"Shattering the young boy's kneecap was the furthest thing from my mind at that moment. The American boys looked at each other, their eyes wide. Then one said something to the other that I will never forget. He said, 'President was right. Heavenly Father protects His missionaries.' Then they both began to cry uncontrollably. I wondered why they were crying; I hadn't broken anything yet.

"Several soldiers entered the room. One, a large brusque fellow, surveyed the scene and began shouting at the two young men. He raised his fist to strike the bigger one, but I told him to stop. I ordered the soldiers to take them back to their cells and leave them alone.

"I spent two days in the hospital, unable to walk or even to feel my legs. Hélène came and cried over me, and I told her about the strange experience. Hélène said she thought God's angel had struck me, and that I'd better not hurt those boys or He might kill me. I thought a lot about that. I thought about it long and hard while I lay unable to move in that hospital bed.

"Then, on the afternoon of the second day, I woke up, got out of bed, and dressed before I realized what I'd done. My strength had returned. I went immediately to the cells where the boys were kept. I could see they were miserable. They hadn't eaten or bathed since they were returned to their cells. No water, either. They seemed surprised to see me there. I moved them upstairs into a room saved for visiting dignitaries. I ordered the boys fed and their clothes cleaned, and I allowed them to bathe. Then I went to see them again and I gave them back their things.

"I asked them to explain what had happened. The two young men looked at each other, and then the younger one spoke. 'Heavenly Father must love you, Captain,' he said. 'He wants you to hear our message about the restored gospel.'

"I told them my wife believed they were messengers from God and that He sent an angel to stop me.

"The young man sounded relieved when he said, 'Your wife is very wise, Captain.'

"I asked them more questions. 'You told me you were missionaries for a church. Can you tell me more of what you teach?' I was startled when they both seemed eager. The oldest said, 'We will tell you everything you wish to know.'

"I asked as many questions as I could think of and listened closely to their answers. They showed me a book they carried with them called the Book of Mormon. It was written in English, and they seemed impressed that I could read it. They shared several passages from the book, explaining that it was a record given to prophets in the American continent, and that it contained scripture that would help us live as the Savior wanted us to live.

"When the young men told me about eternal marriage and families, it struck a chord deep inside me—perhaps because Hélène and I were so deeply in love. Perhaps because we had our first child on the way. Or perhaps it was the Spirit touching me for the first recognizable time.

"Hélène and I prayed together that night—also a first. We knelt beside our bed and I held her close, and I told Heavenly Father we wanted to be an eternal family. I told Him I was grateful for His intervention as I was about to destroy two of His servants. I thanked Him for the miracle of repentance and forgiveness, and I asked Him to help me to know what I should do to help the two missionaries that were in my custody.

"I immediately received the impression that I needed to get them out of Germany the next morning. I was to take them wherever they wanted to go and help them in any way they needed. I told Hélène, and she insisted on coming with me. She spent a good portion of the night packing and making preparations. I insisted that we would only be gone a day and would need nothing, but she was adamant that we should be prepared just in case.

"The next morning I told the missionaries my plan. They were relieved and seemed grateful that I was to accompany them. We departed and headed north toward Denmark.

"While we were traveling, Hélène and I carried on a conversation with the boys about the scriptures. They told us more about the Book of Mormon, and Hélène held the book and studied it—the younger elder explained that it had been a gift from his mother before he left home. One of the missionaries promised he would try to get one to me, although since all the missionaries were leaving the country it might be difficult.

"At the border, no one on the side of Germany questioned what a Nazi captain was doing—gratefully. We said our farewells, and the young men trudged the remainder of the way into Denmark. Suddenly the younger of the two stopped and ran back to us. He handed me the Book of Mormon. 'Take it, Herr Schulmann, and may you and your wife be blessed because of it. Thank you. Thank you!' To my surprise, he embraced me before turning to run back to his companion.

"I still felt a nagging urgency about something. I could not figure what it might be. We started back in the direction of home, and Hélène opened the book. On the inside of the front cover someone had scribbled in French, *'May you have success and safety throughout your missionary journey and for the remainder of your life. With love, your brother in the gospel, Félix Larouche.'*

Marie's eyes widened. *"Félix?"*

Rolf nodded. "Because of those two brave missionaries, Félix Larouche became a part of my life before you ever had a chance to meet him."

Marie stared at him. Her face flushed warm as memories of her dead fiancé flooded over her. How long ago it seemed! She again felt her frustration at his apparent indifference to her presence in France, the fear she had felt that she might fail him, the hope that the differences she sensed between them would not cause irreparable damage to their future together. And she remembered the strange words he had spoken in front of the gathering of Résistance leaders in Belley.

"I remember he mentioned he knew . . ." She hesitated. ". . . one good German." Her voice wavered. "He—he meant you." It was not a question.

Rolf blinked, visibly moved by her words. "If he meant me, then I feel even worse for what happened that night in the mountains." He glanced down at his hands, and Marie reached for them, touching them gently and not resisting when he trapped them tightly in his own. Several moments passed as they stood in silence, both struggling with their own feelings and emotions, and both hesitant to speak, as if Félix's memory might be desecrated if they dared pollute it with words.

The fire had died down to soft embers, flickering ever so slightly. On the couch, Alma stirred in his sleep, then opened his eyes and lifted his head. He searched the room, dazed and disoriented. When he saw his father and Marie near the window, he reached out his hand. "Mami?"

Rolf smiled at her and nodded toward his son. "Go on. He needs you."

Marie approached the small boy and sat next to him on the couch. She murmured softly to him and he crawled into her arms and immediately returned to sleep, his father's gift cradled in one arm. Rolf watched them both from his position near the window, and when Marie's gaze lifted and locked with his she was amazed at the intensity in their blue depths.

Rolf left the room and returned with a blanket. He sat on the couch next to Marie and spread the blanket over her lap and over his sleeping son. He draped his arm across the back of the couch and finally continued his story.

"Below the inscription in the book was an address and hurriedly scribbled directions to a villa near Paris. Hélène and I both knew what we had to do; we needed to be baptized into this strange new faith. We needed to find this person in France who was our only known link to the two young Mormon missionaries who had changed our lives. We needed to find Félix Larouche immediately.

"It was going to be difficult for a Nazi officer to get across the border; on one side we would need a German guard who was easily intimidated, and on the other, a sympathetic French patrol. God was with us that evening. We had both.

"We traveled to the address inside the book. A woman answered and told us her son would be home soon. We were lucky—he was visiting between school terms. When Félix Larouche arrived, Hélène chatted with Madame Larouche in the kitchen while I explained our situation to Félix. I could tell he was suspicious at first—how often does a Nazi officer wander into your home and ask you to tell him about the plan of salvation? He finally began to believe me when I showed him the Book of Mormon the young missionary had given us, and he smiled as he read his own message on the inside cover.

"I told Félix everything that had happened over the past few days. He listened silently, and when I relayed the incident in the basement his face was solemn, and he leaned forward, listening intently. After I told of the missionaries' safe arrival in Denmark, he sat studying me thoughtfully. 'At first I did not know what to think of you, Monsieur Schulmann,' he said. 'It is not every day I receive a visitor from the hated Nazi party.'

"'I know this is all very strange,' I replied.

"'Yes. But it is because of the strangeness of it all that I have no choice but to believe you,' Félix said. He went on to tell me of his visit with the missionaries while at the university, of his conversion, and how his name came to be inside the cover of that book: He told me the elder insisted he give him his address so they could write, and because Félix was his first convert, the young missionary wanted to remember him every time he opened his scriptures. Félix explained that he and the elder actually had plans to meet after his mission, to complete their education at the Mormon university in the United States."

Rolf paused, glancing at Marie. "When I interrogated you in Belley you probably wondered why I was so interested in the name of the university you attended with Félix."

"I admit I did. Now I understand."

"I told Félix why we had come to see him. He was the only link we had to these two young men who had so dramatically altered our lives. We wanted to be baptized, and we had nowhere else to turn.

"Félix said, 'If that is what you and your wife want, I will take you to talk with the branch president.'

"'Why can't *you* baptize us? Here? Now?' I wanted to know. I felt a profound desire to accomplish what we'd come for immediately.

"Félix smiled but shook his head. 'There are procedures that must be followed.' He invited us to stay the night, and he and his mother made us comfortable in their tiny home.

"Hélène and Madame Larouche seemed to become fast friends. Félix and I went to meet the branch president and his wife. They were quite amazed by the whole situation and, although very amiable, seemed fearful of whom I represented. The branch president came with us to Félix's house and interviewed both Hélène and me extensively. I had never been ashamed of who I was before that moment. I determined that when we returned to Germany I would resign my commission and leave the army.

"The next morning Hélène and I drove with Félix and his mother to the banks of the Seine. There, a small group of men, women, and children had gathered—the branch president and his wife had been busy the night before. He came up and shook my hand warmly. He must have come to terms with the incongruity of the situation during the night, because he showed not a sign of concern.

"He asked if I would like to baptize my wife. I was surprised and told him I thought I had to be a member and hold the priesthood in order to do so. He agreed that I was correct, but said that they could ordain me a priest as soon as I was baptized, and then coach me so I would know what to do. I had not dared to dream that I could do something like that. It would mean so much to me. Hélène looked happier than I had seen her in a long time. I agreed to the suggestion.

"Félix's mother brought a white dress for Hélène. She took my wife to a nearby home to change and when they came back Hélène looked like an angel. Someone tied Hélène's hair back with a ribbon. Someone else had a camera. He wanted to have both of us in a photograph, but I wanted just a picture of my wife."

Marie smiled. "You showed me that picture the first time I was in your office."

Rolf nodded. "I was not looking forward to your interrogation. Your interest in the photograph gave me a little more time to compose myself."

"I thought you were trying to soften me up."

He laughed. "I guess in a way I was."

"So did Félix perform your baptism?"

"He did. I remember how calm I felt when he raised his right hand and said, 'Rolf Ahren Schulmann, having been commissioned of Jesus Christ . . .'

"When I went under, the cold water took my breath away. But the warmth I felt inside is as memorable to me as the cold. Then Félix, the branch president, and three other men laid their hands on my head and confirmed me a member of the Church and ordained me to the Aaronic Priesthood. Hélène was crying. I took her hand and walked her down into the freezing current. Félix stood by and prompted me, and when I lifted my wife out of the water I felt the most profound sense of peace. I felt a deep love for each and every person who had come to witness the baptism. And I felt a bond between Félix and me that I was sure could not be broken by any war."

Rolf paused, and Marie said nothing. The only sound was the *Kuckucksuhr* ticking in the background.

Finally Rolf said softly, "I told Félix of my gratitude, and I promised him I would be there for him if he ever needed anything."

Marie shifted uncomfortably, remembering the nightmare above Izieu.

"When Hélène and I returned to Hamburg, the Gestapo had come looking for the two Americans. Our favorite captain was there with them."

Marie shuddered. "Captain Dresdner seems to be in every important scene in your life."

"He does make a good villain, doesn't he?"

"He scares me. He's power hungry and corrupt to the core. He was going to torture me the whole way to Lyon."

"I'm not surprised. He *is* power hungry. He has ambitions that include the downfall of any who oppose him, and he cannot stand beauty—especially beauty he cannot have." Marie looked up at Rolf. His eyes studied the contours of her face, slowly, methodically, as if he knew he had all the time in the world. "Dresdner was not in charge of the raid, but he was one of the higher ranking officers. He insisted I tell him where I had taken the two Americans."

"You told Dresdner you escorted them to Denmark?"

Rolf nodded. "Believe me, he was not pleased. He let me know in no uncertain terms how unhappy he was. He went immediately to his superiors, and I was called to Gestapo headquarters for questioning. I handed the officer in charge the report of my interrogation. It was my duty to convince my superiors that the boys were not a threat to the Reich, so I went into great detail about the things they told me. The Gestapo major read the report and responded reasonably—he praised me for doing my job in a professional and thorough manner, and he called off the investigation. But Dresdner decided to ask a few questions of his own. 'Did you believe what they told you?' he asked. I told him of course I did. 'Did you join their church?' I told him my wife and I had both been baptized. Then Dresdner turned to his commanding officer and told him the Führer would never trust a Mormon and that I should be relieved of my command. The major responded by sending Dresdner from the room."

Marie smiled. "And so the rivalry begins."

"Actually, it began in SS training camp. But that's another story."

"What happened? Did you take his glory? His rank? His lunch tray?" she teased.

"Worse than that."

"What could be worse than taking his lunch tray?"

"I took his girlfriend."

Marie lifted her head and stared at Rolf. *"Hélène?"*

Rolf nodded. "Hélène and I met at a bar. Not the most uplifting place to meet your eternal companion, but I wasn't thinking much on the things of eternity at that time. Hélène came with Dresdner and she left with me. Dresdner was angry and drunk, but I laughed him off and didn't think much of it."

"So was this incident with the missionaries the first time you'd seen him since then?"

"No. We had plenty of opportunities to see each other before that. He tried to discount my service record several times before then, but I managed to get promoted anyway. Hélène and I were married in 1938, and Dresdner came uninvited to the wedding. Drunk and dangerous. My soldiers carried him outside and tossed him on his head. Later he joined the Gestapo and transferred to Paris, and then, in the winter of '42, moved to Lyon."

Marie said, "Last I saw him, he was under attack by Hans and his men disguised as *maquisards.*"

Rolf smiled faintly. "He's not going to give up easily."

Marie leaned her head against Rolf's chest. She felt the warmth of his breath in her hair and the steady rhythm of his son's heartbeat under her arm. "Rolf?"

He waited, his face close to hers.

"Thank you."

"For what?"

She touched his face. "For telling me." She reached up and kissed him.

The three of them stayed that way while the fire died in the fireplace and the candles on the Christmas tree wavered and went out, one by one.

NINETEEN

December 26, 1943

"Marie."

She felt the warmth of a hand on her arm. Opening her eyes, she saw Rolf's face close to her own in the darkness. With a start she sat up, pulling the blankets to her chin. His face was inches from her own as he whispered to her, and at first she did not understand his words; the surprise of seeing him close to her and the suddenness of her awakening made comprehension impossible.

" . . . go with me to Baiersbronn . . ."

"What?"

His words were beginning to register, but the shock of seeing him had not yet worn off. He had been gone the whole of Christmas Day, and when she retired late last night he had not yet returned from helping Hans. Now he was here, close to her, and she desperately wanted to throw her arms around him and tell him how much she'd missed him. Instead, she pulled her blanket closer and tried to comprehend his words.

"I want you to see something. Will you go with me?"

"Where?"

"Baiersbronn. It's a ways from here."

"Baiersbronn?"

"It takes you a while to wake up, doesn't it?" He smiled in the darkness and kissed her.

She murmured against his lips, "I missed you, Rolf."

He looked pleased. "I missed you, too. Amazing, isn't it, how long a day can be?"

Abruptly, he stood and backed away from her. She felt the sudden tension in the room and realized he was fighting an urge to take her in his

arms. His retreat at that moment both dismayed and pleased her, as she realized he was an honorable man. But she felt the separation as a physical
thing, and she wondered if there would ever be a time when he would not
have to leave. She shook her head against the thought, her defenses rising as
the fogginess of sleep left her—it could never be.

"Are you coming?"

"Yes." She hesitated. "I need you to leave the room first."

"I'll wait downstairs." He walked to the door. "Oh, by the way . . ." He
stopped, his hand resting on the doorknob. "Today's Sunday. I was
wondering if you would like to go with me to sacrament meeting . . ."

"Rolf! I haven't been able to go in ages! Not since before . . . since
before . . ." Her excitement trailed off. She could not bring herself to say,
"Since before Izieu."

Rolf understood. "I know. I'm sorry. It's not easy for a German officer
in France, either. I'll meet you downstairs."

He closed the door behind him, and she could hear his footsteps disappearing down the hallway.

* * *

Fifteen minutes later she joined him next to the darkened Christmas tree.
Rolf was standing near the window where they had stood together on
Christmas Eve. He was in full uniform, with his dark overcoat resting
loosely over his arm. He watched her descend the stairs.

"Why are you in uniform?" she asked.

He indicated his suitcase by the door. "When we get back I'll be leaving
immediately for France."

Even though she'd known he had to leave today, she was disappointed.
She would miss him—desperately.

"Did I ever tell you about that dress?"

Marie looked down at her blue dress, the one she had been wearing
when Rolf and his son brought in the Christmas tree. "What do you mean?"

"There's a story behind it."

"I was sorely lacking in clothes. Hans said it would be all right to
borrow things from the armoire . . . I liked this one best."

"That was Hélène's favorite, also. I gave it to her on our first wedding
anniversary."

"Oh, Rolf!" Marie's hands flew to her throat. "I'm so sorry. I didn't
know . . ."

He brushed aside her worry. "It looks beautiful on you. I want you to
have it."

"But if it has so many memories attached to it . . ."

"All good ones." Rolf's hands warmed her shoulders as he rubbed the soft fabric between his fingers. "But it's just a dress. It would be mildewing in a villa in France if you were not here to wear it."

Marie looked at him hesitantly. "When I wear it, do you see her?"

"No." He kissed her lightly. "Hélène's dead. Her memory doesn't haunt me, and because of Félix and two American boys, I don't find myself pining for her. When you wear it, I see *you.*"

* * *

The roads were icy in the early-morning darkness. Marie found herself clinging to the seat as Rolf negotiated slippery curves, his headlights catching an occasional deer or small forest creature with eyes glowing luminously in the brightness. Rolf drove silently, and Marie had plenty of time to study him in the darkness. She realized he was one of the most handsome men she had ever known, and she wondered when he had begun to seem handsome to her. Certainly not that morning last November in the mountains above Izieu. He had seemed a monster then—a murderous monster. She remembered how he'd stood over the body of her fiancé in his black boots and dark uniform, and how when he'd bent near Félix Larouche his face had registered surprise, recognition, and . . . and sorrow. Now she realized that was what he had been feeling, and she ached for him. Interesting, how time and circumstance could change one's perspective. Marie watched Rolf's profile as he drove. Same black boots, same dark uniform—she knew she should be terrified right now; of the icy road, of the war, and especially of his presence here beside her. She was surprised that she was not.

And yet, there was an element of fear in her situation. She knew she had fallen in love with him. She wondered when it had started. Was it when he cared for her wounds in Belley? Was it when she realized he was the one who had rescued her from Dresdner? She couldn't pinpoint the exact time. But still she could not escape the dark truth that was at the root of her fear—that he was a Nazi. She shivered. She was wearing the coat Rolf had given her for Christmas—worthy of a Schwarzwald winter. But she was not shivering from cold.

"We're almost there. See the lights up ahead?"

"I see something. Baiersbronn?"

"Part of it. Baiersbronn is actually more than one village, and what you see is just the beginning of a larger community that curves a bit around the mountainside."

Rolf resumed his focus on the road ahead, struggling to negotiate a particularly icy stretch. A few moments later the Citroën's wheels again took hold of the road and Marie relaxed slightly. They rounded a curve and saw the beginnings of a town, floating in the whiteness of the snow as if on a cloud. Here and there, lights were beginning to appear as darkness turned into the chilly haze of morning. Rolf pulled the car carefully to the edge of the road and turned off the engine. He switched off the headlights and they sat in darkness for a moment, the town ahead of them only visible because it stood out in dark relief against the snow, and because there was the illusion of morning light caused by a sun threatening to rise.

Rolf glanced at her shoes and stockings. "I took the liberty of bringing you these." He reached past her into the back seat and produced a pair of heavy winter boots. Marie noticed that they were similar to those worn by Hans when he hiked the mountains with his troops.

She looked at him questioningly. "Are we planning to climb the mountain?"

"That's right." He smiled and handed her the boots. He reached back a second time and produced a larger pair for himself. "There's something I want you to see. Alma loves it when I bring him."

"Speaking of Alma, there's something I've been meaning to ask you. How did you decide on his name?"

Rolf smiled at her. "Remember in the Book of Mormon when Alma tells his son Helaman of his miraculous conversion? Alma and his friends were trying to destroy the Church and an angel stopped them. The angel says to Alma, 'If thou wilt of thyself be destroyed, seek no more to destroy the church of God.' Alma fell to the earth and couldn't move or speak for three days."

Marie watched him intently, and her eyes grew wide. "It reminded you of your own conversion, didn't it?"

He nodded. "After the missionary gave me his Book of Mormon, Hélène and I spent many evenings reading together, and when we read the account of Alma and the angel I knew I wanted to name our newborn son after that Book of Mormon prophet."

"You've given him quite a legacy."

"Berta thinks I was a fool."

Marie laughed. "I know. She told me." She kicked off her shoes and slipped one foot into a boot.

"Does it fit?" Rolf had pulled off his uniform boots and was donning his own pair.

"You must think I have really big feet."

Rolf laughed. "Actually, that was the smallest pair Hans could find. He said any smaller and the soldier who wore them had no business joining the army."

Marie smiled. "Next time you see Hans, tell him they were perfect."

Rolf opened the door and stepped out into the snow. His feet sank to his ankles as he moved around to open Marie's door.

The mountain was not as steep as it had looked, nor as high. With Rolf's strong hand to guide her and Hans's ample winter boots, Marie was able to climb the slope without too much trouble. She wished she and Rolf could have more such mornings together—before he had to return to reality in Belley. She found herself reaching for the support of his hand more than might have been necessary, just for the chance to feel his strength as he pulled her up to stand next to him. The cloud of her breath mixed with his more than once as they negotiated the incline together in the semi-darkness. They laughed and talked, and Rolf seemed to her more alive and happy than she had ever seen him.

She realized she was feeling the same. Certainly it had to be more than just the exertion and the cold that was bringing color to their cheeks and life to their eyes. Their camaraderie at that moment was so intense it was easy for Marie to forget the war and the reason she was here with this man in Germany. At this moment, there was nowhere in the world she would rather be.

Far too quickly, they reached the top. Rolf wrapped both arms around her waist and brought her back firmly against him. Marie surveyed the scene before them and gasped at the sight. Spread out below her, covering the entire width of a valley that snaked in and out of the dark forested hills, was the most beautiful winter wonderland she had ever seen. The cluster of villages that was Baiersbronn was slowly coming alive. The sun had not yet peeked out from behind the mountains, but its glow was beginning to spread in the sky. Below the blackness of the mountain slopes lay the white-blanketed community where morning lights flickered in hundreds of windows as blackout curtains were raised and villagers began to awaken. There was no sound. Even the sound of their own breathing was muffled. Marie knew no photograph would be able to do the sight justice; a photo would lack the intensity of the colors, and the lights—and the feel of Rolf's chest against her back, rising and falling with each breath as they stood there together there on top of the mountain.

"Rolf . . . It's beautiful."

"I thought you'd like it." Together they stood and watched as the sun finally rose, catching the colors of the villages below them and altering them, and at the same time dimming the intensity of individual lights as the greater light spread over the valley.

* * *

Sacrament meeting would be held in a small school near the center of town. As they drove, Rolf explained that the government permitted them to hold gatherings as long as they allowed representatives of the military to observe their meetings whenever they wished.

When they arrived and entered the school, the room was empty except for a middle-aged man carrying two sacrament trays. He looked up as Rolf and Marie entered the back of the room. With an enthusiastic greeting the man approached, his arms outstretched to Rolf. Marie watched Rolf and the man's reunion with interest. Rolf gestured for her to join them, and he introduced her to the man in French.

"President Wagner, this is Giselle." Marie accepted the proffered hand and was shocked to feel half his hand missing. She smiled back at the man as Rolf completed the introductions. "Giselle, this is our long-time branch president, Horst Wagner." The man's brown eyes crinkled when he smiled, and his nose was almost lost in a bushy salt-and-pepper mustache.

Rolf explained, "Giselle is very special to me. I will tell you this because I know I can trust you: I tell people she is my son's tutor, but in reality I brought her here as a prisoner of war under house arrest—and I have managed to fall in love with her."

Herr Wagner smiled. "War can bring people together under the strangest of circumstances." He nodded kindly at Marie. "You are welcome, Giselle. If Rolf has fallen in love with you, you must be an extraordinary person."

She thanked him, amazed at his easy acceptance of the situation. She was relieved when he changed the subject and turned his full attention to Rolf. For her benefit, he continued to speak in French.

"Tell me how long you are here, Rolf. We could use your help in the branch."

"I have to leave soon after the meeting."

"The war is calling you back, I imagine?"

"Unfortunately, yes."

Horst Wagner turned to Marie. "Your friend here is my trusted counselor. He tried to make me release him when he was assigned to France, but I refused. I couldn't find a better man. Not in all of Europe."

"A lot of help I am to you, living over five hundred kilometers away."

"Ah, but you're still alive. That's a big help in itself."

Rolf looked stricken. "Franz is . . ."

President Wagner nodded. "Last month. Mathilde is beside herself with grief."

"I am so very sorry."

"Yes, well, that is war." Herr Wagner tried to sound nonchalant, but his voice caught noticeably as he spoke. "Especially on the eastern front. I think we both knew it was coming." Marie watched the man, and her heart broke for him as he struggled to keep his emotions under control.

The branch president continued, "But your son—Alma . . . He must be four years old by now. Is that right?"

Rolf nodded. "His birthday was in September. He is healthy and strong." His voice was solemn, as if he realized how cruel it might seem to talk about the health of one's son when another's was lying frozen on a deserted battlefield somewhere in Russia.

"That is how it should be."

A door opened in the back of the room and a frail woman entered. Her gray hair and thin face attested to the rigors of war life, and in her hands she carried a tattered hymnal as she headed toward an old upright piano. When she saw Herr Wagner with Rolf and Marie, her eyes widened and she let out a cry and hurried as fast as her tiny frame would carry her toward the gathering.

"Rolf! You've come home!" She threw her arms around his neck and kissed him on both cheeks. President Wagner introduced her to Marie. "Mathilde, this is Giselle—she is visiting with Rolf from France. Giselle, this is my wife, Mathilde."

Marie smiled and held out her hand to the woman, relieved that President Wagner would not be telling his wife the whole story.

Frau Wagner had a kind face and soft, worried eyes. She smiled and grasped Marie's hand. "What a beautiful girl you are." Her French was good, and with uncanny discernment she added, "Our Rolf needs someone like you. He has been alone too long. Welcome."

"Thank you, Frau Wagner."

Mathilde turned again to Rolf. "How good it is to see you. If it is possible, you have grown even more handsome than before."

Rolf laughed. "I think you mean 'distinguished,' don't you? I'm also a bit older than before."

"You are still young enough to be my son." Frau Wagner's voice wavered slightly.

Rolf wrapped his arms around the fragile woman and held her close. "I am glad you think so," he said gently. "Nothing would make me more proud."

Marie looked at Rolf in awe. His words were exactly what the older woman needed to hear. With a sob, Mathilde kissed him again and stepped back. Brushing moisture from her eyes, she managed a smile and turned to include Marie in her look. "There now, see what a good man he is? You could never find one better."

"Now you're embarrassing me in front of Giselle."

Frau Wagner laughed. "Come along for dinner after the meeting and I will embarrass you more."

Rolf shook his head. "Much as I would love to eat your wonderful cooking, I need to decline."

"But why?" The woman looked almost stricken, and she turned to her husband for assistance. The branch president put his arm affectionately around her shoulders. "Rolf has been called back to the war, Mathilde. We will have to invite him and his friend next time."

Frau Wagner looked disappointed but seemed to understand. She nodded. "I see. Next time, then."

"Yes. Next time."

Marie noticed several people begin to enter the room and take their places on hard wooden benches. She still had not become accustomed to the scarcity of men in the villages; most of the men who entered now were either too old to fight or disabled, like Herr Wagner.

She felt a slight touch on her arm, and Frau Wagner excused herself to go with her hymnal to the piano.

The branch president was speaking to her. "Fräulein Giselle, you will allow Rolf to sit with me in the front?"

Marie smiled at Rolf. "Of course."

Rolf caught her hand in his. "Sit on the front bench, next to Frau Wagner. That'll mean a lot to her." Marie nodded, amazed again at how much he cared.

As Marie sat down she looked around and saw several people that she knew lived in Schönenberg. She smiled at them, and they smiled back. She felt the truth of her father's words, spoken when they first attended their new ward in America: "The Church is a family. Wherever you go you will never be without family."

Frau Wagner's music filled the room. The piano was slightly out of tune, but no one seemed to mind. Marie watched as several German officers and soldiers in uniform entered and sat on the bench closest to the back. One soldier made his way through the congregation to the front of the room, shook hands with Rolf and the branch president, and took his place on the bench opposite Marie, facing the sacrament table. Another man from the congregation sat beside him, and two more sat on chairs behind the table. Marie watched them with interest—especially the young German soldier. He seemed completely at ease, unaware that he was attracting anyone's attention. Marie thought it an odd sight—even a little disturbing—to see a German soldier ready to pass the sacrament.

Then she remembered Rolf. He was also in full Nazi uniform, sitting next to the branch president as his counselor. She turned to look at him and realized he had been watching her closely, obviously aware of her unrest. He had a question in his eyes, and Marie felt ashamed. She dropped her gaze to her hands.

Rolf rose and faced the congregation. He spoke a few moments in German and then switched to French. Marie knew that even though most of the congregation understood at least elementary French, he was doing this for her benefit.

"On behalf of your president, I would like to welcome you to our sacrament meeting. We will sing 'Silent Night,' after which we will ask Frau Schmidt to give us an opening prayer. After the prayer, we will sing 'Come, Follow Me,' and then we will partake of the sacrament, prepared and passed by members who hold the priesthood."

Rolf returned to his seat. Marie watched him and felt sick inside. His words reminded her that the uniform did not necessarily represent the worthiness of the man. Frau Wagner began the first strains of "Silent Night."

A few minutes later the sacrament hymn ended and Frau Wagner moved to sit next to Marie. She took Marie's hand in both of hers and held it in her lap. Marie felt like she was going to cry. She was as accepted here as she had ever been in any ward or branch of her past. And she was sitting here having doubts about at least two men in the congregation—two men who had been required to serve their corrupt government in an unjust war. Who was she to judge these people?

She did not understand the words of the sacrament prayer. But she knew their meaning, and the feeling of reverence was unmistakable. She watched as the two trays were distributed, and the German soldier carried his tray to the front of the room, offering the sacrament first to President Wagner and then to Rolf. The other man began passing the sacrament to the congregation on the other side of the room, and suddenly Marie looked up into the face of the German soldier. With a pleasant smile he offered her the tray and she took a morsel of crusty black bread in her right hand. He smiled again, nodding to her before turning his attention to Frau Wagner.

Marie hesitated, staring at the bread held limply in her hand. Suddenly she closed her eyes and begged her Father in Heaven's forgiveness for her unkind thoughts toward the young soldier. Feeling remorseful, she put the bread in her mouth.

* * *

After the meeting was over, several people came to visit with Rolf. When they displayed curiosity about Marie, he stuck to his story that she was a tutor from France, living with his sister-in-law and tutoring his son. They received several more dinner invitations, all of which he respectfully and regretfully declined. She felt overwhelmed by the love and appreciation for Rolf displayed by the congregation. She looked around for the young German soldier who had passed her the sacrament, but he had already left with his comrades.

Rolf caught her arm. "I have a few things I need to discuss with President Wagner, and then I will be ready to go. Will you be all right?"

Marie nodded. "It looks like Mathilde could use some help. I'll keep her company until you get back."

He kissed her on the cheek and left.

* * *

Rolf and Marie said nothing as the car drove through the village toward his estate. His fingers laced themselves through hers and she felt their strength as he held her hand tightly.

She stole a glance in his direction. His face looked flushed and his jaw was clenched. He felt her scrutiny and glanced at her briefly. His mouth pursed together and he gripped the wheel so tightly the knuckles of his hand went white. Marie wondered what she could say to lessen the tension she felt, and was sure he was feeling. She could think of nothing.

As they approached the main house Marie realized her time with Rolf was drawing to an end—perhaps forever. With a shudder she realized how much she would miss him. His love for her was unlike anything she had ever experienced. Félix had come close, with his fun-loving ways and admiration for her determination to help with the Résistance. But Rolf—what she felt for him—and from him—was so deep that the thought of him going away was like her heart being wrenched from her chest. How was it possible for two people to feel this way about each other and have no chance of being together?

Rolf turned off the engine, and for a moment he sat silently staring out the window at the house. Then he turned to Marie. His eyes looked desperate, haunted. He opened his door and stepped out of the car, pulling Marie after him. He wrapped both arms around her, pulled her close, and kissed her.

"We need to talk." His arms gripped her even more tightly as he spoke, and Marie felt frozen in place, as if some life-changing event was about to occur. She watched his face quietly, waiting. "I can't stand the thought of leaving you, Marie." Rolf took a deep breath. "I know you have concerns— about us, about my part in this war—but leaving you now . . ." He stopped, his eyes studying every inch of her face. "I want to marry you."

Time stood still. If not for the pounding of her heart against his, she might have thought she was imagining this moment. He wanted them to take the step she so desperately wished to take, but never could. In all her regard for him, she could not begin to resolve the differences between them—the conflicts in their chosen paths. Never would she find someone that awakened in her such deep emotion, such incredible longing. She could not imagine life apart from him.

Neither could she imagine a life with him. A Nazi wife? It was unthinkable. She pictured them going to Nazi party gatherings together, him associating with people like Dresdner—and Hitler—and she, swapping household hints with other Nazi wives. Her children would become Hitler Youth and be raised in the shadow of their benevolent Führer. Rolf would go to work and do unimaginable things and then come home to kiss her and his children good night.

It was impossible. It was unthinkable! Even though he was a member of the Church, he would be required to do things he would otherwise never consider. She could not imagine the thought of always wondering what he had done during the day, whom he had interrogated—and how.

Did she not have enough faith in his conversion? Did she doubt his conviction? Did she doubt *him?*

Her mother had said, *"Trust him."*

Her mother was dead. That had been nothing more than a dream. Taking a deep breath, Marie did the most difficult thing she had ever done. With both hands she reached behind her and loosened Rolf's embrace. But at the same moment, she could not bring herself to let go of his hands. She desperately wanted him to understand—to understand why her answer had to be no.

"Marie . . ." His eyes were like those of a hunted animal as he recognized her meaning. He grasped her hands fiercely between his own.

"I . . . I'm so sorry, Rolf! If you only understood how much I love you . . ."

"But you still fear me."

"I fear what you represent, Rolf—not you. I love you more than I thought was humanly possible."

"Then how can you tell me no? If we stay close to God, the rest should work itself out, eventually. We just need to trust each other . . ."

"Rolf—" Marie could hardly see him through the tears in her eyes. "I— I can't. I just *can't.* I'm so terribly sorry . . ."

"I can't imagine losing you."

"Please forgive me!"

Rolf looked down at their hands, clasped together as if they had fused and could not be separated. Marie felt tears cascade down her cheeks. She wanted desperately to throw her arms around his neck and hang on for dear life.

But something held her back. And when his eyes looked again into hers she saw that they had become masked, unreadable, as if he had forced his emotions behind a barrier and locked it securely.

"I can understand your concern." His voice was controlled. "I can accept it."

"Rolf, you are one of the best men I've ever known."

"But that's not enough, is it?" His voice had taken on a slight edge, and Marie cringed.

"It would be more than enough—if it were not for . . . for . . ."

"For the fact I'm a Nazi."

"Rolf, Berta told me why you stayed in the Nazi party—to protect your son, and them . . . I'm so sorry it had to come between us."

He spoke bitterly now. "Funny. I always thought my being a Nazi was what brought us together."

Marie gasped. She realized he was right and felt her hands trembling in his. "Perhaps soon the war will be over . . ."

"Would that change your opinion of me? If Germany wins, I will continue to be a Nazi. If Germany loses, I'll be hated because I *was* a Nazi. Your family, your country . . . no matter what happens, the whole world will still see me as a Nazi."

"Maybe not." Marie tried to sound hopeful. "Maybe they will look instead at the good you have done . . . at your religious beliefs."

Rolf shook his head. "Many Nazis have Christian beliefs, Marie. That doesn't stop them from shooting communists or shipping Jews to extermination camps."

"*Extermination* camps . . ." Marie stared at him in horror. She remembered the conversation with the Gestapo major on Christmas Eve. "The trains . . ."

Rolf nodded. "I'm not supposed to know. Many Nazi officers truly believe deportations are just to relocate the Jews. But that's not true. Shuffling trainloads of Jews around the continent will never accomplish the Führer's real purpose. Hitler is determined to cleanse all of Europe."

"But you—you wouldn't!"

Rolf cradled her trembling hands in his. "I won't. But I'm in a dangerous situation, Marie. You realize they would murder my son if they thought I was not following orders?"

She lifted her chin. "I will watch over him." She realized as she said it she was in no position to do so. Wasn't she a prisoner herself? And she was in the middle of enemy territory with nothing hiding her true identity but a wig and a set of counterfeit identification papers.

He looked at her in surprise. "How could I ask you to risk your life . . . ?"

"I don't know how, but I *will* keep him safe." She gave him a half smile. "And you know if we keep the commandments we will be protected. Didn't Heavenly Father save those two missionaries from a madman?"

Rolf looked at her solemnly. "And saved a madman from himself."

"Then why can't we expect He will save this madman's innocent son—if we have the courage to do what is right?"

"Marie, you are a blessing to me."

She felt Rolf's hand touch her cheek in the way she loved, bringing with it a flood of emotions. Would she ever be able to be free of this feeling? She sighed and closed her eyes. "If only . . ." Her voice trailed away.

"What is it?" Rolf's fingers stilled on her cheek as he waited for her reply.

She opened her eyes and looked at him. "My mother used to say, 'What's right for one is right for all.' Maybe if we just focus on staying alive and getting through this war . . . Perhaps the rest will work itself out."

She felt his hand begin to tremble against her cheek. "You realize you've given me something to hope for. I'm afraid to imagine what it is, but I can feel it hiding in the shadows of your mother's words."

She gave a sigh of relief. The look on his face warmed completely through her. "I don't know what it is, either, Rolf. But I am willing to hope for it too."

* * *

She returned to her room, fatigue and emotion sapping her of energy, and found a ring on her pillow with three emeralds embedded in a thin gold band, and the silk WOK he had confiscated in St. Victor-sur-Loire threaded through it. She fingered the silk thoughtfully, her fingers running over its lines of characters, and she held the ring in the palm of her hand and wept for herself, for Rolf, and for his little son.

TWENTY

It was eleven P.M. On the Avenue Berthelot in Lyon, the *École de Santé* was just coming alive. All along the tree-lined street, vehicles were parked in a festive but orderly abandon. In a city famous for its conservative attitudes and cool compliance with the occupation, Gestapo headquarters was the place to be on New Year's Eve 1943.

A black Citroën pulled into an unlikely parking place—over a curb and onto the snow-covered grass between two trees. Captain Bernard Dresdner waited impatiently for his driver to open his door, and he stepped gingerly over a gutter overflowing with filthy snow. He straightened his uniform jacket and glanced up at the building in front of him. *Four stories of impressive architecture,* he thought, thinking how his carpenter father would have appreciated this sight. His thought for a father who had long ago disowned his son was brief. *No need to bring that contemptuous old man into the picture to ruin this evening's pleasures.*

He adjusted his eye patch. While working, he always dispensed with this ridiculous accessory—his damaged eye actually seemed to accentuate the fear and loathing he tried to establish, thereby making both his inferiors and his prisoners more manageable.

But a party such as this, with an assemblage of his peers, was no place to strike fear and loathing. Tonight he needed to command respect and admiration. A good image was vital to his career goals.

Anyway, Deidri was uncomfortable looking at his damaged eye. He turned and stiffly offered the woman his hand as she stepped from the car. Deidri was a beautiful necessity. No good arriving at this event without a date of some sort, and Deidri would hang prettily on his arm, keep quiet, and make him look good. In the absence of time to scrounge up some other lucky Fräulein, Deidri would have to do.

Holding Deidri's arm, he led her across the wet street and up the steps to the entrance of the *École de Santé*. Inside, he dropped her arm and surveyed his surroundings. The foyer was crowded with Gestapo officers drinking, sampling hors d'oeuvres, and carrying on loud conversations in groups. A young girl in uniform took his coat and Deidri's fur wrap, handed them receipts, and headed for the coatroom.

Captain Dresdner looked for familiar faces, pulling Deidri by the elbow as he wound his way through the crowd. He left the foyer and entered the main room, also crowded to bursting with officers and their dates. Smoke hung thick in the air, and a veritable beehive of waiters navigated their way through the laughing assemblage carrying trays loaded with their offerings. Deidri recognized one of the officers' dates and squealed with delight at the discovery. She twisted her arm from Dresdner's grip and trotted off to share the latest gossip. Dresdner stood in the doorway, alone and unaccompanied, feeling idiotic. Silently he cursed Deidri for her sudden departure and himself for not being quick enough to contain her before she bolted. *I should have been more selective in my choice of date,* he thought angrily, and he stepped into the room.

"Captain Dresdner!" Dresdner turned and saw his superior officer, Major Nieman, standing with a group of Gestapo officers from Paris. Straightening his shoulders, Dresdner walked toward the group. This was a golden opportunity to get his name recognized by the most important leaders in France.

"Welcome, Captain. You finally made it, I see." Major Nieman looked around Dresdner. "I'm surprised to see you alone. Where's your date?"

"Powdering her nose." Dresdner clicked his heels and bowed.

"Ah, yes—mine, too." Major Nieman gestured toward the group of officers. "Gentlemen, Captain Bernard Dresdner. Probably the most talented young officer in Section Four—if he can remember to use his talent to further purposes of the Führer instead of his own career."

The officers laughed and Dresdner smiled tightly. Not exactly the welcome he was hoping for, but he could handle the major.

"Captain Dresdner has a knack for getting the job done, if you know what I mean."

One of the officers spoke. "Captain, you worked in a Paris *arrondissement* at one time, did you not?"

Dresdner nodded, grateful the man remembered. "Yes, Major Knopf. I completed a *rafle* at one time in your district."

Major Knopf's brow knit as he contemplated. "Yes, I think I remember . . . You performed admirably, I'm sure." He smiled politely.

Major Nieman indicated his comrades. "Paris has sent these fine gentlemen to brief us on the successes of northern France in implementing the Final Solution. We are honored to have them here. Southern France is woefully deficient in this area."

Dresdner acknowledged the group. "And what do you see must be done?"

One of the officers spoke. "All Jews of foreign birth must be transported from the city of Lyon to Drancy, the gathering place north of Paris. Berlin will decide where they will be sent from there. Barbie is in the process of convincing the Ministry of Transportation that Lyon needs more trains."

Another officer spoke, gesturing with his champagne glass. "Not only Lyon. The surrounding *départements* need to contribute too. Those areas have been safe havens for foreign Jews long enough."

Dresdner was interested. "Who would be included? What local elements would be considered deportable?"

The officers took turns voicing their opinions. "Barbie insists on us being specific on that regard. He still cares about public opinion."

"All Jews of non-French origin in the vicinity. Also, Berlin has authorized the inclusion of naturalized Jews, if their naturalization took place since 1919."

"It's 1919 now? I had heard '27."

Major Knopf explained. "Yes, now it's 1919. In '42 the deportations depended upon the change."

Major Nieman nodded. "It makes perfect sense."

"Barbie plans on sending trains to the southern areas in the spring. Several *départements* have already been alerted, and we are preparing lists for them now."

Knopf shook his head. "No more disasters like Bordeaux."

Dresdner looked at Major Knopf. "Bordeaux?"

"Hans Bordes was the officer in charge. In '42 he ignored orders and refused to make the appropriate arrests. That July the train scheduled for Bordeaux had to be cancelled. Eichmann was furious."

"With reason, I'm sure." Dresdner nodded. "Bordes was, of course, punished?"

"On the contrary," Major Knopf drank from his glass. "Bordes was able to convince his superiors there were not enough non-French Jews to fill the train."

"And so the law was amended to include naturalized elements after 1919."

"Ah, but the formerly unoccupied zone is volatile. The Vichy will never agree."

"The Vichy no longer have any say in the matter."

"Maybe not, but they carry public opinion."

Dresdner spoke up. "Perhaps Vichy cooperation is no longer the solution."

"How so?" The Gestapo officers from Paris looked at Dresdner with renewed interest.

"The *Milice française* is easily persuaded," Dresdner pointed out. "And it's less expensive in the long run."

Major Nieman agreed. "They will be clean and efficient. No mistakes. They may be renegades, but they're resourceful. The Final Solution in this corner of Europe may well depend upon them."

"And upon the continued support of the *département* leaders," one of the officers concurred.

"Of course."

Dresdner thought about Belley. "There have been rumors of insurrections."

"Insurrections?" Major Nieman looked inquiringly at the captain.

"Well, civil disobedience. Small instances—on the part of the commanding officers."

A Paris officer shook his head. "Even small disobediences can undermine the Führer's plans."

"Of course."

"Lyon needs to have its own commission for the organization of the *rafles*."

"Barbie has orchestrated that already. The round-ups of the Jews are of utmost importance to him and he himself will take control of the organization."

"Each area needs to have its own *rafle*."

"Barbie will take care of that."

Another officer took a drag on his cigarette. "There is also rumor of an Allied invasion, in the springtime."

Major Nieman shook his head. "They will try. They will also try to involve the Résistance, the Maquis."

Dresdner was contemptuous. "The Résistance is fading. And the Maquis are motivated, but ineffectual. They will be easily silenced."

"But not, perhaps, before the invasion."

Several women approached, taking the arms of their respective husbands. Out of deference to the women, talk of war and business was set aside. Conversation turned to fine French architecture and the weather. Dresdner moved to his commanding officer's side. "Major Nieman, may I speak to you a moment?"

"Of course. What is it, Captain?"

"About the minor insurrections . . ."

"You have heard something?"

"I have my suspicions—about Belley's leadership."

"Major Rolf Schulmann? You have mentioned him before. What do you suspect?"

"Major Klein and his wife spent the Christmas holiday in the Schwarzwald. They saw him there."

"He has family there, a son and sister-in-law. Nothing suspicious about that."

"Perhaps not. I hear he has a new girlfriend. A beautiful blonde from France."

"A surprise, but again, nothing irregular." Major Nieman was irritated. "What are you trying to tell me, Captain? I have guests who need my attention."

"My apologies, Major. It was a comment Major Klein made that bothered me."

"What was that?"

"He said Major Schulmann seemed annoyed by the possibility of a train in his *département*."

The major sighed. "He would not be the first officer to feel that way. But in the end, the Führer's wishes are always respected and orders are always carried out."

"They were not with Bordes in '42."

Nieman did not answer for a moment. He studied Dresdner. "So are you implying there is chance of another Bordeaux incident? In Belley?"

"I believe there is a very good possibility, Major."

"Major Schulmann's record is impeccable."

"His religious preferences are such, sir, that they preclude any action against foreign nationals."

"You are guessing. There has never been any hint of insubordination in his conduct."

"Maybe not—but never before has a train been ordered for his region."

Nieman scowled. His brows furrowed as he digested this information. "Then, Captain,"—his voice was brusque—"what do you recommend?"

"As you said, there is no record of any misconduct. I would like to be assigned to look into it, sir. For as long as it takes."

Major Nieman set his empty glass on the edge of a table. "Captain Dresdner, as opposed to Major Schulmann, you *do* have a record of misconduct." His scowl deepened. "What would compel me to give you any control in Belley?"

"I have reason to believe, sir, that Major Schulmann is hiding an enemy spy."

"You mean the American girl? The one *you* allowed to escape?"

Dresdner cleared his throat. "I believe it was a carefully orchestrated coup, sir. And I am almost positive Schulmann is the one who organized it."

The major shook his head. "Those are serious allegations, Captain."

"I'm aware of that."

"You've been trying to prove your innocence since you lost the girl. You realize if these accusations against the major prove unfounded you could be court-martialed?"

Dresdner swallowed. "I understand, sir. But I believe I have enough evidence that I should be allowed to investigate further. The success of the Belley *rafle* and the Final Solution in that region may depend on it."

Again Major Nieman scowled, his round face turning red. "You would do well to tend to your responsibilities here, Captain. You've been complaining about Major Schulmann for months. I have no idea why you dislike him so much, but you're allowing a personal vendetta to endanger your career. Which—" the major leaned close, his eyes narrowing—"it will." With an irritated click of his heels, Major Nieman saluted, turned, and left the captain to his thoughts.

Dresdner was furious. He'd expected resistance to his idea, but not flat out refusal to cooperate. How could these people be so blind? Could Schulmann have them wrapped so completely around his little finger they could not see the evidence in front of their faces? When before had Dresdner ever let a prisoner escape? Certainly there had been attempts, but many had died. He had never lost a prisoner before now, and that portion of his record was unarguably impeccable. And the other incidents? Insignificant mistakes. Surely there was nothing worthy of such a fuss. When it came to his abilities as an interrogator and as an investigator, his record was above reproach—even the despicable Mormon could not boast such accomplishments. Hadn't he proved himself with Jean Moulin in June of '39 and again with the same communist in '43? The Résistance leader's interrogation and death certainly counted as a prize worthy of a little respect—if not a promotion!

He felt a hand on his arm. Deidri had returned and smiled demurely at him, her heavy lipstick smudged. For some reason the slight imperfection annoyed Dresdner and he ordered her sharply to the washroom to repair her face. Hurt, she left him to his murderous thoughts.

Schulmann was a problem—a threat to Dresdner's career. He needed to be taught a lesson, and Dresdner could think of no better way than exposing the Mormon as the slippery traitor he was. How the Third Reich could let a man as dangerous as Schulmann retain such power was beyond him. Something had to be done.

The clock chimed the approach of the New Year. All around him, his fellow officers and their dates were toasting the event with champagne glasses raised high. Dresdner wondered what was taking Deidri so long. She was probably crying in the washroom. How he detested weakness.

And then, as the liquor flowed and laughter bubbled, he made his own New Year's resolution. The thought of it lifted his spirits, and Major Nieman's harsh words no longer bothered him. He lifted a glass for himself off a passing garçon's tray and even took one for Deidri, who returned a moment later, her lipstick repaired but her eyes red. He handed the glass to her with a forgiving smile, and they toasted the New Year together.

Dresdner's resolution made him joyful. He wrapped his arm around Deidri's waist and raised his glass high. "Here's to a wonderful new year, full of possibility, opportunity, and . . . victory."

TWENTY-ONE

Sunday, January 23, 1944

Rolf pulled the collar of his coat up around his chin and followed the small Frenchman out of the café and onto the sidewalk. The snowfall had lessened but the wind was raising swirls of white powder, impeding his vision. The streets of Belley were, for the most part, empty. An occasional pedestrian took a wide berth to avoid the major and his companion, trying to look as unimpressive as possible in order not to capture the attention of the German officer.

"This way, Monsieur Schulmann. The man went this way."

"What makes you think he's the one we want?"

"He keeps the same schedule every Sunday, monsieur."

"Did you see exactly where he went?"

"*Oui*. He knocked on the door of a house five blocks from here. Someone let him inside. I could see there were several people in the room behind."

"Were you seen?"

"No, monsieur. You can be sure of that. I am extremely careful."

The two men walked in silence for a while. Rolf was disgusted with this man, one of a multitude of *collabos* ready to sell out his fellow countrymen for a price. He would return to his friends and brag about spying for the German invaders. And he would buy drinks for all his buddies with the spoils of his betrayal. He would never know what it was all about—nor, after a night with his drinking buddies, would he care.

"Just a little farther, sir." The Frenchman picked up his pace, eager to receive his reward and be back with his friends on this day of rest. Rolf was eager for another reason.

They passed a parked car and several bicycles. Rolf knew they would be left a distance from the actual meeting place and discreetly distributed throughout the neighborhood to alleviate suspicion of any illegal public meeting. He noticed several more bicycles parked in alleyways, and they passed a baby stroller abandoned against a brick wall.

"There, monsieur—across the street." Rolf and his guide had reached a corner, and the Frenchman pointed with one dilapidated glove. He waited expectantly for Rolf's reaction.

"The one with the candle in the window?"

"Oui, monsieur."

"You have done well. *Merci.*" Major Schulmann deposited a pile of francs and ration coupons into the Frenchman's outstretched hand and nodded his dismissal. Without another word the Frenchman touched his cap and disappeared in the direction they had come.

Rolf turned his attention to the home's front porch. The candle in the window burned steadily at about half mast—it looked as if it had been doing so for an hour, at least. Obviously it was a signal, a guide to inform certain individuals of what was happening inside. Rolf's boots crunched in the snow as he approached the house. All was still, but he knew the meeting inside would be kept intentionally quiet. Discovery could mean arrest, deportation, or even death. He removed one glove and lifted his hand to the door. As he did, he heard the almost imperceptible strains of a song quietly sung. He recognized the melody and he felt a shiver go up his spine. *How I've missed . . . !*

His knock brought an abrupt end to the song. The quiet voices, male, female, and child, broke off in mid-phrase, and Rolf could feel a sudden tension in the air. He waited.

After several long moments Rolf heard a latch being lifted, and the door opened a crack. He saw the hesitant face of a woman peering through the narrow opening. When she recognized Rolf's uniform, her face went white and her attempt at composure shattered. Her voice shook when she spoke. "M-may I be of assistance, monsieur?"

"I would like to come in please, madame." What could he say that would lessen the terror caused by his presence? Not much could diminish the fear his uniform would bring to these people. Nevertheless, he had to do this. It had been too long.

"I will speak with whoever is in charge of this meeting."

"We are not trying to cause trouble, monsieur . . ."

"May I come in?"

"Of course." The woman hastily stepped aside, and her eyes glanced fearfully behind her at the assembled crowd. Major Schulmann pushed the door open with his boot and stepped into the room. His eyes followed the woman's terrified gaze.

There were close to twenty people in the parlor. Bodies crowded the small space, facing the far wall. In front of the assembled group a woman stood clutching a hymnal to her chest. To her right, two young men stood behind a table covered with a simple white cloth. On the tablecloth was a metal plate and two cups. The boys were holding broken loaves of black bread, suspended in frozen hands. To the left of the boys sat three Frenchmen, their chairs facing the assemblage. All faces in the room were turned to Rolf and the woman at the door. All present were frozen in place, as if a sudden arctic wind had swept the room at his entrance and forever preserved the moment in ice. Rolf could smell the fear as he strode purposefully toward the three men seated facing the group. As he passed chairs and seated people he heard the terrified whispers of children to parents. One woman let out a sob.

The woman with the hymnal dropped into a chair and averted her eyes. Major Schulmann stopped and faced the three men. They stood, and one with white hair and kind blue eyes approached Rolf. He extended his hand and Rolf took it. In German the man asked, "How may we help you, sir?" Although Rolf detected a touch of fear, the man's voice mirrored the kindness in his eyes.

You are all under arrest for holding an illegal public meeting. Rolf knew the penalties these men and woman were facing, and he spoke carefully. "I wish to speak with the congregation."

"Of course, Major." The white-haired man nodded at the two young boys standing behind the table, and they sat down abruptly, their faces petrified. Then he gestured to Rolf to accompany him to the front of the assembly.

Rolf turned and studied the people in the room. They watched him with anxiety and fear. They knew his power and they knew they had broken the law. Rolf watched their anxious faces as he spoke. "My name is Major Rolf Schulmann. I am the officer in charge of civilian compliance for this region of France." Schulmann could see several of the men avert their eyes. *Résistance sympathizers,* Rolf thought, and he continued. "I represent the Third Reich. I know that it is not your desire that I be here with my soldiers. I know most of you wish things could be as they were before the occupation. You and I are different in almost every way. I am German and you are French. I am a servant of your German conquerors and you are the conquered. But there is one subject upon which I believe we can find common ground. That common ground is the gospel of Jesus Christ."

Hesitant murmurs of surprise reached Rolf's ears. He turned to glance at the white-haired gentleman standing behind him. The man looked stunned, and tears glistened at the corners of his eyes. Rolf fought back his own emotions and again addressed the congregation. "I wanted to join you this afternoon and tell you I have a testimony of our Lord and Savior Jesus Christ. It is rare that I have the opportunity to share this. I miss the fellowship of my brothers and sisters in the gospel. And I wanted to apologize on behalf of my government, whom I serve because I must, for your discomfort. My hope and my prayer is that this war will soon be concluded, and that the outcome will be what is best for all.

"I see God's hand in my life, and His love and protection of my family. I pray you see the same, and that you can feel peace even under persecution." Rolf felt his voice catch and he swallowed hard. "I want to have your permission to meet with you and worship with you whenever my schedule allows. I want you to know that I will protect you with all that is in my power and help you as much as I can for as long as I am stationed in your community."

Rolf concluded and turned back to the Frenchman behind him. With open arms the man welcomed Rolf to their meeting and introduced himself as the branch president. Someone found another chair, and the branch president asked Rolf to sit beside him. Rolf felt the feeling change in the room—from fear and mistrust to love and peace. He closed his eyes and said a silent prayer of thanks for this moment, and for these Saints who were willing to forgive him and welcome him into their midst.

The meeting continued. Rolf sang the sacrament hymn with the congregation and partook of the sacrament. The branch president stood and shared several scriptures from the Book of Mormon, discussing each and bearing his testimony. He asked Rolf to tell the congregation about himself. Rolf stood and told them of his conversion. He told them of his struggles to do what was right as a disciple of Jesus Christ and as a German officer. He told them of his home in Germany and of his son and deceased wife. He told them of his small hometown branch and of his desire to once again be with the Saints. And he bore his testimony of the truthfulness of the gospel, of his love of the Book of Mormon, and of the Savior.

When the meeting ended, Major Schulmann waited until the last member had left, and then turned to the branch president and his wife. "Thank you for your hospitality. I apologize for the commotion I caused. I want to make a suggestion, if you would be kind enough to consider it."

"Of course, Major Schulmann."

"I have tried to make my men act as orderly and gentlemanly as possible."

"Your troops are very affable, considering the circumstances."

"I have wanted to find LDS members in this area for as long as I have been here. I am happy to finally have that search concluded. However, I need to warn you that the only way I was able to find you was by following up on a lead provided me by one of your fellow countrymen—a *collabo* eager for a few extra francs. He came to me last week and told me he suspected that your home was the location of illegal public meetings. I wondered if it was not a gathering of LDS Saints, because the informer said you always met at the same time—on Sunday afternoon—and at the same place."

The branch president and his wife watched Rolf silently, their faces betraying their worry.

"I suggest you vary both the time and the place of your meeting. The Gestapo would arrest you if you were discovered. Please forgive me, but I must strongly suggest that you watch yourselves."

"I understand."

"The Gestapo has almost limitless authority. They are allowed to do as they please—as long as they can convince the Führer that their actions are in the best interest of the Reich."

"I see."

"You must understand, President, that I and my men will do all in our power to help you. But the Gestapo captain who might soon be coming has a deep hatred of Mormons."

* * *

Marie Jacobson stared at the wall behind the kitchen sink, eyes focusing on some faraway memory the wall could not hide. She did not hear Berta's constant chatter as she set out plates for their meal. Nor did she hear Walter enter the kitchen from his workshop outside, stomping his boots and shaking snow from his coat. Alma played with his panzer tank and toy soldiers near the fireplace in the other room, and Bandit whined from the front porch, still not accepting that he wasn't allowed in Berta's home. Unconsciously Marie fingered the thin gold band hanging from a string around her neck, realizing as she did so that this was becoming a habit whenever she felt anxious or her memories of Rolf hovered a little too near the surface. She shook her head to clear it of a fog that threatened to spirit her away from reality and bent again to her task.

"You miss him."

It was the first thing Marie had heard Berta say. She turned and stared at Berta before she realized the significance of the woman's words.

"I miss him."

"Why don't you wear his ring?"

Marie hesitated. Berta probably wouldn't understand her reasons for not wearing the band, but Marie always felt that wearing a ring meant commitment—an engagement, in this case. And she knew that could never happen with Rolf.

"Giselle, I think he would want you to wear it." Berta walked to her side. "He loves you. He would understand that you consider it a reminder of his affection and not necessarily a promise, although I cannot understand how two people who love each other more than is humanly possible can be so cruel to each other . . ." She shook her head.

"I can't, Berta. Not yet, anyway." Marie reached for a dishtowel. "Perhaps someday it'll be possible—as a remembrance of a man who saved my life, who I'll always cherish."

"Giselle . . ." Berta seemed ready to reproach her and then changed her mind. She returned to her task still shaking her head.

"It's complicated, Berta." Marie paused, wanting this kind woman to understand but finding it difficult to formulate her thoughts. "A ring is, well, to me it's a symbol of love and promises that can't be taken lightly. I'm not engaged to him, and I don't want to imagine I am."

"Why not? What could be wrong with thinking about him in that way?"

Marie felt her eyes become moist, and she turned away so Berta would not notice. "It's too painful, Berta. Thinking about how much we love each other tears me apart inside—and I can't take that much hurt."

TWENTY-TWO

March 22, 1944

Major Rolf Schulmann saw the man limping across the Place des Terreaux and tried not to look overly interested. He drummed his fingers against the small café table and looked nonchalantly the other direction. He knew the man instantly: middle-aged, gaunt, and of average height, the Frenchman rolled violently to the side with each step, which indicated that one leg was shorter than the other. Rolf knew the man was balding underneath his leather cap, and that the face partially hidden behind a thick wool scarf and *chapeau-mou* was thin and unimpressive. The Frenchman did not even glance in Schulmann's direction, but Rolf knew he had seen him. At the street corner the man paused to light a cigarette, balancing on the curb as he took his first deep drag. He hesitated just a second longer before continuing his irregular gait across the cobblestones. Rolf waited until the man had disappeared around a corner before he rose casually to his feet.

"Wait here."

The young lieutenant with him nodded and settled back into his chair. Two more soldiers sat a block away in an unmarked Renault, watching the café. Rolf stepped off the curb and walked in the direction the small man had disappeared. He caught up with him in a narrow alleyway three blocks from the café.

"Major." The man dropped the butt of his cigarette and ground it with his heel into the dirty snow.

"Trotter." The major's greeting was clipped. Schulmann produced a photograph. It was of a man leaving a street corner café with a young woman clinging contentedly to his arm. Although the photograph was taken from a discreet distance, the subject's defined cheekbones and crooked nose were easily discernable. "I am looking for this man. This is your establishment at the corner of Place des Terreaux and Chapelle that he is leaving. Do you know him?"

Trotter studied the photo but did not take it. "I know him."

"The man in the photograph is Monsieur Jacques Bellamont. We call him Bruno, and we've been tolerant of his crimes long enough. Have you seen him lately?"

Trotter nodded and extracted another cigarette from inside his coat. He lit it, inhaled slowly, and looked at Schulmann. His expressionless brown eyes were set deep in folds of wrinkled skin. He looked at least a decade older than his forty years. "He visits my café often. He gestured with his cigarette. What's my assignment?"

Schulmann returned the photograph to the inside pocket of his uniform and straightened his jacket. "An Allied plane went down six kilometers west of here, near Izieu. Three days ago we found a parachute. We have reason to believe the Résistance has him hidden here in Belley. Izieu is close-knit and small—too small to hide a downed pilot. The Résistance wouldn't risk it. They've brought him here. I need to find him."

Trotter grunted and pulled on his cigarette. He exhaled in Schulmann's direction. "They've got him, all right. Saw him yesterday. He's got a badly broken leg and can't be moved—at least for a couple of weeks."

Schulmann nodded his satisfaction. "Tell me where Bruno's keeping the pilot."

"I can do better than that, Major." Trotter's eyes squinted as he glanced down one end of the dilapidated alley and then the other. Schulmann could tell he was getting impatient with the length of the meeting. The major was also aware of the risks of an extended *rencontre*. Trotter continued. "They've called a meeting for tomorrow morning. The Maquis are planning to interview the pilot—find out what he knows about a rumored Allied invasion."

"We've heard the rumors."

"They're planning to meet at Madame Guilbert's home on the rue de St. André."

"I know the place. In fact, we've suspected the woman for some time now. Continue."

"Everyone important will be there. They'll expect me to be there." Trotter scowled. "I'm not ready to get shot, Major."

"You won't be there. Plan to have influenza. Tell someone you're taking the rest of today off—and make it believable."

"Thank you. Anything else?"

"No. Don't contact me for any reason. I will see you next time."

Trotter nodded, flicked the ash from his cigarette, and disappeared from the alley, moving surprisingly fast for a man with a disability. Shoulders hunched and hands jammed deeply into his pockets, he did not look back. Rolf exited the alley on the opposite street and circled back in the direction of the café. He rejoined the young lieutenant, sitting opposite him at one of the small curbside tables. The lieutenant remained silent, knowing better than to ask any questions. Without a word, Schulmann gestured curtly for the garçon.

* * *

March 23, 1944

When the door opened, it did so with such force that it splintered as it hit the wall. The men inside never had a chance. Schulmann entered after two of his soldiers demolished the door and positioned themselves on either side of the opening, machine guns trained on the assemblage. Rolf's gaze swept the room: twenty men, frozen in various positions with assorted expressions of shock, fear, and hate. Some of the men assembled were probably leaders of the mountain Maquis—a group that begged for attention and nipped at Nazi heels like an English terrier when they received it. Most of the men he did not know or had seen around town but never met. Most were probably the local Résistance leaders, bent on sabotage and not necessarily murder, like the Maquis. He recognized Jacques Bellamont from that fateful morning in the mountains above Izieu. And he could not help but recognize the English pilot. Jacques was seated near the pilot's mattress with a map of France in his hands. He, like his comrades, was frozen in position. Whatever he had been doing the moment the door disintegrated was the last movement he had made. Except, of course, when Schulmann's soldier shouted for all hands to be raised, gesturing toward the ceiling so that they would understand.

Schulmann spoke in French. "Everybody please stand. Except of course for you, sir." The last was said with a deferential nod in the wounded pilot's direction. "You may stay where you are. But please raise your hands. I do not think you want to die today." Schulmann addressed the men, who were all rising slowly to their feet. "I'm sure none of you wish to die today. So I will tell you that Madame Guilbert's home is completely surrounded, your vehicles have been disabled, the men you left at the gate and behind the house have been apprehended, and there is a squadron of my men armed with machine guns ready to escort you to my headquarters. So please do not try anything foolish."

No one spoke. Major Schulmann continued. "You will please exit the room in an orderly manner. Please form a line and allow my men to assist you. Move."

Everybody except the pilot moved. The men followed Schulmann's instructions perfectly, forming a sullen line and shuffling silently out the door. They were submissive in body, but Schulmann could see the expressions of defiance and hate in their eyes as they passed him. A split second of weakness and he would be dead at their hands, he knew. They would kill him and in turn be killed. To a Maquis guerilla, an SS officer would be worth the sacrifice. He was very careful.

Two soldiers arrived with a field stretcher for the wounded pilot. Gently they lifted him and placed him on the carrier, taking care not to jostle the broken limb. Schulmann asked, "Has a doctor looked at that leg?"

"You must be joking." The English pilot grimaced. "And have them come snitching to you?"

"You need medical attention. My doctors will see to you."

With one gloved hand Major Schulmann singled out the Résistance leader known as Jacques and motioned for him to stand aside from the line. The remainder of the men exited the room and continued out of the house to the waiting trucks. Schulmann gestured for the two guards to wait outside the door. In the empty room the two enemies studied each other warily.

"Your name is Jacques." Schulmann nodded to the Frenchman.

Jacques did not respond.

"My name is Major Rolf Schulmann. I am stationed in Belley."

"I know you."

"Perhaps you remember our brief encounter in the mountains last year?"

Jacques hissed, "How could I forget?"

"I admire your escape. You outwitted my men and gave them significant trouble."

Jacques said nothing, but his eyes smoldered.

"I am sorry about your friend Félix Larouche."

"You killed him, remember?" Jacques's words were soft, menacing.

"An unfortunate accident."

"Your men are outside the door," Jacques growled. "What would stop me from causing another 'unfortunate accident' right now?"

"Nothing—except, perhaps, your desire for two things."

"What things?"

"The preservation of your own life and a desire to hear what I have to offer."

Jacques said nothing, but Schulmann caught a glimmer of interest in his dark eyes. Just as quickly, hate and disdain closed over his expression like a black curtain. "You have nothing to offer me. I'll die before I lift a finger to assist you or the evil you represent."

"If it helps, Jacques, you're not alone in your feelings."

Again Jacques's eyes flickered almost imperceptibly.

Rolf watched him closely. "I know my government is corrupt."

"Then why do you wear that uniform?"

"That is complicated, monsieur."

Jacques turned abruptly. "Right and wrong are never complicated. People like you are the ones that complicate them."

"I agree." Schulmann sat on the edge of a table and removed his gloves, setting them carefully beside him. He kept his Luger ready in his lap. Reaching into his jacket he extracted a folded document. "I've received orders from Lyon. I thought you might be interested in seeing them."

Jacques glowered at the major before glancing down at the paper in Schulmann's hands. He took it and studied it closely. "What's this?"

"An order from the head of the Gestapo in Lyon—Klaus Barbie. I am to arrest all the people listed there and ready them for deportation."

Jacques hands began to shake. "There are forty-seven people on this list . . ." He counted silently. "Fifteen different families."

"That's right."

Jacques looked more closely at the names and swore softly. "My fiancée's name is here—her whole family." Shocked, he looked up at Schulmann. "Why are you showing me this?"

"Your fiancée is Jewish, is she not?"

"Yes. What does it matter?"

"Every person on this list is a Jew."

Jacques slowly sank into the nearest chair. He held the paper tightly in both hands and said nothing.

"My soldiers and the local Milice will go to their homes tomorrow morning before dawn. We will ransack their homes and confiscate everything of value. We will load the families and their belongings into trucks and deport them to Drancy—a detention center north of Paris. There, the men will be separated from their wives and the women will be separated from the children, and they will be loaded on a train bound for Poland." Major Schulmann paused. "You need to understand, Jacques, that even SS officers are only told what they need to know. If we ask where the prisoners are being sent, we are told they are going to Poland to work until the end of the war. I have a feeling this is not true. But I have no way of confirming my fears."

Major Schulmann spoke deliberately. "If Aimée is still at her home in the morning, I do not think you will see her again. Not if the Allies invade, not at the end of the war—not ever. Do you understand?"

The paper crumpled in Jacques's fist. "You would do this? You would tear people from their homes—decent, law-abiding people—and send them to their deaths?"

"I have no choice. If they are still in my district in the morning, they will have to go." Schulmann studied the man in front of him carefully. "Will you help me?"

Jacques stared at Schulmann, still in shock.

Schulmann continued. "I know you have influence, with the Maquis, with the other Résistance leaders, with these families." He indicated the list in Jacques's hand. "You can save their lives. I cannot."

"What if you ignored the order?"

"I've been receiving these orders for three months. I've ignored them for three months. Lyon is not pleased. The Gestapo will be visiting this area if I do not make some effort to comply this time."

Jacques smoothed the crumpled paper on one knee. "I still hesitate to believe you are truly concerned about these Jews. It could be a ploy to arrest more of my fighters."

"Yes, it could be," Rolf agreed. "But are you willing to risk Aimée's life on that assumption? The lives of her mother, father, and little sister? The lives of all forty-three others? I can do nothing. There is a train leaving this month and I *must* comply—or at least make an attempt. My hope is that the belongings of the families will be enough to appease my superiors in Lyon. I don't even know if that will work, but I have to try. I *have* to try." Schulmann stopped abruptly. He had displayed more emotion than he had intended. Jacques was watching him closely, curiously.

After a moment of silence Jacques spoke softly. "You said Félix's death was an accident. An 'unfortunate accident.' What did you mean by that?"

Schulmann let out a long sigh. "Félix Larouche was my friend. In a way, he saved my life." Jacques looked stunned. He said nothing, and Schulmann continued. "I knew him just briefly—in August 1939. He taught me about God and—and repentance."

"You joined his church?"

Schulmann nodded. "It's not *his* church, but yes, I did join the Mormon Church."

Jacques gave a short, sardonic laugh. "I should've known." He stood and began pacing the room, his hands fumbling for a cigarette. "Félix Larouche was a good man. But he had a lot of crazy ideas—most of which I don't believe." He held his cigarette in one hand and turned to look at Schulmann. "Félix was crazy to join the Mormon Church. But Félix was a man of his word. That much I admired."

Rolf said nothing.

With his eyes on the major, Jacques lit a match and touched the flame to the tip of his cigarette. He shook the match and tossed it onto the floor. He took a deep drag and exhaled thoughtfully. "Does your church teach you to be a man of your word?"

"Yes."

Jacques sat next to the major. "If your church teaches you to be a man of your word, I will help you."

"Then I will help you in return."

* * *

Alma crouched beside Marie and pushed as hard as he could, his little hands in their mittens partially over hers and his eyes screwed tightly shut. The snowball had already exceeded the boy's height and weight, and Marie felt the enthusiasm and exertion in his small frame as he bent to his task. He let out a grunt or two, perhaps as he remembered from his father, and Marie had to laugh.

"*Das ist sehr gut,* Alma!" Marie formed the alien words with difficulty around her French tongue, and Alma laughed, answering her with a barrage of German that overwhelmed her small vocabulary. "Now, wait a minute, munchkin! How in the world do you expect me to follow that? Slow down!" She might as well let him ramble on, she thought, realizing he didn't seem to mind that she didn't understand.

She made a show of wiping her forehead, demonstrating to the boy that the snowball had exhausted her. "Let's leave it right here, all right?" She ruffled his hair affectionately. "That way Berta can see the snowman from the kitchen window when it's done. *Verstehst du?* Do you understand?"

The next half hour flew by as the two intrepid builders rolled a medium-sized snowball followed by one the size of a basketball, placing one on top of the other until Herr Snowman faced them with a blank expression. Then Marie scoured two stones for his eyes. "There, Alma. He has a little more character now, don't you agree?"

Alma spouted German and pointed at the location for his nose.

"All right. Let's see what we can find."

Alma discovered a moldy corn cob next to the barn picked clean by winter birds and half-frozen into the mud. He kicked it with his boot until it came clear and carried it triumphantly back to Marie.

"Way to go, honey. We've got a nose."

She turned from the snowman to watch as Hans Brenner's large car pulled to a stop next to the guest cottage. It was the weekend, and she could see Derek waiting anxiously at the window, scrubbed and decked out for a night on the town with the lieutenant. It was Lancelot's turn to stay and guard the American prisoner while his two comrades combed the Schwarzwald for every drop of liquor and every available Fräulein they could find.

Hans waved and Marie returned the greeting. He left Derek climbing impatiently into the car and walked across the snow toward Marie, Alma, and Herr Snowman.

"Rolf sent you a letter, princess. Thought I'd bring it by."

Marie felt her heart leap at his announcement, and she smiled at the lieutenant. "I appreciate it, Hans. I've been wondering if he'd ever write."

Hans swept a shrieking Alma up into his arms and tickled him mercilessly. Amid the boy's howls the lieutenant grinned back at Marie. "He's written thousands of letters to you, Marie—only they're all in his head. It's dreary, time-consuming work, being in a war. He doesn't have a lot of time to write."

"I never thought he did." She accepted a writhing Alma from Hans and set the boy back on his feet beside her. Hans reached inside his coat and produced an opened envelope. Marie accepted it and looked questioningly at the open flap. "Have you read it?" she accused.

"Sure." Hans nodded. "And so have a dozen other people en route."

"In America that would be considered a crime." Marie tried to joke, but she felt a little indignant.

"In Germany it's what's inside that might be a crime, Marie." He shrugged. "It was delivered to me opened. Seems our friend has his share of enemies."

Marie looked down at the letter, curious what she would find inside. In the automobile, Derek leaned on the horn.

"Gestapo might be just a little suspicious," Hans said and turned to go. "So don't expect too much from that letter."

"Thanks, Hans. I appreciate you bringing it to me."

"*Tschüss, Fräulein.*" He raised a hand to wave, then trotted off in the direction of his car.

Marie grabbed Alma's hand. "Let's go see if Tante Berta has anything to eat, all right?"

"Tante Berta" meant "food" to Alma after a romp in the snow, and Marie's mention of his aunt sent his legs churning toward the kitchen door.

Marie followed at a more leisurely pace, pulling the single sheet of paper from the envelope as she did so. She opened it and held it at an angle to take advantage of the afternoon sunlight and eagerly read the French writing:

> Fräulein Giselle:
>
> In the interest of my son's education and for his own good, I expect you to implement the following in his daily routine: Each day you must require that he study the *Hitlerjugend* pledge: *"I promise to do my duty in love and loyalty to the Führer and our flag,"* until he can recite it by heart. I expect him to pronounce it daily before break-fast. His future in the Fatherland's glorious Third Reich is of paramount importance, after which will follow his other subjects, mainly reading and French. You will geve the utmost atention to strict obedience and character development. No son of mine will be a disgrace to his country.
> —Major Rolf Schulmann

Marie held the single sheet of paper in her hand and stared at the words, speechless. Of all the things he could have written, this was the last thing she expected. She refolded the paper and put it back in the envelope, dazed and confused. Her feet transported her the remainder of the way to the house and she walked into the warm kitchen where Alma sat happily munching bread and honey at the table.

Berta saw the expression on her face. "What is it, Giselle?"

"Rolf wrote me a letter." Numbly she handed it to the woman and slipped quietly into a chair. Berta extracted the letter and read silently. She glanced once at Marie and then continued reading.

"Seems a sensible letter to me. It *is* important for the boy to begin to prepare for what will be expected of him . . ." Berta returned the letter to its envelope. "Although I must say it does seem a little cold."

"A little."

Berta gave the letter back to Marie, studying her face. "Are you concerned he no longer loves you?"

"It's not that, Berta." Marie shook her head and struggled to explain her feelings to the woman. "It's just that I've been waiting for a letter from him for so long, and now that it's come I guess I was hoping . . ."

Berta exploded. "You won't even wear his ring! What exactly are you wanting, Giselle? If he had filled his letter with endearments would you have been satisfied? *Why won't you wear his ring?*"

Marie stood and took a deep breath. "You're right, Berta." She forced a smile. "You are always right."

Berta calmed. "I'm sorry I shouted at you. I shouldn't become involved, and I shouldn't judge you." She smiled sadly at Marie. "You're a grown woman—and an intelligent one, or you wouldn't have been selected to spy for the enemy. I cannot tell you what to do." She turned away and busied herself at the sink.

Marie studied Rolf's sister-in-law and realized she had grown close to the woman. *What a strange, twisted world we live in,* she thought, *where enemies become friends and those who are friends kill each other.* She had a fleeting memory of a German officer bending agonizingly over a lifeless form in a frozen, moonlit meadow, before she stepped close to Berta and touched her shoulder gently. "I love you, Berta. And I love Rolf. Please don't ever think I don't." She sighed. "Everything's so confusing . . ."

Berta smiled. "I'm sure he loves you too. Maybe he just doesn't know how to say it."

"You're probably right." Marie kissed the woman on the cheek, surprising her. Then she took the letter and walked out of the kitchen, up the staircase, and to her bedroom, where she opened a drawer and placed the envelope inside. She began to close the drawer and hesitated. In the back of her mind she recalled something Hans had said to her at Rolf's villa in France—something about Rolf's education. She concentrated, her hand resting on the half-closed drawer. She remembered the river and the walk with Hans along its banks. He had told her about Rolf's experiences in America, and had said that he graduated with a degree in law . . . *cum laude!*

She recalled Rolf's letter contained a couple of misspelled words, words he should have been able to spell easily. And someone who graduated at the top of his class from a renowned university and spoke three languages as well as educated natives from any of those countries was not going to write like a peasant. Her heart beat faster as she retrieved his letter and read it again. She had not thought much of the mistakes when she first read it, instead focusing on its disappointing subject matter. Now she read with a critical eye, and with her free hand rummaged blind in the open drawer for a paper and a pencil. She sat on her bed and found only two misspelled words—"give" and "attention"—which she transferred onto the paper. Then she crossed the room to the closet and retrieved her boot with its hidden silk WOK. Rolf had some motivation for returning it to her, and she had always thought the reason was sentimental—a forgiveness of some kind—but now she wondered if his reason might have been more practical than she had originally thought. She returned to her bed with the silk and spread it out on the pillow, ready to give Rolf's letter the attention he desired.

She studied the WOK and then turned back to Rolf's letter. Somewhere in the text he needed to indicate which code key she was to use. There were enough keys on the silk to encode several dozen messages, and there were not enough hours left in her lifetime to try them all. If she used the wrong key she would be working away at deciphering the message until doomsday, never sure if she were using the wrong key or if Rolf had made mistakes in his encryption. But if she knew the correct key she could figure the message out eventually, even if Rolf's coding skills were not necessarily on par with those of his *Funk Horchdienst.*

She scanned the brusque message closely and wrote "Third" from *Third Reich* on her paper next to the two misspelled words. Then her index finger found the third code key on the silk and she began to work. The two misspelled words would be Rolf's transposition keys, and she debated at first whether he expected her to correct the spelling first or use them as they were. She decided to leave them as they were. Then she began the torturous process of numbering her key-phrases, using the third WOK key as her guide and praying she—and Rolf—could remember how to use it properly.

She assigned a number to each letter and encoded a series of numbers using the double-transposition keys on her WOK. Her impatience to discover Rolf's message cramped her hand and she had to pause and massage it while she studied the mess she had made of the paper. Finally she bent again to her task, working backward from number to letter, then from letter to second letter, according to the random design chosen by some bleary-eyed WOK designer at SOE. When the solution made no sense in French, she switched to English, followed the same pattern, and finally wrote the words,

I love you.

Marie held the paper in both hands and stared at the three simple words that meant so much to her. Then, without a word, she broke the string around her neck and slipped the ring onto her finger.

TWENTY-THREE

March 24, 1944

The morning of Friday, March 24, was unbelievably cold. Major Rolf Schulmann stood on the steps of Belley headquarters with two of his aides and watched the group of men in the courtyard. German soldiers and Milice stamped their feet in the pre-dawn darkness and wrung their hands, waiting impatiently for orders. Clouds of steam erupted as they talked with each other, their voices muffled behind gloved hands.

It was impossible to get warm. Rolf's feet felt numb in their heavy woolen socks and black boots. His gloves did little to warm his fingers, and his whole body shivered. It was one of the coldest mornings he could remember. He turned to one of his aides, a young officer of twenty-two. "Tell Monsieur de Lorme to get out here with his men. It's not right for him to be enjoying his coffee by the fire while his men stand freezing in the cold."

"Yes, sir." The officer disappeared up the steps into the château.

Rolf turned to again study the men. They knew little of what would be happening this morning. And when they did find out in a few moments, many of them would be concerned. Others, mainly the Milice, would unfortunately find pleasure in this morning's activities. He looked across the stone wall at the other end of the courtyard and counted the dark shapes of eight trucks: three for his men, three for confiscated goods, and two for Jewish cargo.

Cargo! It was amazing how easy it was to dehumanize a person by referring to him as "cargo." In disgust, Rolf turned his attention back to the men.

They were becoming impatient. Their talk and laughter were becoming more raucous and their complaining more intense. Rolf turned to his other aide.

"Divide them into five groups. I want each group to have a lieutenant in charge and two Milice. Tell each lieutenant to choose one Milice representative to come with him and report to me here."

The aide saluted and headed for the courtyard. The sun would be up in three hours, and Rolf hoped to have the operation completed before it was fully light. He stamped his boots in a futile attempt to return feeling to his feet. Monsieur de Lorme exited the château, his face rosy from a hot breakfast and the heat of the fire. His beard carried several breakfast mishaps, and his eyes showed his displeasure at being forced out into the cold before he was absolutely ready. His fur cap had the ear flaps pulled down over his ears, and his incredibly large paunch was buttoned tightly inside a fur-lined winter coat. He had the impressive appearance of an overstuffed sausage. The director of the Belley Prefect stopped beside Major Schulmann and surveyed the courtyard with distaste. "It seems your men are having a difficult time organizing themselves this morning, Major."

Irritated, Rolf snapped, "They are cold and hungry, and they were waiting for us to organize ourselves, Monsieur de Lorme."

De Lorme mumbled something into his beard and adjusted his hat. He said nothing more but waited for Rolf to tell him what to do.

Rolf watched the organization of the troops in the courtyard: five groups, each with at least four regular troops, an officer, and two Milice. He pulled lists from his coat pocket and turned to de Lorme. "Two of your men will be posted with each of our officers. I want one of your men from each group to be in charge, to work under command of my officer."

"But Major, why *under* your officer? Why not at the same level? They could each have equal say in—"

"Monsieur de Lorme, I do not know where you were in June of 1940, but I seem to recall that your government surrendered to mine. I do not remember the Führer declaring this country—or my *district,* for that matter—a democracy."

"But, sir, you have been quite congenial with us up until now . . ."

Rolf snapped, "I'm not in the mood this morning to be 'congenial.'"

The second aide returned to Rolf's side. "Groups are assembled, Major Schulmann."

"Have one Milice and each officer report to me."

Rolf watched as the officers assembled on the steps below him. They were all young—younger than he—and most were inexperienced. In a way, Rolf felt he had done them a disfavor; their military service with him up until now had been relatively easy—comparatively trouble-free. They were assigned to an area of France with reasonably few problems. His men had been told to be polite to the citizens in his jurisdiction and to treat them with respect. Someday, likely as soon as these officers were transferred, they would have a rude awakening to the realities of war—and to what was often expected of a Nazi officer.

Today was going to be that someday. Klaus Barbie had officially organized the *rafle* system for southern France, and this morning these young, inexperienced officers would get a taste of Hitler's Final Solution.

"Gather 'round, please."

Five officers and five *Milice* huddled near, blowing on their frozen fingers and stamping their cold feet, anxious to receive their orders. Rolf turned to Monsieur de Lorme and indicated the five *Milice* in the group.

"Are these men agreeable, monsieur?"

De Lorme nodded impatiently and indicated with a wave of his hand for the major to continue. Rolf turned back to the ten men. "First, we will establish seniority in your groups. My officers will be in command. Members of the Milice will be second in command. Final say lies with my officers." There was a grumble or two from the Frenchmen, but Rolf continued unperturbed and showed them the lists. "We are privileged—according to Section Four—to take part in this *rafle*. Each group will receive a list of three families, or a group of individuals, for which they are responsible. You are to knock on the door of each home, and when they answer you are to swiftly enter their homes and detain all you find there—men, women, and children. You are to confirm their names on these lists and load them into the provided trucks. Do not enter the home until the truck reaches your vicinity. I have numbered your lists based upon the routes of the trucks. Make sure you keep on schedule, or you'll be hiking home with your prisoners.

"After you detain your prisoners, you are to gather everything of value from the home—furniture, silverware, bedding, clothes, jewelry, money—and load it onto the next truck, provided for that purpose."

Rolf handed the lists to one of his aides, and the man began to distribute them among the officers. There was a murmur of voices as names were read and families recognized. Rolf gave them a few moments to familiarize themselves with the names and addresses and then continued. "Undoubtedly, problems will arise. Many will refuse to go. You might be threatened with weapons. But I must insist that there be no killings. These are *detainees*—not criminals. I repeat: No killing."

A lieutenant spoke up. "What if they refuse to go peacefully?"

"I will be supervising the operation with my aides. I should be close to wherever you are. Send a member of your group to find me and I will talk to them. Perhaps I will be able to convince them to comply. If not, I will authorize the use of force."

"Yes, sir."

Rolf surveyed the group. "Are there any other questions?"

No one spoke.

"You are not to keep any of the possessions you find. That is called looting, and you will be severely disciplined. We hand over everything to Section Four, as ordered.

"If a home is empty, check the surrounding homes and grounds. Perhaps the family has been forewarned and is hiding somewhere nearby. More soldiers are at your disposal if a search is necessary."

Major Schulmann stopped and studied the faces of the ten men. "You are cold. I know that. Get your task done as quickly as possible and there will be a hot breakfast waiting for you when you return."

There was a murmur of approval and several grateful looks in his direction.

"That is all. Return to your men and find your assigned trucks. Let's get this job done." The men turned and descended the steps, rejoining their groups and migrating in the direction of the trucks.

Rolf felt a nudge at his elbow and turned to see Monsieur de Lorme shivering beside him. "They're gone. Can we go back inside now?"

"You may go. My driver should be here any moment, so I will stay here."

De Lorme turned and scurried up the stairs like a very large, furry rat.

* * *

Rolf's driver turned down another street and pulled forward slowly. Rolf caught a rapid movement in the darkness, coming from a street to his left. "Any activity in that neighborhood?" he asked.

One of his aides shuffled quickly through the list. "Yes, sir—Lieutenant Meer's area."

"Stop the car."

Schulmann's driver applied the brake, and the Citroën ground to a halt. Rolf and his aides exited the vehicle and watched as a soldier approached them at a run. He stopped in front of Rolf, breathing heavily. "Major Schulmann, sir . . ." The boy gasped for breath. "Lieutenant Meer requests your assistance with one of the families on the list."

Rolf felt a knot forming in the pit of his stomach. "Problems?"

"Yes, sir."

"Come with us in the car. Tell me on the way." They climbed into the Citroën, and Rolf ordered the driver to follow the soldier's directions. Rolf turned to look back at the soldier in the back seat.

"Tell me what's going on."

"Well, sir, this family . . . well . . . they're shooting at us, sir."

"Shooting at you?"

"Yes, sir."

"Anybody hurt?"

"No, sir—we moved back and I came to find you."

"Good. Which family is it?"

"Monsieur Gustav Stern. He fled Germany in '39 with his wife and three children."

"I see."

"We're almost there, sir. Do you want us to park away from the house—since he's shooting at us?"

"I'm sure that would be wise, since he's shooting."

"Yes, sir."

The car pulled to a stop underneath the hanging branches of a tree. Major Schulmann exited, along with the soldier and his aides. Rolf told his aides to stay at the car and gestured for the young soldier to follow him.

Lieutenant Meer joined them. "The man has himself barricaded inside his home, sir. His wife and children are in there with him. He keeps insisting he'll shoot the first man to step onto his property."

"Thank you, lieutenant. Where are your men?"

"Surrounding the property, sir. Waiting for your orders to go in."

"Is he heavily armed?"

"I don't know, sir. He claims to have quite a few guns."

"Is that the house?" Rolf pointed toward a small cottage a few doors down the street. The windows were dark. Curiosity had brightened the windows of several other homes, the light visible in slivers beneath blackout shades.

"Yes, sir."

"I'm going to talk to him."

The lieutenant shook his head. "He'll shoot you, Major. He's already shot at several of my men—and they were nowhere near his property."

"All right. I want you to tell your men to gather back here—away from the house. Do not let him see you moving in the darkness. He'll think you're planning something—and then I *will* get shot."

"Yes, sir."

Rolf took a deep breath and walked down the middle of the street toward the house. As he approached the house he heard a shout from inside one of the darkened windows. A shot rang out, the bullet whistling somewhere over his head. Screams from inside the house followed the shot, and a woman's voice begged her husband to put down his gun. The man shouted again. "Who's there? Stay away! I already told ya I'd shoot!"

"Gustav—it's Major Schulmann. Remember, we spoke last week in your café."

There was no response.

"I need to talk to you."

"Major Schulmann?"

"That's right."

"You got a weapon?"

"Only my sidearm."

There was a pause. Rolf could hear a child crying inside. His heart beat so loudly he almost imagined Gustav could hear it, too. Then Gustav spoke. "Throw it down."

"What good would that do, Gustav? I have seven armed men outside your house."

"Throw it down 'n' I'll talk—but only to you. You tell all those other *boches* to stay back."

"All right." Rolf removed the Luger from its holster and dropped it at his feet. It thudded heavily against the gravel of the road. "Now may I come in, Gustav?"

There was a long pause. Even the child had stopped crying. It was as if all in the house held their breath to see what Gustav decided.

After a heavy silence Rolf heard a latch being drawn back, and the front door opened a few inches. He hesitated a moment and then walked through a small picket gate, up a cobblestone path, and through the front door. The room was in darkness. Rolf could barely make out the shapes of furniture and a small table. At the far end of the room, standing in a corner, was Gustav. His dark form was all Rolf could see, and the form was pointing a rifle at Rolf.

"Put down the gun, Gustav."

Gustav hesitated and then laid the gun next to him on the table.

"I'll put it down for *you,* Major—but just 'cause of what you did for my li'l girl."

"How is she?"

"Better. She woulda died. There's no way I coulda paid for—"

"Never mind that, Gustav. I'm here to see how much time you need to get your family ready to go."

"No way I'm goin' back. You got no right—"

"Gustav, you have no choice."

"Major Schulmann, I got a bad feeling 'bout this relocation business. I think if we go, my family'll be taken away from me."

Rolf nodded. "That is possible. That is why I need you to listen closely. Are you listening?"

"Yes, sir."

"I am going to walk out of this house with every one of your guns. Then I'm going to take all of my men—*all of them*—and go on to the next name on our list. Are you listening?"

"I got only this one gun. I'm almost outta bullets, too."

"That's fine. Now pay attention. I will walk out of this house with that one gun. We will leave. In twenty minutes we will be back. Twenty minutes. Do you understand?"

Gustav stood speechless in the corner. Rolf moved a step closer. "Twenty minutes. That's how much time I can give you to make any—arrangements."

Gustav shifted his position and gave a little gasp. Monsieur Stern was not the brightest of men, but Rolf could see he was beginning to understand. Silently, Rolf prayed for guidance. "When we return—in *twenty minutes*—you and your family will have to come with us. Do you understand, Gustav?"

"I understand." The man sounded like he was about to cry.

"All right. Hand me your gun."

Gustav picked up the weapon, turned it around, and obediently handed it to Rolf, stock first. Rolf secured it under his arm. "If there are any more shots fired from this house we will have to kill you. I cannot allow my men to be harmed. Please don't shoot anymore."

"I just gave you my only weapon."

"Very well. I'm leaving now. Please have your family ready in twenty minutes."

"Yes, sir."

Rolf turned to leave.

"Major Schulmann?"

"What is it, Gustav?"

"God bless you."

Rolf walked out of the house and across the street. Lieutenant Meer waited nervously next to Rolf's car, his six men milling about behind him.

"What are your orders, Major?"

"What number is this family on your list?"

"Two."

"I promised Gustav if he gave me his weapon I'd give him twenty minutes to get his family ready. Take your men and go to the next address."

"I'll leave a couple of my men . . ."

"No need. All of you will go."

Meer looked confused. "Won't that give him a chance to—"

"I said you'll *all* go." Irritated, Rolf turned on the young lieutenant. "Question my orders again and you'll get guard duty for a month."

"Yes, sir."

"Did you deliver the first family to the trucks?"

"No, sir." Lieutenant Meer shifted uncomfortably. "There was no one there."

* * *

Lieutenant Meer found no one at the third address on his list. He ordered his men to search the surrounding houses and the field behind. They found nothing. Lieutenant Meer and his soldiers loaded everything of value from the house onto the truck and returned to Gustav's residence.

It was deserted. Lieutenant Meer stood in the front yard of the cottage and watched while his men ransacked the place and searched the fields behind the house. He lit a cigarette and leaned against the small gate, studying the front door thoughtfully.

* * *

Rolf paused his dictation and turned away from his secretary. The young aide handed him the list.

"Are all the groups back?"

"Yes, sir."

"How many detainees?"

"Not one, sir."

"*None?* Out of forty-seven?"

"None."

"Have the officers report to me immediately. And tell the soldiers breakfast is ready." Rolf nodded his dismissal to his aide and the secretary, and the young man and the woman exited his office. Rolf sat behind his desk and dropped his face into his hands.

He realized he was trembling. "Heavenly Father, I've put myself and my loved ones in danger. I'm grateful for your help this morning—but I'm concerned about the effect my actions will have on my son . . . and everyone else I love. Please protect me. Please help my family to be safe—somehow . . ."

TWENTY-FOUR

March 25, 1944

Captain Bernard Dresdner of the Section Four Gestapo, his face mottled with rage, stormed down the hallway of Gestapo headquarters in Lyon and entered the office of his superior, Major Albert Nieman. His secretary looked up in alarm as Dresdner approached her desk at a frightening speed. "I must speak with the major."

"But sir, he is on the phone with the *Obersturmführer*. You will have to w—"

"Get him for me. Immediately." Dresdner slammed his hand palm down on the desk, his dead gray eye inches from the woman's face. Terrified, she leaped to her feet and scurried like a frightened squirrel to the major's inner office.

Dresdner paced several times about the perimeter of the room, fuming and swearing, before the secretary returned. "The major will see you now." She shrunk from the captain as he passed her, his face only a few shades closer to its normal hue.

Major Nieman was hanging up the receiver of his phone and seemed neither pleased nor surprised to see Dresdner. "What is it now, Captain? You interrupted an important call. An emergency, my secretary said—"

"More than an emergency. A disaster!" Dresdner approached the major's desk and leaned into it, his hands tightening into fists. "Remember, at the New Year's party I warned you this would happen."

"What would happen?"

"Insurrection! Treason! Just like Bordeaux—the train will have to be cancelled."

Major Nieman leaned back in his chair, lacing his fingers calmly across his middle. "The train has not been cancelled—only postponed a few weeks. I had a chat with Major Schulmann this morning, immediately after I received his report. He explained the situation to me—quite calmly and professionally, I might add." Nieman glanced distastefully at Dresdner's red face and turned to select a document from his desk. "I have his report here. Barbie has read it and he feels the same way I do—that we need to give the major another opportunity. This time we will allow him to compile his own lists."

"What excuse could he possibly have for such a disastrous failure? How could forty-seven Jews out of forty-seven be unavailable?"

"His reasons are actually plausible, Captain. Most of the registrations were outdated. Some by as little as a year—others by as much as ten. These people could have moved out of his *département* years ago. For the next *rafle* he will have a completely updated list—because he will compile it himself."

"You said he had more than one reason."

"Ah, yes." Major Nieman chuckled. "Actually, the other reason is rather embarrassing to Section Four. It was *our* mistake."

"What's that?"

"Major Schulmann informed us the *rafle* we ordered took place in the middle of spring holidays. Many of the families had school-aged children, and at least half of those would have been vacationing at that time anyway, regardless of whether the registrations were up-to-date."

"That can't be correct. It seems a little early . . ."

"That's what I thought. But Major Schulmann gave me the name of the minister of schools in Belley—a Monsieur Jacques Bellamont. I called him, and he confirmed that it was indeed their holiday season."

"I refuse to believe it. Major Schulmann has found a way to trick you—to deceive the whole section. I told you his religious beliefs would keep him from—"

"Captain Dresdner, let me make one thing clear." Major Nieman pushed himself out of his chair and walked around his desk. "Major Schulmann's religious beliefs, although curious, make him an honorable man. I respect the major. I do not, regrettably, hold you in such high regard." The major moved to the door and opened it. "After this, when my secretary says I am busy, it means I am busy. Do not storm into my office again. You are dismissed."

Dresdner stood dumbfounded, trying to think of something to say. Angrily, he saluted his superior officer and exited the room.

* * *

Captain Dresdner sat behind his desk, drumming his pen incessantly against its smooth surface. He had a difficult time remaining still and jumped to his feet to pace the room. His bad eye was bothering him—it seemed every time things did not go as planned, his eye hurt. He cursed his father for the millionth time and tried not to think of that drunkard's fist hitting him over and over . . .

Something had to be done. Major Schulmann had them all deceived. Only Dresdner knew who he really was, and what he was capable of doing. Schulmann's list of offenses continued to grow, Dresdner thought, and he seemed to be the only person astute enough to see it. Helping an American agent escape and assaulting an officer of the Third Reich, hiding the girl, lying to his superiors, withholding information . . . Dresdner mentally added the latest and worst deceit to his list: refusing to fulfill his Jewish quota and cooperate with the Führer's Final Solution.

Captain Dresdner was tired of waiting for permission to act. He had a feeling that if he did not resolve the situation now, it would be too late. Dresdner's future was at stake, and he had to convince his superiors that the future of the Führer's Reich was endangered as well. It was time to get the evidence he needed. Opening the door to his office, he called to his secretary. "Helga, get Kuester and Siegfried for me. Tell them to meet me in my office in five minutes."

TWENTY-FIVE

March 26, 1944

Because of his successes in Berlin and Amsterdam, *Obersturmführer* Klaus Barbie was transferred in 1943 to southern France to find and annihilate Résistance cells in Lyon and the Rhône-Alpes. The mountainous region east of Lyon acted as a natural hiding ground for Maquis guerillas, and from there the *maquisards* staged massive resistance to the *boches'* occupation.

On March 26, a military convoy under the command of Major Rolf Schulmann left Belley and headed toward Lyon. From the back seat of his staff car, Rolf turned to study the three trucks behind him. The first carried a contingent of his soldiers, and the second was filled with Maquis prisoners from the raid three days before. The final truck was filled with munitions, supplies, and surplus from his warehouse purportedly for transfer to Lyon. It looked like a typical transfer of prisoners, like those carried out at least once a month from his district. No one would blink an eye.

Snow had ceased to fall, making the transport easier both for himself and for his troops. Rolf knew the prisoners must be suffering in the cold truck, but there was nothing he could do about it. Not now, anyway. He turned to face forward again and thought about what lay ahead.

They still needed to pass the first checkpoint, and Rolf was beginning to feel impatient for this unpleasant business to be over. He shifted in his seat and thought about the raid. It had been a complete surprise, netting ninety percent of the known Résistance and Maquis leaders in his *département* in one fell swoop. He credited Trotter for his ingenuity, and he made a mental note to have the man transferred away from his district as soon as possible. Transferred far away—it would be no good to have Trotter bumping into Jacques still running free and deciding to go to the Gestapo. No, Trotter's invaluable services would be needed immediately elsewhere—

with a large cash reward and the profound gratitude of the Führer, of course.

Major Schulmann saluted the checkpoint guard, who recognized him and saluted smartly back. The German private waved the convoy through without the mandatory document check. There were advantages to being a dreaded Nazi officer, Rolf thought wryly. He settled back in the leather of his seat and checked his watch. A quarter to nine. The mail truck would be through at exactly ten thirty, carrying his troops' mail: letters from sweethearts, mothers, grandmothers, and sisters—practically all the living family these unfortunate boys had left in their German homeland. The letters would tell them to follow their leaders, not question orders, and make it home as safely and as soon as they could. Their willingness to follow this excellent counsel was about to be tested. He pounded the back of the driver's seat and ordered him to pick up the pace.

At nine fifteen the convoy left the main road and followed a slightly more rural route, backtracking to the northeast. They would pass through the Rhône-Alpes region where Lieutenant Hans Brenner had been stationed before Rolf ordered his transfer to the training grounds of the Schwarzwald. *God bless that man*, Rolf mused. He'd saved Rolf's life and reputation more than once in this dirty business. Didn't matter that Hans thought Rolf an imbecile for joining the Mormon Church—he was the best friend anybody could have, criticisms and all. Rolf couldn't resist smiling at Hans's reaction to Rolf's newfound belief: "Listen, friend. Don't tell me about angels, gold plates, and boy prophets. I have my own religion: I believe in angels that keep me warm, gold I can spend, and boys I can beat into soldiers. That's enough religion for me."

Rolf thought about the last time he had seen Hans—at Christmas in Schönenberg, skating on the lake and touting his signature ear-to-ear grin. Rolf thought about that day with his son—and Marie. He thought about the stolen kiss and the surprise with which she'd stared up at him afterward, her soft brown eyes big and round and . . . fearful. He shifted uneasily in his seat and glanced out at the snowy landscape. What he wouldn't do to erase that fear from her eyes—to be able to replace it with . . . with something else.

"Will this do, Major?"

The driver's words brought Rolf's thoughts back to the present. All around them pine, oak, sycamore, and maple trees rose steeply, blanketed in thick layers of snow that would disguise them until late spring. In other, happier circumstances, this mountain meadow might be peaceful and serene—a place not unlike the Black Forest meadows Rolf's father used to take him to for their hunting trips. But there was nothing beautiful about what had to be done this morning. He surveyed the scenery outside his window and grunted his affirmation. "Stop here. We'll just be a minute."

The driver nodded and carefully tapped the brakes. Gingerly the vehicle slowed and inched toward the edge of the icy road. Behind them Rolf heard the downshifting of gears as the trucks tried not to slide into each others' backsides. Rolf's driver exited the vehicle and came around to open the door for the major. The man's expression was closed, professional. Rolf knew he did not like this business any more than he, but the driver knew to keep silent. A mass execution was not an everyday occurrence—but neither was it unheard of. And a group of cutthroats like they had in the truck back there would definitely be considered a candidate for such a maneuver. Approve or not, the driver kept silent and did his job like a good Nazi.

Rolf's inexperienced young soldiers would also do their job. This morning's events would be forever imprinted on the minds of every one of these boys, and whatever they did for the remainder of the war, they would revisit this experience constantly in their minds. Of that Rolf was certain.

The major watched soberly as his soldiers pulled the prisoners from the back of the truck. With shouts of *"Schnell! Schnell!"* Prisoners were thrown bodily into the snow. Some slipped on the icy road and fell on their backs, grunting and struggling to rise. Rolf felt momentary pity for them, but he pushed it aside. This business would be over soon enough and the prisoners would no longer have to suffer. Rolf walked toward the shackled Résistance fighters, his shiny boots sinking deep into the snow. The prisoners stood huddled in an awkward circle, their eyes on the tall, impeccably dressed Nazi major coming toward them. He circled them silently, face devoid of emotion as he studied their shivering forms. Many stared back, some defiant, some pleading. He knew they understood what they were facing here in this remote meadow. Rolf spoke calmly to his soldiers. "Take them to the other side of the clearing and move them into position." His boys immediately sprang to action, using their rifles to prod the prisoners into a line and ordering them to march. The snow was so deep they could not lift their feet free of its grasp, so the unfortunate prisoners at the front of the line had to break a trail for their companions. Three soldiers unloaded a large machine gun and bipod and followed the line of prisoners and soldiers, holding the weapon high over their shoulders as they negotiated the path cut by the group through the snow.

Major Schulmann followed with two more soldiers, leaving the driver and three soldiers to guard the supply trucks. Rolf stepped gingerly around puddles wherever he could and sank to his ankles wherever the men's footprints hit water runoff from the surrounding mountains. The snow deepened to near knee-height at the center of the clearing, and then lessened again as the ground began to slope upward toward the far tree line. They would need a place with firm soil to set up the gun, and Rolf wondered for a moment whether they would be able to find one. He had not been prepared for this much snow—but perhaps it could work to their advantage.

"Halt!" The prisoners had reached the opposite tree line, their boots sinking only a few inches into the snow. This would have to do. Rolf gave the order, and the soldiers in front of him began to assemble the machine gun, securing the bipod and feeding a disintegrating metal-link belt containing two hundred fifty rounds into the carbine.

"Line up the prisoners parallel with the tree line." His troops hastened to obey. Rolf could see that a few of his young *grenadiers* were beginning to turn green. Perhaps it had finally dawned on them what was happening, and he felt sorry for them and wished he could change the situation.

One of the prisoners hissed loudly in his direction. "You'll rot in hell, Nazi!" Another began to pray, moaning piteously under his breath.

"The gun is ready, sir."

"Very good. Wait for my command."

Rolf studied the prisoners in front of him. Half of them were already resigned to death, huddling together against the cold, and the other half strained uselessly at their bonds, ready to kill him with their bare hands.

"Courrez. Run."

His order carried sharply in the cold air. Surprised, no one moved. Both the prisoners and those of his soldiers who understood French or English stared at him as if he had ordered them to dance a jig.

He repeated the command in German, this time with more urgency. *"Lauft! Schnell!"* Still not one prisoner moved. He heard one whisper to another, "He wants to make it look like an escape—not an execution."

Swiftly Major Schulmann unholstered his Luger and pointed it deliberately at the center of the speaker's forehead. Terrified, the man's eyes locked with his, and Rolf said, "If you value your life, *run.*"

Without another word the man turned and plunged awkwardly through the snow for the tree line. After a bewildered second his companions followed, their arms still shackled behind their backs and panic in their eyes—but the panic was mixed with the hope that they might actually be granted the luck to outrun the bullets of an MG 34. Major Schulmann watched their frightened, headlong dash for the trees, his face emotionless.

After ten seconds he gave his order. "Open fire."

Immediately the clearing erupted with the sound of machine-gun fire. It echoed off the surrounding mountains and the din was deafening. Major Schulmann watched gravely as the fleeing prisoners stumbled toward the tree line, struggling to keep their feet under them on the snowy hillside. The machine gun continued to stutter as the handcuffed prisoners ran in a panicked, headlong dash for the trees. No one fell. Within a matter of seconds not one prisoner remained in the clearing.

The huge gun fell silent. Major Schulmann glared down accusingly at the gunner, who looked back at him, terrified. The boy seemed ready to cry. "I . . . I . . . I'm so—"

"What happened, soldier?"

The boy gulped, his eyes bulging from their sockets. "I . . . I don't know, sir! I opened fire—just as you said . . ."

Rolf glowered at him. "Looks like we'll have to work on your marksmanship, young man." He turned and strolled back across the clearing.

* * *

Rolf reached the edge of the clearing in time to see the truck carrying ammunition and supplies moving rapidly away from the line of vehicles, its gears grinding angrily and its wheels spinning in the snow. Rolf picked up his pace, while behind him his bewildered soldiers made their way as quickly as they could through the quagmire of the snow-covered meadow.

Rolf's driver ran toward them, his face ashen.

"What happened?" Rolf asked the driver. He looked around at the remaining trucks. "Where are the three soldiers I left to guard the convoy?"

"I—I think they were taken prisoner, sir."

"By whom, Lieutenant?"

"Maquis!" The driver pointed down the road. "They arrived soon after shots were fired, sir—and they forced the watch at gunpoint and stole the truck . . ."

"Maquis?"

The driver nodded. "Who else could it be? We're in their territory. They probably saw us arrive and decided to ambush us for the supplies."

Rolf studied the meadow thoughtfully. "We need to find our men and get that truck back." Rolf ordered his men into the two remaining trucks, and they followed the road taken by the supply truck.

Three kilometers farther they found the three missing soldiers, roped together at the side of the road and shivering with no coats and no boots. Rolf jumped out of the truck and approached them. The three men tried to struggle to their feet. Except for their shackles and missing clothing, they were in good shape.

One of them spoke. "Maquis, sir! They took the truck and supplies. They forced us to come with them . . ."

"Yes, we know."

"One of them told me to give you a message."

"A message? What message?"

"He said to tell you you're as crazy as the other one."

* * *

Rolf Schulmann sent Marie several more letters—each one detailing how he wanted his son educated, insisting she prepare Alma for his glorious future as a member of the Hitler Youth organization and espousing the virtues of loyalty to the Führer and dedication to the Fatherland.

And he persisted in misspelling words. Berta commented on his mistakes once and surmised that Rolf was under a lot of pressure and could use a holiday with his son. "Then you'll see," she said, patting Marie's shoulder. "He really does love you—this war is just wearing him down."

"You are wise, Berta. Thank you."

Rolf never forgot to tell her he loved her, and Marie worried at times that parts of his letters might begin to look familiar to whoever was reading his mail. Over a series of several letters he also warned her that things were getting difficult and that he might soon be in trouble. He promised to warn her if she needed to take Alma and disappear, saying she should contact Hans in town if she needed to leave immediately. One weekend when Hans arrived to collect one of her guards for an evening of revelry, he leaned close and confirmed his assistance if she ever needed his help. She hoped it would never come to that.

TWENTY-SIX

March 27, 1944

Major Rolf Schulmann stood just outside the heavy cell door, looking through the barred window at the form stretched on the bare mattress. One leg lay encased in a mammoth cast and the other contorted periodically at the knee. The man was obviously in a great deal of pain. "How is he?" Rolf glanced at the medical officer beside him.

The Nazi surgeon shook his head. "His leg will be fine. It's his head that poses the greatest risk."

"To himself? Has he attempted suicide?"

"Nothing like that." The heavy-set doctor glanced through the window at the patient. "He hates Germans, Major—and keeps describing what he would do to them if he could get out of here."

"Is he dangerous? In his present condition?"

"Only if someone leaves a weapon within his reach."

Rolf turned again to watch the prisoner. "How long?"

"Until he can be safely transferred?" The doctor shrugged. "Two, maybe three weeks."

"We need to transfer him tomorrow."

The doctor stared at him. "I'm sure you have your reasons, Major. It's just that—"

"Tomorrow." Rolf turned the key and entered the cell. The wounded pilot looked up as he entered, and there was no mistaking the hostility in his pain-filled eyes.

"What is your name, pilot?"

"Andrews. What's yours?"

Rolf sat on the edge of a chair and faced the wounded man. "My name is Rolf Schulmann. I'm a major in the Allgemeine SS. For purposes of your confinement I will need to know your rank."

"What's my rank got to do with anything?"

"Prisoners who are officers receive deferential treatment, Mr. Andrews."

The pilot smiled. "I'm a captain."

"Where are you from, Captain?"

"I should think it obvious, Major. England."

"I meant, from what part?"

Andrews pulled himself up to rest on one elbow. "Dover. East cliff. You ever been there?"

"No. I've not had that pleasure. But seven years ago I passed through Deal, just along the coast from Dover. I did see the cliffs. Kept back from the edge, though. It's a bit nerve-wracking, don't you agree?"

The captain nodded. "Been known to drop chunks into the channel without first asking a bloke's permission. Wouldn't want to be taking a gander over the edge when she does that." He leaned back, a faraway look of pleasure in his eyes. "But the view is unparalleled. My brother and I spent many a grand summer day traipsing along the edge . . . Did you know that on a clear day you can see the coast of France? Used to explore from Dover Castle all the way to the Western Heights. Ever heard Vera Lynn singing 'The White Cliffs of Dover'?"

Rolf nodded. "Nobody sings it better. Does your family still live there?"

"Been there for generations. Be there for generations more if I have any say . . ." He broke off and looked up awkwardly at Schulmann as if he had just remembered to whom he was speaking. He cleared his throat and dropped back to the mattress. "You really had me going there, Major. I guess I may never see those cliffs again."

Rolf shrugged. "There's always a possibility. But you were detained in German territory and will have to serve your time as a prisoner of war."

"No chance of clemency, eh, Major? No special consideration for a wounded man? I've got a sweetheart at home, praying I'll be home before too long . . ."

Rolf folded his arms and studied the captain. "Why should I be lenient with you? What makes you think you deserve special consideration? We all have wives, families, sweethearts. Every German pilot you shot down has someone at home weeping for him. Our hospitals are full of your 'clemency' and your 'special consideration' for *our* people. If I allow you to return to England you'll be back on one of the next planes to Germany, dropping your bombs on the homes of my friends, my family, my people."

The captain scowled. "Well, now, Major. You've made a fine show of good will, pasting me back together and buttering me up like you have. You almost had me convinced that you were human."

"I've done what my conscience required."

Andrews swore. "You're nothing more than a bloodsucking *Kraut*. As far as I'm concerned, you and your people have caused more pain and suffering in this war than we British could ever repay. And you're wrong, Major."

"About what?"

"You said I'd be on *one* of the next planes to Germany. But I won't—I'll be on the very first."

* * *

No snow had fallen since the morning before, and the clearing, although in shadow because of steep mountains on either side, was beginning to thaw. Captain Bernard Dresdner, always proud of his foresight, had provided thick winter boots for himself and the young German soldier at his side. Now as they followed the trail of footprints left by yesterday's line of prisoners, Dresdner studied his surroundings carefully.

"What a beautiful place. Don't you agree?"

His companion mumbled something as he struggled to keep his footing in the muddy snow.

Dresdner indicated the steep mountains around them. "My father used to take me hunting in mountains such as these. Did your father take you hunting as a boy?"

"Often, sir."

Captain Dresdner smiled at the young soldier. "You're doing the right thing, you know."

Private Theo Fleischer looked confused. "What do you mean, sir?"

"I mean you were correct to come to me with this information. If there's a problem with Major Schulmann's weapons it's a dangerous situation for you and your fellow soldiers." Dresdner shrugged helplessly. "Yesterday you were only shooting escaping prisoners. What if you had been facing a charging enemy and your life depended upon the proper function of your weapon?"

The boy went white. He got the picture.

"Think of the good you're doing! You're saving lives. The Third Reich needs soldiers like you." Dresdner could see the soldier was pleased. He continued. "You told me you were assigned to man the machine gun for the operation. Is that correct?"

Theo nodded.

"Did you see anything unusual about the weapon as you and your comrades assembled it and made ready to follow the major's orders?"

"No, sir. It was not the newest model, but the gun went together perfectly, the same as in all our drills. It seemed to function properly."

"And you said not one prisoner was injured?"

"Not one, as far as I could tell."

"What do you mean, as far as you could tell?"

"Well, sir, some of the prisoners stumbled when I began shooting, but they got up again and continued into the trees. There." Theo pointed slightly to their left. "Over there." Captain Dresdner looked where the boy pointed. The tree line was thick with underbrush. An army could hide there, he thought—or a Maquis rescue party, if they knew in advance where their comrades would be released.

"And this is the spot where you and your companions assembled the gun?"

"Yes, sir."

Dresdner studied the ground around them. The indentations from the base of the machine gun's bipod remained visible in the soft ground and were filled with dirty water, and bullet casings lay everywhere. He bent and picked up two.

"Who fed the belt into the machine, soldier?"

"My friend Gerrold. He's new in the army, reassigned from his Hitler Youth regiment. I know he wouldn't have done anything—"

"Of course not. Don't worry, soldier. You and your friend are not being charged with any crime. It's not your fault the major's weapon malfunctioned."

". . . and Major Schulmann—he was really decent about it, sir. He didn't yell at me or threaten to have me reassigned or anything. He just said I had to work on my marksmanship."

"I see. And do you?"

"Need to work on my marksmanship? I didn't think so, sir. I was always top of my Hitler Youth group back home. My friends used to tease me that I could shoot a flea off a mutt's ear."

Dresdner laughed appreciatively. He worked the shell casings in circles around each other in his hand, his mind occupied with yesterday's catastrophe, for that was how Klaus Barbie would see it—a catastrophe. Perhaps with this boy's help Dresdner could also unveil the treason behind the catastrophe.

"Do you like your assignment to Major Schulmann's district?"

"Yes, sir."

"What do you like best about it?"

"He treats us with respect. He feeds us well. He makes sure we get our letters from home and copies of *Das Schwarze Korps* to read. He makes us be polite to the locals."

"That's good. You must be a very responsible soldier."

"I try to be, sir."

"What would you do if Major Schulmann ordered you to do something wrong?"

"Wrong? He would never do that."

"Of course not. But what if he ordered you to do something that was against what you had been taught in your Hitler Youth group?"

"I was taught to always do what I'm told, sir. By my commanding officer, that is."

Dresdner shifted to his other foot and tried a new tactic. "Let me give you a scenario: Suppose you arrested a murderer—one who had murdered your best friend, or maybe even a family member. You brought him to your commanding officer, and your commanding officer ordered you to let him go."

Theo's brow wrinkled as he contemplated the situation.

Dresdner watched the boy closely. "What would you do?"

"I wouldn't think it was right, sir. I'd be angry."

"But what would you do?"

"Like I said, sir, I do what I'm told."

"Whether or not you like it?"

"That's right."

"Did Major Schulmann order you to shoot over the heads of the escaping prisoners, Private Fleischer?"

Shocked, Theo jerked his head up and stared at the Gestapo captain. "No, sir! He told me to open fire. That's all."

"Good for you, son." Captain Dresdner clapped him on the shoulder and gave him a reassuring smile. "Then it's obviously the gun that malfunctioned."

Dresdner slipped the shells into his pocket and gestured to the boy. "Come. You've been more than helpful. Let's get you back to your unit."

TWENTY-SEVEN

Monday, April 3, 1944

Klaus Barbie, *obersturmführer* and director of Section Four Gestapo assigned to southern France, sat down to his dinner at the *École de Santé* in Lyon. He stared thoughtfully at his wine glass, his brown eyes focusing through the amber liquid at some spot far away, and his mind on plans for the near future. He often took his meal in the privacy of his office—one of the benefits of being in command—because the next few weeks were going to be complicated, and he needed to have time to think and to plan. The operation in Saint-Claude was going to take all his time and energy. He knew the Maquis would be crippled if he could flush them swiftly from their hideouts in the Rhône-Alpes. Of course, the success of Operation *Frühling*—Operation Spring—depended upon complete secrecy. Another reason he liked to be alone. No need telling his officers until everything was planned and all the details had been worked out.

He was a social creature, so he usually only insisted on privacy when he had an operation to think over. He respected and needed the opinions of his officers—most of the time. This was not one of those times. At least not yet.

The Maquis had become a threat. Allies dropped supplies to them on a regular basis in the mountain clearings, and even though the supplies were often intercepted by Barbie's troops, enough slipped by to be a concern. Although Hitler's Final Solution still held highest priority, Klaus Barbie knew the Maquis had to be dealt with swiftly and effectively. It was becoming more and more difficult to get a train through to Poland without multiple acts of sabotage to the lines, and continuously re-routing trains was becoming a logistical nightmare. Not only were the *maquisards* sabotaging the railroad tracks, but they boldly attacked German outposts and checkpoints, stole supplies, and even impersonated German officers. It seemed the rumors of invasion had energized their ranks and given them courage. They continued to infest the Rhône-Alpes, growing in numbers daily. Soon the only way to rout them would be to burn the villages that aided them. Guerilla warfare was not Barbie's strength, and he was not about to send his troops to be slaughtered in their mountain hideaways—at least not yet. He had to crush them now before the Maquis spiraled completely out of control.

There was a hesitant knock on his door and his aide peeked around the doorframe. "Sorry to disturb you, sir—there is a Captain Bernard Dresdner here to see you."

"Dresdner?" He wrinkled his forehead in distaste. "I'm busy. He will have to come back later."

His aide cleared his throat nervously. "He said you would want to hear what he has to say."

Irritated, Barbie laid down his napkin. "Tell him to be quick."

"Yes, sir." The aide withdrew his head and opened the door. Captain Dresdner entered in full uniform and saluted the *obersturmführer,* clicking his heels smartly.

Barbie was unimpressed. "I'm busy, Captain. What is it?"

Dresdner approached the desk, reached across, and deposited two shell casings next to Barbie's wine glass. Barbie looked at them in disgust and then up at the captain. He made no move to touch them. "What is this?"

"Blanks, sir. These shell casings were blanks."

"And why are they lying next to my dinner?"

"Do you remember the Rhône-Alpes incident last week, sir?"

"I don't have time for guessing games, Captain."

"Major Rolf Schulmann. Belley *département.* The Maquis attacked and stole a supply truck, and all the prisoners escaped."

"Ah, yes." Barbie nodded and reached for the casings.

Dresdner explained, "These are from the site of the escape."

Barbie silently studied the casings in his hand.

"There were many more like these. I brought these two and gave them to our forensics expert. He confirmed what I suspected, sir. They were blanks."

"Go on."

"Schulmann wrote in his report that the gun malfunctioned. It was an older version of the MG 34. He said the firing mechanism jammed, and—"

"Never mind. I understand how weapons malfunction."

"I have tried to get Major Nieman to allow me to go to Belley and investigate this and other concerns . . ." Dresdner paused. He knew he was treading dangerous ground admitting to circumvention of his superior's orders. Licking his lips, he continued. "I am requesting permission from *you*, sir, to go immediately."

Klaus Barbie studied the captain for a long time. To Dresdner it seemed like an eternity, and he felt sweat building at the base of his uniform collar and his eye under its patch began to throb. He clenched his fists behind his back, fighting the urge to explain himself further. Anything he said right now would sound like babbling. He had said what needed to be said. Now he must wait.

Barbie pushed back his chair and stood, his medium height barely surpassing that of the captain. "You may have a point, Captain. I have been concerned that the trains are ready to depart at the end of this week—and there is no word from Belley of a successful *rafle*."

Dresdner said nothing. Klaus Barbie walked around his desk and stood before him, planting his feet slightly apart and clasping his hands behind his back. His handsome face was solemn. "What would make me want to assign this task to you, Captain Dresdner?"

Dresdner's pulse pounded. "I may have blights on my record, sir, but not where it affects my loyalty to my Führer." He cleared his throat. "I was your aide when you interrogated the Résistance leader—Jean Moulin—in '43. Before that I successfully led several *rafles* in Paris and the surrounding *départements*. I have a record of success as an interrogator that is unparalleled in southern France." He hesitated, then added, "Except of course by *yours*, sir."

Barbie nodded. "I remember you were quite helpful with Moulin."

"Thank you, sir."

Barbie turned back to the desk. "I will see what I can do." He placed the shell casings on its surface and studied them thoughtfully. "This bit of evidence certainly sheds new light on the situation in Belley."

"Yes, sir."

"You may go. I will talk with your superior officer."

"Perhaps . . . perhaps it would be better not to—"

"Captain, you are out of order. I will follow correct procedure and discuss the possibility with your superior officer. Dismissed." Barbie returned to his meal.

"Yes, sir." Dresdner did not like the idea of Barbie telling Major Nieman of his visit, but there was nothing he could do about it. He knew his future hung precariously in the balance at the moment, and all depended upon what Barbie said to Nieman. His back ramrod straight, Captain Dresdner saluted the *obersturmführer* and left the office.

* * *

Marie heard the knock on the door but kept her focus on Alma. "There you go. Choose another color. The picture's coming along nicely."

Alma dipped his paintbrush carefully in the small cup of water and then chose blue paint for the eyes of his stick soldier. "Do you think Papa will like it?"

"I'm sure of it." Marie knew her German was rough, but ever since she'd promised Rolf she would look after his son she had felt an urgency to learn as much as she could. She spoke German all the time now with Berta, and Berta corrected her pronunciation as much as possible. Sometimes Berta would throw her hands in the air and complain that it was useless: a French accent just did not work with German. Marie was used to the soft, flowing beauty of French and the practical choppiness of English. She guessed only a native could love German—to her it was all spitting and shouting.

Well, not exactly shouting. Berta had a way of making it sound halfway presentable. And Rolf's words were beautiful in whatever language he spoke.

She usually tried not to think about Rolf. She missed him—so deeply it hurt. She remembered how they had stood together at the top of the mountain in the early morning hours of December twenty-sixth, looking down at the incredible sight of Baiersbronn, and she mulled over the moment of his proposal multitudes of times, each time wishing she had answered him differently. In her mind she found a thousand different justifications for his military service. She imagined what it would be like to be his wife, and when she wrapped her blanket around herself at night, she imagined it was Rolf's arms keeping her warm and safe. And she found herself turning the ring around and around on her finger, much the same way a bride might, whenever she thought about him.

Berta's voice carried up the stairs, calling for her to come down. She sounded worried. Smiling encouragingly at Alma, Marie rose to her feet and descended the stairs. Two men dressed meticulously in dark business suits and hats stood inside the front door. One of them carried a briefcase, and the other had an overcoat slung casually over one arm. They were young, clean-shaven, and serious, and something about them terrified her. They were undoubtedly Nazis—possibly Gestapo. She felt her pulse quicken.

One of the men touched his hat. "*Guten Morgen,* Fräulein. *Guten Morgen,* Frau Sandler."

"*Guten Morgen.*"

"My name is Herr Kuester, and this is my associate, Herr Siegfried." The younger of the two held out his hand to Marie and smiled what he probably thought was a friendly smile. Hesitantly, Marie allowed him to shake her hand.

"We would like to see your papers, please."

"Are you with the police?"

"No, Fräulein. Department of Immigration. We want to make sure everything is in order."

Marie hesitated. She could see Berta standing in the doorway trying to mask her fear. Berta was also convinced they were lying.

"It won't take long. Your papers, please."

Marie reached into her pocket and extracted the identification papers Hans had given her the day she was delivered to the estate. Berta had warned her always to carry them on her person. Getting caught without one's papers was grounds for imprisonment. Marie handed the documents to Herr Kuester, and he gave them no more than a cursory inspection. He looked up and studied her. "How long have you been in Germany, Fräulein?"

"Less than four months."

"And what is your purpose here?"

"I am a tutor for the son of Major Rolf Schulmann. He is, unfortunately, unable to tutor the boy himself."

"Ah . . ." Kuester nodded slowly, his eyes studying her thoughtfully. "And how long were you planning to stay?"

"Until I am no longer needed."

"I see." He handed back her documents. "And why are you wearing a wig?"

Marie started. She wasn't expecting the question. She wondered if perhaps her own hair had escaped from beneath. But she had taken extra care this morning to make sure she looked presentable because Berta was taking her and Alma to the village later that morning to buy supplies.

The look on his face told her there was no use denying it. "The major said it would make his son more comfortable," she lied. "The boy's mother had blonde hair."

"Interesting." Without warning Kuester grabbed her wrist and lifted her hand, singling out her ring finger. "And are you having an affair with the major?" Marie instinctively tried to pull away, and he tightened his grip, crushing her wrist. He studied Rolf's ring closely. "A beautiful ring, Fräulein—worthy of a beautiful tutor."

"Herr Kuester—" Marie could hardly form the words past the dryness in her throat. "These are strange questions for the Department of Immigration. I must protest." She tried to sound incensed.

"Remove your wig, please, Fräulein." Kuester dropped her hand.

"What?"

"Remove your wig."

"You have no right—"

"I will do it for you if you do not comply immediately."

With shaking fingers Marie reached and loosened the pins holding her blonde curls in place. She removed the wig and let it fall to her side. Both men studied her dark brown hair, and Siegfried spoke for the first time. "You are pretty enough with brown hair, Fräulein. You shouldn't cover that hair with a wig."

Marie said nothing.

"And what is your nationality, please?"

"I am French."

"Your last name is Frank? Giselle Frank?"

"Yes."

"'Frank' is a German name."

"My father was obviously German."

"You will check with the Department of Immigration before you leave the Schwarzwald."

"I understand."

"You are not to leave the country unless you receive exit papers from the Department. Do you understand, Fräulein Giselle?"

"Yes."

"Very well." Herr Kuester touched his hat. Siegfried followed his example, smiling cordially. Kuester repeated the gesture to Berta in the doorway of the kitchen. Then both men turned and left the house.

Marie caught Berta's eye. The older woman's face was pale. She whispered, "Gestapo."

Marie nodded. Could Captain Dresdner have found out she was here? But how would he have known? She turned to a window and watched the men's car drive away. She wished Rolf would contact her and tell her what to do. Certainly if Dresdner was beginning to be suspicious, Rolf would know of it. And he would send his telegram.

TWENTY-EIGHT

April 4, 1944—Morning

The rumble of approaching trucks was enough to cause Major Rolf Schulmann to cut short his instructions to the morning patrol. He sent his men on their way and walked around to the front of the building, where three military transports, each holding at least twenty men, were parking in the courtyard directly in front of Belley Headquarters. A large black Renault pulled to the front entrance and the driver opened the door for Captain Bernard Dresdner.

And so it begins . . . Taking a deep breath, Rolf squared his shoulders and advanced toward the Gestapo captain.

* * *

Rolf walked around his desk and sat in his chair, facing Captain Dresdner. "Will you take a seat? Can I bring you something to drink?"

"I will stand. I have a letter from your superiors that you will read." Dresdner held out the envelope, his posture stiff and businesslike. Rolf stood and took the letter, then picked up his opener and sliced through the seal. Dresdner watched with a triumphant smirk playing at the corners of his mouth as Rolf extracted two papers and began to read.

Rolf read the first page silently, slipped it behind the other, and continued to read. After a few moments he refolded the letter. He spoke calmly. "These accusations are unfounded. I have fulfilled my duties as requested. Always. My references are impeccable." He indicated the papers in his hand. "'Probation—pending the outcome of an investigation'? There is no reason for this."

"Your superiors are beginning to think otherwise. As stated in the letter, Major Nieman has recommended to them that I be assigned the task of investigating each and every one of these allegations. If even *one* of them proves founded, I am to arrest you and have you delivered to Lyon for trial."

"You seem to have received quite a promotion, Dresdner. Has Major Nieman forgotten your little disaster outside Belley?"

"Oh, I plan to look into that quite thoroughly while I am here." Dresdner picked up the small picture from Major Schulmann's desk and studied it, running his index finger across Hélène's form. "In fact, I have two men in your home village of Schönenberg right now—investigating the possibilities." He looked up and smiled at Rolf. "They should be here some-time tomorrow to tell me what they have found."

Rolf felt his heart begin to race. "And what else do you have planned for your little visit?"

Dresdner tossed the picture back onto Rolf's desk. "*Obersturmführer* Barbie has appointed me officer in charge of the Final Solution in your district." Dresdner was gloating. "From this moment on you will leave all matters related to the Jewish Question to me."

"There is no way we can fill a quota by this weekend."

"I think you are wrong, Major Schulmann."

"You will not find them."

"Again, you are wrong. There is always a way to do the Führer's bidding." Dresdner smiled sardonically, leaning over the desk toward Rolf. "If it eases your discomfort any, Barbie has instructed me to give highest priority to filling your Jewish quota—before I dedicate all my energies to investigating your conduct."

Rolf was silent.

Dresdner straightened. "I'm on a tight schedule—the train cannot wait. I brought my own men, so most of yours will be temporarily reassigned to other duties until your superiors can decide where they will be needed."

"I expect to have access to my office staff."

"Of course. You are on probation—that is all. You are still expected to work. This is not a holiday."

"I never imagined it was."

Dresdner turned toward the door. "I will be taking that office down the hall. You are to send any visitors to me, and I will read any and all reports."

"One more thing." Rolf spoke, his voice firm. "You have come to Belley determined to discredit me. You said any evidence these accusations are founded will send me to trial. Keep in mind the opposite also holds true, Captain. Any evidence these accusations are false and you could be shot. I know Major Nieman. He trusts me. You have obviously circumvented his orders to get to Barbie, and that has gotten you this far. But perhaps you are just digging yourself a more elaborate grave."

"Take care, Mormon." Dresdner's voice held ice. "Or you and your son may find yourselves on that train. And understand, Major, its destination is not what you think."

TWENTY-NINE

April 4, 1944—Noon

Major Rolf Schulmann glanced up from his desk as two Frenchmen entered his office, hats in hand. He had seen both before, although their presence in his office surprised him. The first, Lucien Bourdon, was a farmer who lived between Belley and Izieu. He was well-known by the Germans in Belley and spent many an afternoon drinking with Schulmann's officers at the café Nevy along the Place des Terreaux. He was a dirty, foul-mouthed drunkard, and Schulmann detested the man. The other man was a friend of Bourdon's, Schulmann knew—Antoine Wucher, a *collabo* who would turn in his fellow countryman for a price.

"We regret the intrusion, Herr Major. But we would like to speak with Herr Dresdner, of the Lyon Gestapo. We understand he is now in charge?"

Major Schulmann's lips twitched. *Word travels fast in the drinking circles of Belley,* he thought, and gestured toward the outer office. "Wait in the other room. He will be with you as soon as he finishes his meal." The two men bowed their way out. Schulmann called to his secretary and relayed the message to her. She went to the private dining room and whispered in Captain Dresdner's ear.

* * *

Captain Dresdner set down his fork, dabbed at the corners of his chiseled mouth, and leaned back in his chair. The two men standing in front of him, wringing their hats in their hands, were vaguely familiar. He thought he might have met one of them before—perhaps on one of his earlier visits to Belley. He gestured for the two men to approach.

One of them spoke. "Herr Captain, we were informed you are now in charge, and that you can help us with our problem."

"Tell me your names."

"I am Monsieur Lucien Bourdon. I have a farm in Brens, near the tiny village of Izieu—a few kilometers from Belley."

"Ah, yes. I have seen you before—at the café in town, I think."

"And this is my friend, Antoine Wucher."

Dresdner acknowledged Wucher with a nod and waved both men to seats at the table. "Join me for refreshment?"

"Thank you, Herr Dresdner." Bourdon and Wucher moved to the table and sat down. Dresdner could see the look of surprise and gratitude in their eyes at his unexpected invitation, and it gave him a feeling of superiority. There was something stimulating about having others at one's beck and command—to know that one was the giver of gifts and the benefactor to someone as poor and degenerate as these two fools before him.

Dresdner nodded impatiently to the small French servingwoman, and she scurried to bring two more steaming mugs of German coffee. Wucher grabbed his cup and immediately began to drink, a look of pure pleasure glazing over his eyes when his taste buds recognized not foul *ersatz* coffee, but a genuine German blend. Bourdon was more controlled, and he held his cup gratefully between his two rough palms. "You are most kind, Herr Captain. Most kind."

Dresdner said, "And what do you do, Monsieur Wucher? I have not had the pleasure of meeting you before today."

"I am a mechanic, sir. A mechanic and handyman for a Madame Zlatin and her *colonie d'enfants* on the mountain above the river."

"I see. I have heard of the place, but only a little. I hope to spend time becoming acquainted with all my neighbors as soon as possible." Dresdner now turned to Bourdon. "What problem do you have, monsieur?"

Bourdon still sat with his hands wrapped around his coffee mug. He cleared his throat. "It is about a pressing matter of business—a matter important to the war effort, Herr Dresdner."

"Continue."

"Well, sir—" Again Bourdon cleared his throat, this time nervously. "As you know, I am a farmer—"

"Yes, yes." Dresdner nodded impatiently and reached for his coffee.

"As Monsieur Wucher began to tell you, there is a *colonie d'enfants* run by a Madame Zlatin in Izieu. It is in a most beautiful spot, Herr Captain, overlooking the Rhône—"

"Do not waste my time, Monsieur Bourdon. Tell me what you came here to tell me." Captain Dresdner took a drink from his cup.

"But that is what I am trying to do, Herr Captain. The *colonie d'enfants—La Maison d'Izieu*—it is filled with Jewish children."

Captain Dresdner carefully set down his cup. "Repeat that, please?"

"Madame Zlatin—she has opened a home in Izieu for Jewish children whose parents are missing or have been sent to work in Poland. She has at least forty there at present, if I am not mistaken."

Dresdner glared at Bourdon. "And how did you come by this information? You are nothing but a farmer."

Bourdon flinched. "But I am here hoping to be more than a farmer to you, Herr Captain."

"How did you find out? About the children?"

Bourdon shrugged. "Izieu is a small community, sir. Everybody knows— or at least, everybody suspects. But I decided to devise a plan to find out if it was really true." He smiled at the memory of his own cleverness.

"And what was this plan?"

"I went one day last month to the home and asked Madame Zlatin, 'Do you have a big boy who can give me a hand with my crops?' Madame Zlatin was very accommodating and sent a fifteen-year-old boy named François to help me. He stayed with me for most of the month and helped me on the farm. When I asked, he told me that he was Jewish and that all the other children were Jewish as well."

Captain Dresdner watched him silently, his hand motionless on his coffee cup.

Encouraged, Bourdon continued. "My friend Antoine was also helpful in confirming the news." Antoine Wucher drained his coffee and nodded, smiling. The French servingwoman filled his cup for the third time. "Antoine asked Madame Zlatin to take in his eight-year-old boy, René, because his mother was sick at the hospital and it would give Antoine more time to work. Madame Zlatin agreed, and the boy brought home much news of the goings on in *La Maison d'Izieu*."

Bourdon stopped talking. Captain Dresdner continued to stare at him. He felt nothing but disdain for this weasel of a man and his greedy companion, who would sell out children for a cup of coffee and a few words of praise. He knew Bourdon could probably read the disdain on his face, but he did not care.

"Well." Dresdner placed both hands definitively on the table and stood. The moment of uncomfortable silence was at an end. Bourdon rose also, glancing at his untouched coffee. Wucher stood and drained his cup. Captain Dresdner forced a thin smile to his lips and moved toward the door of the dining room. Uncertain, the two men moved to follow.

"Monsieurs Bourdon and Wucher, you have been most informative. I will certainly look into the matter." He moved to the door, clicked his heels sharply, and bowed his dismissal. Bourdon opened his mouth as if to say something more, but then closed it again, confused.

Wucher spoke for only the second time since they had entered the room. "One thing I ask, sir."

"What is that?" Captain Dresdner snapped. He was ready for them to be out of his sight.

"My son—René. I would ask that he be spared, and returned to me."

"Your son will be cared for. Good-bye."

Dresdner watched thoughtfully as the two Frenchmen escaped past his aide and negotiated the staircase, exiting into the courtyard. He felt his left eye begin to twitch, and he imagined for a moment he could see again through the damaged pupil. That always happened when he was excited. He could almost imagine that his left eye was again sending impulses to his brain and forming pictures as it had before his father beat it to a pulp. Secretly he thought of it as his intelligent eye—functioning normally whenever he was hit by one of his incredibly ingenious ideas.

A children's home, filled with available Jews. He felt like a child on Christmas Eve—viewing for the first time the Christmas tree loaded with candies and fruits. Barbie would be pleased.

Barbie. He needed to call Klaus Barbie! If he acted quickly, the train would be able to leave as scheduled, with no delay and no need for a full-blown *rafle* among the citizens of Belley. Dresdner was being handed an opportunity to fulfill his orders with minimal inconvenience to himself—or to Belley. That would make it more likely the good citizens would cooperate with him on future operations. He called to his aide. "Get me *École de Santé* on the line. *Obersturmführer* Barbie. And go after those Frenchmen. Tell them I will accompany them tomorrow morning to see what they have to offer."

THIRTY

April 5, 1944

On April fifth, Major Rolf Schulmann woke at four in the morning, rolled to his knees, and begged his Father in Heaven to protect his family. He explained that his situation seemed to be rapidly getting out of hand, and he was concerned that he and his family might be in danger. He told his Father in Heaven about Dresdner's all-consuming hatred for Mormons and of the captain's desire to destroy him. Then he opened his ragged copy of the Book of Mormon and read silently from Alma 46: *"And it came to pass that he rent his coat; and he took a piece thereof, and wrote upon it—In memory of our God, our religion, and freedom, and our peace, our wives, and our children— and he fastened it upon the end of a pole."*

Rolf took a small stub of pencil from the table next to his bed and wrote in the margin next to verse twelve: *"Hélène. Alma."*

After a slight pause, he added, *"Marie."*

For a long time he thought about Marie. He felt her warmth in his arms and saw her wide brown eyes looking up into his. He ached inside at the thought of her. He turned a few pages to chapter 48 and read: *"Yea, and he was a man who was firm in the faith of Christ, and he had sworn with an oath to defend his people, his rights, and his country, and his religion, even to the loss of his blood."*

Beside verse thirteen, Rolf wrote a question: *"Am I like Moroni?"*

The Nephites were faithful at that time and had been blessed with protection from their enemies. Rolf read verses fifteen through seventeen:

> *And this was their faith, that . . . God would prosper*
> *them in the land, or in other words, if they were faithful in*
> *keeping the commandments of God that he would prosper*

them in the land; yea, warn them to flee, or to prepare for war, according to their danger;

And also, that God would make it known unto them whither they should go to defend themselves against their enemies, and by so doing, the Lord would deliver them; and this was the faith of Moroni, and his heart did glory in it; not in the shedding of blood but in doing good, in preserving his people, yea, in keeping the commandments of God, yea, and resisting iniquity.

Yea, verily, verily I say unto you, if all men had been, and were, and ever would be, like unto Moroni, behold, the very powers of hell would have been shaken forever; yea, the devil would never have power over the hearts of the children of men.

Rolf again lowered his head. "Dear Father," he prayed, tears playing at the corners of his eyes. "The Nephites were promised if they kept Thy commandments they would be protected from their enemies. I know I have my faults, but I am trying to do the best I can. Thou knowest me. I am Thy son. Please help me. Please warn me when to flee—and help me to warn Marie. Father, I love her so much. I would do anything for her . . ."

There was a polite knock at the door, followed by the muffled voice of his aide. "Major Schulmann, sir, Captain Dresdner wishes to see you in his office." The aide sounded hesitant, as if the message were awkward for him to deliver.

Rolf looked at his watch. It was five thirty. "Thank you. Tell the captain I will be there in ten minutes."

Rolf stood, placed his Book of Mormon on the table, and began to prepare for the day.

* * *

Without preamble, Captain Dresdner informed Rolf he was needed in Lyon—to discuss temporary reassignment of his troops. Rolf sensed Dresdner was anxious to get him out of Belley, and his feeling of foreboding deepened. As he gathered his troops to be reassigned and readied them for departure, he mulled over the possibility of sending a telegram to Marie—to warn her that she was in danger. But he decided to wait.

* * *

Dresdner watched Major Schulmann's convoy leave the Château de Lafont with a great deal of satisfaction. Klaus Barbie would keep the Mormon busy while Dresdner took care of business in Belley. He called for his aide. "Tell Monsieurs Bourdon and Wucher I will be ready in an hour. Have them wait for me downstairs."

"Yes, sir. Anything else?"

"Call headquarters. Inform the *obersturmführer* that Schulmann is on his way. Everything is in order for tomorrow."

"Right away, sir."

"And one more thing. When you call headquarters, see if Kuester and Siegfried have returned. I want them to report to me personally—this afternoon, if possible."

THIRTY-ONE

Rolf pulled off his gloves and sat wearily behind his desk. The building was quiet—only his office staff and a skeleton crew of Gestapo remained in the château. He wondered where Dresdner had gone, and the captain's absence brought back Rolf's sense of foreboding. He sensed the captain was up to no good and had orchestrated Rolf's removal from the office in order to accomplish something without his interference.

Rolf had the feeling he needed to find Dresdner quickly. Something was happening—something Rolf knew he would regret for the rest of his life if he did not try to prevent it. He walked out of his office and called to Dresdner's orderly. "Where is Captain Dresdner?"

The man shook his head. "I'm sorry, sir. He told me if you returned early you were not to be informed."

Rolf made a beeline for the man and took him firmly by his shirt front. "In the absence of your superior officer, I am in command. Tell me where he went."

The man shook his head. "I'm sorry, sir." He had the shadow of a smile on his lips. Rolf flung him away and turned back toward his office. It was uncanny, he thought, how an army could be so divided! Supposedly they all fought on the same side, but the Gestapo had been given so much power that at times it seemed they fought on nobody's side but their own.

That was what made men like Dresdner so dangerous. Rolf remembered several examples in the Book of Mormon of people who had received great power and had used it for evil. Nehor was a tool of the adversary, receiving great power from that source. The Gadianton robbers were notorious for their abuse of power. And Amalikiah, the king of the Lamanites, received that position and almost infinite power by murder, fraud, and deceit. Rolf entered his office and closed the door. He thought again of

Moroni. Yesterday he had read about the greatness of the Nephite captain and his faithfulness in keeping God's commandments. Didn't the scriptures say Moroni never sought for power? On the contrary, he was always seeking to pull it down.

Again, that question: *Am I like Moroni?* Rolf's hands clenched and he spoke to the framed image of Hélène. "Am I willing to have that kind of courage?"

He needed to find out what Dresdner was doing. He had the terrifying sensation that many lives depended on it. And he had another impression— one so frightening it took his breath away. Quickly he grabbed a clean sheet of paper and began to work. Five minutes later he folded the paper, took a deep breath, straightened his shoulders, and stepped into the hallway. "Bernice?" His secretary looked up from her typewriter and he smiled at her. "I have a telegram for you to send. Will you take care of it right away?"

Bernice glanced fearfully at Captain Dresdner's orderly, standing guard at the captain's office near the head of the stairs. "Yes, sir. Immediately." Accepting the folded paper from Rolf's hand, she scurried toward the stairs. As Rolf had expected, the orderly grunted and reached for the paper, and she surrendered it to him, glancing apologetically back at Rolf.

The Gestapo orderly read the paragraph and glanced up quizzically Rolf. Then he re-folded the paper and handed it back to Bernice. The woman took it and disappeared down the stairs.

Except for Rolf and the orderly, the second floor was deserted. Rolf left his office and walked toward the stairs, approaching the Gestapo orderly. Casually, his fingers closed around the handle of his gun and slid it from its holster, his eyes meeting the smirking gaze of the other man. Lightning-quick, Rolf raised his weapon, knocking the butt of his Luger squarely through the man's sneering teeth. Caught off guard, the orderly gurgled strangely and went down, half his front teeth broken or completely missing. Rolf secured him by the back of his collar and dragged him into Dresdner's office. The man did not object when Rolf picked him up by his collar and the back of his pants and threw him bodily onto Dresdner's desk. He moaned and tried to turn away from Rolf, and several teeth and a fair amount of blood stained Dresdner's latest report to headquarters. Rolf followed him onto the desk and planted his knee in the orderly's abdomen, grabbing him by the throat and pressing the business end of the gun deep into the man's neck. "Now I will give you one last chance." The man stared back at him with terror in his eyes. "Where is Captain Dresdner?"

The orderly coughed blood. "Izieu."

Schulmann was surprised. Izieu was such a small community. He already knew there were no Jews there. Except for . . .

Suddenly Rolf felt sick. His voice began to tremble. "What's Dresdner doing there? How long has he been gone?"

The orderly grinned, his mouth and gums stained bright red, and said nothing. Rolf reversed his gun and hit the man again, knocking him unconscious. Then he jumped from the desk and left the office, locking the door behind him.

He raced for his car and his driver trotted over from a nearby café, apologizing profusely for his absence. Rolf told him not to worry—Rolf would drive. Surprised, the driver stepped out of the way as Rolf gunned the engine and swung around in the street. Shrugging, the driver returned to his meal in the café.

* * *

On any other day—under any other circumstances—the climb to *La Maison d'Izieu*, the Izieu Children's Home—would have been a scenic pleasure. Izieu itself was a village of only a handful of inhabitants, and the children's home sat high on the side of a mountain overlooking the Rhône River. As his vehicle struggled to make the climb, Rolf shifted into a lower gear and passed two military vehicles—two lorries—on their way down from the village. He glanced at them and had the dreadful impression he was already too late. He passed the barn full of animals lovingly cared for by the children, and he immediately recalled the morning he had visited with Madame Sabine Zlatin and her husband, Miron Zlatin, after capturing Marie Jacobson and hearing her admit she was supposed to work there. The Zlatins had been gracious and affable, offering to show him their facilities and giving him a tour of the grounds. He had even met several of the children, and he had promised the Zlatins he would protect them.

The two-story children's home appeared ahead. A troop convoy was parked near the entrance to the tiny courtyard, and two Gestapo were posted guarding the door. Rolf pulled to a stop next to the truck and walked quickly through the courtyard toward the house.

The place seemed deserted. Gestapo orderlies guarding the front door did nothing to stop his entrance. Stepping inside the home, he paused, hearing nothing but the rustle of a paper and a shutter creaking on its hinges. Rolf looked up the stairs. Not a sign of life.

He moved into the refectory, and his heart caught in his throat. He saw tables and chairs, some broken, some overturned on the floor. On the long tables cups with chocolate sat half consumed, cold and unattended. In a daze, Rolf walked through to the schoolroom and his boot crunched paper. Absently he bent to pick it up and saw that it was filled with childish scrawls.

He began to read and what he read was more than he could take. Slowly he sank onto a chair and his shoulders hunched as he stared at the letter, written by a young girl—Liliane—one of the children he had met on his visit:

> *God? How good You are, how kind and if one had to count the number of goodnesses and kindnesses You have done, one would never finish.*
>
> *God? It is You who command. It is You who are justice, it is You who reward the good and punish the evil.*
>
> *God? It is thanks to You that I had a beautiful life before, that I was spoiled, that I had lovely things that others do not have.*
>
> *God? After that, I ask You one thing only: Make my parents come back, my poor parents protect them (even more than You protect me) so that I can see them again as soon as possible.*
>
> *Make them come back again. Ah! I had such a good mother and such a good father! I have such faith in You and I thank You in advance.*
>
> *Liliane*

Through his agony he heard footsteps behind him and he stood, the letter still clutched in his hand. Captain Bernard Dresdner stood in the doorway of the schoolroom, watching him with a sneer on his lips and his one good eye unnaturally bright. Behind him stood the two Gestapo who had been guarding the front door. Dresdner spoke. "I'm glad you came. I don't know how you found me, but I'm glad you did." He pushed a chair aside with his boot, hands clasped behind his back. "Do you realize what a full morning this had been?" The captain sat on the edge of a desk and swung his leg. "Forty-four children and seven adults. You should be pleased, Major—that more than fulfils your quota.

"I do admit I was annoyed when one of the children escaped—jumped from the second story into the garden. My men and I are just returning from looking for him. Slippery little devil. We couldn't find him." Dresdner sighed and pulled off his gloves. "They went easily—what are children against grown men? We threw them into the lorries like sacks of potatoes! Monsieur Zlatin protested violently—said that they had been given a promise by some benevolent SS officer that they would be protected." Dresdner smiled at Rolf's shock. "He believed in you wholeheartedly."

Stricken, Rolf deliberately folded the letter and placed it inside a desk drawer. The Gestapo captain continued. "Monsieur Zlatin, though, kept demanding to talk with you, and I had to inform him you are no longer in charge." Dresdner smiled. "You probably passed the lorries going down while you were coming up. Your prisoners will be transferred immediately to Drancy, and from there, probably to Auschwitz-Birkenau." The captain shrugged. "I really don't care where they're taken. My job is done here. And now—" Dresdner stood and moved toward Schulmann. "I can focus on the next interesting phase of my mission." He reached inside his coat and extracted a photograph. "Do you know who this is?"

Rolf felt dead inside. He did not immediately take the photo from Dresdner, but stared numbly at the captain.

"Take it, Major. It's a beautiful picture—it will make you feel better . . . just like it did me."

Rolf took the picture. It was of Marie, walking in the village with Alma. A tiny wooden toy grasped in Alma's raised hand seemed to be the focus of the boy's attention, and Rolf could almost hear the sounds of the panzer engine created by his son's puckered lips. He looked back at Marie. The day must have been lovely, for she was carrying her coat over one arm, her slender frame erect and lovely in the dress he had given her. She was holding his son's hand and smiling down at the boy's make-believe.

"No, God, please no."

"She is beautiful." Dresdner looked joyful. "I can see why you kept her to yourself. Two of my men took this photograph just three days ago in your hometown. She was wearing a wig, but she took it off for my men when they asked her politely. This picture was taken later that same day. She seems to be very happy."

"What have you done with her?"

"Unfortunately, nothing yet." Dresdner held out his hand for the photograph. "I sent my men on a whim—just to see this lovely young tutor Major Klein kept raving about. I wanted to make sure my suspicions were founded before I requested permission to act."

Rolf faced the smaller man. "I have seriously misjudged you, Dresdner."

"I'm sorry to hear that." The Gestapo captain smiled.

"All these years I've thought you an odious, evil man. I've even pitied you for what your father did to you."

"And now?"

"Now I have no words to describe the kind of man you are. In fact, in my mind, you have ceased to be a man."

Dresdner shrugged indifferently. "What you think of me is not important. You should worry instead what Section Four thinks of you."

"With your help, I'm sure it's not good."

"It's not. In fact, as of five thirty this morning I have been placed in complete control in Belley. You, Major Schulmann, are under arrest for treason." Dresdner gestured to the two guards. They entered and moved to Rolf's side. "Hands behind your back please, Major. That's good. I was not expecting you to show up here. I thought I would have the honor of arresting you when we returned to Belley. But this is better. Much better."

"You only have a photograph. Without that photo there is nothing to accuse me."

"How about warning forty-seven Jews to escape?"

"I did not warn them to escape. Ask my officers. Not one of the families was home. I already explained to Nieman why that was so."

"You underestimate your officers, Major." Dresdner shook his head as if to an errant child. "One of your lieutenants came to me yesterday with the strangest story I have ever heard—of a family being given twenty minutes to prepare for departure . . . and then disappearing. I was quite intrigued. And I understand your *rafle* supposedly failed because it occurred during the spring holidays? You claim in your report it was so. What a surprise when I called the minister of schools in Belley and a Monsieur Bastien Adophe answered the phone instead of a Monsieur Jacques Bellamont."

Rolf remained silent.

"How long did you think it would take me, Mormon? Do you think I am so stupid as to miss such glaring facts?" Impulsively, Dresdner slapped Rolf across the cheek with the back of his hand, leaving a bloody scratch from his ring.

Rolf glared at the Gestapo captain. "You will pay for what you did here today, Dresdner. You will pay someday with your life."

"You are mistaken. It is *you* who will pay." Dresdner laughed and struck Rolf again. "I could shoot you for treason right now. No one would bat an eye. But I have a more dramatic end planned for you, and it involves your American girlfriend and your son."

"Leave them alone."

"I am flying to Germany today to arrest them both." Dresdner turned his back on Rolf, gesturing for the guards to bring him along.

"My son is only four." Rolf could hardly form the words.

"Yes. And his father is a traitor."

THIRTY-TWO

April 6, 1944

"Rolf sent a telegram."

Marie had been preparing Alma's breakfast, and now her hand froze, Alma's bread halfway to his outstretched hand. "What does it say, Berta?"

"More about the boy's education. I must admit he surprises me with his persistence . . ."

"Berta." Marie's voice wavered. "Give it to me."

Surprised at Marie's intensity, Berta unfolded the single sheet of paper and handed it to Marie.

> GISELLE REQUIST YOU DEDICATE
> MORE TIME TO SONS FRENCH
> STOP UNACCEPTABLE AMOUNT
> OF FREE TIME STOP ONE HOUR
> ONLY STOP MAJOR SCHULMANN

Marie stood, and the bread in her hand dropped unnoticed to the table. She placed one boot on the chair and extracted her silk WOK from its hiding place, much to Berta's surprise and consternation. Alma strained to grab the slice of bread from several inches out of his reach while Marie spread the silk on the table. Berta opened her mouth as if to comment, and Marie could imagine mental gears turning as her friend made the connection between Rolf's strange letters and Marie's present actions.

"A pencil and paper please, Berta. No, never mind. There's no time." She quickly scanned the telegram for errors and found only one misspelled word. Rolf had chosen to leave the first code key for this message, and she mentally thanked him for leaving the fastest and least likely confused code key for the most important message. Rolf obviously wanted this message deciphered as quickly as possible. Berta and Alma stared while Marie worked through the double transposition keys, whispering her conversions in a steady monologue that probably had Berta thinking she had gone mad.

Run.

Berta started to tremble. "I guess I hoped it would never come . . ." She brushed at a tear. "I'll get Alma ready. We probably haven't got much time."

Marie held the woman close. "I'll miss you, Berta. You've been a good friend."

"I'll miss you, too."

* * *

Holding Alma's mittened hand firmly in her own, Marie entered the small bookshop and asked to use the telephone. She paid the woman several Reichsmark notes and picked up the receiver. "Schönau, please. Yes, I would like to speak with Lieutenant Hans Brenner, of the Alpine SS. Will you connect me? Yes, I will hold . . ."

The woman watched her suspiciously while she shelved books. Marie smiled at her. "Yes, I'm still here. What did you say? Oh, I see. Yes, I understand it would be quite impossible for him to come to the phone . . . Yes, I will leave him a message . . . This is Giselle Frank. I tutor Major Rolf Schulmann's son. That's right—Giselle Frank. Are you lieutenant Brenner's secretary? This message is very important . . ."

Marie glanced back at the owner of the shop. The woman still watched her, unsmiling.

"Yes, I'm still here—he said to wait for him where? . . . Yes, I know where it is." Marie breathed a sigh of relief. "Please ask him to hurry!"

Marie hung up the receiver and thanked the woman. Grasping Alma's hand again in hers, she pushed open the door and hurried into the street. The wind whipped at her coat and she squeezed Alma's hand reassuringly.

Alma tugged on her hand. "I'm hungry."

"All right, munchkin." She smiled down at the boy. "When we get to the hotel we'll eat something Tante Berta packed for us." Marie glanced at the clouds. They were moving fast, and she wondered if they would slide by and miss them altogether. Perhaps Baiersbronn would get snow—but that would not be a problem. Hans would be with them and they should reach their destination before the roads became impassable. Marie held Alma's hand firmly as she crossed the street and entered the two-story home that served as the village hotel. She smiled at the proprietress and asked if the two of them could wait for a friend in the warmth of her living room.

The proprietress, a thickset woman in her fifties with ruddy cheeks and wire-rimmed spectacles perched impossibly on the end of her nose, stared suspiciously, taking in the slender visitor and her tiny charge with the air of a martyr. "This room is for paying guests only, Fräulein." She flicked an imaginary dust particle off the arm of a chair and lifted her chin, challenging Marie to dispute her regulations.

Marie hesitated, wondering what to do next, and glanced about the room as if the faded décor would give her a clue. She turned back to the woman and smiled sweetly. "I am meeting an officer of the *Gebirgsjager*. I don't think he would be happy if he heard you threw me out into the street."

"You're meeting an officer—with *him?*" Appalled, the proprietress pointed one fleshy finger at Alma, clearly surmising that Marie was meeting a man to consummate a romantic liaison.

Marie caught the insinuation and felt her cheeks flush, but she raised her head and faced the woman squarely. "What I do with my life is none of your concern. And I'm sure he will not keep me waiting in your living room overly long." Stubbornly she sat down, pulling Rolf's son onto the sofa beside her.

The woman glowered as if she would like to pick her stained teeth with Marie, or at least throw her out into the street. Then she shrugged. "As you wish." She sniffed and returned to the other room.

Marie took a deep breath and smiled reassuringly down at Alma. "Tante Berta sent us bread and goat cheese, Alma." She opened her purse and withdrew two wrapped sandwiches. "Doesn't it smell good?"

Alma accepted his portion gratefully, devouring it with the voracious appetite of a five-year-old. Marie ate hers more slowly, carefully watching the street outside through a dingy lace curtain. She wondered how long Hans would be. If Rolf were concerned for their safety, certainly the danger would extend to being caught in town. Schönenberg was small—and not a good place to hide. She knew they needed to get to Baiersbronn as soon as possible.

Evening approached, and Alma clamored for the wooden tank his father had carved for him at Christmastime. When Marie produced it from her purse, Alma accepted it gladly and immediately began crawling all over the tattered sofa and obliterating imaginary troops up and down the faded cushions. The proprietress periodically glared from the adjoining room, her waning patience obvious. Shadows were lengthening across the street when Alma crawled onto Marie's lap and nodded sleepily against her arm. Marie gently removed the precious toy from the boy's loosening grasp and returned it to the safety of her purse.

Darkness fell and Hans still had not arrived. Several travelers entered
the hotel and secured rooms for the evening, and Marie carefully studied
each man that entered, relieved when none of them were Kuester or
Siegfried. The two men that approached her at Rolf's home had followed
her into the village that afternoon, and Marie had tried to ignore them and
seem unconcerned. As she assisted Berta and Alma with their shopping they
had not bothered her, and she had not seen them since.

Suddenly Marie's head shot up at the sounds of car doors slamming,
and she looked out the window to see two large automobiles parked outside.
Four men and one woman in Gestapo uniforms exited the vehicles. The
woman and two of the men waited outside while the other two officers
approached the entrance of the hotel. Marie's blood ran cold, and in a panic
she shook Alma awake and pulled him to his feet. He mumbled and
complained, trying to snuggle next to her again. "Time to go, little one!"
Her voice did not sound like her own.

Unable to arouse him sufficiently, she wrapped one arm around him
and half carried him toward the back of the room. Through an open
doorway she could see a dimly lit kitchen with the proprietress working
feverishly at a tub of laundry.

"You have visitors, ma'am." She strode purposefully through the kitchen
toward the woman, who straightened in surprise to see Marie and Alma
invading her kitchen. "They look to be in a hurry."

The woman seemed ready to complain, but she turned at the sound of
the front door opening and walked into the living room to greet the new
arrivals. Marie pulled Alma through the door at the rear of the kitchen and
turned to see the Gestapo officers approach the woman. There was something
familiar about the small man who pulled a photograph from his coat pocket
and held it up for the proprietress to study, and his voice sent her senses
reeling. "Have you seen this woman? She escaped a military prison . . ."

The woman nodded. "Yes. She is here with a small boy. She said she was
waiting for somebody . . ." She pointed triumphantly toward the kitchen,
and the Gestapo officer turned to look.

Marie met his gaze and found herself face to face with Captain Bernard
Dresdner. In a rush of panic-induced adrenaline she turned and ran, drag-
ging Alma down a dimly-lit hallway toward the back of the hotel. She could
hear Dresdner's deliberate tread behind her and she realized he was not
concerned she would escape.

The hall turned and darkened, and Marie felt with her hand for an
escape—any escape. Her hand contacted a door and she scrabbled for the
handle, her breath coming in panicky gasps as Dresdner's voice came from

behind. "Marie Jacobson! Rolf sends his hello. He asked me to bring you to him."

Marie's hand found the door handle and she thrust it downward. Miraculously it was not locked, and she escaped into the cold night air. Behind her the door was captured before it had a chance to close, and she heard Dresdner calling for his companion to get the car. She ran as fast as she could with Alma in tow, the small boy complaining in muffled rebellion at the suddenness of her flight.

Dresdner's voice behind her sounded amused. "You won't get away, Fräulein. You might as well stop." Suddenly she felt her arm jerked violently, and she turned to see Dresdner gripping Alma's other arm and reaching for his gun. Without a second thought Marie launched herself at his evil face, clawing and scratching, gouging at his eyes and furiously pummeling his head, nose, neck, and whatever else she could contact. Surprised, Dresdner released the boy and turned on her, viciously backhanding her and sending her sprawling into the dirty snow. He released the catch of his gun and stepped close, his dead eye drifting and his working eye glinting with a mixture of amusement and hate. "Give it up, Marie. You're no match for me."

Alma cowered a few feet away, whimpering as he watched his surrogate mother struggle to rise. Marie fought the dizziness that threatened to engulf her and tried to focus on her tormenter. She forced herself to maintain consciousness and pushed back the nausea that made her weak.

"You and I have been apart too long, and to tell the truth, I've missed you." Dresdner leered at her, stepping closer. "Last I saw you, you were praying. Are you a Mormon—*like Schulmann?*" The thought was new to him. "Is that why he protected you?" The revelation lit his face with joy, and he kicked her viciously. Marie recoiled, gasping in agony as horrific pain shot through her body, and Alma's whimpers grew louder. "Go ahead! Pray to your Mormon god!" The captain's voice rose in triumph and he laughed out loud. "You'd better get started, woman, because soon you won't be able to speak."

Marie tried to think past the thundering agony in her body, to plan what to do. Alma's pitiful moans wrenched her heart and deepened her terror of the man above her, and she realized she was in need of a power greater than her own. She took her tormenter's advice and silently poured out her heart to her God.

Suddenly Dresdner's face twisted darkly. "A traitor and a spy. The only thing worse than that combination is a *Mormon* traitor and a *Mormon* spy. "Get up, Fräulein. I'm through playing with you."

Marie stared up at the small man towering over her and felt her defenses crumbling. For a moment she gave in to the defeat her mind was insisting she accept. Then a split-second memory transported her back to her training, and she heard the monologue of an officer reciting from an SOE training manual: *The Gestapo's reputation has been built up on ruthlessness and terrorism, not necessarily intelligence . . .*

With a strength and speed that astonished her, she swept her legs forward and back in a scissor motion, imprisoning the diminutive captain's ankles between her knees, and before he had a chance to react she forced his legs out from under him and threw him violently onto his back, his head striking the frozen ground with a hollow thud. She heard his lungs release their air supply in one tremendous whoosh. His gun fired into the trees before he dropped it, shattering the darkness and bringing a terrified shriek from Alma. Instantly Marie was on her feet, kicking the gun away from the Captain's reach and dodging his outstretched hand as she moved to grab Rolf's son. Clutching the frightened boy into her arms, she ran as fast as she could toward the dark shadows of a stand of trees behind the hotel.

Dresdner rose to his feet and pursued her, his footsteps closing rapidly behind her and his foul curses hinting at what he would do to her when he caught her. In her terror she almost gave in to the overwhelming temptation to surrender. But something inside her warned her to keep running, and she forced herself to continue. She could hear his breath now, coming in short, angry bursts, and knew he was going to overpower them before they could reach the trees. She felt his proximity and recognized he could reach out and grab her at any moment, and the realization that Dresdner felt in control terrified Marie even more than his proximity. She felt his rough hand on the back of her neck at the same moment her feet contacted open space, and she fell, feeling his fingers rake painfully through her hair as he tried unsuccessfully to restrain her.

The suddenness of her fall knocked the breath from her body, and with a mighty splash, icy blackness enveloped her as she went completely under water. Shocked by the cold, she fought for the surface, her feet searching frantically for solid footing and eventually finding the soft squishiness of the river bottom. She stood, and her head and shoulders rose above the water. In her arms Alma sputtered and shrieked, his panicked fingers clawing at her neck and struggling for something to hold onto, and she wrapped her arms around his tiny body and held him close, whispering soothingly in his ear until he began to relax. Above her, she heard the Gestapo captain cursing and threatening in foul, breathless spurts. He did not follow her, but stood at the edge of the embankment yelling over his shoulder for a flashlight.

Alma was shaking uncontrollably, and so was she. Holding the boy's head as high out of the water as her strength would allow, Marie moved away from the riverbank with its cursing Gestapo officer. He called after her. "You'll die of the cold, Marie Jacobson. It's going to snow tonight."

She continued to push through the water away from him, clutching Alma close in her arms.

"In the morning we'll find your cold, frozen, beautiful body. The major will be heartbroken."

Marie prayed silently for help, her lips shaking uncontrollably. She could hardly think straight, she was so cold. In her arms, Alma was still crying softly, and she was thankful because it meant he was still alive.

THIRTY-THREE

April 6, 1944—Evening

Major Rolf Schulmann stood at his bedroom window and watched the alley below. The sun continued to set through a depressing mist, and other than a stray cat sifting through garbage on the curb, the alley was deserted.

He was a prisoner in his room. Rolf thought back to the days when he would have reached for a cigarette in a moment like this, and he thought about the two missionaries who had taught him and so completely altered the course of his life. He blessed those two American boys for their courage and conviction. He thought about the many times he had hovered on the brink of spiritual disaster since then—moments when his decisions could have resulted in his condemnation and certain eternal misery. He thanked his Heavenly Father for the companionship of the Holy Ghost during those dark moments. He thanked his Maker for Hélène's love and the promise of a future together with her and their son. He felt an overwhelming gratitude for the good people who were risking their lives to care for Alma and Marie. And, with a yearning so great he could hardly endure it, he thought about Marie.

Now he stood at his window, waiting for a Gestapo death squad to transfer him to Lyon, where he would be executed for high treason. He was guilty of orchestrating Marie's escape from Dresdner. He was guilty of hiding an enemy spy, allowing Résistance leaders to escape, lying to his superiors, assaulting a Gestapo orderly, collaborating with the Résistance, and withholding information vital to the Third Reich. He did not dispute these charges. He watched the alley below his bedroom window and listened for the convoy from Lyon.

He could hear the sound of their vehicles on the other side of the château as they approached along the Place des Terreaux. At the same time in the alley below him he noticed a man on a bicycle with his hat pulled down over his eyes and wearing an old overcoat and gloves. The man did not notice the Nazi officer standing alone in the second-story window, but Rolf heard the faint sound of the bicycle's bell as the man hurried past on his way home from work. Dejectedly, Rolf observed the man until his bicycle disappeared in the mist, and then he turned his attention to the sound of the approaching convoy. He could hear several large trucks entering the courtyard and circling, then parking near the main entrance. Doors slammed, and he could hear voices approaching the château's main entry. They would invade his privacy at any moment, yanking him out of his room and roughing him up as much as they dared.

He heard footsteps climbing the main staircase, and he turned from his bedroom window. Taking a deep breath, he straightened his shoulders and stood ready to face them, his pulse pounding violently. He knew he would die. They would not even waste space in a POW camp for traitors such as himself. His trip to Lyon would be the last trip he would ever take in his life—in this life, at least. He took a wavering breath. That was another thing he was thankful to those two American boys for: a knowledge that life continued after death. And in spite of his trepidation, he recognized a tiny burst of joy at the thought that Hélène might be on the other side waiting for him. Peaceful warmth enveloped him at the thought as he waited for the door to open.

He started, shocked, when the first man came through the door. It was not the Gestapo escort he had expected—instead, his intrepid Gestapo guard shuffled into the room with his arms raised and his face as colorless as the sky outside Rolf's window. He was followed by the barrel of a very dangerous, very efficient-looking Schmeisser which was connected, finally, to the mischievously evil grin of Jacques Bellamont in the stolen uniform of a Gestapo captain.

The Frenchman's grin widened when he saw Rolf standing by the window, and he addressed the terrified guard. "I'm proud of you. You brought me directly to him without any foolishness." He jabbed the guard in his solar plexus with his weapon to show his gratitude. "Major, I was worried we'd missed you. Good to see you're still in one piece."

Rolf exhaled a sigh of relief, a mixture of bewilderment and gratitude on his face. His brow puckered. "How in the world did you—"

"Alcohol will do strange things to a man, Major. And headstrong young Gestapo are no exception. With a whole lot of drink and a little persuasion, we were able to convince one of Dresdner's men to tell us what we needed to know."

"*Gentle* persuasion, I'm sure."

"Well, it started out that way . . ." Jacques's voice trailed off noncommittally.

"Captain Dresdner would approve of your methods."

"Of course he would." Jacques nodded. "I wish I could demonstrate them for him." He jabbed the guard again. "'Ugly' here was intelligent enough to keep his mouth shut and do what I said. Now we'll see if you're as smart as your guard. Let's go, Major—in three minutes this building is going up in smoke."

"My secretary . . ." Rolf reached for his uniform jacket and empty holster.

"The woman cowering in the corner downstairs?"

"I don't want her hurt."

"We'll make sure she's out before this place falls apart."

"And the others?" Rolf thought of Dresdner's staff.

"They'll be useful—like Ugly here." Jacques loved that solar plexus routine. "*Maquisards* can interrogate prisoners as well as you Germans."

"My escort from Lyon is expected at any moment," said Rolf as he accepted the gun Jaques tossed to him and moved toward the door.

Jacques followed with the whimpering guard. "I guess that means we'd better hurry. I'm not equipped to take on the whole German army, so move quickly, please." He barked orders to one of his men waiting outside the door, and the man, dressed in another pilfered uniform, relieved Jacques of his prisoner and prodded the unfortunate man toward the stairs. Rolf ducked into his office to retrieve his Book of Mormon and the picture of Hélène from his desk, while Jacques hovered impatiently near the doorway. The Frenchman seemed relieved when Rolf reappeared, and they continued down the marble staircase to where Bernice huddled in a pitiful heap on the floor. Rolf helped his secretary to her feet and placed his arm around her, supporting the terrified woman through the front door and down the steps. He spoke soothingly. "Don't worry, Bernice. This has nothing to do with you. Go on home." He gave her a gentle push away from the château.

She took a few steps before turning to look at him. "Will—will you be all right, sir?"

"I will now, Bernice. Thank you."

She smiled hesitantly, seemed about to say something else, then clutched her sweater about her shoulders and fled.

Jacques nudged Rolf's shoulder. "Get in the car. I'll finish up here and then we'll go find someplace to celebrate."

"That sounds wonderful." Rolf smiled at the Frenchman's sense of humor. "I can hardly wait." He turned and ducked into the nearest truck and settled next to the driver while Jacques and three of his men attached charges at intervals around the foundation of the old Château de Lafont. They connected each charge in sequence and tied them all to one main fuse, which Jacques then unrolled across the courtyard to a safe distance and attached to a small detonator. Urgently he waved to the truck drivers, who pulled the trucks away from the building. Rolf's rescuers returned with their prisoners to the trucks, and three of the four vehicles pulled away, turning into the Place des Terreaux and continuing into the evening mist. Jacques glanced up at Rolf seated inside the one remaining truck, hesitated, then hunched his shoulders and forced the handle down into its base. For a split second it seemed nothing happened, and then, with an explosion surprisingly muffled for its size, the ancient château that had survived the Great War and who knows what other conflicts imploded inward and upward, disintegrating windows and violently twisting the stone walls until the structure collapsed into a magnificently grotesque mountain of fire, rubble, and choking dust.

* * *

The sun had just disappeared behind the skyline when Jacques ordered the driver to pull the truck to the side of the road leading to a military airfield near Lyon. He swung to the ground and waited for Major Rolf Schulmann to follow him. Jacques offered the major a cigarette, then returned it to its case with a shrug when Rolf refused. "I'll never understand what you Mormons have against cigarettes and coffee." The Frenchman lit his own cigarette, cupping one hand protectively around the match until the end glowed warmly in the evening darkness. Then he dropped the still-flaming match into the gutter and nodded to Schulmann. "But you've proven your mettle in every other way, and I guess I can forgive you your Mormon idiosyncrasies."

Rolf watched him soberly. "Thank you—for my life."

Jacques scowled. "A lot of good it did. You're throwing it away and it'll be your fault. You know that."

"I know." Rolf agreed. "But I can't let it go. I couldn't live with myself. I need to do this for Félix—and for Marie."

Jacques studied the major soberly. "It took me a while to put two and two together, you know."

"What do you mean?"

"Félix." Jacques explained. "You said he saved your life. At first I didn't make the connection between you and the German friend Félix kept talking about." He grinned. "It makes perfect sense now—I can see that this would be a difficult burden for you to carry."

Rolf said nothing.

Jacques balanced his cigarette in the corner of his mouth and pulled a small scrap of paper from his pocket. "I found her." He handed the paper to Rolf. "She's in a safehouse south of Paris—in Beaune-la-Rolande. Local Résistance hid her last year at Félix's request, and they hired a caretaker for her home so no one would suspect she had disappeared. Seems Félix was under suspicion with the Germans for some time, and his mother's cottage was under surveillance just in case he returned."

"I never heard of his Résistance connections—I only knew of you." Rolf studied the man in front of him for a moment before he looked down at the address in his hand. "I guess I never considered that he might become involved. I misjudged him, and misunderstood him completely." Rolf shook his head. "I've been so blind."

Jacques shrugged. "What difference would it have made if you had known? Would you have helped us then?"

"Probably not," Rolf said. "But I would have been torn—it would have been infinitely more difficult for me to do my job. And I would always have worried that I would catch him in some act of sabotage and have to arrest him. It would have haunted me constantly."

Jacques pulled on his cigarette. "Félix arrived in Belley not long before you. Somehow he eluded the authorities and got his mother out also. It seems she's been in hiding ever since, although he never mentioned anything about her whereabouts to me. I didn't even know she was missing until you approached me." He shook his head in wonder. "Whoever would've thought? A Nazi and a *maquisard* . . . We're an odd friendship, all right."

"War creates extraordinary relationships, I'm discovering," Rolf said, feeling the strange miracle of it all. He smiled at the Frenchman. "I will always be grateful to you. You have probably saved not only my life, but in a roundabout way the lives of my son, the American girl, and everyone on my list for that hellish *rafle*."

"Not bad for a day's work," Jacques quipped.

* * *

Snow fell heavily outside. Marie held Alma close, burrowing herself as deeply as possible into the hay. The farmer didn't know they were there. She had watched, shivering, from the forest until he and his wife finished milking the goats and closed the barn door behind them, and then she had slipped quietly inside with a sleepy, freezing Alma in her arms.

She dropped her sodden coat and shivered uncontrollably as she worked on the little boy. She was so cold she could not undo the buttons of Alma's coat. She prayed silently for help and was eventually able to loosen them with fingers so frozen the joints were stiff.

She cried at the sight of the boy when she finely got him undressed. He was pale and past shivering, and she prayed fervently for his safety while her hands vigorously rubbed his chest and limbs. He responded in time, calling her "Mami" and allowing her to hold him in her arms. She hung their outer clothing across the milking rail and burrowed into the goats' pile of hay, ignoring the animals' complaints. Soon the goats settled down and disregarded the woman and boy, grazing around them as if the intruders were not there.

Marie fought an uncontrollable urge to sleep, knowing she needed to keep track of Alma's breathing. She could feel him warming slightly, and she cautiously allowed him to sleep in her arms. But she was terrified that as soon as she allowed herself to drift off, he would die.

So she stayed awake. She stayed awake as long as she could, but realized she had been slumbering when the sound of heavy boots in the barn awakened her. At first she thought it might be the farmer. But the intruder was not using the lantern the farmer had had with him when he exited the barn with his wife. This person had a powerful flashlight, and he was searching for something with the determination of a person who knows the thing he searches for is somewhere nearby. Terrified, Marie slumped down until her head disappeared under the hay. Alma was already completely covered, and she watched the flashlight dart silently from one corner of the barn to the other. The goats started to complain, pulling at their ropes and crying loudly. Too late Marie remembered her and Alma's clothes drying on the milking rail. The beam of the flashlight caught the garments hanging there, and it stopped.

"Marie?"

Marie's breath caught in her throat. It was Hans. With a cry of relief she called out to him and he turned the flashlight on her briefly and then swiftly crossed the barn to her side. She threw her arms around his neck, so overcome with desperate sobs she could hardly breathe, and he held her tightly, allowing her to cry until she had no more tears.

"How did you ever find us?"

He chuckled. "The owner of the hotel doesn't want trouble with the Gestapo. She was ready to tell everything she knew to whoever wore the right uniform. I followed your footprints—and Dresdner's. Yours dropped off into the river, and I knew I'd better find you as fast as I could. Dresdner, on the other hand, seems content with picking your frozen body out of the snow tomorrow. He's off to bed."

"How did you find me in the dark? In the snow?"

"Mademoiselle, next to your friend Rolf, I'm the best tracker the Führer's got. I'm in the *Gebirgsjager*—the Alpine Elite—remember? I do this for a living." He made his voice sinister. "You'd better be glad I'm on your side."

Marie laughed softly. Alma stirred in his sleep and she looked down at him. His skin was not as ghostly as it had looked when she first undressed him, and he seemed to be comfortably asleep. Perhaps now, with Hans here, the worst would be over.

Hans spoke. "Much as I'd love to nestle down with you and stay this way all night, I think we'd better get going. Besides, there's a man who loves you desperately, and he wouldn't like it if he heard I'd spent the night with you—in the hay."

Marie touched Hans's face. "You might not agree with me, Hans, but I think you've got a good heart." She kissed his cheek. "You'll make a wonderful husband—whenever you decide to settle down."

Hans smiled in the darkness. "Got any sisters?"

She laughed, and he released her and rose to his feet. "Your clothes seem almost dry," he said. "Anyway, we'll have to take what we can get—we've got to get you to Baiersbronn. Rolf told me to be ready to take you there when you called."

"The clothes will be fine. We'll survive."

"Alma looks rather worn out. Want me to help him while you get ready?"

"I would appreciate it. Thanks."

The trek with Hans through the snow was excruciatingly cold, but this time he carried Alma and she was able to hold onto Hans. Their clothes had not completely dried, and the shivering started all over again. The only difference this time was that Hans accompanied them, and even though Marie felt almost as miserable as before, she felt safe.

It took them half an hour to reach Hans's car, and when they did, it took a while before Hans could get it started in the cold. After several fruitless attempts the engine began to show signs of life and eventually turned over. Marie held Alma close in the back seat, and his eyes drooped with fatigue. Hans glanced back at Marie. "Go ahead and sleep. I know where to go."

"Do you know where the Wagners—"

"Rolf explained how to get there."

"Thank you, Hans." Her voice was soft. "We owe our lives to you tonight."

"What are friends for, right?" Hans gripped the steering wheel and turned the car into the snow.

* * *

Someone shook her gently. "Marie . . ." She stirred and opened her eyes. For a moment she didn't remember where she was. "Time to get up."

Marie sat up, Alma's head still in her lap. She blinked a few times, saw Hans, and remembered.

Hans whispered, "Leave Alma here for a minute. He'll be all right."

She took his hand and allowed him to pull her out of the car. He steadied her and chuckled. "Rolf said you take a while to wake up."

"Whatever do you and Rolf talk about?"

He laughed again and softly closed the car door. Alma slept on.

Holding her hand, he led her to the front door, and Marie noticed that the snow had stopped and a few stars were beginning to appear. It was bitterly cold. Hans knocked firmly and then waited through a long silence. He knocked again, and finally the door opened a crack and the branch president peeked out.

He recognized Hans's uniform first and opened the door quickly. Then Herr Wagner saw Marie and his eyes widened in surprise. "Giselle!" He hesitated, glancing at Hans. He was obviously confused.

Hans spoke. "Herr Wagner, your friend Rolf Schulmann is in danger and the Gestapo is trying to capture his son. Giselle is an American, and she is also in danger. I need to know right now if you are willing to hide her and the boy." Hans paused. "If you are not able to do so, please tell me quickly so we can be on our way."

President Wagner looked overwhelmed.

"Who is it, Horst? It's almost midnight." Mathilde Wagner appeared in the darkness behind her husband, her grey hair rolled in curlers that escaped from beneath her scarf. She saw Marie and Hans and her eyes grew wide. "What is happening?" she gasped. "Where's Rolf?"

Hans spoke calmly. "We think the Gestapo has arrested him for protecting Giselle. She and Rolf's son need a place to hide. The Gestapo is searching for them both."

Mathilde looked terrified. "The Gestapo . . ." She glanced at her husband.

"Of course we'll hide them." Herr Wagner lifted his chin. Marie felt an outpouring of gratitude for the man and his wife, and she fought back tears.

"Rolf will come for them as soon as he can—if he can. Otherwise, we'll have to make other arrangements." Hans squeezed Marie's hand briefly. "I'll go get Alma."

Mathilde stretched her arm past her husband's nightshirt and grasped Marie's coat. "Come. We must get you inside." She felt the moisture in Marie's clothes and shook her head disapprovingly. "We must get you dry."

A moment later Hans returned and handed the sleeping Alma to Herr Wagner, then turned back toward the car.

Marie turned to Mathilde and touched her arm. "Frau Wagner, there's something I must do first." She slipped past the branch president and ran after Hans. "Hans, wait!" Her voice was soft, but it carried in the stillness of the night.

Hans stopped and turned, his eyes searching Marie's face.

"Hans—how can I ever thank you?" She hesitated in front of him. He moved as if to touch her, and then stopped.

"I'll think of something," he said.

"Will I ever see you again?"

Hans shrugged. "If you decide to marry that crazy Mormon, you can count on it."

THIRTY-FOUR

April 7, 1944

Captain Bernard Dresdner tapped his gun impatiently against one uniformed leg and waited. He hated to wait. He knew he should have followed the woman yesterday evening, but the day had been long and he had been feeling out of sorts and tired from his long trip.

He hadn't been able to believe his luck when he'd seen the American girl and Hélène's son in the hotel. His luck had been running high since early that morning when he'd cleared out the children's home in Izieu and arrested the traitorous Mormon. Now it looked like he would be able to wrap up the whole inconvenience that was Schulmann and his family within twenty-four hours.

His future possibilities looked bright. Nieman would be required to forgive his insubordination, and Barbie would give him his long-overdue promotion. Yes, his future looked bright.

With superhuman effort he pulled his thoughts back to the inconvenience of the task at hand. Fräulein Jacobson's body was out here somewhere. He could just leave it, but for two considerations: He needed the girl and the major's son in order to complete the Mormon's humiliation and defeat, and, deep inside, he had a nagging feeling that they were not really dead.

Last night had been impossibly cold. Reason dictated that the woman and boy would soon be found, huddled together under a tree and frozen solid. There was no way they could have survived the night after that swim in the river. Dresdner watched as his men searched the forest. They were not the best trackers in the Reich, but under the circumstances, they would have to do. Calling in the *Gebirgsjager* would be his next step if the bodies were not found within the next few hours.

But the American girl and Hélène's boy could not have gone far. Dresdner holstered his weapon and walked toward the village doctor, who was standing under a tree and looking uncomfortable. "Herr Becker, I apologize for the delay. I am sure we will find them soon."

The doctor shook his head. "There is no way they could have survived if, as you say, they fell in the river."

"But you are here just in case, Herr Doctor. If they are alive they will need medical attention before I can take them with me."

"Captain—" The doctor cleared his throat. "You're an optimist. The chances of the woman and boy surviving—even for an hour after exposure of that sort—are so slim as to be almost nonexistent."

"But perhaps they received assistance of some sort and were able to survive through the night."

"Perhaps." The doctor did not sound convinced.

"We will find them. Soon we will discover their tracks and then it will only be a matter of time."

"Remember, Herr Captain, it snowed most of the night."

Before he could respond, Dresdner heard a shout and turned in the direction of the sound to see one of his searchers approaching with a local resident in tow. The Gestapo agent pointed to the small man who was wringing his hands nervously as he stared at Dresdner's eye. "Captain, this farmer has something to tell you."

Dresdner turned impatiently toward the nervous man. "Well?"

"Sir, I was readying myself for bed last night when I heard my goats bleating in the barn. They are usually very docile and sleep well at night. That is, if I remember to feed them properly and—"

"What is this about?" Dresdner had no time for this farmer's ramblings.

"Well, sir . . ." the man was obviously terrified. ". . . the goats are actually good watchdogs, sir. They tell me when wild animals are nearby or a prowler is approaching, ready to shoot the missus or me . . ."

"Farmer, I'll shoot you myself if you don't conclude your statements within the next five seconds."

The man was visibly shaken. "I went to the barn, sir—to check on my goats—and . . . and there was a woman there, and a boy, and an officer . . ."

"An *officer?*"

"Yes, sir . . ." The man sensed he had the full attention of the Gestapo captain and relaxed slightly. "He seemed to be one of the *Gebirgsjager* that train here in the area—"

"And the woman and boy—they were alive?"

"Yes, sir. The woman was talking with the officer."

Dresdner scowled darkly. "Did they see you?"

The farmer shook his head proudly. "I hid behind my tools outside the door and listened . . ."

"Listened?" Dresdner stepped closer. "What were they talking about?"

"Well . . . " The man shrunk from the Gestapo captain's approach. "I— I didn't hear much, really . . . The goats—"

Dresdner swore, describing in detail what he thought of the man's goats. "Tell me everything you heard, farmer."

* * *

Frau Wagner glanced up from the table as Marie pulled a shirt heavy with water to arm's length and allowed the excess water to cascade off the garment's surface into the washtub. "You had me fooled, Giselle." She punched her bread dough with strong hands, folding it in upon itself and then repeating the process. "I truly thought you to be French."

"You heard?" Marie folded the shirt in half and twisted a good portion of the remaining moisture into the water below. She glanced at the woman.

Mathilde nodded, rolling the dough expertly between her strong hands. "When you arrived I heard the officer with you tell my husband you are an American."

Marie watched her closely, water from the shirt dripping down her arms and off her elbows into the tub. She spoke softly. "And how does it make you feel?"

The woman hesitated. "I meant it when I said Rolf needs someone like you." Disappointment wrinkled her brow. "I just didn't imagine the person he chose would be an American. I guess I should have known—I suspected that Horst and Rolf were not telling me everything that Sunday we first met. But I never thought it was something important enough to put Rolf's life in danger."

"Rolf's life is in danger because he has protected mine." Marie tried to ignore the sting of Frau Wagner's words, bending to her task with increased determination. "He protected me even when he wasn't sure I would return the favor if the tables were turned. He knew I was an enemy, yet he risked his life for me." She blinked back tears and turned to smile at Alma, who had just entered the room looking for her.

Mathilde straightened her back and glanced lovingly at the boy, her hands idle for a moment. Then she shook her head and her expression saddened. "Are you even a member of the Church, Giselle?"

"Yes."

"Probably 'Giselle' isn't even your real name."

"No."

The older woman looked tired. "I guess I would do everything in my power to protect someone *I* loved—if that person were in danger." Her voice caught, and Marie wondered if Mathilde's memories of her son made her feel even more protective of Rolf. Mathilde said, "I cannot fault him for doing the same."

Marie met her gaze, and for a moment the two women shared an uncomfortable oneness—the older woman feeling the acute loss of her son, and the younger, the separation from the man she loved and to whom she owed her life. Marie tried to think of something to say that would lessen Mathilde's anxiety, but she could think of nothing. She heard rapid steps approaching from the living room and turned to see President Wagner hastening through the door, his face pale.

"The Gestapo is searching the village."

Mathilde stared fearfully at her husband. "When will they get here?"

"Any moment." The branch president took a deep breath, trying to steady his breathing. "Frau Sussman sent her daughter to warn the neighbors."

Brushing dough from her wrists, Frau Wagner grasped Alma's tiny hand and hustled Marie and the boy up the stairway. In the bedroom she pulled a ladder from the closet and leaned it against the frame of the attic opening. "Up here, Giselle." Her voice bordered on panic, and Marie wrapped one arm about the small boy's waist and carried him like a sack of potatoes up the ladder. She pushed the attic door open and hoisted Alma up inside. Then she grasped the edge of the opening and pulled herself through. As she pulled her feet into the attic Frau Wagner spoke, her voice a frantic whisper. "Hide behind something as best you can. They will most likely send someone to search the attic. It's the best we can do."

Marie nodded.

"I will remove the ladder. Wait for me to come for you."

"God bless you, Frau Wagner." Marie knew the branch president and his wife were risking everything for her and for Alma. Carefully she closed the attic door.

By now Herr Wagner had let the Gestapo into the house. There was not much in the way of insulation between the floor joists and wooden planks that separated her hiding place from the rest of humanity below, and Marie could hear voices. Although their words were muted, she could still make out what they were saying.

"*Guten Morgen,* Herr Wagner. We are sorry to bother you. May we enter?"

"Of course, Lieutenant. You and your men are always welcome in my home."

Marie could hear the heavy boots of several men entering the large living room below. She heard the muffled voice of the Gestapo officer again.

"We apologize for the intrusion, Herr Wagner, but we must search your home."

"Excuse my boldness, sir, but why? We are law-abiding citizens . . ."

"That may well be. However, we have received information that a woman and young boy are hiding in your village. The woman is wanted for murder."

"We would never hide a criminal, Herr Lieutenant. There is no murderer here."

"If that is true, you have nothing to fear."

The branch president's response was hidden by a cacophony of heavy boots stomping across Frau Wagner's tidy floor, and footsteps entered the kitchen where Mathilde had most likely returned to her bread making. Through the high attic window Marie could hear soldiers moving about outside. Then she heard heavy footsteps ascending the main staircase.

"Come, Alma. Tread softly. We must find a place to hide." Obediently, Alma took her hand and tiptoed with her across the attic floor. Boxes, bags, and various pieces of furniture dotted the perimeter of the room, and at the far end under a boarded window lay a large mound of burlap sacks filled with corn husks and wood chips. The pile was haphazardly thrown together, the bags piled on top of each other until they reached halfway to the ceiling. Marie guided her small companion in that direction. Either it would be the best hiding place in the attic, or it would be the first place the Germans looked when they came through the attic door. Marie did not have time to look elsewhere—she heard voices in the hallway below her, and footsteps entered the bedroom and paused. Marie heard a shout and knew they had discovered the access. They would search for the ladder, and in a minute they would be in the attic.

Gingerly, Marie moved a burlap sack aside. "In here, Alma." She gave him a gentle push. "Let's pretend we're playing hide-and-seek, all right?" Alma disappeared inside. Cautiously Marie followed. It would not do for the soldiers below them to hear her movements, or for a bag to become dislodged and fall to the floor. Marie squeezed her body through the small natural opening between the pile of burlap and the slope of the roof where it met the floor. A cold draft chilled her back as she moved the burlap sacks carefully over the entrance and settled with knees tucked beneath her chin and her arms around the terrified boy.

"I'm cold!" Alma's words were a whisper, but Marie shushed him with a gentle finger on his mouth.

"We mustn't talk, *liebling*. Be very still." Marie felt the little boy stiffen against her in a courageous effort to ignore the cold draft hitting his back-side, and the tiny fingers that gripped her skin felt like ice.

In the room below, the soldiers found the ladder. Marie could hear it scraping across floorboards as it was pulled from the closet. The end of the ladder hit the frame of the attic door with a sharp thud, and Marie heard a soldier climbing toward their hiding place. She pulled Alma closer and tried to keep her breathing shallow, but her heart beat so rapidly she felt like it would pound a hole in her chest.

The access door opened, balanced at its highest point, and then crashed backward to the attic floor. Against her side Alma whimpered softly, and Marie placed a gentle hand over his trembling mouth and held him as still as she could. There was a silence, probably while the German soldier allowed his eyes to adjust to the gloom. Then Marie heard his boots hit the wooden floor in one swift movement as he swung himself into the attic and stood. Marie heard his comrade below asking questions. The soldier in the attic replied abruptly and moved into the room, and through a crack between the bags she could see his back as he searched the opposite end of the attic behind the furniture. Carefully and methodically he moved pieces aside from their original positions, taking an inordinate amount of care not to break anything. Satisfied that the two fugitives were not behind the furniture, he moved to the left and began rearranging piles of bedding and boxes of kitchen supplies. Marie's breath quickened as she realized the man was determined to search every inch of the attic. Unless a miracle occurred, he would find them.

A head appeared through the attic floor, and the second German soldier barked a question. His comrade in the attic shook his head and gestured for his companion to wait below. Marie was relieved when the head disappeared.

Her relief diminished as the soldier on the opposite end of the attic rapidly worked his way toward their hiding place. Marie frantically searched the floor around her with one hand, desperate for anything usable as a weapon. Her fingers touched nothing but sawdust and small chips of wood, so she grabbed a handful and waited.

The soldier reached the pile of burlap bags. He paused, then commenced removing sacks and throwing them aside. Alma whimpered, and the soldier started and reached for his gun. His eyes searched the pile of burlap and his hand pulled bags out of the way. He couldn't see them yet, but he knew they were there.

The German soldier picked up the last burlap bag separating him from their hiding place and threw it aside, and Marie saw the man's face clearly for the first time. She stifled a gasp. He was one of the German soldiers who had been in sacrament meeting on the day after Christmas—he had passed her the sacrament. He stepped back, his face registering shock as he recognized her, also. Marie and the German soldier stared at each other for a long moment while time stood still and Alma sobbed quietly, clinging to Marie. The soldier lifted his gun awkwardly, as if he were uncertain what to do.

Marie whispered, "Please . . ."

"Hast du sie gefunden?" A voice from the foot of the ladder shattered the silence, and time sped on its way.

The soldier in the attic had not moved, and when his comrade at the foot of the ladder asked what he had found, the voice seemed to jostle him back to reality and his chin lifted defiantly. His eyes locked with Marie's, and without breaking eye contact he holstered his gun and picked up a bag of corn husks. *"Nein, ich habe die Frau nicht gefunden!"* He threw the bag over Marie and Alma's hiding place and turned on his heel. A moment later he hoisted himself down onto the ladder and disappeared, pulling the attic door solidly shut behind him.

Marie shook violently. Her heart pounded and she felt incredibly cold, and it had nothing to do with the draft at her back. Something had just happened, something miraculous. Tears fell and she buried her face in her knees and began to sob. Her tears intrigued Alma, and he stopped his own sobbing to watch her closely. "Mami?" A tiny hand touched her face. Marie lifted her head and smiled at him through her tears.

She recalled the smile the soldier had given her on the Sunday after Christmas as he passed her the bent metal plate with its scraps of coarse black bread. She remembered the look in his eyes just now as he stared down at her in the attic. And she thought about the love that the Savior had just shown her. He had sent that particular soldier into the attic to look for her and kept the other in the bedroom below. He had helped the soldier recognize her before he had a chance to betray her to his companion, and He had softened the Latter-day-Saint soldier's heart so that he did not betray their hiding place. With a sob of relief, Marie kissed Alma's unruly hair and settled down to wait for Frau Wagner.

THIRTY-FIVE

April 7, 1944

Marie held Alma close for several minutes, shocked by what had transpired and humbled by the obvious miracle that she and the boy had just experienced. She listened to the silence and waited for Frau Wagner to inform them the soldiers had gone. Gradually, Marie's body again registered the cold of the attic and she began to notice the boy's shivering in her arms. She kissed the top of his head and murmured comfortingly to the bewildered child while she listened for Mathilde. Her mind raced, trying to formulate a plan.

They needed to get out of Germany. Perhaps she could ask the Wagners to help her find somebody who might help them cross the border into Switzerland—somebody who had knowledge of the fastest and safest route through the Alps. If Captain Dresdner believed she were here, he would not leave until she were captured. She could not begin to imagine why she might be so important to the man—unless his hatred of Rolf and his determination to be exonerated of any wrongdoing in her escape was what formed his all-consuming ruthlessness.

Eventually Marie heard the shuffle of feet and the creak of the ladder. It was Herr Wagner's head that finally emerged through the attic door, and as he peered into the gloom, trying to locate Marie and Alma, Marie pushed aside the bags and stood on shaky legs, relieved the Gestapo's search party had moved on. Alma clutched her hand tightly as they approached the branch president. Marie asked, "They'll be back, won't they?"

"Yes, probably they will." President Wagner reached for Alma, pulled him close, and descended the ladder with the boy in his arms. He reached up to assist Marie with the last few steps and then returned the ladder to the back of the closet. "One of the searchers is a member of our branch, posted with the local *Hitlerjugend.* He comes to our meetings as often as he is permitted and helps pass the sacrament."

"I know. I remembered him." Marie still felt the wonder of the miracle she and Alma had just received, and she shared the experience briefly with Horst Wagner. He listened solemnly, his eyes shining with emotion as she relayed how the soldier had decided not to betray them to his comrade solely because he recognized her from the meeting that Christmas Sunday.

Mathilde Wagner waited for them in the kitchen, her hands wringing agitatedly in her apron. "Will Rolf come for you?" she asked Marie.

"I don't know if he can, Frau Wagner. Hans thinks Rolf might have been arrested. Hans told me yesterday that when he received my message he immediately called Belley headquarters and the operator couldn't connect the call." Marie's voice wavered. "I'm afraid something terrible has happened."

Herr Wagner gazed sympathetically at her and then turned to glance at the major's son, consternation puckering his brow. Alma stood in the doorway clutching the tank his father had given him for Christmas, his anxious eyes traveling from one adult to another. The branch president shook his head. "We'll have to get him out of the country. If he stays here it's inevitable he will be caught." He looked at Marie. "Both of you need to get out." He scratched his chin thoughtfully. "Rolf would want us to help you."

Marie licked her dry lips. "I have already put you in enough danger, President. If the Gestapo discovered you had helped us—"

"Do not worry about us, Fräulein. God has been looking out for us in miraculous ways—as He did you. We will be all right. Somehow, we will get through all of this." He placed a comforting hand on her shoulder. "For good people such as you and Rolf, God has many special miracles reserved. I believe He will see both of you through this war."

Marie blinked back tears. "You have incredible faith, Herr Wagner. I am glad I got to know you."

Herr Wagner struggled with his own emotions. "I wish we had time to get to know each other better, Giselle. You are a steady, responsible girl, and I wish I could have told you how Rolf has blessed our lives. If God is willing, you will see him again—in this life."

"There is nothing I would like more," Marie said softly. "Thank you, President Wagner."

Herr Wagner stepped back and took a deep breath. "Now we must figure how to get one American girl and one small boy past a military checkpoint without raising any suspicions." He frowned thoughtfully.

"Perhaps there is someone in my branch who has clearance to travel—maybe that person might know a way . . ."

Mathilde Wagner made a strangled sound deep in her throat, and she stared fearfully at her husband as he paced, concentrating. She wrapped her arms around her own frail shoulders and began to moan softly and rocked back and forth. Marie went to her and placed an arm around the woman, and even though Mathilde remained rigid in her embrace, Marie felt her begin to sob. She wished she could know what to say to comfort her, but the stiffness of Mathilde's shoulders suggested the older woman would not be receptive to anything Marie had to offer. Frau Wagner had been through unimaginable heartache already with the loss of her son in Russia, and the idea that she and her husband might have to endure more because of a fugitive enemy agent was likely more than she could take.

The branch president turned to face his wife, his face kind. "You know we have to do this thing, Mathilde. We need to do it for Rolf—and for his son."

She nodded silently and said nothing.

Her husband looked thoughtful. "Frau Salzmann has a son who works for a bank in Zurich. He makes deliveries and comes home regularly to check on her—the doctor does not like her to be alone with her weak back for too long." He reached for his coat. "I will go talk to her."

His wife shook her head. "It's too risky, Horst! The Gestapo will still be searching—"

"We have no time to waste." Herr Wagner bent to kiss his wife tenderly before pushing his arms through the sleeves of his coat and reaching for his hat. "I will be careful." He glanced at Marie. "And I will hurry. You must get across the border before the soldiers decide to do a more thorough search." He smiled ruefully. "A blessing given by our Father in Heaven may be withdrawn if we do not do our part when we have the chance."

Marie nodded in agreement and watched silently as he opened the door, looked furtively to the left and to the right, and then slipped out into the street.

The branch president returned less than an hour later with Frau Salzmann's seventeen-year-old son in tow. Horst introduced Marie to the boy, who nodded at Marie and extended his hand. His grip was firm and steady for a teenager, and she was intrigued by the self-confidence illuminating his eyes.

"President Wagner told me you are Alma's tutor, Giselle," he said, smiling. "I am pleased to meet you. My name is Roderick." He stepped back and glanced down at Alma, asleep on a blanket on the floor next to the stove. "And this is Alma, I presume?"

"Yes. He is small, and shouldn't take up too much room . . ."

Roderick nodded. "He should fit just fine."

"Fit?" Herr Wagner looked quizzically at the young man. "What do you mean?"

Roderick looked at the branch president in confusion. "You did say you wanted me to smuggle him across the border?"

"Yes, but—"

"I ride a *motorcycle,* President Wagner. I will have to fit him into one of my saddlebags."

Marie gasped. "You can't do that do a small boy! He'll die of fright!"

Roderick shrugged. "That's all I can offer. The patrol at the border will not search my bags because I carry financial documents for the *Hitlerjugend.*" He paused. "That is my job for the Third Reich, President—I thought you knew."

There was an uncomfortable moment of silence. Herr Wagner glanced at the major's son peacefully sleeping near the warmth of Mathilde's baking bread. He murmured, "I didn't know you rode a motorcycle . . ."

"It is very efficient—uses very little petrol." Roderick spoke matter-of-factly, as if the branch president should have known that a motorcycle was the preferred means of travel. "I'm sure I can get him to Zurich safely, if that is what you wish."

Herr Wagner looked helplessly at Marie and then back at the boy. "I was hoping Giselle could accompany you too . . ."

"Oh, no!" Roderick shook his head emphatically. That would not be possible. They would detain her without question at the border—and then Major Schulmann's son would be in danger. You *do* want him to reach Switzerland, don't you?"

"Of course." Herr Wagner looked tired.

"Besides, I would lose my job—maybe even be *disciplined.* If I am to smuggle anything across the border for you it must be able to fit inside my bags."

"How do you plan to fit a small boy . . . ?"

"It's easy." Roderick demonstrated in the air with his hands. "I pack him in the bag like this . . ." He motioned lifting the lid and sliding something inside. ". . . until his feet and bottom are completely covered. Then he leans close to my back and wraps his arms around my waist, and my rain-coat covers him. The only thing they see at the border is the sack on the back of my motorcycle. I carry things in sacks all the time, and they have not looked yet—I am an officer and I have a pass." He straightened, looking pleased with himself.

Still the uncomfortable silence prevailed in the Wagners' tidy kitchen. Marie was the first one to speak, her voice strained. "He will be terrified, but at least he'll be safe." She felt the familiar fear building at the base of her throat at the thought that she would not be able to go, but she swallowed against it valiantly. "I want him to do it."

Herr Wagner looked at her in concern. "What about you?"

Marie knew her continued presence in this house would be more than the branch president's wife could take, and she smiled courageously. "I will return to France." She would find a way to contact the Résistance and petition their help in crossing the border. "It will be all right, Herr Wagner. I will make it." She smiled at him, her eyes moist. "You have been a blessing to me. I am so grateful to you both." She moved closer to the branch president's wife. "And I thank *you*, Frau Wagner, for your kindness. I know it has not been easy."

Mathilde shook her head. "I *want* to like you, Giselle—for Rolf's sake." She smiled cautiously. "Perhaps after Germany has won the war . . ."

Marie decided to let that pass. She returned the woman's smile. "Yes. Perhaps."

Roderick cleared his throat. "What have we decided, then?"

Herr Wagner looked soberly at Marie, then across to the sleeping form of Rolf's son. He hesitated and then said to Roderick, "Are you certain he will be safe? Will you get him there?"

"I am certain."

"Very well." The branch president sighed, resigned. "When you arrive in Zurich, take him to a local hospital and tell the nurses you found him wandering alone in the streets. They will know what to do with him."

Suddenly Marie panicked. "Where will I find him?" Herr Wagner and his wife turned to stare at her and she realized what she had said. She paled. "I mean, where will Major Schulmann find him after the war? He'll look for him as soon as possible, I know."

Herr Wagner studied her thoughtfully. "The hospital will assign him to an orphanage where he can stay until his father comes to get him. Children are displaced all the time, and parents look for them as soon as they are free to do so."

She felt awkward under his scrutiny. What had made her say that? She shook her head and turned away, subdued. "I will get his things."

* * *

Darkness fell, bringing with it a chance for Marie and Alma to slip from Herr Wagner's home and join Roderick in the tiny shed behind his mother's house. His motorcycle had seen better days, Marie thought, trying not to worry about Alma's safety with a member of the Hitler Youth. She knew he was a member of the Church, and President Wagner seemed to trust him. Yet Marie couldn't help thinking it was a little like entrusting a spider with a fly. She wondered what the branch president had said to the young man, what he had told him about Rolf that would make a young *Hitlerjugend* officer agree to do such a dangerous thing.

"We must hurry, Fräulein. Curfew begins in ten minutes and you must be back inside Herr Wagner's home before then, or I will have to arrest you."

Marie peered at the young man, curious as to whether he was joking, and was intrigued to see that his expression seemed perfectly serious. His comment seemed odd when he was in the process of breaking the rules himself. Yet he appeared unable to make the connection between his actions and hers, probably justifying his actions based upon his military position and whatever Herr Wagner had told him, whereas she was just a civilian being warned not to break the rules.

Roderick briskly took command of the situation. "Please lift the boy to the back of the seat, Fräulein." He donned his sidearm, checking to make sure the flap across the handle was snapped shut and his belt securely fastened. Marie thought sadly that Roderick was too young to be a man, yet that was what it seemed he had been forced to become. He looked like a boy playing at soldier, donning a toy gun and an attitude and preparing to annihilate the enemy single-handedly. She felt a twinge of pity for him, locked into this world of hate and killing that seemed to be the required path of all German youth at this stage of the war. Gently she lifted Alma onto the motorcycle and crouched to look him in the eye. "Do you know what is going to happen, sweetheart?"

Wide-eyed, Alma stared at her and said nothing.

"This is Roderick." Marie pointed to the young man, who was busily donning his raincoat. "He is going to let you ride with him on this motor-cycle—all the way to Switzerland." She tried to smile.

"Are you coming with me?" Alma sat rigidly, clutching her hand tightly in his own.

Marie shook her head, crying inside. "No, dearest. I cannot come with you."

Alma's gaze wavered. "I don't want to go. I want to stay with you."

She had dreaded this moment, wondering how in the world she was going to explain to this tiny boy the reason for their separation. "You *must* go, Alma. There are bad men trying to hurt you—and Roderick can take you far away to where they cannot get you."

He understood about bad men. Bad men made you jump in a river so cold your lungs burned when you tried to breathe. Bad men stomped and yelled and chased you into the attic. And bad men made you have to go away with an impatient stranger, your feet folded uncomfortably tight against your bottom in a bag, and a smelly raincoat suffocating the breath from your body.

Marie felt nauseated. She tried to position Alma's body more comfortably but was startled when Roderick barked at her imperiously, pushing her aside and swinging his leg over the motorcycle. He glanced back at his young passenger, saw the tears, and softened somewhat. "Go ahead, Fräulein—take one minute more. I must get through the checkpoint before it is closed for the night, so one minute is all I can give you."

"Why are you sending me away?" Alma's eyes were pleading. "Don't you love me anymore?"

"I love you, Alma." Marie felt her throat constrict as she looked into his tear-filled eyes. "I love you so much that it hurts. But this is for your own good—so you can be safe."

Alma thought about what she had said, and a large tear fell silently, following an already shining path on one smudged cheek. He watched her carefully while she wrapped the blanket Frau Wagner had given him tightly around his shoulders, securing it with a pin so it would not fly off and betray his position under Roderick's coat.

Marie forced herself to speak calmly. "You must be strong, Alma—and mind what Roderick tells you. He will help you get to a safe place."

"Where no one tries to hurt me?"

"That's right." Marie forced a smile. "Where no one tries to hurt you."

"Papa said *you* would take care of me."

Marie hesitated. "Yes, Alma. Your papa wanted me to keep you safe. I've done my best, and now . . ." Marie swallowed past the lump in her throat. "Now it's Roderick's turn."

Alma continued to watch her soberly, his eyes betraying his fear. "I don't want to go," he said again, this time subdued.

"I know. And I'm so sorry." Marie pulled him close and felt her own tears falling. His hair pressed against her cheek felt warm and familiar, and his miniature body fit comfortably in her arms. She held him close for one long moment, and then took him gently by the shoulders. Her eyes locked with his and she felt the shock of his father's penetrating gaze in his five-year-old eyes. "You are a strong boy, Alma. You are brave like your father. You will be all right."

With one tiny fist he brushed a tear from his cheek. "Will you come and find me when the bad men are gone?"

Marie flinched. She realized it would be cruel to commit to something and then have him be devastated later. What if she did not survive? Or what if she found a way to get home and could not get back? She loved Alma deeply, but there were too many variables—too many things that could go wrong. She remembered when she would call her father from school, complaining about something or other—a roommate, a school assignment, a broken faucet . . . Her father would remind her that life had unimportant things, important things, and things that mattered most. He suggested that she spend the days allotted to her on the things that mattered most.

What if she were supposed to be a part of this boy's life? She could not dispute that her destiny and his had been thrown together and entwined over the last months in a way that was difficult to separate—even with physical parting imminent. As Marie held him close, she realized she did not sense the finality that usually accompanied permanent separations—such as she had imagined this would be. In fact, she felt the same confusion and loneliness that had accompanied the separation last Christmas from Alma's father—a feeling that the story was not yet complete, the book not yet closed. It could have been wishful thinking—a desire that things would work themselves out, or that a dream would ultimately mesh with reality. Yet, she knew this love she had for Rolf's son carried a value far above that of other things she could be doing with her life. What if she did find a way to escape war-torn Europe and return to her father in Utah? What would she do with the nagging worry that would pester her for the remainder of her days—the worry that Alma still needed her?

She realized that Alma deserved an answer, and that the answer she gave him in the next few moments could possibly determine the course of her life—perhaps her entire future. And most importantly, it could determine his. The thought overwhelmed her and she took a deep breath. *The things that matter most . . .*

"I promise." She pulled him closer in her arms. "Dear, sweet Alma. I promise I will find you!"

* * *

The last sounds of the small motorcycle with its precious cargo faded into the darkness, and as the night grew silent about her Marie stood for several minutes, looking unseeing in the direction Alma disappeared. Her eyes had long ago adjusted to the darkness, and she studied the empty road with a numbness that enveloped her whole body to a point where she no longer felt the cold wind penetrating her unbuttoned coat and stiffening her unprotected fingers.

She felt too numb to be uneasy, her loss paramount in her mind, dwarfing all else—even the fact that she was an enemy standing alone in a darkened street past the beginning of curfew. She stared blankly past rows of darkened cottages and a church, with its white steeple rising eerily to a point somewhere in the night sky. She did not even try to think, to reason, but just allowed herself to drift aimlessly, as if she were one with the wind that tugged haphazardly at her skirt and pulled her hair from beneath her hat to tumble down the back of her neck. "Alma . . ." Her whisper made no noise, exiting more as a thought than a sound. Her lips formed his name over and over until it became no more than a string of syllables in her head repeating themselves unendingly.

She shuddered, shaking off the stupor and forcing herself to focus on the task at hand. She would return to the branch president's home, gather her few possessions, and leave immediately. From that point she had no plan, other than to find her way somehow back into France and into the care of the Résistance. Her mind still refused to reason, saving her from the harsh reality that she probably would not make it. She turned and followed the road back in the direction she had come.

A tall figure walking toward her seemed familiar, but in her numbed state she did not at first recognize the broad shoulders or the relaxed stride that so intrigued her about Major Rolf Schulmann. When he reached her she felt life flowing back into her veins, and her senses registered a relief so profound that she could not speak. Instead, she launched herself into his arms with the desperation of a thirst-crazed man approaching a reservoir, her arms tightening around his neck as if she would squeeze the life out of him. Rolf's arms closed around her with the same desperation, a sob escaping his throat unbidden as her head nestled against his shoulder and neck. He pressed his cheek against her hair and for several minutes neither of them spoke, the stillness and darkness around them growing loud with a multitude of unanswered questions.

Rolf whispered, "President Wagner told me what you did for my son."

"Rolf . . . I've missed you . . ."

Rolf lifted her chin and kissed her gently. "Thank you, Marie. Thank you for protecting him."

She shook her head. "It was the Wagners, Rolf—and Hans. I couldn't have made it without Hans . . ."

"I know," Rolf said. "Horst told me about your run from Captain Dresdner, the river, the barn, Hans, the attic . . ." He paused, taking a deep breath. "How can I ever repay you, Marie?"

"I told you I'd take care of him, Rolf."

"You've had quite a harrowing two days, haven't you?"

"I'm sure you have, too." She touched his cheeks with her hands, still awestruck at his presence, and a little unsure he was real. Concerned, she asked, "Did the Gestapo come after you?"

"Yes."

"How did you escape? What did they want from you . . . ?" She trailed off, realizing that she had too many questions for him to answer at the moment.

"I'll tell you about it sometime, Marie." He took her hand in his own, his large palms warming her cold fingers. "I need to talk to you—about many things."

"I wish you could've seen your son before he left . . ."

"I guess I was hoping I could get here in time . . ." Rolf sighed. "But it's better this way. It would've been too hard on him—and on me. He would not have wanted to go." His voice wavered slightly. "Now he'll be safe until the war is over." He walked with her back to Herr Wagners' house, holding her close and whispering questions in her ear as they walked down the darkened, empty street.

Rolf's appearance had a mellowing effect on Mathilde, and for the duration of the evening the woman seemed at peace with Marie's presence in her home. She prepared a meal for them, providing a loaf of her freshly baked bread and a jar of homemade apple butter. Then she lingered, watching Rolf eat and telling him everything that had happened that day. Marie stayed silent, observing the conversation and marveling at the change in Mathilde. She felt sorry for her; the woman had never come to terms with the death of her son, and Rolf's presence in her home seemed to fill that void, soothe her nerves, and calm her fears. Marie wondered what her own response would have been had she been forced to show hospitality to a German or a Japanese spy. Certainly she would not have responded with such grace as Frau Wagner—and Marie had not half the reason for hate as did Mathilde. She knew she could not fault the woman for her fear and distrust. Perhaps propaganda spouted by her government had tainted her opinion of Americans—as American propaganda had turned Americans against the Germans, Italians, and Japanese, Marie realized. She did tend to agree with most of what she had been told, but still she knew that Mathilde's reasons for distrust did not make the woman any less a Christian. Marie analyzed her feelings for Frau Wagner and realized what she felt for her was sorrow—sorrow and pity. She decided that if it had not been for the war they could have easily been friends.

Rolf spoke to Marie. "We need to get you to Switzerland. You can contact your friends there and find your way home to America."

President Wagner stood and reached for his coat. "I will make inquiries. I will ask members of our congregation if they have any ideas." He moved toward the door.

"Do you trust them?" Rolf stood and followed him as far as the door.

"I'll be careful. There are several I can trust." He captured Rolf's shoulders in his hands and smiled at him affectionately. "You are much loved in our little branch." He stepped out into the street.

Mathilde asked, "What about you, Rolf? Aren't you also in danger?"

Rolf hesitated. "I'll be all right."

"What are you going to do?" Now that he was with her, Marie felt panic-stricken at the thought he might leave her again.

"I have business in France."

Frau Wagner's eyes widened in shock. "You're returning to France? What about the Gestapo? How do you plan to avoid arrest, Rolf?"

Marie realized that for once Mathilde was on her side. Frau Wagner continued, her voice rising in volume. "If they capture you they will kill you, Rolf. Please be reasonable! Whatever business you have in France can wait until after the war." The older woman seemed on the verge of tears. "Please, Rolf, go with Giselle to Switzerland and find your son. Alma needs you. He misses you . . ." She slumped to the table, burying her head in her hands. Rolf stood, crossed over to her, and placed his arms around her shoulders as she sobbed, "I can't lose you, too!"

Rolf whispered soothingly, "You will always have me, Mathilde."

She took a deep breath and forced herself to control her emotions. "You are not my son, but you fill my heart and comfort my memories of him." She smiled bravely at him through her tears. "I know you will do the right thing." She stood, glanced uncomfortably in Marie's direction, and left the kitchen.

Rolf sat beside Marie, took her hand in his, and said nothing for several moments. He seemed lost in thought, and she waited, sensing he had something difficult to say. Finally, he spoke. "I am going to Beaune-la-Rolande, near Paris." He looked down at their entwined hands. "Madame Larouche, Félix's mother, is in a safehouse there. I need to see her."

Marie gasped. The unexpected mention of her former fiancé and his mother shocked her, and she could think of nothing to say. Rolf continued. "She's been on my mind since the day I—the day Félix died. It's as if my conscience is telling me that I need to talk to her, make sure she's safe, tell her about her son's death, and . . . apologize to her." He stopped, and Marie saw the look of pain in his eyes. "Perhaps then I can have peace." His voice broke. "Perhaps then I can be forgiven."

"I'm going with you." Marie's resolve surprised her as much as it surprised Rolf.

He stared at her. "Absolutely not, Marie."

"I need to go with you—to be with you when you tell Madame Larouche about Félix." She realized it was impossible to explain how she felt—how her heart leaped at the news that he would be going, and how she felt an urgency to be included. "I realize it will be dangerous, Rolf. But I need to go. Dresdner thinks I'm here, and he's going to keep looking for me here. He'll never suspect I'm with you, and he won't believe we would dare return to France. And then I'll go to Switzerland immediately afterward . . ."

Rolf studied her thoughtfully. His eyes searched hers in the way that so disconcerted and thrilled her, and then he spoke softly. "You're a brave woman, Marie." He paused. "You realize, don't you, that it will be dangerous trying to get past the Westwall into France—let alone back into Switzerland afterward."

"You have a plan." She smiled confidently. "I cannot imagine you wouldn't have thought it completely through."

Rolf nodded. "We'll head north, pass through Freiberg, and cross the Westwall at Saarbrücken. We'll try to stay a step ahead of the news of my escape, and I'll use my influence as an officer to get us through. Strasbourg is closer, but that would be the obvious choice—and by now we need to assume the army there has been warned about me. It is, after all, my route home, so they will be watching for me."

"You said 'we.'"

Rolf smiled. "You're determined, so what can I say?"

"Let me come, Rolf, and afterward I promise I will go wherever you say."

He stood, pulling Marie up with him. "I have a friend who might be able to help both you and Madame Larouche. He'll have connections to get you through the Rhône-Alpes and across the border to Geneva."

THIRTY-SIX

April 8, 1944

The garden lay unattended and stark, last year's plants still in a ground blackened by frost and snow. Through that dismal blanket Marie could see glimpses of bright green cotyledon leaves forcing their way stubbornly upward through last year's sodden mass. Given another week the garden would be breathing again, hiding its dark past underneath newborn green until the wilted rejects of the preceding summer disintegrated into the soil and became nourishment for the new living growth.

Marie followed Rolf past the stone wall separating the garden from the house and up a series of steps to the doorway. Like the wilted garden, the doorway needed a new beginning—in this case, a breath of fresh paint, perhaps a shade lighter than its current depressing brown. In fact, the white-washed cottage could have used a cheerful helping hand on every side so the small residence would once more enjoy the charm it had probably once possessed.

Rolf caught her hand in his own and reached to knock on the heavy wooden door. He stepped back to wait, and Marie noticed a bead of sweat sliding down the back of his neck. Other than that, he remained his calm, collected self, although what he might be suffering inside Marie could only guess.

After a long moment of silence the door opened a full inch. "May I help you?"

Rolf removed his visor cap and held it close to his chest. In his uniform and black boots, he looked to the casual observer like any of a thousand other Nazi officers on the streets of occupied Paris on any particular morning of the week. Marie's disguise followed along different lines: a standard working-class gray skirt and red blouse, a wool coat, sensible shoes, and the illusion of hosiery accomplished by carefully drawing a single dark line up the back of each calf—common during these years of war-inspired creativity.

"Madame Larouche?" Rolf spoke through the semi-open door. "This is Major Rolf Schulmann." There was silence on the inside of the door, so Rolf cleared his throat and explained. "I visited your home in Paris back in '39 with my wife Hélène. She and I wanted to be baptized. Do you remember?"

There was an audible gasp from behind the door. "Major Schulmann?" The door opened significantly, and Marie caught her first glimpse of the woman who had given birth to the man she thought she would love for the rest of eternity. Madame Larouche's head barely reached Marie's shoulders, causing Marie to wonder if Félix's height had stemmed from his deceased father's side of the family. The woman had wrinkles on top of laugh lines on top of worry lines, creating an incredibly complex pattern of memories, sorrows, heartaches, dreams, and old age. Her white hair, swept back in a tight bun at the base of her neck, betrayed her advancing years, and her back displayed a definite stoop. Marie could tell that the woman's body had begun to waste away, and she wondered if her health had been compromised by the war and probable knowledge of her son's death.

"What a wonderful surprise, Rolf!" Madame Larouche took his hands between her own bony ones and squeezed affectionately. "How in the world did you find me?" She hesitated, consternation wrinkling her brow for a brief moment at the thought that a German officer could discover her hiding place.

Rolf quickly put her mind at ease. "Don't worry, Madame, you are safe. I would not betray your location to anyone." The relief on the woman's face touched Marie. Rolf continued. "I have been looking for you for some time."

"Why?" The older woman again looked concerned.

"May we come in?"

At Madame Larouche's invitation, Rolf and Marie entered the sparsely furnished yet immaculately clean interior and moved with their host toward the kitchen. "I don't have much to offer . . ." Madame Larouche spoke apologetically, glancing about the kitchen as if something edible might sprout at any time from some hidden location. "I am dependent upon others for my supplies and—"

"Don't worry about us, Madame Larouche." Marie smiled reassuringly at the woman. "We're not hungry." Marie's free hand pressed against her stomach to suppress an untimely growl, and Rolf glanced over at her in quiet amusement.

"Adèle," the woman said to her. "Call me Adèle."

"Adèle, I need to tell you about your son." Schulmann's straightforward introduction brought instant tears to the woman's eyes, and her hand flew to her throat. Slowly, she sat on a chair across from Rolf and Marie, her eyes on Rolf. "What about my son?" She clutched her hands together in her lap. "I already know he's dead."

"Yes, but do you know how he died?"

Madame Larouche shook her head. "He was working, that is all I know. At least he died for what he believed."

Without preamble Rolf told her what had happened above Izieu. He did not spare himself or his part in the events, nor did he make excuses for himself or for his men. His description of the morning's proceedings was straightforward and thorough, and as she watched him Marie again felt the wonder of his goodness. His honesty touched her and made her feel protected, and even though his narrative brought back the familiar pain of Félix's death, she realized with a sense of wonder that it had been tempered by her growing relationship with this man. Rolf spoke directly to Félix's mother, his eyes haunted yet determined, the relief at finally sitting in the same room with her evident on his face. He spoke for a long time, and Madame Larouche listened without interruption, alternating between wringing her hands and wiping at her tears with a small embroidered handkerchief.

Finally Rolf paused, and his voice began to tremble. "When Félix died I was devastated. I felt that not only had I betrayed my best friend—I had betrayed my God. After arresting—" He hesitated. "After taking my prisoner to the truck, I went back alone to the valley and . . . buried your son there."

Marie stared at him, her eyes wide. He had never shared this with her, and she understood how this courageous personal experience could be a difficult thing to reveal.

"I buried him," Rolf continued, "and then I knelt next to his grave and begged Heavenly Father to forgive me. I told him how much Félix had meant to me and how sorry I was that the war had destroyed our friendship and taken his life. I asked God to help me know what to do, and the thought came to me that I needed to protect the people he loved."

Marie fought back tears as she watched Rolf. He lost his battle to control his emotions and let out a tortured sob. Marie took his hand in hers and felt it trembling.

"I decided I needed to take care of the woman Félix was planning to marry. I knew it was because of her love for him that she followed him to France. She was willing to put her life in danger in order to fight at his side for the thing she knew he loved most." He turned and smiled at Marie, his face flushed with emotion. "Madame Larouche, I would like you to meet Marie Jacobson—Félix's fiancée."

For a moment the older woman looked confused, and her eyes searched Marie's face as if looking for confirmation there of this incredible truth. "I have heard about her . . . have been hoping to meet her someday . . ." She smiled softly as the fact began to sink in, and she said, "Félix told me so much about you, Marie Jacobson. I have wanted terribly to meet you."

Marie moved closer to Félix's mother, sitting beside her and taking her in her arms. For several moments she and Madame Larouche embraced, their tears mingling as they mourned Félix and silently shared his memory. Marie looked over the woman's shoulder at Rolf, and his eyes met hers. She smiled at him, feeling her love for him deepen and feeling a returning love from him. Yes, she mourned Félix. And yes, his death would always be a difficult memory. But it no longer stood between Rolf and herself, she realized, feeling a wave of relief.

Rolf turned his gaze back to Adèle Larouche. "I wanted to tell you that I am sorry. I am very, very sorry." He had to stop speaking while he took control of his emotions. Then he said in a wavering voice, "I am responsible for your son's death."

The room was completely still. Madame Larouche looked at them both, overwhelmed by Rolf Schulmann's words and the presence of her son's fiancée at her side. Marie watched as she wiped her eyes, studying Rolf carefully. Then she responded in a way that shocked both Rolf and Marie. She stood up and crossed the room to where he stood. She reached up and captured his tortured face between her gnarled hands and looked deeply into his eyes.

"My Félix spoke often of his friendship with you, Rolf Schulmann. He saw the good in you, and I see it too. I forgive you. *I forgive you.*" Rolf began to sob, dropping his head and burying his face in his hands. She pulled him down into a tender embrace, her tears falling on the immaculately tailored shoulder with its braided epaulet. "I love you—and I know my son loves you still." She kissed him tenderly on both tear-stained cheeks. "Someday he will tell you so himself."

"I am looking forward to that day, Adèle."

* * *

Rolf asked, "If you had the opportunity to leave France, would you take it?"

Madame Larouche's eyes misted and she turned to look out into the garden, the frozen ground thawing in a desperate attempt to welcome a reluctant spring. "I have a sister in New York," was all she said, but the ache in her words told Marie that the woman was incredibly lonely and homesick for family.

Rolf nodded as if he understood, then he turned to Marie. "Do you remember Jacques Bellamont?"

Surprised, Marie nodded, remembering the photographs and Rolf's interest in the man during her interrogation. "Of course I remember him." She wondered why Rolf would bring the name of the man he had been searching for into the conversation. "Jacques was Félix's friend from the Résistance—and a good man."

"One of the best," Rolf agreed. He looked at Madame Larouche. "Jacques helped me find you and has assisted me several times over the past few weeks. He told me to get in touch with him if I ever need his assistance, and I believe I will ask him to help you contact the Allies."

Marie shook her head in wonder. "You've been busy, Rolf."

"So has Jacques." Rolf smiled at her. "Someday I hope to have the opportunity to tell you all that Jacques has done."

* * *

Toward late morning Madame Larouche showed Marie to the guest room, apologizing again for her lack of preparation. Marie shook her head and smiled at the woman's concern. "If things go as Rolf hopes, then tomorrow Jacques will take us away, Adèle—there is no reason to worry about my accommodations. Believe me, I am thinking more about what tomorrow will bring than whether or not my sheets have been ironed."

Madame Larouche smiled. "I would like to have known you under more favorable circumstances, Marie Jacobson—I can see why my son fell in love with you."

"I'm glad I came, Adèle. I have heard so much about you, from both Félix and Rolf."

The woman studied Marie carefully. "Rolf Schulmann is a good person."

"Yes, he is."

"He will not take the place of my Félix, but I can see that you love him very much."

Marie met Adèle's gaze steadily. "He will never take Félix's place. That would be impossible. Félix has a place in my heart that is reserved only for him, Adèle. At one time I thought he would fill my whole heart, but that was not to be. So I keep his memory warm right here . . ." Marie laid a hand over her heart. "And I take it out often to remember what we had together."

"Does it bother you—what Rolf has done?"

Marie nodded. "It used to. But that feeling has faded." She responded to the question still in the older woman's eyes. "And, yes, I have fallen in love with him. I could not begin to tell you all the reasons why."

"He seems to love you, too. It is evident in everything he says and does." Adèle paused and let out a deep sigh. "I believe Félix approves."

"Thank you, Madame Larouche." Marie felt a peaceful feeling wash over her. "I'm glad you think so."

There was a soft knock on the doorframe, and Marie and the older woman turned to see Rolf standing in the doorway. "I contacted Jacques and he will be here tomorrow morning," he said. "He wants you both ready to leave as soon as he arrives—it will be dangerous for him to stay too long." Turning to Madame Larouche, he reached and hugged her close. "I'm glad I found you, Adèle. I'm sorry it had to be under such terrible circumstances. God bless you for your forgiveness."

She kissed his cheek. "This is sounding very much like a farewell, Rolf Schulmann."

"It is, unfortunately. I must go before someone recognizes me." He moved to Marie's side. "Can I speak with you for a moment?"

She nodded and he took her hand. He led her toward the front door, and on the porch he turned to her, his eyes worried. "Will you be all right?"

"Yes." She lifted her chin, determined to be brave. "Jacques will take care of us."

"Jacques seems to be good at that."

"And you? What will you do now?"

"Find my son." He placed his hands on her shoulders. "I will tell him you are thinking about him."

"I promised him I would come."

Rolf shook his head. "Not this time, Marie. And I won't change my mind." He kissed her gently. "It's time for you to return to your father in America. You will have to let me fulfill your promise to Alma. And then, maybe after the war . . ."

Marie met his gaze steadily. "I was wrong, Rolf. There is no confusion, no conflict."

"What do you mean?"

Marie took a deep breath before continuing. "You are the only one I could ever imagine spending my life with. I cannot imagine a life without you near me—or without Alma. I never thought I could feel love this deeply."

"Marie—"

She gently pressed her finger against his lips, silencing him. "You ceased to be my enemy the moment you saved me from Dresdner near Belley—it's just that I was never willing to admit it to myself. I refused to let go of my prejudices and the hate that I had allowed to fester inside of me. I had you thrown in along with the whole Nazi stereotype and I was not willing to see you for who you really are. And I denied my feelings for you because of that stereotype. I am so sorry."

Rolf captured her face in both his hands and held it against his own, their foreheads touching and tears falling. "You are the one who saved *my* life, Marie." He tood a deep breath. "And your words will comfort me until I can see you again."

"When will that be?"

She heard the anguish in his voice as he answered, "I don't know, Marie. I honestly do not know."

She was desperate to keep him close to her for a moment longer. "When I jumped from that plane I never imagined my life would turn out as it has. It's as if each of our lives is a story—an adventure we are living every breathing moment of our existence—and each choice we make helps determine the outcome of that story."

Rolf managed a smile, touching her cheek affectionately. "I like the way our stories have merged."

"So do I."

"In a perfect world, our story would end right here, with us in each other's arms and the war fading into a horrific memory behind us."

"I wish this were a perfect world, Rolf."

Rolf's hand traced the curve of her jaw. "So how is our story going to end?"

Marie smiled faintly. "Maybe instead of how it *ends,* we should think of how it will *begin* again."

"And *when . . .*"

"I love you, Rolf Schulmann."

He wrapped her in his arms and held her close, and his final kiss took her breath away. "I love you, too, Marie. And I will think about you every single day until we are together again."

* * *

Horst Wagner's head hit the floor with a solid thud, and for several seconds he lay still while the room spun dizzyingly around him.

"*Aufstehen!* Get up!"

Slowly, excruciatingly, the branch president willed his limbs to obey, pushing against the dead weight of his torso until he knelt on the wooden floorboards. Then, clutching first the seat of a chair and then the edge of the kitchen table, he managed to finally pull himself to a standing position. It was a terrible, excruciatingly painful process, with blood pounding in his ears and the wound above his temple disorienting him to a point that he could not keep his balance. He continued to grip the table for support with one hand, and with the other he wiped at his eyes, trying to clear them of blood so he could focus on the small man in front of him. He blinked rapidly and again saw the wrinkled, disfigured eye socket in the Gestapo captain's diabolical face. Then the room lurched sideways and his hand slipped from the edge of the table as he fell to his knees in front of the diminutive man.

"Your perseverance is admirable, Herr Wagner, but useless." Captain Bernard Dresdner smiled pleasantly. "One of your Mormon friends realized his responsibility and reported your activities to the authorities—said you were trying to find a way to smuggle a woman out of the country." He leaned close to the kneeling man, his voice mocking. "I thought you Mormons protected each other."

President Wagner said nothing.

"I was surprised to hear Rolf Schulmann is in the neighborhood, Herr Wagner. I thought I'd arrested him." Dresdner shook his head. "I'll have to look into the matter." He lifted the branch president's chin with his rubber club, forcing him to look up into his face. "I will ask you again, Herr Wagner: Where did Schulmann take the girl?"

The sound of the front door opening distracted Dresdner, and he turned to see Mathilde Wagner standing in the doorway, her coat buttoned against the cold and a basket on one arm. The other arm was securely held by one of Dresdner's men, and her ashen face stared at her husband kneeling in the middle of the kitchen floor. She let out a muffled scream and Horst looked up and saw her, then closed his eyes with a groan. He whispered, "Mathilde . . ."

"Welcome home, Frau Wagner." Dresdner smiled at the terrified woman. "Won't you join us?" He nodded in the direction of a kitchen chair next to the wall, and Mathilde's captor escorted her firmly across the room. "We were just discussing the whereabouts of Major Schulmann and the American woman."

Mathilde could not tear her eyes from the huddled form of her husband, and she clutched her basket in her lap with white knuckles. Huge welts covered a good portion of the branch president's face, and blood coursed unchecked from a gaping wound over his forehead and eyes. Dresdner continued. "I am going to ask your husband one more time, Frau

Wagner, and then I will hurt him." He turned back to the man on the floor. "Where did Schulmann take the American woman, Herr Wagner?"

Horst lowered his head to his chest and said nothing, his lips working silently and his eyes closed.

Dresdner leaned close. "Are you praying? *Praying?*" He stood and raised his club. "I'll show you what good praying will do you, Mormon . . ."

"Wait!" Mathilde Wagner began to sob, and the basket tumbled to the floor as she stood, wringing her hands. "Please don't hurt him! He doesn't know anything. He—he was gone when Rolf left with Giselle . . ." She hugged her arms around her shoulders and shook uncontrollably. "*I* heard where they were planning to go, sir. They—they didn't know I was listening . . . Please don't hurt him, sir—he's all I have left . . ."

* * *

With aides tightly on his heels, Dresdner stormed the nearest hotel and approached the desk. "Give me your phone." Dresdner snatched the receiver from the hotelkeeper's hand and disconnected the startled man's call with one swift jab of his forefinger.

The man recovered quickly. "Excuse me, sir—will it be a local call?"

"Of course not," Dresdner snapped, dialing furiously. "Who would be worth calling in Baiersbronn?"

After a succession of phone operators, he succeeded in reaching the department in Paris that he required. "Major Knopf? This is Captain Bernard Dresdner from Lyon. You recall we talked at a New Year's party at Section Four Headquarters. Major Nieman introduced me to you . . . yes, that was me. You have an exceptional memory, Major." Dresdner hesitated. "Yes, I agree that would be hard to forget . . ." He cleared his throat nervously and then straightened, his determination returning. "I must request a small favor . . ." He continued to outline his plan, emphasizing that the fugitive Major Schulmann was to be included in the catch, along with an Allied agent and several Résistance leaders. When he hung up the phone, he had approval from the Paris Gestapo to borrow seventy-five men, guns, ammunition, three panzer tanks, and transports as necessary for an operation in a small town south of Paris the following morning.

THIRTY-SEVEN

April 9, 1944

Marie was startled awake by the staccato of machine-gun fire, and she jumped from the bed to the floor, startled into action by the sound. Madame Larouche's panic-stricken voice called from the next room, and Marie threw on her dress and slipped on her boots. Running into the parlor she looked out through the curtains, shocked to see soldiers patrolling the main road leaving the village. A glance out of the kitchen window revealed several troops assembling a machine gun in a snow-covered field. Military convoys moved slowly past the houses, depositing armed soldiers at intervals along the streets, and Marie realized with a shock that they had surrounded the town. A sick feeling began to grow in her stomach as she wondered what they were looking for. A bullhorn on the roof of a truck sounded on the street, terrifyingly close to her window. "Citizens of Beaune-la-Rolande! Please evacuate your houses and congregate in the village *platz* immediately. All citizens are required to congregate immediately in the village *platz*..."

The bullhorn continued to vibrate windows as it moved slowly down the street, and Marie watched as residents cautiously left their homes, uncertain as to what to do. Hesitantly, they all began obey the order to migrate in the direction of the village square.

Adèle Larouche looked shaken. "It has happened before, Marie. Do not worry. They will talk to us, maybe threaten us a little, and then allow us to return to our homes."

"Are they searching for us?"

"I don't know." The woman was agitated. "I don't know how they could have found out..."

Marie reached for her coat. "It would do no good for us to hide?"

"No. They will search the houses while we are gathered in the square. We will have to blend into the crowd."

Marie and Adèle hurried across the icy street and joined a large group of people making their way toward the square. Marie saw women in bathrobes and house slippers clutching warm coats around their bodies or carrying crying babies in their arms. Older citizens shuffled along as best they could, half dressed and shivering, and children hung onto parents' hands, bewilderment evident on their sleepy faces. As they approached the center of the village, Marie noticed the truck with the bullhorn parked in the center of the village square. The engine still idled and its bullhorn repeated the call through the crisp morning air. Marie and Adèle Larouche mingled with the villagers and waited.

For half an hour the residents of Beaune-la-Rolande stood in the frozen street, talking among themselves in uneasy whispers and shifting from one foot to the other in an effort to keep warm. Mothers comforted children, and fathers blew on stiff fingers. Everyone watched fearfully as German troops advanced to surround the crowd, and Marie recognized several Gestapo uniforms among the soldiers. Then she saw Captain Dresdner giving instructions to a man with a bullhorn in his hand. Shocked, she took a panicked step backward and glanced quickly around her, instinctively searching for a better place to hide than the middle of a village street. Adèle placed a calming hand on her arm and warned her to be still.

Dresdner finished his instructions to the man, who nodded and turned to climb to the roof of the truck so all could see and hear. "Citizens of Beaune-la-Rolande, you have a criminal in your midst." He paused for effect, and then continued with more enthusiasm. "The woman we seek is guilty of murder, theft, and treason. Her name is Marie Jacobson, and she has eluded capture by hiding in your homes. We have been informed she is here." The crowd murmured uneasily, looking at each other and shaking their heads. Marie wondered how many in the crowd were Résistance sympathizers. She studied the faces of the villagers, and she was startled when she met the gaze of Jacques Bellamont on the opposite edge of the crowd. He nodded almost imperceptibly, acknowledging her presence before looking away.

The announcer on top of the truck continued. "The Führer is a forgiving leader. He does not wish to upset you or interfere with your peace and happiness. Therefore he has this offer for you: Surrender this woman and you may return to your homes unharmed."

The man paused, lowering the megaphone. Marie hazarded a glance in Captain Dresdner's direction and saw that he watched the crowd closely, his damaged eye roving uselessly as he searched. Under his scrutiny the villagers stood frozen and quiet. No one spoke or moved for fear they would be singled out for questioning, and Marie's breath came tight and hard as she waited to see what the Gestapo captain planned to do next. The silence lasted for several minutes. To Marie's relief, no one spoke up. She squeezed Adèle's hand hopefully.

Captain Dresdner glanced up at the man with the megaphone and nodded for him to continue, and Marie's relief was dashed into a thousand horrifying pieces. "The Führer gave you a chance to save yourselves, and no one stepped forward to become a savior for the people. Now we have no choice but to show you what happens when you hide an enemy in your midst."

The man stopped talking and nodded to the soldiers surrounding the square. Instantly they sprang into the crowd and began randomly separating women and children from their families. Terrified and confused, the villagers protested loudly. Adèle's hand was torn from Marie's grasp, and the older woman was forced toward the front of the crowd to join the others. Soldiers herded the women and children into a line in front of the truck, and Marie watched in stunned disbelief as their captors assembled a large machine gun in front of the prisoners. Near the center of the line Adèle wrung her hands, terrified. Many of the panicked hostages tried to re-enter the crowd and return to their loved-ones but found an unyielding wall of German weapons forcing them back.

Captain Dresdner reached up and gestured to the man on the truck, who handed him the megaphone, and Dresdner's oily smooth voice spread over the audience. "Citizens of Beaune-la-Rolande, I will give you one more chance to surrender the American woman. If Marie Jacobson does not show herself within one minute, one of your neighbors and friends will be shot. If Mademoiselle Jacobson continues to remain hidden, a prisoner will be shot every minute thereafter until she surrenders. We will continue shooting your friends until you yield the woman to us, or she is the only person left standing in the *platz*."

Marie cringed at the evil in him.

"You have one minute," Dresdner finished.

Marie felt sick. This could not be happening. She looked around her and saw horror and shock on the villagers' faces. Several had sunk to their knees to pray, and a woman in the line of prisoners screamed and began to babble uncontrollably. A father pulled his little girl close as she cried for a mother standing with the prisoners. Marie could hardly breathe past the bile rising in her throat, and she felt as if she were the one facing the firing squad, knowing her life was seconds away from being extinguished. It was wrong—horribly wrong!

Suddenly, with a calm that surprised her, she knew what she had to do. It was the most difficult thing she had ever done in her life. Knowing she had no time to lose, she took a deep breath and stepped forward. She caught a glimpse of Jacques shaking his head violently, warning her back, and then she glanced at Madame Larouche and felt an outpouring of love for the woman. She pushed her way through the crowd, determination keeping her terrified form upright and moving her forward. Stepping from the crowd, Marie stood and faced Captain Bernard Dresdner. Their eyes locked, and Marie felt his evil penetrate her very soul.

"Stop!" Her voice broke and she began sobbing. "I'm here."

He stood and looked at her for one long moment, then without breaking eye contact he signaled the soldiers to release the prisoners. Crying, children lunged for mothers and grandparents spirited away terrified grandchildren. One woman whispered, "Bless you, *amie,*" as she passed, but Marie felt nothing but the chill wind of death. Out of the corner of her eye she saw Jacques with his arm around Félix's mother, his lips moving urgently next to her ear. And then Captain Dresdner approached Marie, his gaze a mixture of triumph and murder. She felt her knees weakening as she faced him, and she wavered on the verge of collapse.

"So we meet again, Marie Jacobson." His voice, silky and smooth, cut like a razorblade. "Your friend Major Schulmann will not save you this time." Lightning quick, his gloved hand connected with the back of her neck and she felt her body slip into darkness.

THIRTY-EIGHT

April 9, 1944

Major Rolf Schulmann watched as the line of white-clothed figures zigzagged their way down the mountainside. *Five students and a teacher.* Rolf did not need to see uniform insignia to know who instructed and who learned; the students' technique lacked the grace and confidence of their teacher. The figure out front was Hans—the best ski instructor this side of the Swiss Alps.

Rolf watched them impatiently. They seemed to be taking an inordinate amount of time navigating the slope. To them it would seem they were flying, but from his vantage point they seemed to be moving at a snail's pace.

The skiers disappeared behind a low mountain rise. Rolf knew that in a moment they would reappear in a path that would cross his exact position, and he shifted his skis expertly to move off to the left of the route. No good them coming around the bend and mowing him down—Hans would never forgive an attempt to derail him in front of his students. To Hans, appearance was everything. But his friend would recognize him and wait for him at the base of the mountain. Schulmann watched for the reappearance of the soldiers.

A few seconds later they came around the bend. He admitted their speed was impressive, especially with rifles, bedding, and survival gear strapped to their backs. Thirty-two kilos of dead weight on their backs did not do much for morale—but it would help their speed and trajectory. They approached Rolf's position at the velocity of a freight train, and Hans barked at his students. They altered course slightly, escaping the disaster Rolf knew would result if they continued their present route: Ahead lay a drop-off that would have taken them to the base of the Belchen in an embarrassing tumble of broken skis, bones, and bravado.

Rolf watched as Hans and his students approached and passed his position without a hint of recognition, but he knew Hans had seen him and would be waiting for him at the base of Belchenmont. He turned and shoved his skis into the path left by the alpine troops. He would cut his own trail through soft powder rather than rely on the unreliability of soldiers in training. He didn't want to find himself straddling a tree trunk or stumbling over a dropped backpack and ripping his legs from their sockets as he tumbled the rest of the way down the slope. Better a new trail and reliable, fresh powder.

Hans was the better of the two when it came to downhill skiing—but perhaps by just a margin. Rolf could hold his own and always felt a hint of longing for the slopes. Sometimes he wished he had gone with Hans when he enlisted with the *Gebirgsjager.* Now Rolf could see the base of the trail, and he began to tighten his switchbacks in order to absorb more of the shock of deceleration. A blinding flash of snow as his skis cut perpendicular to the slope at stopping would be dramatic—but not practical. Below him Rolf could see several students pulling just such a maneuver, and he knew there would be swift reprimands. An alpine unit needed to be swift and discreet—and a cover could be blown and battles lost by carelessly displaced snow hurtling down a mountainside.

Major Schulmann arrived at the base of Belchenmont and waited at a discreet distance for Hans to give final instructions to his students. Then with an exuberant yell the soldiers headed for the lodge, released from their lessons for a weekend of drinking, revelry, and general lack of responsibility. Hans stooped and appeared to fumble with his boot. Rolf knew better, and he nimbly dodged the mammoth snowball that a moment later was hurled past his face.

Hans laughed. "You're getting quicker, Mormon."

"*Nein.* You're getting slower."

Hans laughed. With a shove of his ski poles he maneuvered his large frame even with that of his friend. "To what do I owe this pleasure, Major?"

"I'm an outcast—just like you predicted."

"I've heard." Hans grinned. "Superiors fed up with your preaching, eh?"

"Something like that." Rolf briefly returned the lieutenant's smile, then he became serious. "Actually, Captain Dresdner has accused me of treason. Most importantly, he's captured Marie." He frowned. "A friend told me the Gestapo arrested her this morning in Beaune-la-Rolande."

Lieutenant Brenner swore. "So now what?"

"I need your help, Hans."

"Of course. But what can I do?"

"Since I'm a hunted man, I need you to be my eyes, ears, and legs."

"Well, now . . . I don't know." Hans folded his arms and considered Rolf thoughtfully. "Word is you've got a price on your head so high a fellow like me could turn you in and retire in style. It's tempting . . ."

Rolf's lips twisted in a wry smile. "Glad to know you're such a loyal friend."

Hans smiled back, then turned serious again. "Do you think he has a guard posted at your house?"

"I'm sure of it—waiting for me to check on the family."

"Sounds like Dresdner. I swear I'm going to kill him this time."

"I won't try to stop you."

"That surprises me, Mormon."

"If you'd seen what Dresdner did in Izieu, it wouldn't "

"Tell me later. I don't need you to convince me of anything. Right now, we need to find out what happened to your woman." Hans swung his ski poles over one shoulder. "And your son—what of him?"

"He's safe in Switzerland. The Wagners sent him there with a member of our congregation."

"You Mormons sure are a close-knit group, aren't you?"

"You have no idea."

"Anyway . . ." Lieutenant Brenner smiled. "It's good to see you, friend." Hans extended his gloved hand and Rolf grasped it warmly in both of his.

"It's good to see you, too."

Rolf glided next to Hans toward the warmth of the lodge. Hans spoke. "So Marie—what is she to you, anyway?"

"She's an Allied agent."

"She's more than that, Rolf. Admit it."

Rolf smiled. "I love her, Hans, if that's what you mean." Rolf hesitated. "And I'm not so sure being an Allied operative is such a bad thing right now."

"You planning to betray your country?"

"According to the Gestapo, I already have. Don't think I can turn back now."

"So what'll they do with you if they catch you?"

Rolf shrugged. "Send me to die on the eastern front. Or work in a labor camp. Shoot me. But my career's over, Hans. They'll never give me back my command."

"That bad, eh? Your God didn't save you, I guess?"

"Maybe He did."

"What do you mean? You're a hunted man, remember?"

Rolf smiled. "I guess I'm learning what matters most, old friend. My son is safe, and I don't have to fight my conscience anymore."

"I banished my conscience to the eastern front ages ago. I think a sniper bullet killed it. Now I'm blissfully free of conscience."

Rolf chuckled. "Must be nice."

"Sure is." Hans grinned at his friend. "I don't miss it at all. Especially when some beautiful young thing offers to keep me warm on a cold winter night."

Rolf rolled his eyes. "What's new?"

"So how about Marie?" Hans looked sideways at Schulmann. "She kept you warm yet?"

Rolf turned to face the lieutenant. "That is none of your concern. But since you asked, I'll remind you that I believe in reserving sexual relations for marriage . . ."

Hans held up his hands in an attitude of surrender. "All right, all right! Spare me the lecture, Mormon! I just can't imagine you losing a moment's time with that one . . ."

"Then you don't know me as well as you thought."

"Maybe not." He slugged Rolf's shoulder. "Okay, so she's a 'hands off' American agent, and you've fallen for her—if it's possible for a chaste Nazi like you to fall in love with a woman . . ."

"Believe me, it's possible. And I have. I won't argue that point. Only I don't know what to do about it."

"Kind of like a bird loving a fish, eh?"

"Pretty much."

"So let's suppose you married the girl. Where would you live? Seems Germany is out of the question—unless Hitler loses the war."

"I don't know, Hans."

"What's wrong? Doesn't she like you?"

"She says she does."

"Then what's the problem?" Hans asked. "You like her, she likes you . . . Sounds like the perfect formula for an incredible relationship."

"Hans, what do you know about relationships? Ever been in love?"

"No. But I've been in lust. That's close to love."

"Not even remotely."

"All right, *Herr Lover*—tell me what love is. If it's not physical, what is it?"

Schulmann thought carefully. "Love is physical, yes. Very physical. But there's more to it—something deeper."

"This I've got to hear."

"Remember Hélène?"

"How could I forget her?"

Schulmann continued. "Hélène used to say she loved me. But then she would add that not only did she *love* me, she *liked* me."

"What's that supposed to mean?"

"That love was more than nights in each other's arms and bearing children." Schulmann paused, and his eyes locked with Hans's. "That love meant commitment. Honesty. Fidelity . . ."

"I can't imagine being faithful to one woman."

". . . and most importantly, *eternity*."

"Eternity, huh?"

"You ever think you could stay with a woman for eternity?"

Hans shrugged. "To be honest, I've been too busy living for the moment. Too busy to give *eternity* a thought."

"Well, try giving it a thought right now. We've got a few moments." Schulmann bent to unlock his skis from his boots and prop them against the outer wall of the lodge.

Hans did the same, his face thoughtful. "I think I could begin to imagine an eternity with Marie . . . or someone like her." He gave his friend a mischievous smile. "So let me know if you two don't work out."

"Be serious, Hans."

"When have you ever known me to be serious?"

"For the next few hours might be good."

"Sure thing." Hans sobered. "I'm very serious about wrapping these two hands around Dresdner's neck and squeezing—"

"Good for you, Hans."

Hans pulled off his white parka and tossed it across the tops of his skis. "You have a car, or did you come all the way from France on skis?"

"Parked on the other side of the lodge. I borrowed the skis."

The two friends entered the lodge. Most of the troops in training had already disappeared for the weekend, eager to leave the rigors of military life behind for a few days. Hans gestured toward the kitchen. "Want something to eat?"

Rolf shook his head. He watched his friend thoughtfully. "Hans, it's dangerous to help me."

Hans's smile spread from ear to ear and he faked irritation, punching Rolf in the shoulder. "That's why I'm doing it, you imbecile! I need excitement this weekend. I'm bored and I've had enough of these idiot troops."

Schulmann was sincere. "I appreciate it."

"Good. Then let's get going."

* * *

Marie felt as if a hot poker was gouging the base of her head. She opened her heavy eyelids and tried to focus on the vague shapes moving about the room. Her head, when she tried to move it, sent shooting daggers through her eyes into her brain, and she moaned.

"She's regaining consciousness, sir."

"Sit her up."

Rough hands forced her to a sitting position and propped her against the wall. Her head rolled forward, her neck useless, and she again felt the searing heat tearing at her skull. Someone grabbed her by the hair and forced her head back against the wall.

"Marie Jacobson." The voice was hauntingly familiar, and she stared at the face hovering close to her own. "Can you hear me?"

Marie mumbled something incoherent in reply.

"Good." The face smiled at her. Marie didn't think she liked that smile.

"Tell me who helped you escape near Schönenberg."

Marie did not answer. Her eyelids drifted closed again.

The hand lodged in her hair shook her sharply, and she opened her eyes. The face in front of her was becoming more distinct. Defined eyebrows framed one sharp blue eye and one gray, useless eye. High cheekbones and chiseled lips pressed in a thin line. She remembered him and recoiled.

"Stay where you are, mademoiselle." Captain Bernard Dresdner's hand held her head firmly in place. Marie's eyes watched him fearfully, and the side of her head where he had hit her in Belley seemed to throb. Dresdner smiled. "More beautiful than last time—if that is possible. I hate to damage such beauty. So, mademoiselle, will you please answer my questions quickly? Who helped you escape that morning in the farmer's barn?"

Marie said nothing, her lips parting slightly.

"Was it your friend, Major Schulmann?"

"No."

"Perhaps he was not at the scene of the crime—but was it his idea?"

"I—I don't know."

"Yes, you do."

Marie was silent.

"You Mormons help each other out, don't you?"

Marie felt her eyes rolling back in her head. She tried to focus on the corner of a window behind the captain's head, but it kept floating in circles.

"Give her scopolamine."

Marie felt the sleeve of her dress pushed up to her shoulder and the sharp pinch of a needle. A moment later nausea enveloped her as the truth serum mixed with her blood and pulsed through her body.

"Now you will answer my questions."

Marie looked at the captain, her eyes refusing to focus.

"Somehow Rolf Schulmann has managed to escape. I have been informed that he brought you here. Why?"

"To find Madame Larouche."

"Larouche?" Dresdner contemplated the name, wondering where he had heard it before. He had the distinct impression that the name had been important to him in the past, and the thought prompted another question. "Has Larouche been involved with the Résistance?"

"Yes."

Dresdner remembered, and he smiled. Of course. Félix Larouche, a young university professor living in Paris under suspicion for Résistance activities. He disappeared early in '43, and soon afterward, his mother did also.

"Where is Félix Larouche?"

"He died."

"And his mother?"

"On her way to America."

Dresdner returned to his favorite subject. "Where is Rolf Schulmann?"

"I don't know."

"He was here with you. Where did he go?"

"To look for his son."

"Frau Wagner told me his son is in Switzerland. Where will Schulmann try to cross the border?"

She mumbled incoherently, her mouth refusing to cooperate.

"What was that?" Dresdner leaned close. "Where will Schulmann cross the border?" A thought occurred to him and he asked, "Will he go home first?"

"Yes."

Dresdner grinned. "To visit his sister-in-law and her husband . . ."

"Yes."

Captain Dresdner released her, and she sank onto the mattress. In her fog, Marie heard the door of the room open. She tried to open her eyes but her heavy lids resisted.

"Orders for you, Captain."

Dresdner snapped, "I'm busy."

"It has to do with the woman, sir."

There was a long pause. Marie heard the shuffle of papers, and Dresdner swore softly. "This isn't what the *Wehrmacht* promised! Major Knopf said I could take care of the problem myself."

"It says Major Knopf's *Funk-Horchdienst* unit has intercepted a coded transmission from a suspected Résistance cell near Paris, sir, denouncing

Marie Jacobson as a double agent working for the Vichy to undermine de Gaulle and warning SOE operatives not to trust her."

"I know what it says," Dresdner snapped. "I don't believe it. This is Schulmann's last desperate attempt to steal her from me."

The messenger hesitated. "Major Knopf believes the message is genuine, Captain. He has ordered me to take custody of the prisoner and transport her to Paris."

"You can tell the good major I'm not through with her. I'm going to make her suffer. I'm going to torture the truth out of her myself, and when I'm through with her I might let him have what's left."

The messenger cleared his throat. "Major Knopf said you might resist, sir. He told me to relay to you his deepest sympathy that he will not be able to attend your funeral."

Marie heard a chair crash against the wall and more swearing. Then, for a moment, silence. Finally Dresdner spoke again, and he seemed to have regained control of his temper.

"Put her in the car. Lieutenant Meer will accompany you to Paris. Tell your boss I've decided I'm tired of her."

THIRTY-NINE

April 10, 1944

Captain Bernard Dresdner finished a leisurely breakfast at a hotel near Baiersbronn and stepped into the street. Thick clouds hid the sun, and snow had begun to fall. He knew he could be reprimanded for returning to the Schwarzwald—he had received orders to go to Saint-Claude immediately after Beaune-la-Rolande—but Klaus Barbie would forgive him for his little detour. Hadn't he just captured the elusive American woman and discredited the Mormon? What about Dresdner's unparalleled success at Izieu? He had nothing to fear—his reputation was saved and his future bright.

Besides, he couldn't go to Saint-Claude empty handed. He planned to capture the Mormon traitor Rolf Schulmann as he came to bid his sister-in-law a tearful farewell before disappearing into Switzerland. The fool probably didn't even know he was the focus of the greatest headhunt since the war began . . . And the reward Dresdner could receive for bringing him in would make it easy to forgive Knopf for taking Marie from him. Schulmann probably didn't even realize his American girlfriend had been captured. He probably thought he had rescued the girl from harm and now he could disappear into the sunset, like in some idiotic American Western. But this was real life. Real life said there was a firing squad just around the corner for Major Rolf Schulmann. The Mormon had failed to save Marie, and now he would die a horrible death himself. That was reality, and Dresdner was triumphant.

His driver waited with the car. "Where to, Captain? Major Schulmann's estate?"

"As fast as possible." Dresdner settled against the back of the seat and contemplated his plans for the future: first, wrap up loose ends in the Schwarzwald, and second, get this necessary business in Saint-Claude completed. No need to hurry. Barbie would understand. Dresdner was positive Schulmann would turn up near his estate, and it would be criminal to be within thirty kilometers of the man and not arrest him. Dresdner felt satisfied. He had hoped to shoot the American woman and the major's son in front of Schulmann and watch him beg for mercy—perhaps even pray to his Mormon god. But since Marie had been stolen from Dresdner by Major Knopf, then Schulmann's sister-in-law, her husband, the Wagners, and whoever else they could round up in Baiersbronn would have to do.

The car entered a snow-packed curve and began a steep climb, and as the driver followed the bend in the road and negotiated the slippery surface, Dresdner noticed a military checkpoint ahead. This was new. Security probably had been heightened because of the looming threat of Allied air attacks. German refugees—cowards who believed the enemy would penetrate the Fatherland—had begun escaping toward Switzerland, and the Führer was not pleased.

As they neared the checkpoint, his driver slowed and Dresdner tapped on the back of the seat. "Tell them to make it quick. I'm in a hurry."

"Yes, sir."

Two soldiers clad in the white parkas of the *Gebirgsjager* approached the driver's window. One stood near the front of the vehicle while the other walked around to the other side. The soldier near the window spoke. "Your papers, please."

Dresdner leaned forward impatiently. "Lieutenant, I am Captain Bernard Dresdner of the Section Four Gestapo. I'm on an important errand for the Führer, and I must be allowed to continue immediately on my way."

The soldier stared coolly back at the captain. "Captain Dresdner?"

Dresdner had the disturbing feeling he had seen that face before, and he leaned back in his seat, worried. The face made him uncomfortable, and he tried anxiously to remember why it looked so familiar.

"Step out of the car, please."

"I beg your pardon?"

"Step out of the car, Captain."

Suddenly, Dresdner remembered. The hills outside Belley. German commandos dressed as French Résistance fighters. The American woman!

"Drive!" Dresdner's command to the driver was a panicked shriek. Startled, the driver gunned the engine, his haste causing the rear tires to spin uselessly on the snow-packed surface. Both *Gebirgsjager* pulled their weapons and pointed them at the driver.

"Drive! Drive!" Dresdner hated feeling like a trapped animal—even more than he hated his tendency to panic in dangerous situations.

"I can't! The ice . . ." The driver frantically fought the steering wheel.

"Stop the car." The *Gebirgsjager* soldier's command carried easily over the roar of the engine. "Stop the car or I'll have to shoot."

Terrified, the driver glanced back at his passenger. Dresdner pumped his body frantically back and forth, shrieking obscenities and pummeling the back of the seat and the driver's head. "Drive, you fool! Don't listen to him! *Drive!*"

Calmly the lieutenant at the window pointed his Luger at the driver's right kneecap and opened fire. Screaming horribly, the driver released the steering wheel and grabbed his leg. The engine immediately died as the gas pedal was released, and slowly, deliberately, the car began to slide backward down the ice-encrusted road. Dresdner reached across the seat and shook the driver hysterically by the neck. "Drive, imbecile!"

"I can't . . . My leg . . ." The man sobbed hysterically, and Dresdner shoved him aside, trying to reach the steering wheel himself. In his crazed panic, one clear thought drove him: If he could keep the car on the road until it reached the base of the hill, he would climb over the seat, throw the wounded driver out of the vehicle, and make his escape.

A bullet shattered the windshield and sprayed him with tiny shards of glass. Screaming, he clutched his good eye and sank back into his seat. He felt blood on his hand and thought he had been shot. But when he did not immediately lose consciousness, he realized he had merely been blinded by the glass. The car continued rolling backward with no one in control, picking up speed as it went.

The road turned. Without a driver at the wheel, the vehicle left the road, dipped deeply through a ditch, hesitated lazily on the opposite side, and then continued its downward trajectory cross-country. Dresdner heard the slap of branches and a hideous scraping sound as rocks demolished the undercarriage, ripping at the body of the car in horrible, metallic shrieks. He screamed again and again, blindly clawing for a handhold. There was no sound from the wounded driver in the front seat, and Dresdner felt as if the whole world was imploding on top of him as the tearing and shrieking outside the battered vehicle continued endlessly. With his one eye useless and his other filled with glass shards, all was horrible darkness.

He felt a horrendous thump, and the car bounced so violently his head hit the ceiling. He bit his tongue deeply but did not feel the pain. Clutching at his scalp, Dresdner cowered down as far as he could in the seat. Then the car seemed to pause, groaning like a wounded animal as it rocked back and forth, and he tried to scream again but could only gurgle piteously, his mouth full of blood.

The vehicle tipped, its rear end hooking on an outcropping and its front end turning over in a wide, graceful arch. Then there was a horrific silence where it seemed the whole world stilled and time passed in silent slow motion, and then the car landed on its roof on the forest floor twenty feet below.

* * *

Rolf shouldered his weapon and followed Hans down the steep embankment. Everywhere strips of metal and shards of glass littered the forest floor. The captain's vehicle had shed parts of itself the entire way down, and at the end, where it had made its one-hundred-and-eighty-degree turn through the air, Rolf and Hans found the twisted rear bumper still pinned between two jagged rocks. The car itself lay upside down at the bottom of the ravine, twenty feet below where they stood.

"I guess this might change our plans a bit, eh, Major?" Lieutenant Brenner sounded chagrined.

"I have a feeling he's still alive."

"Is that God telling you, or just your heart?"

Schulmann shook his head. "He's got to be alive. We need to find out where he's taken Marie."

"Guess we could rough up a few more Gestapo agents—some of the ones he left sipping beer in the hotel waiting for you to show your face."

"I think our luck's running a bit thin, don't you?"

Hans nodded. He started down the face of the ravine. "Let's have a look inside. Maybe God *is* on your side this morning."

They reached the car. It had flattened considerably under the weight of impact: twenty feet of free fall could do irreparable damage to even the heaviest steel frame. There was no sound from the interior, and Major Schulmann crouched to look inside. Glass blanketed everything, including the two figures lying perfectly still.

Heavenly Father, I need Thy help. Dresdner needs to tell me what has happened to Marie. Please let him survive long enough to tell me . . .

The body in the back seat twitched and moaned. Hans joined Rolf at the edge of the car and they each grabbed hold of a boot, pulling the moaning figure unceremoniously from the back seat out into the snow. Dresdner howled. "I think I broke my leg . . ."

Rolf leaned close. "Where's Marie Jacobson? What did you do with her?"

Dresdner stopped moaning. He could not see the shape leaning close to him, but he would recognize that voice anywhere. Smiling grotesquely, he gave a short, sardonic laugh.

"Major Rolf Schulmann. What a surprise."

"Where's Marie?"

"Every time something goes wrong in my life, you're behind it."

Hans leaned close, his voice pleasant. "Tell the major where the girl is or *I'll* be behind the next thing going wrong in your life."

"She's dead."

Rolf rocked back on his heels, feeling like he'd been stabbed. "Did you kill her?"

"No. But she's as good as dead." Dresdner gurgled deep in his throat. "So are *you,* Mormon."

Rolf unholstered his Luger. "Tell me what you've done with her and I might let you live."

"I should have ordered you shot in Izieu."

"Tell me what you did with her, or I'll kill you."

"You've already killed me."

"A broken leg isn't a death sentence. You might still make it if you tell me where she is."

Dresdner laughed a horrible, unearthly sound through the hole that used to be his mouth. "She's on her way to Ravensbrück. I told you—she's as good as dead."

Rolf holstered his weapon and stood. He'd learned all he wanted to know. Without another word he turned his back on the Gestapo captain and walked away. Hans followed behind.

"What're you going to do, storm the place?" Dresdner cackled and then swore. "It'll take you months and all you'll get for your efforts is a firing squad."

Rolf Schulmann and Hans Brenner continued walking away, ignoring him.

"You'll never get her back, Schulmann!"

Rolf and Hans began to climb out of the ravine.

"Haven't you forgotten something, Mormon?" Even in his wounded state Dresdner sounded triumphant. Rolf and Hans paused. Captain Dresdner continued. "Your sister-in-law? Your Mormon friends in Baiersbronn? The Wagners?" Dresdner cackled gleefully. "Every one of them will pay for what you've done. While you're running after your girlfriend I'll be ordering them arrested. And when I bring your son back from Switzerland I'll order every Mormon in the Schwarzwald rounded up and shot."

Rolf turned and walked back toward the captain.

"You can't kill me, Schulmann. Your religion has made you weak. You'll let me live, out of the goodness of your heart, and then I'll have my revenge on your fam—"

In the split second it took for Rolf to walk back to the captain with Hans, a thought darted through his mind: *"In memory of our God, our religion, and freedom, and our peace, our wives and our children . . ."* Rolf and Hans drew their weapons and fired at the same time. Both bullets entered the captain's skull in basically the same spot, and without another sound Captain Bernard Dresdner shuddered and lay still.

FORTY

June 5, 1944

Marie tried to turn over, the bones of her shoulder painfully contacting the wooden slats at the edge of the straw mattress. Her bed-mate, a hardened prisoner of five months, swore and punched her. "Hold still! What d'you think this is, the Ritz?"

Marie held still. Her stomach hurt and she shivered with cold. The others had laughed when she'd asked if there were any blankets. She rubbed one arm with her other hand and thought about Alma. She remembered his bright blue eyes and rumpled hair. Even now she felt the softness of his tiny hand in hers. She was concerned for his well-being and hoped Rolf had found him. She worried about the Wagners' safety, and Berta's and Walter's. What would the Gestapo do to them for aiding her escape? She wondered if Madame Larouche had reached safety. Marie felt tears in her eyes but blinked them back quickly. No use crying. She needed to spend her energy planning a way to survive.

At least that was what the barracks leader had said four weeks ago when one of the new women with Marie cried when she saw the inside of the barracks: row after row of three-leveled wooden bunks, each less than three feet wide and softened with a moldy straw mattress crawling with lice. Each bunk bed attached to the one next to it, making a row of beds as deep as the block itself. Narrow walkways passed between the rows, and Marie could smell the open-faced toilets in the rear of the barracks as soon as she entered the building.

At first Marie found herself looking to the colored *winkels*—patches shaped like triangles—on their arms for some clue as to why her fellow prisoners were here: Poles, Jews, political prisoners like herself, Jehovah's Witnesses, and criminals. But after days and weeks of back-breaking labor, insufficient food, dirty clothes, and little if any personal hygiene, all the women had begun to look the same: sodden boots, thin bodies clothed in cast-off dresses like hers, and head scarves over thin, scraggly hair. When night fell, the bunks always filled up quickly, each prisoner vying for the center of the bed, away from the rough wooden slats and drafts of cold air.

That first night had been horrific. Marie remembered how exhausted she had been, and by the time she made it through the interminable toilet line the bunks had been full. She broke down then, crouching in a corner and weeping until a woman from her work detail, with a "Jehovah's Witness" mark on her *winkel,* helped her find a bed—one with only three inhabitants. The woman had been her friend ever since.

Seven weeks! It seemed like seven years. Marie could not get back to sleep—a problem she had developed since arriving at Ravensbrück. It didn't help matters that the straw mattress beneath her was a veritable flea factory, or that the woman on her right always snored lustily in her ear. She scratched at her stomach. She knew it was useless—the fleas would invade her clothing no matter what she did.

She lay on her side, wedged between the other prisoners, and thought about her first sight of Ravensbrück: a panorama of long dreary structures spread in even rows as far as the eye could see. Row upon precise row of single-story barracks set closely together with heavy snow covering each long roof and camouflaging the ground. Everywhere she looked the snow had been shoveled from the roads and thrown high against the walls. As the train approached the compound, Marie saw fences. They weren't like at home in her father's cow pasture, but more like those around a penitentiary: tall fences guarded by soldiers with dogs. And tall walls cut them off from humanity in many parts of the camp. Women prisoners shoveled snow at all hours of the day and night, and Marie noticed that only a few women wore coats. The others endured the cold and ignored frozen fingers and toes, continuing to lift shovels, stones, or bricks in painfully slow motion as if they barely had the strength.

After the first few days of snow removal the women no longer paused in their labors to look at the train or the new arrivals. Their backs remained bent and their shovels continued to dig.

It was still incredible to her that her captors would be so inhumane as to leave people stuffed inside train cars for days on end with no water, no food, and no bathroom. On the journey from Drancy the crush of humanity against her chest had been so intense she had had trouble breathing, and when she was able to fill her lungs the stench of their mobile prison had been almost more than she could take. The cattle car smelled progressively more of dirty bodies and human waste, and the crush of humanity made it impossible to sit down. When a woman had fainted on the third day, she had remained standing, pinned between bodies with her head slumped against the shoulder of a crying woman to her right.

The movement of the iron wheels below them had sounded deafening in the crowded cattle car, and the movement of the train had jostled them into the ribs, stomachs, and shoulders of their neighbors. First Marie's legs had hurt from constant standing, and then, as the hours and days dragged on, they had burned. And then, finally, her limbs had become so numb that she was relieved of the pain to a point that she could sleep, her head resting against the back of the tall Polish woman in front of her.

At times during the ordeal her mind had refused to return from its meaningless wanderings, and she would visit fanciful places in her head. She found respite standing on the mountainside with Rolf, his arms around her and Baiersbronn spread like a shimmering Christmas tree below them. She ran through the meadow with Alma and the goat, rolled playfully in the grass with Bandit, and cuddled Rolf's son in her arms under an apple tree loaded with big red fruit, Alma's favorite storybook open on his lap. Always in her daydreams it was summertime, and the warmth of the sun and green of the grass made her heart glad. Perhaps it was because standing in the cattle car she had always been cold and miserable. Perhaps her dreams helped her stay warm.

Then the train had stopped amid a clatter of breaks and abundant clouds of cold air vapor. Soldiers had exited the car ahead of them, making their way through the snow to their door. When they opened the door, yelling *"Alles raus! Everybody out!"* Marie had struggled to untangle her stiff limbs from those of the women around her and stumble on rubber legs from the putrid cattle car.

Seven weeks! In the bug-infested bunk, the woman lying next to Marie snored mightily. Marie thought about Alma's father, and the memory of Rolf's smile took her breath away. She recalled his gentle hand on the side of her face and the warmth of his arms around her. She passed sleepless nights such as this with pleasant thoughts of Rolf Schulmann, grateful for the memories of their time spent together that helped pass the hours. What would happen to Rolf? Had he made it to Switzerland? In one of her favorite daydreams she imagined Rolf and Alma playing together in a large grassy field, Bandit barking enthusiastically as Rolf swung his son high in his arms. The fictitious scene soothed her, and she eventually drifted into slumber.

* * *

When the whistle sounded, Marie sat up, terrified and disoriented. She noticed her bed-mates climbing stiffly down from the bed and she followed, her pulse still pounding from the suddenness of her awakening. Through a dusty curtain she saw it was still dark outside. *Appell*—roll call. A female guard stood stiffly with her whistle in one hand and a clipboard in the other. "Ten minutes," she barked, and then turned and exited the block. Marie followed her fellow prisoners as they migrated toward the toilets at the rear of the room, and she took a place in line for one of the four filthy, overflowing toilets that served the block.

"We have to hurry." Marie looked to her left and saw her friend with the Jehovah's Witness *winkel* in the line to her left. She smiled wearily at Marie. "We'll miss *appell* and have punishment duty for a week."

Ten minutes later Marie stood shivering with her fellow prisoners in the snow outside the block. Marie looked left, then right, and noticed similar groups of women gathering in front of barracks up and down the line. She recognized several women who had arrived at the camp with her seven weeks ago.

Breakfast was the usual watery substance that the prisoners referred to as soup, and Marie accepted her portion and also received half of a raw potato, thrust into her hand after she had stepped past the soup pot. She sat next to the others and ate carefully, realizing she might be starving by her next meal. Her new friend sat next to her, and when Marie stared listlessly at her potato she said, "You'd be wise to eat it all."

Marie drained her soup and slipped her bowl into the pocket of her dress and found her barracks leader. She lined up behind the woman along with her friend and the other women in her work detail, standing patiently until the female guard blew her whistle. Then she marched, her boots rubbing painfully and her back still sore from yesterday's labor, to the supply shed where she was handed her shovel. She continued to follow the barracks leader past row upon row of barracks, until they passed through the perimeter fence and reached their work site.

They dug trenches, fighting first the stubborn permafrost and then the heavy gravel below, piling the soil next to the trench for the wheelbarrow detail to cart away to some undisclosed location. It was the same every single day, and in the early afternoon Marie's back began its predictable complaining whenever she lifted her shovel, and only her fear of the infamous infirmary kept her going. She remembered what a woman had told her when a young girl collapsed and the guards carried her to camp hospital: "A word of advice: If you get sick, don't let anyone know. The infirmary's worse than dying."

No water. No food. One shovelful followed by another. Each shovelful lifted was certainly the last she could lift. But she continued to bend, dig, and lift, and her body did not give out. Finally the sun began to set and the prisoners fell into formation behind their barracks leader to return to their block. Marie's legs shook and she was careful not to let the guard see that her back was bothering her. They again ate soup and formed a line for the reeking toilets, and when she finally reached her bunk she climbed up the end and fell inside, then closed her eyes and whispered a prayer.

Father in Heaven, I am grateful to still be alive. There are women in this room that might not make it until morning. Please bless and help them. And please bless Rolf. I'm worried he's in trouble. I'm worried he may be hurting, or dead. Father, I love him so much. He is such a good man, and he has faith in Thee. Please remember him—and his son. I miss them so much! If it be Thy will, please may Rolf and I both make it through this war alive? Please let me have another chance to see him and show him how much I love him!

Marie felt better. She closed her eyes, ignoring the burning in her muscles and the itching across her stomach and legs, and immediately fell asleep.

FORTY-ONE

June 6, 1944

When Marie awoke in the darkness, she wondered what had awakened her before early morning *appell.* She had no idea what time it was, and she could feel her heart beating rapidly with a growing sense of foreboding. Wedged between her sleeping neighbors she did not sit up but lay still, wondering what had startled her. Unable to calm the nervousness she felt, she closed her eyes and took advantage of the stillness to pray. She had the feeling something important was going to happen that morning. She also had the feeling Heavenly Father was trying to prepare her . . . *Father, all I can think of to do is ask for protection for those I love—especially Rolf. I'm so worried about him! I need him to be all right. Please, please care for him today* . . . And then she hesitated, and added . . . *and if it be Thy will, please allow something to happen soon that will turn the tide of this war. Please bless the Allies that they will be protected* . . .

She drifted back to sleep.

* * *

Breakfast was the same as the morning before, and Marie accepted the watery substance in her bowl and found a place to sit. Numb and weak, she concentrated on consuming the contents of the bowl, allowing her thoughts to drift as they would so she would not have to think about another day of back-breaking labor in the trenches.

"Marie Jacobson!" The female guard's voice rang across the group in the morning darkness. Several heads lifted to see who would answer.

For a moment Marie did not respond. She had not heard her name in ages, and it took a while for the sound to register before she looked up, surprised. Trying not to spill her soup, Marie rose to her feet. "I'm Marie Jacobson."

"Come with me." The guard grabbed her arm, and Marie's bowl fell into the dirt, spilling its contents in all directions. She followed the guard, her feet rubbing painfully in her boots while the woman walked rapidly, barking at Marie whenever she stumbled or lagged behind. Marie looked back and saw her friend and several of her fellow prisoners watching her leave, curiosity evident in their gaunt faces. Why had she been singled out? She looked at other prisoners as she walked past their barracks. Everyone seemed to be watching her; no one else was being dragged away from their group. Marie concentrated on keeping her feet under her, trying to ignore the moisture in one boot that signified a broken blister. Soon the pain began, and as they walked past row after row of barracks the pain intensified until it was excruciating.

"Stand here." They had reached the entrance to the building where she and her fellow travelers had received instructions upon arrival at Ravensbrück. The prison commandant and two other men in uniform stood inside the open doorway. The taller of the two officers talked in a low voice with the warden, but since his back was to Marie she couldn't make out any of his words. The other officer was of medium height and slender, and Marie could tell he was listening intently to the taller officer's dialogue. She watched as the smaller man turned toward the taller man, and on his uniform she recognized the insignia of an SS Major-General. She wondered what could be so important in the dark morning hours that such a high-ranking Nazi officer would be involved.

Marie stood beside the female guard and waited, her curiosity mingling with her fear of the unknown. The three officers inside continued to converse intently in German, and from her position outside the building, Marie could only understand a word or two of the discussion. Something about a fugitive, a surrender, a reward, and a prisoner transfer.

A prisoner transfer? Was she being transferred? She actually felt hopeful. Surely any place was better than here! She shifted silently, and her guard scowled at her, warning her to stay at attention. And then, to Marie's surprise, the woman leaned close and said quietly, "You'll be all right." She did not smile, but her words were so unexpected that Marie stared at her in surprise. The guard did not look at her again, and if it hadn't been for the agony of her feet, Marie would have thought she was dreaming.

The officers inside finally seemed to reach an agreement, and the commandant nodded and shook the hand of the shorter man. He then smartly saluted both officers, and they returned the salute. The major-general signed a document handed him by the commandant, and then gave it to the taller officer, who read it briefly, thanked both his colleagues, folded the paper once, and slipped it inside his jacket. Without another word, the taller man clicked his heels together, again saluted, and turned to exit the building. As he descended the steps, Marie saw his face and felt her knees almost buckle beneath her. It was Lieutenant Hans Brenner.

With a hard look he silently warned her to be still. He approached and took her arm firmly and waited for the major-general and the commandant to descend the stairs. Hans followed them, keeping his grip on Marie's arm and staring straight ahead. Marie ignored her feet and hurried to keep up. She tried not to look up at the officer towering over her, but it was all she could do to keep from whispering his name. It seemed Hans had saved her life again. How would she ever repay him? Finally she hazarded a glance at his face and was shocked to see him fighting back tears. The emotions he was trying to conceal upset her. Something was wrong. Her anxiety returned and she realized this was more than just a rescue. Something was dreadfully wrong.

They paused at the gate of the camp while two guards unlocked it and secured their dogs. The officers and their prisoner passed through the imposing gates, and Marie found herself glancing behind her at the long, endless rows of barracks. She noticed that several of the ever-present snow-shovelers had paused in their labors to watch her departure. Then the gates closed behind them and Marie was escorted toward a cluster of military vehicles parked just outside the perimeter of the camp. As they approached, floodlights from the camp suddenly illuminated the scene, and several armed soldiers beside the vehicles came quickly to attention as the major-general passed.

The commandant and the major-general moved to the center of the group of vehicles and stopped. Hans stopped next to them and waited, his grip on Marie's arm warning her to be silent. He continued to hold Marie firmly, and she could feel the slight tremble in his hand. She looked up at the officers and noticed that they had their faces turned toward the road leading away from the camp, as if they were expecting an arrival.

For several minutes no one spoke, and the officers beside her continued to watch the road. Then, in the distance, Marie saw the headlights of a single vehicle approaching the camp. The major-general and the commandant glanced at each other briefly and then at Hans and Marie before returning their attention to the approaching car. Marie felt the feeling in the group change, as if all present had doubted the vehicle would actually appear but now that they could see it the stress level had diminished somewhat. The major-general actually made a comment under his breath to the commandant, who chuckled.

They continued to watch as the car pulled to a stop across from the group, and when the engine died and the door opened, Marie realized she was curious to discover who it was that held everyone's attention so completely—and what *her* role would be in this whole early-morning drama.

She watched as a tall form exited the vehicle and paused, a gloved hand steady on the doorframe. The man had a commanding presence, Marie could tell, although his lowered head was hidden under a businessman's hat and his broad shoulders drooped somewhat inside his dark overcoat. He seemed to hesitate, as if gathering his courage, and then he straightened his shoulders and lifted his head, and when he turned toward the waiting officers his body was straight and proud.

The floodlights illuminated his face, and Marie found herself looking into the intense blue eyes of Major Rolf Schulmann.

Her knees went weak. She choked back a scream, shaking uncontrollably at the effort as she watched Rolf approach and felt Hans's warning grip on her arm. She was grateful for his death grip—otherwise her legs would have ceased to function and she would have collapsed at his side.

"Rolf . . ." She whispered his name through lips that chattered bitterly. He approached, his stride confident and his frame erect. She watched helplessly as the major-general barked a command that sent several guards to apprehend the unarmed man. They produced a set of handcuffs, and Rolf obediently extended his hands, his wrists close together. He did not say a word when they shackled him and forced him forward, striking his back with the butt of a rifle until he stumbled.

The guards escorted Rolf to stand in front of the three officers, and the major-general signaled to an aide standing nearby. Shaking himself as if from a trance, the aide leaped forward and presented the major-general with a small briefcase, which the officer then handed to Hans Brenner. Hans took the briefcase but then immediately gave it to the commandant, who accepted the proffered item eagerly. The major-general then turned to Rolf.

"Major Schulmann." The greeting was devoid of any warmth.

"Major-General Schellenberg."

"A pity we must meet in this way."

The prisoner in front of him did not answer. Marie held her breath and found she could not take her eyes from Rolf's face.

Major-General Walter Schellenberg must have sensed that all pretense at pleasantries had passed, because he cleared his throat and extracted a document from inside his coat. He produced spectacles and balanced them on his slender nose, then unfolded the document and proceeded to read in a commanding voice.

"Major Rolf Schulmann, you are hereby arrested and charged with treason against the Third Reich. By order of the Führer you have been convicted under wartime law of *Nacht und Nebel* of the following high crimes against the Fatherland: conspiracy to overthrow the government, assaulting and endangering officers of the Third Reich, assisting an enemy spy, conspiring with enemies of the Third Reich, unlawfully releasing prisoners and assisting enemy organizations, lying to your superiors . . ."

Rolf stood ten feet from Marie. His eyes moved to lock with hers as the major-general's voice continued to delineate his crimes. ". . . withholding information vital to the Third Reich, damaging Reich property, resisting arrest . . ."

In the darkness of the morning Rolf's blue eyes said everything his voice could not, and Marie felt his love as completely as if he had stepped forward, wrapped his arms around her, and whispered it in her ear. She found herself crying uncontrollably, tears streaming down her filthy cheeks as she leaned against Hans for support. Rolf watched her, and with his lips he slowly and silently formed the English words *I love you.*

". . . you are to be transported to Sachsenhausen, where you will immediately be executed."

Hans felt her quick intake of breath and managed to cover her mouth in time to block her scream. Quickly he escorted her away from the gathering and thrust her into a vehicle at the edge of the group. He then shut the door and slid into the driver's seat, turning the key as he did so. He immediately gunned the engine and pulled away from the other vehicles, and in a matter of seconds Ravensbrück, Major-General Schellenberg, and Rolf Schulmann were far behind.

"Hans . . ."

"Not yet." His voice sounded tight, and she fell silent. They drove rapidly away from the camp and Marie turned to watch as the headlights of a long convoy of vehicles pulled into the road behind them, moving at a more leisurely pace. She watched numbly as the convoy followed them for a few minutes and then turned off to the south until it disappeared in the darkness behind them. Hans continued driving, his back ramrod straight. After a few more minutes he pulled the vehicle into a small cluster of trees and stopped. Suddenly his shoulders fell and he began to shake, and Marie climbed over the back of the seat to sit beside him, resting her hand softly on his shoulder.

"He was . . . he was my best friend . . ."

Marie nodded and said nothing. With a sob he turned to her, gathered her in his arms, and they cried together. "Rolf found out you were headed to Ravensbrück, and we spent the last two months trying to negotiate your release." Hans shook his head. "He made me promise to bargain an exchange with the director of Ravensbrück—he would turn himself in in exchange for your freedom. I wouldn't have agreed if I thought you didn't love him . . ."

Marie shook, tears coursing down her face. "I do love him, Hans. I've never loved anyone more."

"He loves you, too. He . . . loves you so much."

"Hans, I don't think I can stand this. It hurts too much."

Hans nodded against her hair. "I know. You can't imagine how long I argued with him about this—told him there had to be another way." He took a deep breath. "Last week I even approached Himmler—in charge of all the camps—and he laughed when I asked to have you released on grounds of the Geneva Convention. But when I finally approached Rolf's superior officer, Major-General Schellenberg, he agreed to come with me to Ravensbrück to accept Rolf's surrender and negotiate with the commandant. Rolf followed us and waited a distance from the camp. The floodlights were our signal that the deal was acceptable."

"Certainly the major-general would never have consented to the release of an Allied operative. How did you get him to agree to that?"

"Schellenberg wasn't the problem. He was willing to do almost anything to assure the capture of the traitor. It was the camp commandant who was difficult to convince. He only agreed when I promised him the reward money for Rolf."

The full extent of Rolf's sacrifice hit Marie like a physical blow. She felt Hans's arms trembling around her and she could think of nothing to say. Hans continued. "Rolf made me promise to help you get on a boat to Sweden, and from there you should be able to secure passage to England. Anyway, everyone says the Allies will invade soon . . ."

Marie looked up at the lieutenant. "What about Alma?"

"If his aunt survives she can find him in Switzerland after the war."

Marie shook her head. "I need to find him. Take care of him."

"Marie . . ." Hans shook his head. "Rolf would want you safely home in America."

She brushed stubbornly at her tears. "He has *no one,* Hans—I need to keep my promise." She shuddered. "It's the least I can do for someone who . . . gave his life for me . . ."

Hans said nothing for a long time. Outside, the sun was just beginning to lighten the sky, and in the silence Marie thought she heard the faint drone of bombers. Finally Hans whispered, "All right."

"Thank you, Hans."

"On one condition."

"Condition? What condition?"

Hans kissed her cheek solemnly. "You let me come with you."

FORTY-TWO

November 1944

Marie stood outside the wrought iron gate and watched the children at play. They were a sober lot, she realized, every one of them having gone through a nightmare before they reached this orphanage. Switzerland was receiving a numberless influx of refugees, and children torn from their families were no exception. She watched them intently. She could tell what some of them had been through by what games they played: One little girl huddled with a donated rag doll, alternating between rocking her gently and hitting her against the pavement. Another child, a red-headed boy, was playing soldier—most of his playmates had already been shot at least once this morning, and he was currently lining up a row of enthusiastic volunteers to face a firing squad. It made her ache inside.

She heard a step behind her and Hans spoke. "I found a cottage for you."

Marie turned and smiled at him. "However did you get so lucky?"

"The owner is a woman in her seventies—finally decided to surrender the house and go live with her widowed daughter."

"You've taken good care of us, Hans. I'm grateful to you."

Hans smiled and then nodded in the direction of the children at play. "One of these days the nuns in there are going to accept your offer to relieve them of one small child. They must be overflowing with refugees as it is." He put a casual arm around her shoulders and pointed. "Look at them. They're packed in there like sardines! There must be over a thousand."

Marie nodded. "Yes . . . in an orphanage built for two hundred."

Hans studied the crowded playground. "Do you see him?"

She shook her head. "He's a little late. But he'll be here. Sister Bernadette said I could visit him in the playground today."

"You're here every day. How often does she let you in?"

"Three or four times a week. I help her with their evening meal before I go."

"It must be hard to leave him here every night. Why won't they just let you take him?"

"Sister Bernadette says it's because I don't have written permission from Alma's father—and I'm not his blood relative."

"Here comes the good sister now."

Marie watched the diminutive woman cross the courtyard, her round face rosy from the exertion and her dark-blue habit swinging in the breeze. From the other side of the fence she faced Marie and Hans. "Fräulein Jacobson, Alma has a slight temperature. I thought it might not be wise for him to leave the building today."

"Thank you, sister. It was good of you to tell me. I would have worried when he did not come."

The nun looked relieved, and she took a deep breath. She had something else to say. "You are one of the most determined women I have ever met, Marie. I know you are not his real mother, but you are clearly very devoted to him. You have come every day for five months, and I was wondering . . ." She hesitated, as if unsure whether she should continue.

"What is it, Sister Bernadette?"

The woman shrugged. "I could use your help every evening with the children's dinner, Fräulein—the other sisters are overworked as it is, and you have been such a good help to me."

"I would be happy to help you, sister!" Marie glanced back at Hans and then smiled at the nun.

"There's more." The woman looked relieved. "I cannot pay you . . ."

"No matter. I take in ironing most days and I get along fine."

"I was wondering if, in exchange for helping me in the evenings, you would be willing to take Alma home with you every night. We could use the bed space, and he could still attend school each day with the other children . . ."

"Sister Bernadette! What a wonderful idea!" Excited, Marie reached through the iron bars to hug the surprised nun. "You have given me the most wonderful gift!"

"Then it's settled." Sister Bernadette looked pleased. "I think he should stay here until he feels better. Then you can come for his belongings . . ."

"Oh, Sister Bernadette . . . Thank you! Thank you! You have answered my prayers."

Sister Bernadette laughed. "And you have answered mine!"

* * *

Hans held her hand as he opened the door. "And here, princess, is your new home."

Marie stepped from the porch into the living room. Sunlight played over the floor as the lace curtains fluttered in the breeze. The walls were painted a blush rose, and wooden planks gleamed beneath her feet. Marie walked to the center of the empty room and turned, taking in a panoramic view of the place.

"I can't remember ever seeing a more cheerful home."

Hans set down her suitcase. "I thought you'd like it. The kitchen's through here, and there's a washroom—small, I'm afraid—and two bedrooms."

"Hans, I don't know how to thank you enough—for all you've done for us . . . for me . . ."

Hans cleared his throat. He looked into Marie's eyes. "When we were still in Germany you once asked me what you could ever do to repay me."

"I still wonder. I feel no matter what I do I still end up in your debt."

"Well, I've thought of something."

Marie looked up at him in surprise. His voice sounded strained, hesitant. "What is it, Hans? Tell me."

His hands found her shoulders. "Marry me."

His words sent her reeling, flooding her with emotions that she realized were still too near the surface. She stared at him, speechless.

Hans continued "I'll take good care of you and Alma. I know I will. Rolf asked me a question once, when we were setting out to find you. He asked if I ever thought I could love someone for eternity." He paused, caressing her shoulders. "I don't know much about eternity . . . but I know I could love you deeply for the rest of my life."

"Hans, I—"

"I love you, Marie. I want to spend the rest of my life taking care of you . . . and loving you . . . You have taught me love is possible. I've never felt for anyone what I feel for you. I know you still love Rolf, but we have to face reality: he is just a memory—for both of us."

"He might still be alive."

Hans shook his head sadly.

Marie touched his cheek gently. "You are one of the kindest, sweetest men I know, Hans."

Hans's brow furrowed. "If that's a compliment, I think there's something missing."

Marie touched his face gently. "I love you. But not in the way you're hoping. You've been the older brother I never had. It's like you've protected me from bullies on the playground and bandaged my hurt knee." She caressed his cheek affectionately. "I could never have a brother more wonderful than you."

"But as a husband . . . ?"

"Hans, I need someone who loves me enough for eternity."

"Like I said, I haven't thought much about eternity, but I think I could—"

"It's not just a matter of thinking you can. There are things that have to be done, promises made . . ."

Hans watched her thoughtfully. "Rolf told me once he would love his wife for eternity. Is that the kind of love you mean?"

"Yes. And there is a way Rolf can *live* with his wife for eternity also—not just remember her and love her memory."

Hans shook his head. "I'm lost. How can Rolf live with Hélène for eternity?"

"The Mormon Church teaches that there is a special place where a man and a woman can be married 'for time and all eternity'—not just until one of them dies. Rolf was holding onto the promise that if he lived the commandments of God he would be blessed with Hélène by his side even after they both died."

"And that's what you want, isn't it? To have a marriage like Rolf wanted?"

Marie nodded. "I can't imagine settling for anything less. I want to marry a man who will make special promises to me—promises of love and fidelity made in God's temple to someone who is a worthy member of the Church."

Hans was thoughtfully silent. Marie continued, gently. "Hans, even if I grew to love you as *more* than a brother—as deeply as I do Rolf—I would still feel empty inside, like our marriage to each other was a promise of the *limits* of our love, not the *extents* of it."

Hans lowered his eyes. "So I fall short on every count: You don't love me, I'm not a Mormon, and I can't marry you for eternity."

"Hans, that's not entirely true. Everything you mentioned can be straightened out. I *do* love you, you *can* become a Mormon, and someday you *can* marry a woman for eternity. But it's all up to you."

Hans smiled sadly. "Where does marrying *you* fit into the picture?"

"I'm sorry, Hans. It doesn't. I'm so terribly sorry."

Hans shifted awkwardly, but he did not remove his hands from her shoulders. "If there were any chance I could change your mind, I'd be baptized a Mormon tomorrow."

"Thank you, Hans. That means a lot to me." Marie did not resist when he leaned close and softly kissed her cheek.

"From your older brother, then," Hans whispered. "Although it means a lot more to me." He released her and stepped back. He then walked toward a window and pushed back the curtain to stare outside. After a minute he turned to look at Marie. "I've made up my mind."

"About what?"

"I'm going to return to Germany."

"Hans! You're not serious. The Allies are overrunning France and Belgium. It won't be long before they cross the Rhine . . ."

"I need to find a friend. He's desperately needed in Switzerland."

Marie's dark eyes grew wide. "Rolf? You're going back to look for Rolf? What if he's dead? You keep telling me you're sure he's dead."

Hans shrugged. "Somebody once told me God hears and answers prayers. And I know of a woman and little boy who've been praying for his safety."

"Hans . . ." Marie felt tears in her eyes.

"It's going to be difficult keeping in touch, Marie. Germany's a pretty big mess right now."

"I'm worried for your safety . . ."

"Then marry me and keep me here."

Marie laughed through her tears. "If you find him alive I'll—I'll love you forever."

"Like 'eternity'?"

"Close." She sobered and met his gaze steadily. "You find him for us and you and I will be friends for eternity."

"If that's all you can offer, I guess I'll have to accept it." Hans returned her smile, and then became serious. "Don't expect too much, princess."

"I understand."

Hans turned to go. "I'll help you and Alma move in. Then I'll leave." He stopped. "By the way . . ." He reached into his coat pocket. "Rolf wanted me to give this to you. I keep forgetting." He pulled out a small, well-worn book and placed it in Marie's hand.

She gasped. It was Rolf's copy of the Book of Mormon. She opened the front cover and ran her hand lovingly over the message scrawled in Félix's handwriting. Then she looked up at Hans, her eyes bright. "Seeing this means a lot to me."

"Rolf read that book a lot. Every page is dog-eared. I always wondered what he saw in it."

Marie studied him soberly, then looked one last time at Félix's message. She closed the worn cover and handed the book back to Hans. "I think Rolf would have agreed that you should have this. Maybe it's time to find out for yourself what Rolf thought was so important."

"Will this book teach me more about eternity?"

"Yes, Hans. It will."

"Then I'll read it. I'm not much of a reader, but I'll read it." Hans returned the book to his pocket and turned to go.

"Oh, and Hans?"

He paused at the door.

"When you're ready . . . I'll introduce you to my sisters." Marie smiled. "I have thousands of them."

FORTY-THREE

September 7, 1945

Marie pressed six candles into the top of the tiny cake while Alma watched solemnly, his blue eyes wide with curiosity.

"And then I light them, like so . . ." Marie struck a match and carefully lit all six candles. Shaking out the match, she smiled at the boy. ". . . And then you make a wish and blow them out."

"But you just lighted them," Alma said confused. "Why do you want me to blow them out?"

Marie laughed. "It's just part of the tradition, honey. You wish for something you really want, and then, if you blow all the candles out, you'll get your wish."

Alma looked thoughtful. "*Any* wish?"

"Any you want—within reason, of course." Marie refrained from telling Alma the contingency—that the wish had to be kept secret for it to come true—because she wanted to discover what he wanted for his birthday. If she were lucky, she would receive enough ironing this next week to make buying a little something possible.

Alma nodded. "All right. I know what I'm going to wish for."

"Okay. Tell me your wish, and then blow hard!"

Alma's face lit like a firecracker on the Fourth of July. "I wish for my papa to come home!"

Marie sat back, stunned, and watched as her young charge blew out every candle and then looked up at her expectantly. "I did it! I blew them all out! Now when will my wish come true?"

Marie felt the familiar tightening in her chest—the same feeling she felt whenever Alma asked about his father. "I—I don't know, sweetheart. Only Heavenly Father knows."

"Does Heavenly Father listen to my birthday wishes?"

"Yes, Alma, He does."

"If I kneel down and pray—like you taught me—do you think He will bring Papa home?"

"Alma, I . . ." Marie blinked back her tears. Alma's eager face was looking up into her own, his eyes wide and bright. She didn't want to discourage him—to hinder the faith that was budding inside him. But how was she to tell him about concentration camps, and firing squads, and death . . .

Alma grabbed her hand. "Let's pray right now. Here, on the porch."

Marie stared down at the boy, her emotions tearing her apart inside. But she managed an encouraging smile. "All right, Alma. Let's pray here on the porch."

Alma slipped eagerly to his knees and Marie followed, her tears building near the surface. Alma folded his arms and squeezed his eyes tightly shut. As always, his head refused to bow, as if he did not want to chance missing anything important that might catch his attention around him. He scooted close to Marie until his head and shoulder contacted her side, and he began to pray.

"Heavenly Father, this is Alma. Today is my birthday and I am six years old. I love my mami very much, but I wish Papa would come home and be with us, too. Mami says he loves us very much, and *you* love us very much too. She says you answer our prayers—and even our birthday wishes—like the one I made today that Papa will come home. Please let him come home *soon!*"

Alma closed his prayer and jumped up immediately, a satisfied look on his face. "There. Now Papa will come home."

Marie felt tears on her cheeks and she reached for the happy boy. "Alma, honey, there's something. . . something I think you should know."

"What, Mami?" Alma saw her tears, and his smile faded.

"It's about your papa—and the war."

Alma watched her expectantly, his face showing that he sensed something was wrong. Marie prayed desperately to know where to start. Should she tell him everything—from the beginning? How his father had captured her in the mountains and then saved her from the maniacal evil of a Gestapo captain? How she had found herself falling desperately in love with the handsome Nazi major? How he had warned her to flee and ended up sacrificing his freedom for hers? How he had probably died for her? *Greater love hath no man . . .*

She began softly. "Alma . . ."

But something in Alma's expression made her hesitate. His eyes watched her with a brightness and a hope that startled her, and with a superhuman effort she swallowed the words that would have extinguished that spark forever.

What was wrong with hope? She had no right to crush it—to crush his spirit. Wasn't that what Captain Dresdner had tried to do to her? If she assumed now that Hans's lack of correspondence meant all hope was gone, then the Gestapo captain would have won. He had wanted to see Rolf, Alma, and herself destroyed, and if she broke this little boy's spirit then Dresdner would have gotten what he wanted.

Hesitantly, Alma asked, "Heavenly Father will answer my birthday wish, won't He?"

Marie pulled him closer and kissed the top of his head, wiping a hand across her face to keep her tears from falling into his hair. She used to believe wishes came true. But she had stopped waiting for word months ago—ever since Hans had written that there was no sign of Rolf at Sachsenhausen. Hans's last written words had been *"Keep praying for him . . ."* And before that Hans's letters had been sporadic—sometimes months would pass without a single letter. And when they did come they were already ancient history. *Surely Hans would have written if he'd found Rolf.*

After the war ended Marie had heard that the Allies had freed the prisoners from most of Germany's concentration camps. But Hans had not contacted her again. Perhaps Hans had eventually been captured. Perhaps he was dead, like Rolf. Perhaps . . . She shifted uncomfortably and tried not to think about the multitudes of questions that might never be answered.

"Keep praying for him . . ." She had finally begun to realize that her most heartfelt desire to be with Rolf again—the prayer that had carried her through her escape from Captain Dresdner, her farewell to Rolf's son in Baiersbronn, her internment at Ravensbrück, and her desperate search for a lonely little boy in Switzerland—might never be answered.

Then again, perhaps it had. The thought still made her cry inside, but she had to accept that, in her Heavenly Father's kind and gentle way, the answer might already have been given. And the answer had been no.

But in His infinite mercy Heavenly Father had consented to leave her a little piece of Rolf Schulmann. She looked at Alma and felt the deep love she had for him washing over her. If Heavenly Father would not grant her wish that Rolf might return to her, then she would accept His alternative with a grateful heart.

She gathered Rolf's little boy close in her arms and sobbed quietly against his hair. "Alma, your Heavenly Father loves you very much." She mustered her courage and smiled down at him. "And, yes, my sweet boy, in His own way and in His own time, Heavenly Father *will* answer your birthday wish."

Next from Sandra Grey . . .

TRIBUNAL

PROLOGUE

April–May 1945

Over the gate of the Sachsenhausen Death Camp, steel bars are bent to form letters, and the letters are welded into a phrase that reads *"Arbeit Macht Frei."*

"Work makes you free."

One of the prisoners spat at the foot-high reminder of the paradox that was Nazi Germany. He clutched his treasures to his chest—a bundle consisting of a blanket and a few possessions: a book, a cup, and a toothbrush. He had been one of the lucky few to steal a coat, and in the early morning darkness he held it tightly around his thin shoulders as he passed through the gate.

"Work makes you free."

Inside Sachsenhausen, chaos still reigned on the *Appell-Platz* as frustrated SS guards battled to funnel an impossible mass of humanity into orderly groups. The Czechoslovakians had already passed through the gate. Political prisoners and habitual offenders waited farther back in line, followed by the Polish, criminals, Jehovah's Witnesses . . . In the darkness prisoners fought for blankets, coats, and shoes, tearing them from friends' backs or guarding them with every ounce of energy they still possessed.

A child cried. In a shirt several sizes too large, he stood alone in the midst of the confusion, his cheeks stained with tears and filth and his feet bare. Eventually he was herded along with others toward a group of five hundred Polish prisoners at a gathering point in the line. The boy sat in the dirt and clutched his stomach, staring blankly at the passing feet.

Questions raged throughout the *Appell-Platz* like a whispered storm.

"Where are we going?"

"Someone said we were marching north."

"For what reason?"

"The Russians are coming."

"And the Americans."

"Why don't the guards just leave us and save themselves?"

"I heard they're planning to dispose of the evidence."

A group of German prisoners passed the Polish group on their way to a spot farther back in the line. Criminals, habitual offenders, and deserters blended anonymously—as castoffs from the Fatherland, they huddled together and took their place in the confusion. From his position near the front of the German group, Rolf Schulmann clutched his coat securely around his neck with one hand and guarded his blanket with the other. His emaciated face turned in the direction of the whimpering child who was sitting in the dirt, the tiny sticks that used to be his arms wrapped around a stomach bloated with starvation. Carefully Rolf inched his way closer, cautiously watching the SS guards nearby. He bent slightly and spoke through cracked lips.

"What is your name?"

The boy stared at him mutely.

"Are you cold?"

The child nodded.

Rolf slipped the blanket from underneath his arm and dropped it in the boy's lap. "Hold onto this with all your might. Don't let anyone take it from you. Understand?"

The boy stared at him, dull eyes registering a spark of life at the kindness. Nodding silently, he gathered the thin blanket in his arms and held it tightly against his chest.

"Schulmann!" Rolf straightened at the sound of his name and waited silently for his punishment.

"The commandant wishes to see you."

Rolf followed the SS guard toward the brick administration building, holding his coat tightly around his thin body. He did not waste any energy wondering why Anton Kaindl would want to see him; he had learned to accept whatever came and not worry about the future. If this was finally his moment to die, he would die. Nothing he could do would change that.

But his heart told him this was not his moment to die. Why would Heavenly Father save him from a firing squad and protect him through a year of torture in the Punishment Company, only to allow him to be beaten to death for giving a blanket to a child?

He climbed the steps behind the guard, walked down a hallway and followed him into the commandant's office. Anton Kaindl stood in the center of the room, gathering papers and stacking them in deep piles along the edge of his desk. Periodically he chose one, peered at it through his wire-rimmed spectacles, and then returned it to its stack. He looked up momentarily as the guard entered with Rolf, and then he returned his concentration to the papers.

Rolf stood at attention near the door and waited for the commandant to speak.

"Rolf Schulmann?" The commandant continued to shuffle papers on the desk.

"Yes, sir."

"You used to be a major in the SS, am I right?"

"Yes, sir."

"You were charged with treason."

"Yes."

Kaindl turned to face him, leaning back against his desk. "Why were you spared the firing squad?"

Rolf lifted his chin. "June sixth—last year. The Allies were bombing production centers. The former commandant postponed the execution, anticipating they would come after our factories."

Kaindl folded his arms and studied Rolf. "Postponed indefinitely, it seems." Then, to no one in particular, "Seems strange to postpone an execution on the slight chance a bomber might pass overhead . . . Didn't you ever wonder why you were spared?"

Rolf's blistered lips twisted wryly. "I kept forgetting to ask."

The commandant was not amused. He peered at Rolf over his spectacles. "You're a Mormon, aren't you?"

"Yes."

"Your God must think highly of you to save you from the firing squad."

Rolf said nothing.

"I hate Mormons." Kaindl scowled. "I hate Mormons and I hate turncoats. I should've had you executed along with the Russian POWs at Station Z." The commandant shook his head in wonder. "I've missed several opportunities to rid Germany of a traitor. I should be shot myself." He turned back to his papers. "But since you're still here, you will be put to good use." He selected a paper from the desk and glanced indifferently at its contents. "Do you know where we're going?"

"No, sir."

Kaindl turned again to face him, the paper clutched in his hand. "To the Baltic Sea. You and the other prisoners will be loaded onto barges and drowned."

"Why?"

Kaindl smiled. "Cheating death has made you bold. I could shoot you for asking."

"What am I supposed to do to help?"

The commandant nodded to the guard, who stepped forward and handed Rolf a rifle. Kaindl spoke. "You are to select several men from among the other German criminals and form a 'camp people's unit.' Your assignment is to assist the SS guards in maintaining order on the march. Since I don't trust a traitor—" Kaindl scowled—"I will assign an SS guard to watch you." He returned the paper to the desk. "You might have escaped the firing squad, and your cooperation now could save your life when you reach your destination, but one false move on this march and your carcass will be picked clean by Red Army buzzards. Understood?"

Rolf fingered the rifle and nodded.

"Now get out of here." Kaindl waved his hand in dismissal and turned his attention to his piles of papers. Rolf followed the guard out of the building and back in the direction of his group. He felt hundreds of eyes staring at him as he passed his fellow prisoners, gripping the rifle tightly. He felt awkward and foolish—a skinny shadow of a man holding a useless weapon. He did not imagine for a moment he had been allotted any bullets.

* * *

At the end of the first day Rolf's assigned group was moving toward Neuruppin at a pace designated by the SS guard in charge of the people's camp unit. Rolf noticed the guard limping slightly, as the boots he wore obviously chafed and bothered his feet. Rolf felt his own feet burning from eighteen hours of walking, and he could imagine many of the prisoners in his care were feeling the same. Worried, he glanced behind him at an older man near the back of the group. Johann was beginning to lag behind the others, his thin legs trembling with every step he took, and Rolf knew if the man stumbled the SS guard would shoot him and leave him by the side of the road. Rolf slowed his pace so that he walked next to the man. "How are you doing, Johann?"

The man glanced carefully at Rolf, his face betraying his fatigue. "I'll make it. I have to see my grandchildren again."

"Where are your grandchildren?"

"I don't know. Before the war they lived in Belgium."

"You'll find them. But for now, we need to concentrate on keeping you on your feet. Can you do that?"

"Yes, sir."

"Good for you." Rolf smiled at the man and moved forward. The SS guard stared angrily at him, warning Rolf with a shake of his head.

Three kilometers later, Johann fell, curling into a fetal position in the middle of the road. Rolf pulled him to his feet and lifted him onto the SS supply cart, ignoring shouts from the guard. Within seconds the guard confronted Rolf, his face mottled with anger. "You're disobeying my orders, Mormon. Why did you help that man?"

"Because of your feet, sir."

"My *what?*"

Rolf pointed to the guard's boots. "Your feet. That limp is getting worse, and this man is a doctor. If he dies you'll have no one to look at your feet when we stop for the night."

The guard glanced down at his feet and then at Johann huddled on the back of the cart. With a scowl he swore at Rolf and walked away.

* * *

Johann died before they reached Neuruppin. His body was left at the side of the road with those of several others who had also lost the strength to live. Rolf Schulmann concentrated on placing one foot in front of the other. The column of thirty-three thousand prisoners—men, women, and children—moved slowly. Rolf did not notice much around him. He mostly watched his feet—left foot, right foot, and then he repeated the process—so he was aware when the soles of his shoes gave out and his feet began to bleed.

International Red Cross trucks arrived one afternoon and distributed packets of food to the prisoners. Rolf held his portion reverently and fingered a tiny square of chocolate. He placed it in his mouth and relished the sweetness before letting it melt down his throat, and then he watched as his column ate ravenously, tears of gratitude streaming down filthy faces and mixing with the food in their hands.

They traveled steadily to the northwest, and the guards forced them to move faster, averaging twenty to forty kilometers per day. The pace proved too much for some of the prisoners, and they lagged behind and were shot.

Rolf kept moving. He found a dead prisoner and stripped him of his boots while the guard occupied himself with an escaping prisoner. One night Rolf and his group found a barn to shelter them from the cold, and in the morning the farmer's wife distributed bread and water to the starving men before they continued their march.

Once when they were passing through a village, a second-story window opened and a potato flew through the air toward the marching prisoners. Rolf watched as panic ensued: prisoners threw themselves bodily at the object until a large pile of struggling, desperate humanity clogged the street. Calmly, the guards began shooting, and when Rolf passed the location the potato had disappeared—replaced instead by three lifeless bodies in the mud.

When Rolf found blood in his stool, he tried to limit his contact with the other prisoners, but the dysentery that attacked him spread throughout the column and weakened the weakest until prisoners were dropping at an alarming rate. Rolf began watching his feet again: left, right, then left again . . .

Near the Belower Woods Rolf and sixteen thousand prisoners dug holes for themselves and burrowed in for the night. Shaking uncontrollably with fever and cold, Rolf pulled tree roots out of the dirt and chewed them until he could imagine he was no longer hungry. He slept fitfully, and in the morning the SS guard in charge of the people's camp unit stood over his hole.

"German prisoners are being released," he said without preamble.

Rolf said nothing. He decided it must be a trap, meant to catch him trying to escape. He knew the guard would not pass up any opportunity to shoot him.

"As far as I'm concerned, you're a traitor to your country, Schulmann. You should have been executed long ago." The guard pulled the strap of his rifle over his shoulder and folded his arms. "But much as I hate you, I admire the way you've kept your column in line. I've shot fewer escapees from your group than from any other, and there has been very little insubordination on your part. So I'm going to give you one last command: Find your countrymen and give them the order to report here to me. You've got fifteen minutes."

Still unbelieving, Rolf stumbled through the woods, conveying the message to all the German prisoners under his care. The prisoners met his announcement with blank stares or disbelief, but eventually a crowd had gathered near the SS guard. Rolf listened while the prisoners were ordered to march to a village nearby for instructions, and then he followed the group through the trees to a cluster of homes where a group of SS officers recorded names and handed out freedom passes.

Rolf held his pass in one trembling hand and stared at it, his mind refusing to register his good fortune. Then abdominal cramps forced him to his knees and he crouched in the dirt while around him prisoners celebrated their freedom.

* * *

Rolf Schulmann brushed the dirt from his clothes and climbed out of the empty ditch. Early in the morning the road still teemed with refugees fleeing the Red Army's advance, and Rolf waited for a bicycle loaded with suitcases, bags, and a wilted houseplant to pass before he struggled to his feet and stood weaving for a few moments to catch his balance. His body was on fire and his flesh felt clammy. His boots rubbed in all the wrong places, and he felt blood between his toes. He stepped onto the road and followed the multitudes of people migrating west.

When the sun hovered directly above his parched body he fell by the side of the road to rest. He stayed there longer than he had planned, and when evening approached he struggled to rise. Two young men with a wheelbarrow piled high with belongings stopped to assist him, and when he finally stood on his feet they gave him water and bread. Gratefully, he ate and found the strength to continue his journey.

He continued to walk, certain that the next time he fell would be his last. Throughout the night and into the next day he walked steadily forward, following the masses of refugees and thinking about the two most important people in his life: Alma, with his eager five-year-old face and deep love for his father, and Marie, the woman he loved with all his heart and would never see again.

He continued to move forward, forcing his feet to obey and ignoring the excruciating pain in his legs and abdomen. Several concerned passersby offered him water, but he vomited violently whenever he tried to drink. He fell to his knees and could not rise, so for several hours he crawled forward on his hands and knees. Razor-sharp gravel sliced through the thin fabric of his trousers and imbedded itself in his flesh, but he didn't register the pain, didn't even notice the red stains his hands and knees were now leaving on the road.

Then, when he was sure he would collapse at the top of the next rise, through the fog of his delirium he thought he recognized the sound of someone calling his name . . .

HISTORICAL NOTES

Chapter 1

Martin III Marauder: The British provided several B-26 models to the Free French forces in late 1943.

France surrendered to Germany on June 22, 1940. At that time the Germans divided France into two zones: occupied France to the north and unoccupied France to the south. Southern France's Vichy government (so named because it operated out of the city of Vichy in southern France) cooperated with the Germans and was allowed to run southern France (or at least *pretend* to run southern France) until November 11, 1942 (see Morgan, *An Uncertain Hour,* 177). At that time—disputably because Vichy France was not cooperating completely with Hitler's Final Solution—Germany took complete control of France by overrunning the demarcation line between occupied and Vichy France.

The French Résistance was extremely active in the Rhône-Alpes of southern France. Plenty of small villages provided hideouts for the members and sympathizers.

Maquis: A name used usually to distinguish a guerilla branch of the French Résistance that often resided in the mountains, the Rhône-Alpes being especially thick with the organization. Members of the Maquis organization were called *maquisards.* The Maquis organization strengthened as the war endured, and it became a hiding place for many fugitive Résistance organizations that could no longer hide in the cities and towns because of informer activity or the residents' fear that the Germans would punish their community for harboring Résistance.

Not all Résistance fighters were communists, but a good portion of the Résistance leaned in that direction—especially among the Maquis. Communists were generally among the more violent members of the Résistance, while non-communist members focused on sabotage and espionage. The fictional character Jacques Bellamont would most likely have been a communist.

Jean Moulin: A French Résistance leader betrayed by a turncoat *collabo* (informer/collaborator) to Section Four Gestapo in Lyon on June 21, 1943. Klaus Barbie personally oversaw his torture and murder. Eyewitnesses said a severely beaten Moulin was placed on display in Barbie's office for several days before Moulin died.

Gebirgsjager: Elite German Alpine troops. Their uniforms switched between camouflage and white, depending on the season and the terrain.

Chapter 2

Leo Marks: Head of communications at Special Operations Executive (SOE). He introduced several new coding systems during his tenure, including the silk WOKs depicted in this book, one-time pads, and mental one-time pads, in an effort to replace the longstanding and, in his professional opinion, murderous poem code system. He wrote *Between Silk and Cyanide* about his experiences.

Director Marks's secret meeting with Marie is obviously not factual; however, according to his own account, one of his responsibilities was to meet with agents prior to their departure, and because General de Gaulle's representative Lieutenant Valois did in fact meet with Marks about the need for a new system of coding for de Gaulle's Free French agents, it is logical a meeting like this could have taken place.

Lieutenant Valois: A representative of General de Gaulle in Britain, during the time de Gaulle was headquartered in Algiers. Valois oversaw Free French radio traffic and Signals planning. He would have been involved in any decision to send an Allied agent to France to test a new coding system (see Marks, 301–303).

Grendon (SOE Station 53): Location in Grendon Underwood, a village in Buckinghamshire, England, where the SOE had a wireless station in which young volunteers received and deciphered incoming wireless transmissions from field agents (see Marks, 12, 19–20).

SOE (Strategic Operations Executive): Britain's spy organization throughout World War II.

Baker Street: 64 Baker Street was the address of the SOE headquarters in London, referred to by agents simply as "Baker Street."

WT: Wireless transmitter used by agents in the field.

Funk-Horchdienst: German direction-finding and message interception services—a WT operator's nightmare.

WOK: Acronym for "worked-out key." WOKs were Director Marks's brain-child and his attempt to replace the poem codes commonly used by Allied agents to encrypt wireless transmissions. Marks argued that poem codes (used since the inception of SOE) were a death trap for field agents for the following general reasons:

> 1) Poem codes might be based on poems known (or at least researchable) by the German decoders.
>
> 2) Poem codes required a minimum of 250 words per transmission, there-fore requiring a significant amount of time on the air and therefore a high possibility of detection by the Germans.
>
> 3) Poem codes caused a high rate of indecipherables, putting lives in danger from misunderstood messages and often requiring agents to

retransmit (which meant even more time on the air and even greater possibility of German detection).

4) Poem codes had to be memorized, which meant German captors could torture the code out of a field agent during interrogation.

A WOK, on the other hand, was a square of silk printed with a mission's worth of code keys, each randomly selected, and as original among the hundreds of agents that eventually used them as a fingerprint. As an agent completed his transmission, he cut off the used code key and destroyed it, thus making it nearly impossible for an intercepted message to be deciphered by the Germans, even if the agent was captured and his WOK discovered. WOKs were easily hidden and, if detected, were useless in deciphering already-sent traffic. Also, if an agent were forced to send other messages to the Allies under duress, he could insert prearranged false keys into his message that would alert SOE to his capture.

At the time of Marie's fictitious parachuting into France, many field agents were already using the silk WOK, but de Gaulle was still insisting that his agents use poem codes. He was unwilling to share his "secret French code" with the SOE Signals Directorate, so it was impossible to manufacture silk WOKs specific to his needs until he authorized his representative to approach Leo Marks in the latter part of 1943 to request assistance in making his Free French agents' codes less accessible to the Germans.

Chapter 3

OSS (Office of Strategic Services): American spy organization in World War II, and a forerunner to the CIA.

Basque beret: A beret often worn by Résistance and *maquisards* to recognize each other, it was common enough that its use did not necessarily alert the Germans to their presence.

Sabine Zlatin: A licensed nurse who began taking displaced Jewish children into her home after the 1940 armistice. The local prefect warned her that the Germans would be a danger and suggested that she take her children into the Italian Zone. With the kind help of Marcel Wiltzer, the *sous-préfet* of Belley, Madame Zlatin and her husband, Miron, found a home used for Catholic retreats above the small community in Izieu. Wiltzer told them that Germans had never bothered the village. Madame Zlatin moved her operation to the Izieu site and began to take in more children. (See Morgan, *An Uncertain Hour*, 262–275, for the story of the children's home in Izieu.)

It is probable that Madame Zlatin would have welcomed any help she was offered. Many of her friends had agreed to help her with the children, and the budget for the children's home was extremely tight.

Blackout curtains: Required at curfew, they helped a community remain invisible to overhead reconnaissance aircraft from both sides of the war.

Scopolamine: Used by the Germans as a truth serum in interrogations during World War II.

Klaus Barbie: *Obersturmführer* and head of the Gestapo stationed in Lyon, later referred to as the "Butcher of Lyon" for his intense interrogation methods and murders. His responsibilities included not only the implementation of the Final Solution in southern France but also the discovery and disbandment of French Résistance cells in the area.

In March 1935, Hitler reintroduced general conscription. German men (and eventually boys) were conscripted into the several branches of the military, including the labor forces. Mandatory service was at times enforced with threat of harm to the soldier's family. (See "Interview," www.tarrif.net/wwii/interviews/lothar_seifert.htm and www.assumption.edu/acad/ii/Academic/history/HI14Net/WWIItimelines.html)

Charles de Gaulle: Leader of the Free French—the government he led from Britain for a good portion of the war. He attempted to unify the many different Résistance movements in France with moderate success—enough that Britain, which recognized de Gaulle's government over that of Vichy, was willing to assist in the Résistance's efforts by sending supplies and agents.

Chapter 4

Service du Travail Obligatoire (STO): The mandatory work service order instituted in German-occupied France in February 1943. French citizens were required to labor at Germany's factories and farms during the war, taking the place of German workers conscripted into the army. Approximately 650,000 French workers participated in the program. (See Morgan, *An Uncertain Hour,* 108.)

Vichy government: See chapter 1 notes.

Ersatz: German word meaning "substitute." Usually means an inferior substitute. *Ersatz* ingredients were used in many wartime food preparations.

Collabo: French word for a Frenchman who spied for the Germans or tattled on his neighbors.

Chapter 5

RAF (Britain's Royal Air Force): SOE's drops were coordinated with the RAF and several other military organizations—at least whenever SOE was on good terms with them. An interesting point: In part because of intelligence reports that a high percentage of drops into German-occupied Europe were compromised, the British military put a hold on all SOE drops to occupied countries soon after the time of Marie's fictional drop into France. This hold continued—resulting in a high loss of agents who could not escape and a loss of Résistance confidence in Allied promises—for several weeks, before SOE convinced the military to continue.

Boches: "Rascals." Derogatory French nickname for the German invaders.

Chapter 6

Italian Zone: The geographical area located in unoccupied France until Germany overran the demarcation line, mostly east of the Rhône River. Ted

Morgan, in his book *An Uncertain Hour,* places Madame Zlatin's children's home in the Italian Zone, where she went at the suggestion of a city official in Belley in the hope that the Germans would overlook them.

At least in the beginning, German occupiers in this area were known for their civility toward their French neighbors. Some would even play with children in the streets near their headquarters, and many civilians, cold and reserved at first, warmed to the young men as time went by. French and Germans often met and drank together at the cafés along the Place des Terreaux and in other cafés in the city. Spying on both sides during these rendezvous is an assumption on the part of the author. (See Morgan, *An Uncertain Hour,* 268–269.)

Alcohol was available to French citizens and the German occupiers in the cafes, although to what quantity the author does not know (see Morgan, *An Uncertain Hour,* 268–269).

Major Rolf Schulmann: A fictional *Sturmbannführer* (equivalent of a major) in the Allgemeine SS. As a major in the Allgemeine SS organization, Schulmann's assignment in intelligence would have been a security-type assignment to assist the *Wehrmacht,* or regular military.

École primaire: A primary or elementary school.

Château de Lafont: A fictitious château placed in an area that boasts many fine châteaus constructed in centuries past. The history of the château is also a creation of the author, as is the château's owner, Monsieur Jean-Motier Boisseau. However, German garrisons were assigned to the vicinity, and at one time they billeted in an old school, where they ate their meals chuck-wagon-style in the yard.

American-English spy connection: Aside from a few minor disagreements over the years, the American OSS and British SOE cooperated quite a bit in their efforts to unite Résistance movements and undermine the Nazi war machine long before the formal invasion on June 6, 1944. It was not uncommon for volunteers from one organization to assist—or receive training from—the other in order to fulfill certain missions.

Major Walter Schellenberg: SS intelligence officer given the responsibility to investigate Résistance activities arising from Nazi occupation in foreign countries.

Totenkopf: The skull-and-crossbones insignia found displayed somewhere on almost every Nazi officer's uniform. It signified the death of Germany's enemies.

Allgemeine SS: The Allgemeine SS was a paramilitary organization, meaning an auxiliary organization to the military. It dealt with, among other things, administration intelligence operations (as opposed to the Waffen SS, which did most of the fighting). During the war, many in this organization transferred to other branches of the SS (such as the Waffen). Perhaps only ten percent of original SS officers stayed in this branch of the organization after 1942. Service in the Allgemaine SS was seen by some as an embarrassing assignment because members of this branch of the army often did not see combat.

The Women's Army Corps would have been a logical way for Marie to get to Britain—if she was willing to volunteer with the organization for a period of time.

Section Four: The division of the Gestapo dealing with the Jews. Section Four headquarters was in Lyon, France, at the *École de Santé*.

Chapter 7

The Gestapo often insisted upon being involved in the interrogations of important prisoners. An SS officer might have had one, maybe two, days to interrogate the prisoner on his own before the Gestapo arrived and insisted on taking control of the interrogation. Often the organization that carried out the initial arrest was not even allowed to begin interrogations without the Gestapo present. In the fictional case in this book, Major Rolf Schulmann had superior authority to Dresdner and therefore would have been able to interrogate the prisoner at least partially before Dresdner received permission to travel from Lyon to Belley and take over the interrogation. In the Gestapo's rationale, the rank of officers outside the Gestapo organization would have meant almost nothing.

Captain Bernard Dresdner: A fictional *Hauptsturmführer* (equivalent of a captain) in the Gestapo, who would have felt that as a member of the regular *Wehrmacht* (military) and powerful Gestapo organizations, he should be allowed to circumvent the authority of a *Sturmbannführer* in the paramilitary Allgemeine SS.

As mentioned in the chapter three notes, it was not uncommon for a German soldier or officer's family to be in jeopardy if he did not comply with government orders.

Résistance members were known to impersonate SS officers in order to infiltrate organizations or instigate acts of espionage or sabotage. In this book, the opposite scenario occurs—German soldiers masquerading as *maquisards*. A similar situation occurred at the beginning of WWII, when German soldiers impersonating Polish troops ambushed and murdered men, women, and children in order to back up Nazi propaganda and inflame hatred against the Polish people.

Maquis/Maquisards: See chapter 1 notes.

Chapter 9

Manufacture d'armes: An arms factory. The one mentioned here was in St. Étienne, France (near Lyon).

Gendarmes: The police. In this case, the local Vichy police.

Stéphanois: Citizens of St. Étienne, France.

École de Santé: Gestapo Section Four headquarters in Lyon, under the leadership of Klaus Barbie.

Chapter 10

WOK: See chapter 2 notes.

The Thatched Barn: SOE's "gizmos and gadgets" facility. Here special products were developed for field agents, like pen guns and exploding rat carcasses. The facility even had a complete wardrobe section, where clothing was manufactured exactly as it would be in the different countries the agents would be visiting—using the same fabrics, the same threads, the same stitching, and even the same labels. The clothing was then "aged" by several methods, including throwing the newly made garments on the floor and walking on them for several weeks. After Director Marks requested hiding places for the agents' silk WOKS that would escape the Germans' incredibly detailed searches, inventions like the one described here were concocted by the "engineers" at the Thatched Barn.

Indecipherable: A garbled wireless transmission. If the young volunteers at Grendon were unable to decode a wireless transmission, the "indecipherable" could possibly be deciphered by Leo Marks himself.

Encryption school: A school for cryptographers located in Bedford, England, with an eight-week program for SOE and military hopefuls. This school was separate from training offered by SOE for field agents and couriers.

Grendon: See chapter 2 notes.

Baker Street: See chapter 2 notes.

Funk-Horchdienst: See chapter 2 notes.

"The Road Not Taken": A poem written by Robert Frost in 1916.

Armistice of '40: France and Germany signed an armistice on June 22, 1940, in which France was divided into two zones: occupied France to the north and Vichy France to the south. As a condition of the armistice, Vichy leader Philippe Pétain was required to collaborate with the Nazis in every way.

Commander Henri Giraud: A French general and Free French leader. He and Charles de Gaulle became co-presidents of the Comité Français de la Libération Nationale (CFLN) in June 1943 after several weeks of difficult negotiations.

In January 1943, Giraud and de Gaulle had met with Franklin D. Roosevelt, Winston Churchill, and other leaders in Casablanca, Morocco, to discuss the Allies' European strategy. This meeting became known as the Casablanca Conference.

In November 1943, Giraud lost his co-presidency in de Gaulle's Free French Forces and the CFLN, partly because the Allies and de Gaulle discovered he was maintaining his own intelligence organization and undermining goals of the Free French. Although he claimed to oppose German interference in Vichy France, he was known to sympathize with the Vichy government and with Philippe Pétain. He also aroused General de Gaulle's anger when he arrested French Résistance leaders who supported the Americans.

Chapter 11

Luftwaffe: The German Air Force.

Chapter 13

Belchen: Considered the highest peak in Germany's Black Forest. Belchenmont is used here as a location for training German Alpine troops—the *Gebirgsjager.* There is no historical documentation to validate this idea. The Belchen is, in fact, a ski resort.

There are several examples of house arrest during WWII, but the situation under which Marie is placed under house arrest is unique to this story, and would most likely not have happened if Major Schulmann had not been Félix's friend.

Chapter 15

Until the last years of the war, the Hitler Youth program was considered voluntary for boys and girls in Hitler's Germany. Most youth, however, had a difficult time waiting until they were ten years old to join. Programs were added for younger children, but the real *Hitlerjugend* began at age ten. The boys and girls marched, trained with weapons, participated in parades and Nazi gatherings, ran every type of collection drive imaginable, and enforced curfews. *Hitlerjugend* girls were reminded that their greatest contribution to the Fatherland was to get pregnant and deliver healthy Aryan babies. (Often the emphasis on marriage occurring first was lost in the teaching.) During the last years of the war, the Hitler Youth program became mandatory for all German youth and superseded all work, family, school, and church responsibilities.

Chapter 17

The *Milice:* A French paramilitary organization headed by Charles Darnard. The *Milice* were considered by some to be the "thugs" behind some of the worst crimes in Vichy France. Often referred to as the "French SS," the *Milice* would do the things the *gendarmes* refused to do for the Germans (see Morgan, *An Uncertain Hour,* 105, 191).

Kopf: German for "head," as in "heads of cattle."

Klaus Barbie: See chapter 2 notes.

Hitler and his government accomplished what they did in regard to the Final Solution in large part because of their efforts to dehumanize the Jews and other "undesirables." They utilized terms such as *kopf* and *undesirables, time tables,* and *down payments.* According to Morgan, author of *An Uncertain Hour,* the Germans accomplished their plans by following a "Corporate Model" that transformed human life into a series of "logistical problems" that had to be solved in order for the corporation to function properly. Also, secrecy among the top SS officers involved contributed to this transformation. In this chapter and in chapter twenty of this novel, Klein, Dresdner, and the other Gestapo officers speak in terms that mimic the corporate attitude of the SS as they talk about the Final Solution in Lyon.

Rafle: French for "raid" or "roundup." In this case, the term refers to the deportation of so-called undesirables.

Chapter 18

"Silent Night": Words by Josef Mohr (written 1816), music by Franz X. Gruber (composed 1818).

"O Holy Night" or *"Cantique de Noël":* Adolphe Adam composed this well-known Christmas carol in 1847. The words are a French poem called *"Minuit, Chrétiens"* by Placide Cappeau.

SS Training School: Located in Bernau, near Berlin. Recruits were indoctrinated with teachings espoused by the Führer, such as Aryan brotherhood and racial selection. They were also taught unquestioning obedience—*Befehl ist Befehl*—"an order is an order." (See Morgan, *An Uncertain Hour*, 205.)

LDS missionaries' evacuation from Germany: When he received word from the First Presidency that all LDS missionaries were to leave Germany, President M. Douglas Wood of the West German Mission sent telegrams to all of his missionaries instructing them to evacuate to Holland, as they had done during the "false alarm" evacuation in 1938. But when the 1939 evacuation began, Holland had changed its mind without informing Church Headquarters or President Wood. Therefore, when the hapless missionaries traveled to Holland as they had practiced in 1938, they were turned back at the border. They were not allowed to enter Holland unless they could show proof of passage *through* the country to another destination, such as England or Denmark. However, because of the German requirement that travelers leaving the country not carry more money than basically pocket change—maybe enough for a few meals and a phone call—the missionaries found themselves with no means of purchasing tickets to another location and were forced to return to Germany. Several missionaries were detained and threatened or even interrogated by the Nazis as they attempted to evacuate. (See Boone, Transcript.)

Nevertheless, many miracles occurred during the evacuation of missionaries from European countries during 1939. The miracle Rolf describes in this book, however, is fiction.

The practice of baptizing a man and then immediately ordaining him to the Aaronic Priesthood so that he can baptize his family members is no longer allowed, but it was not uncommon during the time period of this novel.

Chapter 20

The New Year's Eve party depicted in this chapter is an assumption of the author, created for the benefit of the story. However, the SS was a party-going organization (at least in the higher ranks), so a festivity such as this would have been highly probable.

In 1944, trains for the deportation of "undesirables" were scheduled for France starting in February and continuing throughout the year.

Hans Bordes, Bordeaux incident: Not all SS officers agreed with Hitler's Final Solution. In Bordeaux, an SS officer named Luther left the Jews completely alone. The anti-Jewish section in that area was headed by Hans Bordes, who refused to arrest the Jews and was incessantly chastised. The inaction of both these officers ultimately caused a train for that area to be cancelled. Captain Adolf Eichmann, who was responsible for all the deportation trains, was furious, and he expressed his embarrassment at having to inform the head of the Gestapo, General Heinrich Müller, of the cancellation. The reason Bordes gave for his failure to make arrests was that there were not more than one hundred and fifty foreign Jews available in

Bordeaux—all the rest wore yellow stars (French Jews) and under existing German law were not considered deportable.

Arrondissement: French for "district," as in an administrative division, similar to a borough.

Chapter 21

The scene depicted here is based upon the experience of an LDS branch in Czechoslovakia soon after the Germans invaded that country. An SS officer entered the room while sacrament meeting was in session and asked to address the congregation. He bore his testimony and asked to be allowed to worship with the Saints in Prague as long as he was stationed in that area. The members welcomed him with open arms. (See Boone, Transcript.)

Chapter 22

Rafle: French for "raid" or "roundup," in this case of Jews. Lists were compiled based upon the mandatory documentation of all Jews in a *département.* Not registering as a Jew if one had Jewish blood was an offense punishable with deportation or death.

Ted Morgan, in *An Uncertain Hour,* believes not all Nazis knew the truth about the trains—often they, and the *gendarmes* that assisted them in the *rafles,* truly believed the deportations were for the purpose of providing labor for the Reich in work camps throughout Europe (see 193).

Deciphering a coded message using a WOK: See Marks, *Between Silk and Cyanide,* 46–59; 114–116.

Chapter 23

Not all individuals involved in the *rafles* in France agreed with the Final Solution. During the *rafles* there were some gendarmes who would give families an allotment of time to "prepare" for departure, and then would leave the family alone during that time. In one case, a woman insisted upon brushing her little girl's hair before departure, but she could not find the hairbrush. A soldier told the girl to run down the street to the store on the corner and buy one. The clerk at the store warned her not to go home, and the girl's life was ultimately saved. (See Morgan, *An Uncertain Hour,* 158–159.)

Chapter 25

Obersturmführer: First Lieutenant. Even though Klaus Barbie was head of all operations at Section Four Gestapo headquarters in Lyon, he did not receive a higher rank until near the end of 1944. Rank, obviously, did not necessarily denote power or position in the Gestapo.

Chapter 26

"White Cliffs of Dover" (sung by Vera Lynn in 1941): Words by Nat Burton; music by Walter Kent.

Vera Lynn: Born in 1917, Vera was a popular British singer during WWII.

Das Schwarze Korps: The official Nazi newspaper, produced weekly, was mandatory reading for SS officers and others. It espoused the Nazi philosophies and propaganda of the Führer. (See www.jewishvirtuallibrary/jsource.org/Holocaust/Das Schwarze Korps.html.)

Chapter 27

Obersturmführer: First Lieutenant—see chapter 25 notes.

Operation *Frühling*—Operation Spring: Klaus Barbie and his Gestapo were part of an operation in the Jura Mountains between April seventh and nineteenth. The main purpose of the raid in Saint-Claude was to capture as many Résistance and Maquis sequestered in that area as possible. Alpine troops from the Rhône-Alpes were involved in the operation as well. For the purposes of this story, Barbie is named as commander of the operation, although there is evidence to suggest that he was only in charge of his Gestapo troops and that the main command fell to General Pflaum's 157th Alpine Division. (See Morgan, *An Uncertain Hour,* 275–280.)

MG 34: The MG 34 and later MG 42 were two of the most commonly used machine guns during World War II. An MG 34 was an air-cooled weapon that was first issued to German troops in 1934 and could be fired using a tripod or bipod setup, usually depending upon the weight of the weapon and the situation in which it was to be used. Although the guns came equipped with either heavy "saddle-drum" magazines or box magazines, a fabric or metal belt could be used for continuous firing (a fabric belt was reusable, while a metal belt disintegrated as it was used). (See http://www.ima-usa.com/product_info.php/cPath/145_103/products_id/731; http://www.answers.com/topic/mg-34.)

Chapter 29

Lucien Bourdon: A Frenchman often seen drinking with the Germans at the location mentioned here (see Morgan, *An Uncertain Hour,* 268). Bourdon was arrested in 1947 and put on trial in Lyon. To his dying day he professed innocence in the Izieu affair, but several eyewitnesses saw him talking to the Germans outside the home prior to the removal of the Jewish children. He claimed he had been arrested and forced to accompany them to the children's home. Bourdon's sentence was national degradation for life. (See Morgan, *An Uncertain Hour,* 268–273; see also http://www.aidh.org/izieu/3e. htm.)

Antoine Wucher: A mechanic who periodically worked for the Zlatins at the children's home. He told Madame Zlatin that his wife was sick and he needed a place for his son, René, to stay so that he could continue working. Madame Zlatin kindly offered to take the boy. René was an unknowing accomplice in the affair: he was quizzed by his father and dutifully told Antoine anything about the home and its occupants that his father wished to know. See chapter 31 notes for more about René Wucher. Antoine Wucher was later shot by the Résistance. (See Morgan, *An Uncertain Hour,* 267–268, 272; http://www.aidh.org/izieu/3e.htm.)

Chapter 31

La Maison d'Izieu: The children's home located in a large house above the small community of Izieu. See chapter 3 notes for more information.

Leon Reifman was the child who escaped. He heard the call to breakfast and was beginning to walk down the stairs when he saw his sister with three men in the foyer. One of the men asked him to come down, but his sister warned him not to. Leon returned upstairs and jumped out a bedroom window, then hid in thick bushes near the edge of the garden. He later testified that he was sure one of the searching Germans made eye contact with him, but then the soldier just walked away. Leon stayed hidden until after sunset. (See Morgan, *An Uncertain Hour,* 269–270.)

One of the vehicles carrying the children away from the children's home stalled next to the *Confiserie Bilbor,* a candy factory in the small community of La Bruyère near Izieu. René Wucher was sitting on the back of the truck and was seen by his aunt, who happened to work at the factory. René called out to her in French, *"Tatan!"* (his word for "Auntie") and was allowed to jump off the truck and go with his aunt. (See Morgan, *An Uncertain Hour,* 270, 273.)

Tante: German *and* French for "Aunt."

Liliane Gerenstein: The eleven-year-old girl at *La Maison d'Izieu* who wrote the "Letter to God," which was found in a drawer at the home. Liliane died, along with the other children, at Auschwitz. Her mother was deported and died before her daughter, and Liliane's father eventually immigrated to the United States and died there in 1979. (See Morgan, *An Uncertain Hour,* 274; http://www.izieu.com/ new_page_5.htm.)

Several other letters written by Izieu children were also found in the home. Letters can be read in Serge Klarsfeld, *The Children of Izieu: A Human Tragedy,* New York: Abrams, 1985. See also Morgan, *An Uncertain Hour,* 262–275.

April 6, 1944: Historians disagree as to whether Klaus Barbie personally led the raid on the children's home of Izieu. Several sources named him as the commanding officer, while others say he only ordered the raid. On the same evening of the *rafle,* Barbie was in Lyon, where he sent a telegram to Paris outlining in triumphant and very derogatory terms the capture of forty-one children and ten teachers, calling them *kopf.* Barbie misstated the number of children, which suggests he was not personally at Izieu that morning. Also, the next morning he had to be in Saint-Claude for Operation *Frühling,* which would have made his schedule very tight indeed. For the purposes of this story, the author has chosen *not* to have Klaus Barbie present in Izieu. (See Morgan, *An Uncertain Hour,* 270–271.)

Fifty years after the deportation of Izieu's tiny charges, the children's home at Izieu was made into a museum to memorialize that horrific event and many other memoirs of the Holocaust (see http://www.izieu.alma.fr/ and http://beaucoudray .free.fr/izieu.htm).

Chapter 32

In the SOE training pamphlet produced by SOE, and in this chapter refer-enced by Marie in regards to the Gestapo, the paragraph to which she refers is the

following (see Mackenzie, William, "The Secret History of SOE," http://www.
spartacus.schoolnet.co.uk/2WWsoe.htm):

> If you are arrested by the Gestapo, do not assume that all is lost;
> the Gestapo's reputation has been built up on ruthlessness and
> terrorism, not intelligence. They will always pretend to know
> more than they do and may even make a good guess, but
> remember that it is a guess; otherwise they would not be interro-
> gating you.

Chapter 35

Westwall (the Allies called it the Siegfried Line): A German-constructed
defense system that stretched more than 394 miles between Switzerland and the
Netherlands, with a series of over eighteen thousand bunkers and numerous tank
traps and minefields. Facing the Westwall on the French border is the French
Maginot Line, which follows the border of France from Switzerland all the way to
Belgium. Unfortunately, when the Germans invaded France, they moved north
around the end of the Maginot Line and avoided the resistance that the Maginot
Line promised. Germany kept the Westwall heavily fortified up until it was overrun
in a series of devastating battles with the Allies in 1945.

Chapter 38

OSS: See chapter 2 notes.

Scopolamine: See chapter 3 notes.

When Captain Dresdner said the Résistance was "all but wiped out," he was
expressing a belief held by many SS officers assigned to France—the belief that the
Résistance was fast failing. He was, however, grossly mistaken: the Résistance was not
failing, but the members were fading into the woodwork—or into the mountains.
Maquis organizations were still operating strongly, despite operations like *Frühling*.

Chapter 41

Nacht und Nebel: A 1942 decree signed by General Wilhelm Keitel, Hitler's
chief of staff. The English translation is "Night and Fog." The *Nacht und Nebel*
decree stated that in order to quickly and efficiently dispose of enemies of the Third
Reich, a "court-martial" would take place silently and swiftly—under cover of darkness—after which the accused would disappear without a trace. Basically, the decree
gave the German army the right to execute suspects or send them to concentration
camps without a trial.

Reichsführer Heinrich Himmler: Head of the SS and in charge of all the concentration camps. He was second in command only to Hitler. If someone had actually
wanted to approach Himmler about a prisoner, the person would have had more
success during 1944 then at any time in the previous years of the war; at that time
Himmler was beginning to lobby for peace with the Allies—a move which cost him his
career in early 1945 and, ultimately, his life. (See www.auschwitz.ck/Himmler.htm.)

BIBLIOGRAPHY

Text

Ayer, Eleanore H., with Helen Waterford and Alfons Heck. *Parallel Journeys.* New York: Simon & Schuster, 1995.

Beevor, Antony. *The Fall of Berlin, 1945.* New York: Penguin Putnam, 2002.

Böll, Heinrich. *The Silent Angel (Der Engel schwieg).* Cologne, Germany: Verlag Kiepenheuer & Witsch, 1992.

Crankshaw, Edward. *Gestapo.* New York: Viking Press, 1956.

Freeman, Robert C., and Dennis A. Wright. *Saints at War.* American Fork, UT: Covenant Communications, 2001.

Gildea, Robert. *Marianne in Chains: Daily Life in the Heart of France During the German Occupation.* New York: Picador, 2002.

Marks, Leo. *Between Silk and Cyanide: A Codemaker's War, 1941–1945.* New York: Touchstone, 1998.

McIntosh, Elizabeth P. *Sisterhood of Spies: The Women of the OSS.* New York: Random House, 1998.

Morgan, Ted. *An Uncertain Hour: The French, the Germans, the Jews, the Klaus Barbie Trial, and the City of Lyon, 1940–1945.* New York: William Morrow & Company, 1990.

Interviews/Lectures

Boone, David F. "The Evacuation of LDS Missionaries from Europe at the Onset of WWII." Transcript, lecture discussion, Museum of Art, Brigham Young University, Provo, UT, October 21, 1999. (Published as Boone, David F. "The Evacuation of the Czechoslovak and German Missions at the Outbreak of World War II." *BYU Studies* 40, no. 3 [2001] 122–154.) Also derived from

"The World-wide Evacuation of Latter-day Saint Missionaries at the Outset of World War II." Brigham Young University. Provo, UT. 1981.

Schnebly, Harold and Ede (European history teachers). Interviews by Sandra Grey. December 2005–February 2006. Sequoia Learning, Mesa, AZ.

Internet Research

A Brief History of the Gestapo, Extracted from the Nuremberg Charges. Nazi Conspiracy and Aggression, Vol. II, US Government Printing Office, Washington, DC, 1946. www.nizkor.org/hweb/imt/nca/

Flitterman-Lewis, Sandy. *Hidden Voices: Childhood, the Family, and Antisemitism in Occupation France.* www.rci.rutgers.edu/~engweb/faculty/profiles/flitterman_lewis/hidden_voices.html

Foreign and Commonwealth Office—UK. SOE. www.fco.gov.uk/servlet/Front?pagename=OpenMarket/Xcelerate/ShowPage&c=Page&cid=1050510206588

"Timeline of World War II in Europe: Statistics of World War II." www.history-place.com/worldwar2/timeline/statistics.htm

Office of Strategic Services Operational Groups. French Operational Group & Operations in Southern France. www.ossog.org/france.html & www.ossog.org/pics_pages/map_france_01.html

Special Operations Executive. Wikipedia. http://en.wikipedia.org/wiki/Special_Operations_Executive

Trial of Klaus Barbie, The. http://members.aol.com/voyl/barbie/barbie.htm

United States Holocaust Memorial Museum. Collections: The Children of Izieu, Sachsenhausen Death March, and Ravensbrück Women's Camp. www.ushmm.org

Watson, Andrew. "Franklin S. Harris (1921–1945)." BYU NewsNet. 16, April, 2003. http://newsnet.byu.edu/story.cfm/43907

ABOUT THE AUTHOR

Sandra Grey was born in Inglewood, California, into a very large two-generation military family. Her grandfather served honorably in World War II, and Sandra and her ten brothers and sisters spent their childhood following an Air Force father around the world and back again. Her favorite memory is of an early morning in military housing on Yokota Air Force Base in Japan, when she walked down the stairs and saw her father, decked out in his officer's uniform, kissing her mother before he left for work.

Sandra studied humanities at BYU and managed to escape without a spouse. After a mission to Brazil and a bachelor's degree, she moved to Mesa, Arizona, and immediately met Kirk, her future husband. Sandra and Kirk are the proud parents of six bright little children (emphasis on little) who are too kind-hearted, intelligent, and obedient to be real. Sandra has always dreamed of being both a mother and a writer—and is happy to discover that it is possible to be both.